DEATH CYCLE

REED MONTGOMERY BOOK 6

LOGAN RYLES

SEVERN RIVER PUBLISHING

Severn River Publishing
SevernRiverBooks.com

ISBN: 978-1-64875-541-5 (Paperback)

ALSO BY LOGAN RYLES

The Reed Montgomery Series

Overwatch

Hunt to Kill

Total War

Smoke and Mirrors

Survivor

Death Cycle

Sundown

The Prosecution Force Series

Brink of War

First Strike

Election Day

Failed State

To find out more about Logan Ryles and his books, visit

severnriverbooks.com/authors/logan-ryles

For my dogs —
Not that they care.

1

The house on the ridge sat by itself, invisible from the road and sheltered by towering pine trees. A long asphalt drive led from the highway, almost two miles through the pines, guarded by an automatic metal gate, a ten-foot fence, and security cameras.

The jet-black Maserati Quattroporte Trofeo hugged the blacktop, winding through the trees with barely a sound as it approached the house. The gate opened, and the house appeared, automatic lights clicking on to illuminate the way into the garage.

The Maserati pulled in, and the engine died, but the man behind the wheel didn't move. He sat staring at the polished wood-panel wall of the garage and thought about revenge.

Emotions had never been a thing that Aiden Phillips understood. He'd read books—lots of books, in fact—that diagnosed his peculiar condition as an advanced form of sociopathic behavior. Essentially, he lacked the ability to associate his decision-making paradigm with any concept of morality. The books called it a lack of a conscience, but Aiden called it a societal ideal. Life was so much simpler and more effective, and above all, more *efficient*, when social constructs as primitive as morality were deleted from the equation.

That was why Aiden wasn't angry with Gambit for failing, but if Gambit were still alive, Aiden would have throttled him personally. It wasn't a matter of emotion, it was a matter of efficiency. Stephen Yates was useful until he wasn't. When a part fails to perform with efficiency, that part should be replaced.

But Gambit's death at the hands of David Montgomery's son was anything but simple, and the complications that now lay at Aiden's feet ignited a burning sense of frustration deep within him. Why couldn't everyone else see the objective value in perfect efficiency? Why was somebody *always* complicating things?

First, it had been Frank Morccelli, that bastard doctor whose medical genius had planted the seed for Aiden's entire operation. Frank's sense of morality made him the first of Aiden's targets, and an orchestrated drunk driving accident in New Orleans brought his complications to an end.

But then David Montgomery, Aiden's financial guru and money-laundering expert, had overreached. He confused perfect efficiency with maximum profit, and that greed birthed a recklessness that landed him on the FBI's radar. David swore he would never rat out Aiden, but if David failed once, he might fail again, and that was anything but efficient. So Aiden snuck some heavy metals into David's prison food, turning his brain to mush and ensuring no secrets would be spilled.

And at that point, perfect efficiency seemed within his grasp. The product was good—damn good, in fact. All elements of the operation were in place, and every gear clicked and spun with an oiled smoothness that brought Aiden a fulfilling sense of pride. The product was manufactured, the product was imported, and then Mitchell Holiday distributed it via his logistics company . . . and Aiden would make billions.

Everything was perfect until Mitchell grew a conscience. It was then that Aiden finally decided he would never meet his equal—somebody who understood efficiency and how to balance opportunity with risk management. To a man, his former associates had fallen for morality or greed or simple stupidity.

And now there was only Aiden and his operation.

And Reed Montgomery.

Aiden pushed the door open and stepped out of the car, adjusting his jacket and taking the stairs into the house. The home was barely fifteen hundred square feet, which was minuscule for a man worth half a billion dollars, but Aiden saw no benefit in a larger home. He didn't live with anybody, and he didn't own extensive collections of worthless artifacts or paint splattered on canvas. It was only him and his clothes and his books. The house was designed and sized, like everything else in his world, for maximum efficiency.

Aiden stepped into the kitchen and placed his coat on the hook, then stopped briefly at the wall-mounted, touch-screen computer that operated a security blanket over the entire eighteen-acre property. He armed the system, checked each camera, then continued into the kitchen and poured himself a generous helping of brandy.

The liquor was smooth and sweet and took some of the edge off his nerves. He refilled the glass, then walked through the living room, past walls of bookshelves, to a floor-to-ceiling window that looked out over North Georgia.

Tree-covered mountains rose and fell like waves, now naked of leaves as winter set in. Aiden admired the view, swirling his drink as his mind worked like a machine, computing and re-computing the problem at hand a thousand different ways. Aiden's mind was his greatest weapon, and he knew it. He knew he was brilliant and that with extreme levels of education and mental fortitude, maximum mental efficiency could be unlocked. Hence the books and the six different collegiate diplomas hanging on the wall behind him.

Intelligence was the world's greatest single commodity, was it not? It was the only thing that could be developed into a potentially infinite supply, yet was perpetually scarce in every corner of society. Aiden believed in intelligence, and he believed in his own potential.

But he didn't know what to do about Reed Montgomery.

Aiden turned away from the window and sat in a high-backed leather chair in front of a chessboard. No chair was on the other side of the board. No one else ever joined him in his lonely house or ever played him. There were probably only a couple of people on the planet who *could* play him.

Aiden preferred to play himself, setting the board each night and switching from black to white and back again as he unpacked his problems.

Life was like chess. He couldn't control other people—not directly. But he could back them into corners and force their next move. He could limit their options and slowly reduce their resources, constricting them like a python wrapping itself around their chests and squeezing until, at last, they were crushed.

Aiden studied chess the way an astronomer studied the skies—overwhelmed by the infinite possibilities but relentlessly dedicated to understanding—and commanding—them all. The better he became at the game, the better he would become at life.

But the chessboard held no answer for Reed Montgomery. When Aiden ordered Gambit to eliminate Mitchell Holiday, Gambit hired a South American contractor named Salvador, and Salvador hired Oliver Enfield, and Enfield passed the job to Montgomery. Aiden had no idea that David's son had become a professional assassin, and when he found out, he thought it was a marvelous coincidence, but he wasn't overly concerned about it until Reed started closing in on the origins of Aiden's criminal empire. It was then that Aiden first appreciated the threat Reed presented, and threats could not be tolerated. They reduced efficiency.

It was Gambit's idea to hire Reed to kill Governor Trousdale. Aiden liked the plan—it killed two birds with one stone—but it hadn't worked, and now both Reed and Trousdale were in the wind.

More threats.

Aiden stroked his lip, then lifted a black rook and shifted it across the chessboard, bringing pressure to the white queen. He congratulated himself on the brilliance of the move, then rotated the chessboard and immediately embraced the role of the white pieces. Now the black rook was a threat—like Reed. And like the rook, Reed would have to be eliminated.

Aiden turned away from the chessboard and picked up a tablet from a nearby table. He opened an email and scanned through a selection of images sent to him by an intelligence contact in the underworld. They were pictures of Reed and his known associates. A blonde woman—Frank's daughter. Another hellish coincidence. The man they called The Wolf, an assassin from New York. Maggie Trousdale, the governor of Louisiana. And two other women, one of them an ex-girlfriend, the other a fellow assassin from Enfield's company.

Five people. The Reed Montgomery coalition. The single greatest threat to Aiden's empire.

Aiden put the iPad down and lifted the brandy, swirling it a moment and staring at the chessboard. He thought about efficiency and strategy and playing cat and mouse. He'd tried to manipulate Reed, trap Reed, and even recruit Reed. None of those tactics had worked. In fact, they had all back-fired, causing more mess, attention from the feds, and increased exposure to his operation. Things now teetered on the edge of a knife, and if Aiden didn't act quickly, dominos might start to fall.

This was one of those rare moments in life where calculation and even efficiency itself took a back seat to whatever was most effective. The first thing Aiden needed to do was stop the bleeding—to lock the gates and secure his operations against being compromised by the storm to come. And then he could deal with the Reed coalition once and for all.

Aiden drained the glass, then withdrew his phone and dialed a number. If Reed couldn't be defeated by maneuvers or manipulations, then he would be obliterated by overwhelming force.

2

***

The Airbnb was a change for Reed. He was used to staying in dusty hotels on the wrong side of town, checking in with a fake ID or no ID at all, paying with cash, and resting assured that he was unlikely to be discovered.

Renting something online, from a total stranger, with an electronic paper trail, was a bizarre idea to him, and at first it seemed a needless risk. But Governor Maggie Trousdale, his former-prisoner-turned-ally, had argued otherwise. He was impressed by how easily she created a false identity using a false email address, followed by a false trip itinerary, a false reason for travel, and a false number of occupants. She even scored a coupon as a "first-time bnb-er," and they never met the owner of the large condominium outside of town. The door unlocked with a combination they received via email, and they slipped inside without ever encountering a desk clerk or security camera.

I'm getting rusty. This chick's got better tradecraft than a professional criminal.

Three days had passed since Reed and Maggie buried David Montgomery on the muddy banks of Lake Maurepas, and the chaos that now gripped Louisiana was absolute. Every news channel reported around the clock on the case of their missing governor, and even the president made a speech during a press conference. Reed was accustomed to the heat of an impending investigation, but the temperature now climbed to an unprecedented level, and it would only be a matter of time before he had to cut Maggie loose. She was committed to helping him hunt down the criminal mastermind Aiden Phillips, but there were other factors at play. Factors like continuity of government and massive federal investigations that would eventually run Reed into a corner.

Reed stared into a mug of lukewarm coffee and tried not to be distracted by the cloud of confused stimuli that overwhelmed his mind. Maggie stood nearby, staring at a laptop. The internet was provided as part of their stay, and the computer resulted from a shopping trip the day before.

"It's just like I thought," Maggie said, her voice tinged with rage. "Coulier has assumed office as the acting governor. That son of a bitch." She smacked the computer shut and sulked to the coffeepot.

Reed didn't look up from his mug. Over the prior three days, he and Maggie had been hiding in the condo, recovering from the chaotic events of the past week and arguing about what to do next. For Reed, the answer was obvious. He was going to hunt down Aiden, along with his entire organization, and do what he did best—wipe them out of existence.

But for Maggie, things weren't so clear. She also wanted to destroy Aiden's organization for the havoc it wreaked on both her personal life and her home state, but she now fought a war on two fronts—hunting her enemies and protecting her state from falling into the hands of one of Aiden's associates, Robert Coulier, her former attorney general and now the acting governor of Louisiana.

"You should go back," Reed said. He took a sip of the coffee and rubbed a bruised thumb across the mug.

Maggie tossed her dollar store reading glasses on the counter and poured a cup of coffee before slumping into a chair across from him. "We've been over this. If I go back, I'll be useless to hunt down Aiden. You can't imagine the circus my resurrection will trigger. Media, legal protocol, an enraged state assembly . . . I get a headache just thinking about it."

"You worried about Coulier?"

"Not especially," she said. "He's vicious and conniving, but it's not like he'd pull a gun on me. My guess is that after I depose him, he'll cease to be useful to Aiden and then disappear."

"You have the authority to fire him?"

Maggie frowned. "Not really. The Office of the Attorney General is usually an elected position in Louisiana, which puts him out of reach of my direct powers. But I'm sure I can figure something out."

"He's got dirt on you, right?" Reed asked.

Maggie's shoulders remained relaxed. "Nothing terrible, and nothing that wouldn't take him down with me. But honestly, I'm not interested in reelection. I don't even care if I'm impeached. I'm much more interested in hunting Aiden."

Reed looked through the window to the small yard out back, overgrown with dead grass that hadn't been cut the previous summer. "I think you should let me worry about Aiden. Wherever he is, whoever he is, he's not out of reach for a man like me. Nobody is."

"You mean a man with no regard for the law."

Reed shrugged. "Birds of a feather, Aiden and I. The difference is, I don't run a criminal operation. I destroy them."

Maggie slammed her mug down. "I told you, I don't want a quiet, bloody ending with an accident on a balcony or a loose electrical cable in the bathtub. I want Aiden to stand trial. I want him torn down."

A tired smile spread across Reed's face—more resigned than condescending.

"What?" Maggie asked.

"You've never been to prison, have you?"

"Of course not. You have?"

"I served some time in a super-max facility out west."

Maggie looked away, and Reed caught her discomfort in the way she rubbed the handle of her coffee mug.

"Don't worry," he said. "I was there for the best reasons." He drained the mug. "You know what the first thing you learn in prison is?"

Maggie tried to smirk. "Don't drop the soap?"

"That's the second thing. The first thing you learn is that *everything* is for sale. A better cell, better food, dirty magazines, cigarettes . . . Literally, anything you want. And that's in a super-max facility. What do you think it's like in a white-collar lockup like Aiden will go to? Tennis courts and tanning beds, I promise you. For a man like him, with the money he has, you'll lock him up for five or six years, he'll live like a king, then come out with a taste for blood. Your blood."

"It won't be like that," Maggie said. "Louisiana is a capital punishment state. Aiden has done plenty to get the needle."

"Sure he has, and you'll never prove any of it. I know people like Aiden, people who stand at the top of very tall pyramids with layers and layers of plausible deniability between them and the blood at the bottom. Whatever sort of sordid shit Aiden is up to, you'll never convict him. You'll be lucky to write him a parking ticket."

Maggie chewed her lip, her fingers working the handle of the coffee mug.

"I have a name," Reed continued. "It's something they used to call me at my last job. *The Prosecutor*. I'm not sure how it started, but there's a reason it stuck. I prosecute the guilty. There's no judge or jury or needle. But the judgment is just, and it's permanent. It's the kind of justice Aiden Phillips deserves, and the kind he's gonna get."

Maggie gritted her teeth. "I *told* you. That's not how society works."

Reed laughed, unable to conceal the condescension in his tone. "It's not how *your* society works. The world is an iceberg, Maggie. You're sitting just above the surface, looking up at a majestic mountain made of all kinds of fancy words—justice, law, civilization. You don't see anything that's happening underwater. But me? I've lived down there for years. So has Aiden. And that's where he'll die, too."

Maggie crossed her arms. "Not happening, Reed. It's illegal."

It was the same conclusion their arguments had reached for three days straight. Maggie wanted her ideals, and Reed knew they were impossible. What's more, he was growing weary of indulging her self-righteousness. Maybe it was time to throw down a trump card.

"What makes you think you can stop me?" he said. "I respect you, Governor. But you need to get something very, very clear. This man killed my father. He killed Mitchell Holiday. He probably killed Frank Morccelli. When I find him and decide how to kill him, trust me when I tell you that anyone who gets in the way is gonna get hurt. Don't be that person."

They locked eyes for a long moment. He liked what he saw in her steady gaze. There was steel and fire and no shortage of grit. She was an incredible woman, no doubt about it. A formidable force, not so different from him. Except she still believed in the mountain of society, while he had lived underwater too long to remember what it looked like. In her world, maybe she was right. Maybe he was an animal. But this wasn't her world, and he wasn't going to let her call the shots in his.

"Go back to Baton Rouge," he said. "Reclaim your office, and deal with Coulier. We'll stay in touch, I promise. You'll know when it happens."

Maggie's stare chilled into a glare. She scooped up the laptop and stomped across the room, starting up the stairs. She made it only three steps when the knock rang against the door. Reed startled, sitting upright and glancing at his phone. He'd placed perimeter monitors on the driveway, designed to send him an alert if anybody approached the house. The phone's screen was black, and another knock crashed against the wood.

Reed stood up, snatching the SIG Sauer pistol from his hip and jerking his head to Maggie. "Get down! Don't make any noise."

She retreated behind the couch as Reed approached the door, positioning himself to one side. Then he nodded at Maggie.

"Who is it?" she called.

"Luigi's!"

They exchanged a frown.

"Luigi's?" Reed mouthed.

Maggie shook her head. Then a glint of understanding crossed her face. "Pizza?"

"Pizza?" Reed whispered. "You ordered pizza?"

She shook her head.

"Luigi who?" Reed asked, feeling stupid as soon as he said it. Like this was a knock-knock joke.

"Uh . . . Luigi's Pizza?" The voice was low and sleepy. Maybe a stoned teenager.

Reed gritted his teeth and evaluated his options. The door featured a peephole, but Reed didn't use peepholes. It was too easy for somebody to wait for the hole to darken and then unleash a hail of bullets through the door. He could move to the window, but the problem was the same.

"We didn't order pizza," Reed called out.

The kid sighed. "Look, dude. It's paid for. Can I just leave it on the doorstep? The address is right, man."

"Check the name. We didn't order."

"Maggie Mud?"

The blood froze in Reed's veins, and he exchanged a glance with Maggie. "Leave it on the doorstep," he said.

The box hit the porch with a loud smack. Moments later, a four-cylinder engine whined to life, and the kid rolled away in his car. Reed waited five minutes, listening intently for any hint of another person on the porch, then he slipped the door open, leading with the gun, and pulled the box into the room.

The door smacked shut behind him, then he re-bolted it and examined the box. "Is it a real restaurant?" he asked.

"Yeah. A few dozen locations around the state."

"And this is their box?"

"Looks like it."

Reed toed the box with one foot. "Okay. Stand back."

He knelt and flipped the box open with the muzzle of the SIG. A cloud of steam erupted into the air, carrying with it the rich scent of molten cheese and sizzling pepperoni.

Reed waved the steam away and wrinkled his nose. It smelled damn good, and he was hungry, but as the steam faded, something else came into view. A Sharpie-scrawled message on the inside of the lid was written in tight, immaculate handwriting.

BB-60. T-MINUS 18. BRING TROUSDALE. —W

3

_____

The metal walls of the old warehouse were rusted, blasted by decades of salt wind blowing off the Gulf. Cracks and gaps in the roof let beams of sunlight streak into the darkened interior, providing enough illumination to navigate the wreckages of abandoned machinery, ship engines, and oil puddles.

Banks sat at the edge of the warehouse on an upturned metal bucket, her legs pulled close and her chin propped on both hands as she watched Kelly and Lucy spar on an open patch of concrete twenty feet away. They didn't use weapons, just their arms and bodyweight, lunging and twisting, grappling for advantage. Lucy was the unquestionable superior—she danced around Kelly's clumsier strides with ease, darting in and out to deliver light blows to the bigger woman's stomach and thighs, but moving slow enough to allow Kelly to learn the fighting style. She paused every minute or so to offer an instructional tip or corrective lesson, refining Kelly's movements and teaching her what exposures to look for.

Kelly's mutilated face was still twisted into her now perpetual sneer, but the attention with which she pursued the fight betrayed her true emotions —focus, intensity, and a hunger to learn.

"Keep your guard up," Lucy chided. "When you strike, you still have to protect yourself."

Kelly lunged, throwing what could've been a pretty great uppercut if Lucy had been six inches taller and half as agile. She dodged it with ease and sent her left leg crashing into Kelly's exposed ribcage.

"See?" Lucy said, dancing back. "This isn't like the movies. You can only take a couple of those before you're finished. Self-protection is paramount to a quick shot."

The sparring resumed, and Banks found it difficult to focus. She sat near the wall, exhausted, a bottle of water cradled in one hand. Three days of hiding near the coast hadn't been enough to recharge her from the action and trauma of the past two weeks. She didn't know if it was PTSD, fear, or just pure weariness that kept her mind in a perpetual state of edginess, but she couldn't remember the last time she got a good night's sleep or didn't wake up thinking about Reed.

Reed. Where was he? After Banks, Lucy, Kelly, and Wolfgang had finished clearing the house by the lake, where they'd discovered an underground sex trafficking operation, they looked for Reed but found only bodies. He and the governor had vanished into the Louisiana swamps, leaving nothing but footprints and shell casings.

The governor.

Banks closed her eyes and thought about New Orleans. Again, she saw herself standing next to the street as cars whizzed by and Reed appeared on the other side. He stood tall and broad, battered by the world but unbeaten by it, and the rush of happiness she felt when she saw him confirmed in her heart as much as her mind what she already knew—that she loved this man. He was a killer. A criminal. Probably one of the bloodiest people on the planet. Yet she couldn't shake the attraction she felt and the belief she held that somewhere behind the killer was a good man struggling to break free.

Seeing him in New Orleans, all she wanted to do was throw herself at him, but she never got the chance. He saw her, he looked away, and then he kissed the governor, pulling her in and holding her as if they were the only people on the planet. The way he used to hold Banks. The way she longed for him to hold her again.

She opened her eyes, and they blurred. She couldn't see Kelly and Lucy anymore, but she didn't care. Since that moment in New Orleans, only one thing was important to her, and that was tracking down the men behind the brothel she and the others had discovered. Wolfgang was busy digging through computer hard drives they'd recovered on-site, and once he found a lead, they would run it to ground.

It may not bring her any resolution with Reed, but delivering justice against the monsters who sold those girls into a life of torment and horror might be enough to bring meaning into the catastrophe Banks's own life had become.

"Banks!" Lucy called.

Banks blinked, bringing focus back to her gaze.

Lucy chugged on a bottle of water, then beckoned. "Tap in, hot stuff." Banks shook her head, but Lucy set the bottle down and motioned again. "Nope, you've sat too long. Let's go."

Banks reluctantly hauled herself up and stumbled into the cleared patch of concrete.

Lucy smiled and smacked her on the arm, then appraised her stance. "Anybody ever say you've got a fighter's build?" Banks blushed, and Lucy winked. "For real, there's something to work with here. But if you stand that way, you'll be on your ass in a blink. Here, do this . . ." Lucy guided Banks's right foot a half step back, then nudged her left forward, her knee slightly bent, and balancing on the ball of her foot. "Stance is everything. Keep your weight on your right leg until you're ready to strike, then shift that weight to your left foot and lean into the blow. You get more power and stability this way."

Banks nodded dumbly and watched as Lucy fell into an identical stance with all the practiced grace of a cat curling into bed.

"Now, there are all kinds of fighting styles with all kinds of rules," Lucy said. "But the only thing that matters in the real world is winning. So eye gouges, ball shots, fish-hooking . . . anything goes."

"Fish-hooking?" Banks asked.

Lucy darted forward and shot a finger into Banks's mouth with the speed of a striking snake. With a quick twist, she dug her finger into the inside of Banks's cheek and jerked right. The blast of pain ripping through her face was immediate and sent her crashing to the floor with no hope to resist.

Lucy released her as she fell, and then she stepped back. "Fish-hooking. It's not always the best strategy. You can lose a finger, in theory, but the point is, nothing's off-limits."

Banks spit blood from a scratched mouth and climbed to her feet, sudden anger rushing into her body. She lunged toward Lucy, but the smaller woman sidestepped without effort and twisted to the left, driving her elbow into Banks's lower back as she passed. The force was enough to break Banks's fragile balance, and she crashed to the floor amid a cloud of dust.

Kelly chuckled as Banks coughed and stumbled to her feet again. Her knees and elbows were sore from the concrete, and she could already feel bruises forming over her shoulder blades.

"Sorry," Lucy mumbled. "I got a bit reflexive there. I don't like being rushed."

Banks glared and accepted the bottle of water Kelly offered.

"She's a bitch, isn't she?" Kelly said.

Banks swigged the water and handed it back.

Lucy beckoned her forward. "Resume your stance. We're going to take it slow."

Banks planted her weight on her right leg and balanced her left leg on the ball of her foot.

"Close both hands, but not tight," Lucy said. "Hold your left in front of your face, palm inward. This is your defense hand. If I go for your face, you block with that hand. Now, your right hand is your power hand. That's where the real hits come from. Hold it up, same way, but lower than the left . . . yes. Now, duck your chin and relax your shoulders. This is about speed, not density."

Banks did her best to mimic the positions Lucy demonstrated, trying to ignore the pain in her knees and back.

"Okay," Lucy continued. "So, this is a basic boxing stance, but we're not boxing. We're fighting. The method I'm teaching is based on a fighting style called Muay Thai. It involves both hits and kicks."

Lucy stepped forward, smoothly and quickly, but without aggression.

She shielded her face with one hand while striking toward Banks's nose with the other. Banks moved her left hand to block the strike, as she had been told. She felt the impact of Lucy's knuckles lightly on the back of her hand only a split second before Lucy's right leg snapped forward and struck her side, shinbone against unprotected flesh. It wasn't a hard strike, but it carried enough force to knock Banks backward while gasping for air.

Lucy retreated immediately, offering a reassuring nod. "Great job on the block! But you have to look out for my legs, too. There's a lot of power in the leg. Sometimes, all it takes to win a fight is a couple kicks to the ribs."

Banks sucked wind. "How do I stop it?"

"With your leg, shin on shin. It hurts like hell, but shinbones are strong. Try to kick me, and I'll show you."

Banks pivoted her weight onto her left leg before snapping her right leg up and sending her shin crashing toward Lucy's hip. Lucy shifted her weight onto her back leg before lifting her left leg up and blocking the kick in midair. Bone crashed against bone with a sharp thud, and Banks stumbled back. The pain was intense, but much less than the kick she had absorbed only moments before.

Lucy smiled. "See? It's simple."

Banks grinned, a sudden, strange satisfaction replacing the pain and anger. It felt good to understand something, and even better to gain Lucy's approval.

Before Lucy could continue, Wolfgang appeared from across the room. He hadn't shaved in days, and his hair was a disheveled mess, but he walked with energy. "I'm making progress on backtracking the hard drives. I'll need some more time, but I'm hungry. Pizza?"

Kelly grunted her approval. "Yeah. Anchovies, this time. No more of that pineapple bullshit."

Wolfgang raised his eyebrows in offense, but before he could return fire, a sharp knock rang out from the metal door twenty yards away at the end of the warehouse. The four of them started, and Wolfgang snatched the Glock from his hip as Lucy retreated to her swords and Banks ran for her shotgun. They all crouched behind cover, remaining perfectly silent. Seconds ticked into minutes, but no second knock came. Eventually, tires crunched against gravel outside of the warehouse. The sound grew increasingly distant, then faded altogether.

"Okay," Wolfgang whispered. "Everybody stay still. I'm going to—"

Banks ignored him, creeping across the open warehouse with the shotgun held ready at her hip. She'd already used the 20-gauge pump action to execute one of the sex traffickers back at the brothel, and she liked the way it felt in her hands—heavy and solid.

"Wait!" Wolfgang hissed.

"Cover me," Banks snapped. She wasn't exactly sure what "cover me" meant, but she'd seen enough movies to know it had something to do with Wolfgang protecting her while she dashed into potentially dangerous territory.

Banks snuck up to a hole in the sheet metal next to the doorframe and peered out, holding her breath as she surveyed the yard. Abandoned machinery and dockside paraphernalia littered the yard, but she saw no sign of the intruder or his vehicle. All was quiet under the midmorning sun. She bit her tongue and slipped up to the door, lifting the latch and pushing it open with the shotgun still pointed outward.

"No . . . no . . ." Wolfgang pleaded, but she ignored him.

No one was waiting outside. The yard was as empty of humanity as it had looked through the peephole only a moment before, but something lay on the doorstep.

A large pizza box.

4

"Walk me through this again," Maggie said. "We're going to meet a mysterious, genderless, faceless entity on the deck of an antique warship. And why, exactly?"

Reed downshifted the BMW to pass a minivan. The little German car responded instantly to his prompting, the nose lifting just a little as more power churned to the rear wheels. It was far from the sort of raw, semi-terrifying American power he was accustomed to, but all things considered, the BMW wasn't half bad as a sports car.

"The message on the pizza box said 'BB-Sixty,' which is the naval code for the USS *Alabama*, a World War II–era battleship that is now anchored in Mobile as a sort of museum."

"I'm clear on that." Maggie's voice was semi-exasperated. "I'm just unsure why we're following a cryptic code on the inside of a pizza box in the first place."

It was a fair question. Reed wondered the same thing. For all he knew, it was a brutal trap. But he didn't think so.

"Who's W?" Maggie asked.

"I told you. W is shorthand for Winter, an intelligence contact of mine from my years in the criminal underworld. Whenever somebody such as myself needs information on a person, a location, a building, literally anything, you call Winter. And Winter gets it for you."

"But you don't know who Winter is?"

"Nobody knows who Winter is. But I've dealt with them for years. In fact, up until recently, Winter was my primary source of intel for all operations."

"Up until recently," Maggie repeated. "What happened?"

Reed frowned, retracing his memories over the past few weeks. Everything was blurring together. "I'm not sure. After my former boss turned on me, I called Winter a couple times trying to get intel on who was behind it all—specifically, who hired me to kill Senator Mitchell Holiday."

"Your boss didn't order the hit?"

"My boss *brokered* the hit. There was always a customer, but I never knew who. I now believe it was Aiden Phillips, Gambit's boss. But at the time, I didn't know, so I called Winter to find out."

"And?"

"And Winter refused to help. At first, they simply objected. Then they stopped taking my calls altogether. Completely ghosted me."

"Is that unusual?"

"It never happened before."

"And yet, you seem very convinced that this shapeless, faceless, invisible entity has now experienced a sudden change of heart and wants to be helpful. So much so that you're willing to read the inscription on a pizza box and crash headfirst toward what is almost certainly a trap."

Reed frowned for a moment, considering the accusation. On face value, it made sense. But he knew better. "It's not a trap."

"What makes you so sure?"

"A couple things. First, the ship is a big attraction. It's always loaded with Boy Scouts, families from out of state, and international tourists. It would be a really odd place to set a trap and a difficult place to pull one off. There's only one way on board, and the park is fenced off. So, if somebody were setting me up, this would be a dumb place to do it. On the other hand, if somebody wanted to facilitate a clandestine meeting in a place that would be easy to secure, the ship makes a lot of sense."

"Okay," Maggie said, still unconvinced. "And the second reason?"

Reed hesitated. The second reason was a lot less logical and really more of a gut feeling than any sort of arguable position. But that gut feeling verged on conviction, and Reed had learned to trust those.

"Whenever I called Winter about the Holiday mission, and especially when I started asking about who ordered the hit, Winter was strange."

"Your point?"

"I'm not sure. I just had the feeling that this job was different for Winter. Personal, almost."

Maggie shot him an "Are you serious?" look, and Reed dismissed it with a shrug.

"I could be wrong," he said, "but even if I am, the first point stands. The battleship is an unlikely place to stage a setup, and I'm confident in my own ability to dodge one anyway."

"What if the FBI is posing as Winter? You're pretty high on their most wanted list. If they were smart, they'd stage a trap at exactly this sort of place."

Reed smirked. "Even the FBI isn't that vicious. They wouldn't risk me opening fire on a group of Korean tourists to escape custody. Which, in fact, I would never do, but they don't know that. And anyway, if they knew about our Airbnb, they could've just taken me there. No reason to arrange a rendezvous two states away."

Maggie nodded without much conviction.

Reed settled back in the comfortable leather seat and reevaluated his decision to accept the invite. Maggie was right—there were a lot of big, unanswered questions looming about the entire situation. But the possibility that Winter had decided to help him find Aiden was too valuable to ignore. As eager as he was to wipe Aiden off the face of the planet, he really had no idea where to find the man. If Winter could point him in the right direction, well, that was an opportunity worth taking some risk for.

"Why do you think this Winter person specifically asked for me?" Maggie asked.

Reed frowned, puzzling the question out for himself. It was reasonable to assume that Winter knew a great deal about Maggie, her background, and her conflict with Aiden's organization. Perhaps Winter wanted Maggie involved in the war because Winter knew more about Aiden's weaknesses than they did.

"I don't know," Reed said. "I'm sure it's a good reason." He shot her a sideways look. "Are you afraid?"

She shook her head. "No. But I'm not reckless, either."

Reed checked his phone. It was one hundred eighty-six miles to Mobile. They'd arrive just past noon.

5

Special Agent Rufus "Turk" Turkman sat behind his desk in the back corner of the office and shot a cautious glance through the door of his cubicle. The hallway lay empty, but the song of clicking keyboards and quiet voices resounded from not far away. He took a swallow of lukewarm coffee from a paper cup and redirected his attention to his computer, closing out of the training webinar he was supposed to be attending and navigating to his web browser. A news article filled the screen, detailing in bold words the presumed kidnapping of Maggie Trousdale.

The thirty-four-year-old governor of Louisiana had vanished right in front of a dozen TV cameras only a few days prior as her podium exploded into a shower of flames and smoke. The resulting panic that swept the state quickly spilled across the country, and the president himself tasked the director of the FBI with finding Trousdale—dead or alive. Turk wasn't a member of the special task force assembled to conduct the search. In fact, after being booted the previous week from the two-man investigatory team charged with tracking down Reed Montgomery, Turk wasn't a member of any task force. He was now a floating agent, assigned to a mountain of meaningless training webinars while the slow cogs of FBI bureaucracy searched for his next assignment.

Turk swallowed more coffee and scanned down the page, clicking play on a video from CNN that was shot on-site of the explosion. Even without audio, it was easy to follow the train of events that quickly unfolded. Trousdale stood on the podium, one hand raised, her stern features directed at the crowd as she delivered some kind of passionate speech. A moment later, the first blast went off, filling the air with clouds of grey smoke. Then the video slowed, and a yellow circle appeared to one side, highlighting the outlines of the man rushing into the smoke seconds before the next blast hurled the camera to the ground.

Turk rewound the tape, focusing on the shadowy outlines of the big man rushing toward the governor. He was tall, broad, and muscular, dressed in the distinctive uniform of a Louisiana state trooper. His face and most of his physique were obscured by smoke, but Turk didn't need a clear shot to know who he was looking at.

He glanced at the stack of paperwork next to his elbow, borrowed from the unclassified, open-investigation data files available to all agents. They concerned the incident with Trousdale, and unbeknownst to the media, they detailed an unpublicized event concerning a state trooper who was found naked and unconscious in an alley near the port.

The trooper couldn't recall much about his assailant other than it being a man, and that man was big and muscular.

Turk leaned back and stared at the screen. There wasn't a doubt in his mind the "trooper" in the smoke was Reed Montgomery, his fire-team commander from his years in the Marine Corps. Turk and Reed were more than trigger buddies—they were loyal friends. The kind of friends who don't necessarily know that much about each other but don't really need to. Something about being shot at and hauling each other through one shit storm after another built that sort of bond. It was a mysterious thing, and even now as Turk sat next to a mountain of evidence that said Reed Montgomery had become a brutal killer . . . the bond remained. And it called to him. It called him to find the truth and pull his trigger buddy out of whatever shit storm now engulfed him.

Turk lifted the cup, but it was empty. He crushed it between thick fingers and dropped it into the trash can. The FBI had pulled him off the Montgomery case, and he still didn't know why. Montgomery was now classified as a domestic terrorist, and the appropriate department had taken over. Homeland was probably involved. They would run him down, whatever it took, and when they found him, well, there wouldn't be a trial. There wouldn't be a news conference or a beaming bureaucrat taking credit for the hard work of his field agents. No, that wasn't how Homeland operated. They would apprehend Montgomery, extract as much information as possible from him, and then he would vanish.

Turk could almost hear the bureaucrats now, frowning into the cameras and saying, "Reed who?"

It was an odd feeling knowing that your fellow Marine was about to fall victim to the same machine that had crushed numerous foreign nationals in the interest of national security. Turk never had a problem with the kidnapping and questionable interrogation of suspected terrorists. He'd seen too many American soldiers and innocent civilians blown to pieces by the crafty efforts of jihadists to invest much energy into questioning the system that hunted those jihadists.

This felt different. Turk wasn't so conceited as to miss the obvious double-standard his emotions reflected. But nonetheless, he couldn't let this happen to Montgomery. If his old friend really was a domestic terrorist, Turk would be the first to bring him down. But first, Montgomery would explain himself, and there would be no backroom "interrogations" involved.

It might be the Homeland way, but it sure as hell wasn't the Marine way.

The phone on Turk's desk buzzed, and he glanced up. The caller ID read "Whitaker, P.," Turk's temporary boss.

Turk lifted the receiver and spoke quietly. "Turkman."

"My office."

Turk hung up and slung his jacket on as he left the cubicle and journeyed the fifty yards through a sea of cubicles to the glass office at the end of the hall. The blinds were closed, but the door stood open.

He knocked once on the doorframe as he stepped in. "Yes, sir?"

Whitaker looked up from his computer, then motioned to the door.

Turk shut it as he stepped in, remaining stiff and alert as he approached the desk.

Whitaker sighed. "I've told you, this isn't the Corps. Relax."

Turk loosened his shoulders, crossing both hands over his belt buckle and assuming an "at ease" position.

Whitaker ran a hand over his face. "Sit down, Turk."

Turk felt a sudden uneasiness with Whitaker's tone, but he said nothing.

Whitaker rubbed an index finger over his lip. "You've been assigned to a field office. You leave first thing next week."

Turk expected to be reassigned, but the news still concerned him. "Where am I going, sir?"

Whitaker still held his gaze, unblinking. "Anchorage."

Turk squinted. "Alaska?"

Whitaker nodded.

"Sir, with respect, I specifically requested to be kept in the Southeast. For my family."

Whitaker raised one eyebrow, then shifted some papers on his desk and slid a single sheet toward Turk.

An icy hand of anxiety closed around Turk's stomach as soon as he glanced down at the sheet. It was a printout of web browsing history—*his* web browsing history, detailing every news site and web search he'd used on his quest for details about Reed.

"I was in the Air Force," Whitaker said. "I don't pretend that pushing papers at a domestic air base is anything like being a combat Marine, but I get the camaraderie. The loyalty to your guys. So, I'm not going to make a big deal out of this. But I know what you're up to, and I can't let you sabotage your career that way."

Molten fire boiled in Turk's blood, and he gritted his teeth. "They're gonna railroad him, sir. You and I both know it. Montgomery will never stand trial."

Whitaker rubbed his lip again, and Turk saw weariness on his face. Or perhaps it was just simple pragmatism.

"You've got training for the rest of the week, then the weekend off.

Anchorage is expecting you next Wednesday. You'll find details in your email, along with arrangements for your move."

Turk squinted at the sheet, then looked up. "You did this, didn't you? You're exiling me."

Whitaker's eyes turned hard. "If I'm doing anything, I'm doing you a favor. That will be all, Agent."

Turk dropped the sheet on the desk and stood up. He marched back to his computer and shoveled the stack of research documents into his brief-case before logging off the computer and turning to the elevator. He would take his lunch, maybe go down to that Chinese place on the corner, which at that time of day was populated almost exclusively by fellow agents—witnesses to watch him get sick and puke on the floor. Then he'd go home. He'd be sick for a few days—long enough to get out of training.

Long enough to find Montgomery.

6

The park was exactly as Reed remembered—large, open, and full of tourists. The parking lot stretched out to the edge of the bay, where a large gift shop was the only entry point through a high fence. On the far side of that fence was the imposing bulk of USS *Alabama*, a threatening monument to the naval warfare of yesteryear, proudly adorned with the Stars and Stripes.

Standing at the edge of the parking lot, Reed couldn't help but feel a twist in his stomach. He'd visited the ship twice before, almost two decades previously. His father loved history and took Reed to as many historical locations and monuments as possible. The ship was Reed's favorite—hence the repeat visit. On their second trip, David Montgomery had convinced a Boy Scout officer to allow Reed to join his troop for an overnight stay.

Deep in the bowels of the ship, stretched out on the same swinging bunks that US sailors had used decades before during their desperate fight against Imperial Japan, Reed lay awake, listening to the unique sounds of the ship: the creaks of metal on metal and the howl of the wind far away. The boat smelled old, like hydraulic fluid, spilled oil, and old shoes.

Something about the ship ignited Reed's imagination, as though at any moment a siren would call general quarters and then the big guns would open fire. The ship spoke to Reed with the voices of a thousand warriors from an age come and gone.

And here he was, years later, a different kind of warrior, fighting a different kind of war . . . back at the same ship. Reed sucked in a breath of cold air and felt uneasiness settle into his stomach. He suddenly wondered if Winter had picked this place for more than its virtues as a safe rendezvous. What if Winter picked the battleship because they knew Reed and wanted him to know how much.

It was an altogether unsettling thought.

"What now?" Maggie asked. She shut the BMW's passenger door and shot a wary glance around the parking lot. There were plenty of people around, but nobody paid any attention to the woman that half the FBI was obsessed with finding.

Before Reed could answer, he felt a buzz in his pocket and dug his phone out. A text message from an unknown number lit up the screen.

Leave the governor. Go inside and buy two tickets.

Reed showed Maggie the text. She raised both eyebrows, but he nodded.

"It's best," he said. "Stay in the car. I'll keep you posted."

She climbed back in as Reed started toward the gift shop. The breeze blowing off the bay was cold, almost icy. He pulled his coat around him, checking for the reassuring weight of the SIG beneath his arm, and mentally reviewed his plan of action if this turned into a trap. As long as he was on the deck of the ship, he could easily jump overboard or dash for cover, but if he was led into the bowels of the old vessel, where hallways were cramped and many of the passages were walled off to tourists, he would have to rely on his wits to prevent an ambush.

Reed entered the gift shop and navigated between the crowds of children and harried adults on his way to the ticket counter.

"Two, please." He slid cash to the attendant and accepted the tickets, then felt another buzz in his pocket.

Leave one ticket in the third stall of the men's room. Proceed to the ship.

Reed hesitated a moment, his mind spinning, then he punched out a quick message.

Why?

The reply was instant.

Because you want blood. I can help.

Reed pushed into the bathroom and stuck the ticket between the wall of the stall and the toilet paper dispenser. Then he walked through the gift shop and through the back doors into the park.

The ship was even more impressive up close—tall and imposing, like an unstoppable force of domination. He moved down the sidewalk to a concrete gangway, and two minutes later he was at the top, stepping on board amid a flood of tourists: men, women, children, Americans, Asians, and Europeans. They all moved up and down the decks, calling to one another in cheery voices as they pointed and marveled at the soaring towers and massive guns. Reed searched the faces for somebody who stuck out—somebody who wasn't there for the Instagram pictures. His pocket buzzed again.

Follow the signs to Boy Scout Berth C.

The cold touch of uncertainty stabbed deeper into his stomach, and Reed cast another look around the deck. Somebody was watching him. They had to be. They knew where he was, what he was doing, and where they wanted him to go next. He knew nothing, and that left him dangerously exposed.

The next text came through unprompted.

Do it now, or I walk.

Reed gritted his teeth. He either trusted Winter or he left now. It was time to decide.

The second ticket, Reed thought. He glanced over one shoulder. Nobody was there, but somebody would be. Soon.

He found his way to the port-side entrance of the superstructure and ducked through a door. It was muggy inside, warmed by the crush of tourists pressing in all around him. He moved through them and followed the signs for the Boy Scout berths, which lay several decks below. The stairs squeaked under his feet, leading him deeper into the ship. He checked his phone, and his suspicions were confirmed as the last bar of his signal faded away. Whoever had set this up was trying to cut him off from any contact with the outside world. They were trying to isolate him.

But why?

As he slipped farther into the belly of the ship, the tourists faded. Most of them wouldn't journey over this many steps, this deep into the stench of hydraulic fluid and years of paint. After another two flights of stairs, he stepped into an open berth loaded with swinging, multi-level beds suspended from the roof by chains. A black door was mounted into the far wall with a single porthole in the middle. Over the door, painted in white letters, were the words "SCOUT BERTH C."

Reed shoved the phone into his pocket and slid his hand beneath his coat, resting it on the SIG. As he approached the door, he could see a padlock looped through the latch, but upon further inspection, he saw it was unlocked. He cast one more cautious glance around the room but saw no one. He was alone, and even the voices of the hundreds of tourists above him had faded away to almost nothing. A prickling sensation ran down Reed's spine—a practiced instinct honed over years of combat and living on the wrong side of the law—a sixth sense, a voice in the back of his head. Whatever it was called, Reed knew this feeling and had learned the hard way that it was never wrong.

He placed his hand on the lock, lifted it free, and pulled the door open.

The room beyond was dark, lit only by the dim glow of red lamps buried in the ceiling above a tangle of wires and pipes. More berths hung from chains, casting dark shadows over the floor, but nothing moved in those shadows. Everything was deathly still.

Reed stepped through without a sound, placing his feet carefully on the steel floor beyond and moving immediately to the right. He melted into the shadows behind the half-open door and placed a hand on the SIG. It slipped out of the holster without a sound, then he directed the barrel toward the door.

And he waited.

Moments ticked by in slow motion. Reed held his breath and kept his finger extended next to the trigger, only a split second from driving 9mm slugs into the gap of the door. Then he saw a shadow. The light streaming through the door was interrupted, and an arm in a thick wool jacket appeared, followed by a torso.

The figure slid through the door without a sound, one hand jammed into the pocket of his peacoat. He didn't see Reed. He didn't even look into the shadows on either side of the door. Instead, he leaned forward and withdrew his hand from the pocket, clasping a pistol.

Reed waited until the figure took three steps into the berth, walking between a row of hanging bunks. Then he left the shadows and stepped into the hallway behind the man and raised the SIG. Reed said, "One more step, and I drop you."

7

The man froze with his gun held at his side and pointed at the ground. Reed could see the tension in his shoulders, but to his credit, he didn't so much as flinch when Reed spoke. He just stopped and waited.

"Put the gun on the bottom bunk," Reed said.

The man complied without comment, tossing the gun onto the nearest bottom bunk. It landed on the plastic-encased mattress with a thump, and the man's hands returned to his sides.

"Turn slowly," Reed said, keeping the muzzle of the SIG aligned with the man's torso.

The man held up both hands and slowly turned around, light spilling across his face as he moved.

Reed stiffened. "Wolfgang?"

Wolfgang offered an ironic smile. "Well, what do you know? You finally snuck up on me for a change."

Reed didn't lower the gun. Instead, he took a half step forward, closing the distance between himself and Wolfgang but keeping him far enough away that he'd catch a bullet long before he could reach Reed.

"Who's with you?" Reed snapped.

Wolfgang sighed, lowering his hands a little. "Nobody. Not here, anyway. You can put the gun away, Reed. I'm not here to kill you."

A strange irritation boiled in Reed's stomach—a frustration, or perhaps just an impatience. No matter where this strange, endless war took him, he couldn't seem to stop crossing paths with the man they called *The Wolf*, an elite assassin originally tasked with killing Reed.

Wolfgang had almost succeeded, too, only thwarted by Reed's limitless willingness to bring down the house or one of Wolfgang's own bizarre rules. Regardless, Reed could never put his finger on why Wolfgang was still around, and he felt vaguely annoyed by that.

"Why are you here?" he demanded, still pointing the gun.

Wolfgang cocked his head then reached for his pocket.

Reed jabbed with the gun and leaned forward.

Wolfgang held up both hands and sighed. "Geez, man. Chill out. It's not a gun."

He reached for his pocket again, and Reed placed his finger on the trigger.

Wolfgang stuck two fingers into the pocket and pulled out something small and white, then dropped it on the floor. It was the ticket stub Reed left in the bathroom.

Reed relaxed just a little. "You received a cryptic message?"

"Affirmative. On the inside of a pizza box."

"For a meeting here, on the ship?"

Wolfgang nodded.

"Who did you bring?" Reed demanded.

"Only Lucy . . . the chick with the swords. The message was clear on that."

Winter wanted Little Bitch?

That surprised Reed. Lucy Byrne, better known by her code name *Little Bitch*, was a formidable killer on a bad day. On a good day, she might be as good as Reed.

Might be.

"Where is she?" Reed said.

"Who?"

"Banks."

"Gulfport. She's safe."

Reed nodded slowly. Wolfgang's relaxed posture and open face appeared honest, and Reed wasn't really sure what The Wolf had to gain by lying, anyway.

"Why are you here?" Reed asked again.

"I told you, I received a pizza I didn't order. Pretty tasty pizza, I will say. Anchovies for the win."

"I know about the pizza, dammit. I'm asking why you came. What are you after?"

Wolfgang cocked his head. Reed guessed he was evaluating his options, trying to decide if he should show his cards.

"You were at the house?" Wolfgang asked. "The one by the lake?"

"Yeah. I saw you and the women storm it. Quite a show."

Wolfgang grunted. "That it was. Banks really doesn't take no for an answer."

Reed felt a smile playing at the corner of his mouth, but he resisted it. "So, why are you here?"

"That house was some kind of brothel. We found underage girls from outside the country. Cameras. Bedrooms. Apparently, it was a blackmail operation. Whoever owned it invited high-profile people to have intercourse with minors, and then filmed them doing so. I found lots of footage . . . There was a senator, among others."

"A senator? As in a *United States* senator?"

"Yep. I'll deal with him later, assuming Banks or Lucy don't get to him first. But the point is, we found a hard drive with all kinds of data on it. Whoever is running this operation is connected to a child trafficking ring from overseas, and we find ourselves compelled to address that. Currently, our investigation points us back to one Aiden Phillips, and Banks seems to think you know where to find him. That's why I'm here."

Reed frowned. Something still wasn't adding up. "You came here based on a message from somebody you don't know, with the vague hope that they would help you?"

Wolfgang returned the frown. "No, I came here based on *your* message."

"What?"

"In the pizza box. Your message."

Realization hit Reed like a fist in the face. Of course Winter wouldn't have signed Wolfgang's message with a W. Wolfgang probably had no idea who Winter was, and even if he did, he had no reason to trust them. So, Winter signed the message as though it came from Reed.

Brilliant.

Reed holstered the gun. For better or worse, he believed Wolfgang. "The message didn't come from me. It came from somebody called Winter —an intelligence asset who works undercover in the criminal underworld. I've worked with Winter for years, but I guess you haven't, so that's why Winter signed the message as me."

Wolfgang whistled softly. "Well, they must be good at their job. The message mentioned our encounter in Chattanooga—you know, when I snuck up on you at the pier? I was pretty convinced it was you."

Reed should've been surprised, but he wasn't. He had no clue how Winter could've known about his encounter with Wolfgang in Chattanooga, but Winter always seemed to know things like that. It was part of their brand.

"I'm here to find information on Aiden," Reed said. "His man, Gambit, killed my father."

"I'm sorry to hear it," Wolfgang said. He sounded sincere.

"For the moment, it looks like we're on the same side," Reed said.

Wolfgang smirked. "Assuming you're telling me the truth, it certainly does."

Reed didn't counter the point. It was a fair comment. Instead, he gestured down the hall, deeper into the dark belly of the ship. "Shall we?"

Wolfgang glanced over his shoulder, then looked down at the bunk. "Can I have my gun back?"

Reed smirked. "Don't trouble yourself. I'll carry it for you."

Wolfgang pursed his lips, and Reed couldn't tell if he was irritated or amused. Then he turned and started between the bunks, allowing Reed to scoop up the gun.

He's got another. Maybe two more, hidden under that coat.

They navigated between the rows of hanging bunks, Reed taking care not to allow Wolfgang to fall behind him. The path between each row was too narrow for them to walk shoulder to shoulder, and they had to split, walking with one row in between them.

Their feet clicked against the metal, and Reed found himself holding his breath as he journeyed deeper away from the safety of the crowd behind him. He wasn't sure if he felt reassured or further unsettled by Wolfgang. Something about the slender killer made him want to trust him. Maybe it was his manner, his tone, or his gentle relaxation. But he couldn't shake the memory of being almost strangled to death, thrashing about in the water in Chattanooga while Wolfgang pulled a choke wire into his throat.

"Why don't you kill after midnight?" Reed asked.

Wolfgang shot him a sideways look. "What?"

"In Chattanooga, you had me. But then your watch beeped at midnight, and you let me go. You said you didn't kill after midnight. Why?"

Wolfgang ran a hand over his mouth, and Reed saw a strange, distant light in his eyes. He shook his head. "Not now."

The row of bunks ended at a flat metal wall, with only one doorframe in the middle of it. That door hung open a couple inches, and the soft red glow of more lights emanated from the far side. Wolfgang opened the door with a gentle tug, and Reed reluctantly ducked through.

The room on the far side was empty. Perhaps it had been a storage closet or some kind of armory, but now it was nothing more than an empty metal box with another door on the far side that was painted closed. Soft red lights glowed from the ceiling, illuminating a bare floor.

Wolfgang followed him inside, shooting Reed a look that said they were both acutely aware of the fact that they had just willingly stepped into a metal box with only one route of escape.

Reed took a step backward, then he heard the voice—soft, semi-electronic, genderless and toneless, ringing out from the ceiling.

"Hello, Reed."

8

Reed froze in the stillness. He glanced at Wolfgang again and saw that his fellow killer stood with one hand in his pocket, staring at the ceiling. Reed hesitated a moment, searching for the source of the voice. Then he saw the speaker mounted in one corner of the room, a black wire running from the back of it and into the darkness overhead, vanishing among the pipes.

"Winter?" Reed asked.

"Yes." The voice was simple, almost abrupt, and still toneless.

Suddenly, the lengthy journey into the bowels of the ship made sense. Winter had led them into this room to isolate them and to cut them off from cell service. Reed watched Wolfgang's gaze travel along the speaker wire, tracing it into the ceiling. That wire probably ran up to the deck of the ship, where it was connected to a transmitter. It was unlikely that Winter was actually on board.

"Funny to hear your voice," Reed said, his hand still planted on the SIG. "Last time we talked, you made it clear we wouldn't speak again."

"Things have changed, Reed. The landscape has shifted. I am now prepared to offer what I was previously unable to offer."

"Which is what, exactly?"

"Information. And assistance."

Wolfgang broke in. "Information on what?"

"Mr. Pierce . . . Thank you for joining us today. Your participation in the coming endeavor will be essential."

"*What* endeavor?" Wolfgang pressed.

"An endeavor to destroy the life and work of one Aiden Phillips."

A chill sank into Reed's soul, like a hand reaching into his heart and grabbing what remained of his controlled calm. "Where is he?" Reed demanded.

"It's not so simple. I will help you find him, but you must follow my rules."

Convulsing anger surged into Reed, and he stepped closer to the speaker. He wasn't sure why. "If you had helped me when I asked, my father would still be alive."

Wolfgang laid a hand on his arm, pulling him back. Reed tensed, ready to push him away, but then he saw the cell phone palmed in Wolfgang's outstretched hand. It was open to a text message window, with five strong bars of signal in the top corner.

"I have a signal booster," Wolfgang mouthed.

Reed scanned the texts. They were to Lucy.

INSIDE SHIP. REED IS HERE. THIRD PARTY SPEAKING FROM SHORT-RANGE TRANSMITTER. LOCATE SOURCE ASAP.

Wolfgang met his gaze again, and Reed nodded once, impressed by Wolfgang's preparation and quick thinking.

"I'm sorry," Reed said simply, his tone betraying the dishonesty in his words. "I want your help."

"As I said before," Winter continued, "my help comes with rules. You must follow them."

Wolfgang spun his finger in a circular motion and mouthed, "Keep Winter talking."

"Okay," Reed said. "What are the rules?"

"I'll get to those. First, we must discuss Mr. Pierce's involvement. Mr. Pierce, you received my package?"

Wolfgang looked up. "What package?"

"I think you know."

"You mean the vial? At my house?"

"Affirmative. Were you able to ascertain the nature of its contents?"

Wolfgang shot Reed a sideways look, and Reed recalled their last conversation at a park bench in downtown Baton Rouge. Wolfgang had asked him about a package that arrived on his doorstep—some kind of chemical or medical solution Wolfgang was interested in. According to the note attached to the package, Reed had sent it, but Reed knew nothing about it.

"You told him I had more of it," Reed said.

"I did. It is necessary that you and Mr. Pierce work together for what comes next. I needed you to meet."

"So, what was in the vial?" Wolfgang demanded.

"That is the question, Mr. Pierce. What I need from you—"

A clattering sounded from the speaker, then Lucy's clear voice rang through the transmitter. "I've got it, Wolf. There's an RV in the parking lot with a short-range transmitter connected to a long-range unit. As soon as I opened the door, the long-range feed cut off. I think it was set to self-destruct."

Reed cursed and slammed his hand into the wall. He looked up at the speaker, then jerked his hand at Wolfgang.

"Come on. Let's go."

They dashed through the crowds and back down the gangway to the gift shop. Reed shot Maggie an update text as they ran, and two minutes later, they were at the back of the parking lot, where an old RV sat by itself, a giant antenna rising from the rear bumper.

Reed circled the unit just in time to see Lucy stepping out of the side door.

She offered him a tight nod. "Prosecutor."

"LB." Reed never called Lucy by her first name, but he also didn't like the moniker Little Bitch, a call sign that originated from Oliver Enfield and was intended to be derogatory. Lucy never seemed to mind, but Reed still preferred to use her initials.

"The stuff's inside," Lucy said, gesturing toward the trailer. "I already searched the rest of the unit. It's clean."

Reed nodded once. If Lucy said it was clean, he had no reason to suspect otherwise. He swung inside and scanned the interior. It was pretty much what he expected—dusty and worn but empty. Radio equipment sat on the dinette table, and a broken wire lay on the floor. The wire must have been connected to the door, which confirmed Lucy's determination that the radio had been set to self-destruct.

Shit.

But there had to be more to it than that. Winter clearly wanted to help and be involved. This entire apparatus was set up to shield Winter's identity, but Winter had never needed such a primitive radio setup to accomplish that before. For years, Reed's communication with Winter was via phone or email, and Winter always made it secure. So, why the change? Why all the cloak-and-dagger, Cold War–style espionage?

Reed shifted through the junk wired together on top of the dinette. He had no idea what he was looking at and only assumed that none of it was about to explode. Winter didn't need a setup like this to kill him. So, what then?

Reed folded his arms and stared at the table, evaluating the entire setup and considering what made it special.

The ship.

There were a lot of places Winter could have chosen, but Winter chose the ship. Why? Well, it was basically the best cell phone signal blocker in history. In the belly of that giant metal beast, nothing transmitted. So maybe that was it—Winter wanted them someplace where they unexpectedly lost signal. It was reasonable to assume Winter hadn't expected Wolfgang to have a cell signal booster powerful enough to connect through the armored walls of the ship.

But then again, if that were true, Winter wouldn't have given them the rendezvous location ahead of time. Winter would've simply invited them to Mobile, and then at the last minute sent them into the ship, ensuring they didn't have time to arrange a booster. And second, if isolation was the plan, why rig the equipment in the RV to self-destruct? A double-safety?

Maybe. That sounded like Winter. But really, this entire setup was much too exposed for the ghost. Much too obvious . . .

Winter wanted me to find this.

Reed hurried out the door, running to the back of the RV. It bore an Idaho vanity plate with a single word printed across it: MORGAN.

I'll be damned.

"What is it?" Lucy asked.

Maggie appeared around the corner of the RV, brushing hair out of her face as she and Wolfgang followed Lucy to the back bumper. Reed pointed to the plate, glancing around to ensure they weren't being watched.

"Winter wanted us to find the RV. The battleship was never the final meeting place—just a midway point to bolster security. Winter wants to meet in person . . . at Fort Morgan."

Wolfgang and Lucy frowned in confusion, but understanding crossed Maggie's face. "The old Civil War fort."

"Right," Reed said. "It's at the bottom of the bay, about an hour south of here. Pretty isolated. Pretty quiet."

"I don't understand," Wolfgang said. "You see a vanity plate, and you assume this Winter person is arranging another clandestine meeting?"

"Winter is being extra cautious right now. I'm not sure why. Maybe they simply want to see if we'll figure it out. But this whole setup . . . none of it makes sense. None of it is consistent with how Winter operates. *Unless* Winter never intended for this to be the final meeting place."

The four of them stood quietly, staring at the plate.

Wolfgang tapped his phone. "Why doesn't Winter just call us? You know, the old-fashioned way."

"*Who* is Winter?" Maggie and Lucy said in unison.

Reed explained quickly, then turned back to Wolfgang. "I don't know why Winter won't call. I'm sure there's a reason. The bottom line remains . . . The next stop is Fort Morgan."

9

The drive to the coast should've taken forty-five minutes, but the two German cars swung quickly in and out of traffic, chasing each other to the water in less than half an hour. Wolfgang's bigger and heavier Mercedes didn't move with the same precision as the shorter BMW, but with just as much aggression. He was a good driver, but Reed was confident he could still stomp him if he had to. Hell, he already had in a Volkswagen Beetle.

At the bottom of Mobile County, the road ended at Dauphin Island, where Fort Gaines sat next to a golf course. Three miles across the mouth of the bay, Fort Morgan stood as a faithful twin. The Mobile Bay Ferry connected the two forts, running multiple crossings a day, and they reached the dock just in time to catch the midday ride. The BMW and the Mercedes slid neatly on board the flat-decked vessel, joining a dozen other cars packed in tight rows. Then the gate rose, and the ferry steamed away from shore.

Reed stood next to the rail, casting wary glances around the ship before he allowed himself to look out at the grey water of the bay. It wasn't what he'd call beautiful—not in the traditional sense. The bay was dirty and restless, churned to a foam by the dozens of commercial vessels that chugged in and out every day. But there was something about this place—something old, mysterious, and sad. Something that spoke to his soul, a little like the battleship did.

"Are you okay?"

Lucy stood next to him, arms crossed, staring out at the water.

"It's good to see you, LB."

"Likewise."

Reed looked back at the water, then ran a hand through his hair. It was longer than he liked it. There hadn't been time for haircuts lately.

"How did you get mixed up in this mess?" he asked.

Lucy shrugged. "Oh, you know . . . I'm usually mixed up in hunting bad guys. I guess our paths just crossed."

Reed grunted, deciding to take the answer at face value, even though he knew there was more to the story.

"You didn't answer my question," Lucy said.

Reed squinted in the bright light of the sun as clouds parted overhead. He shrugged. "I'm not sure I know what you mean. I'm alive. Makes me pretty okay, I guess."

"I guess what I mean is, are you okay about Banks?"

Reed flinched, and he knew Lucy noticed. He looked left to shield his face, searching for something to say before the silence became obvious. But it was already too late.

"I thought so," Lucy said.

"Wolfgang said she's in Gulfport," Reed said. It was a half-question, half-dismissive statement.

"Maybe," Lucy said.

"Maybe?"

"We left her in Gulfport. She wasn't at all happy about it. And frankly, she impresses me as the kind of woman who doesn't follow orders."

Reed wanted to smile at that. He thought about Banks and her stubborn objection to any sort of instructions she didn't like. She was free-spirited. Independent. From the very first day he met her at that nightclub in Atlanta, he'd known she was a rolling stone. What kind of woman walks away from a family fortune to embrace the life of a starving artist in a big city? The kind that wants to call the shots and do things her way. The kind of woman he found impossible to resist.

"She saw you kiss the governor," Lucy said.

The words blasted through Reed's daydream like a burst of minigun fire, bringing a surge of guilt and sudden awkwardness with them.

"I did that to protect her," Reed said. His voice carried a defensive edge he didn't really intend.

"Bullshit, Prosecutor. You did that to get rid of her. And I'm sure you had the best intentions, but that was a shitty thing to do. A real shitty thing. That woman loves you, and I'd put good money on you feeling the same. There's an adult way to handle her safety, and that sure as hell wasn't it."

Reed wasn't surprised by Lucy's bluntness. Even though he'd never interacted with her on a personal level before, he felt like he knew her better than most of his former associates. Somehow, her familiarity felt natural.

Reed rubbed a hand through his hair again. "You're right."

"You're damn right I'm right. I covered your ass. I told her not to over-think the kiss and that you cared for her. That not everything was what it seemed. But mark my words, I won't do that again. Once we get this bullshit with Aiden sorted out, you're gonna make things right with her. You hear me? She's a good woman. A lot better than you deserve."

Reed nodded again, feeling like a scolded child, but maybe he deserved it. Lucy was right—what he'd done to Banks back in New Orleans was a cheap shot, regardless of his intentions.

Lucy brushed her ponytail across her shoulders, then popped her knuckles with a definite *this-topic-is-now-closed* expression. She smiled into the sun, then sighed. "I feel good," she said. "I feel like I'm about to kick some ass."

The ferry nosed against the dock, and the two cars rolled onto the eastern shore of the bay. Fort Morgan lay less than two hundred yards away, shielded from view by tall sand dunes and towering pine trees. The sun was already sinking toward Louisiana, and Reed checked his phone. There were no new messages from Winter, and he wondered if he'd been wrong. What if this whole thing was a miscalculation on his part? What if Winter really had planned to speak to them exclusively at the ship, and after Lucy barged into the RV, that plan was terminated?

If that were the case, they'd never find Winter. They'd be back to square one.

"What's the play?" Wolfgang asked.

Reed was briefly surprised that the others were so readily surrendering operational control to him, but then again, this whole Fort Morgan business was his idea.

"We leave the cars in the ferry parking lot. Fort Morgan is inside a park, which closes at five. We wait until it closes, then we hop the fence and sneak inside. That way, if something goes down, there won't be any witnesses or potential victims."

The others nodded. It was a reasonable approach.

They moved the cars under a tall pine tree, then Wolfgang produced some light snacks from the trunk of his Mercedes, and they all ate in silence while the sun continued its slow descent. An edginess crept over Reed the longer they waited—a sort of semi-conscious uneasiness.

Don't be wrong about this.

At last, the park ranger locked the gate and puttered away in his little truck, and they departed the ferry parking lot, then crept down the beach to where the fence dove toward the waterline. It was easy to splash around the end before turning back up the dunes and heading toward the park. One more fence blocked their way—a little taller than the last, made of chain link. Lucy flipped across it with the agility of a spider monkey, adding a little more flair than was necessary. Wolfgang and Maggie followed with less skill, leaving Reed to fumble over like an elephant crossing a speed bump.

"I'm curious," Wolfgang said, looking at Maggie. "If we're caught and get a ticket or something, can you get us off?"

Maggie smirked. "No problem. The governor of Alabama and I are real tight."

They trudged up another row of dunes as the sun sank beneath the horizon, leaving only an orange-purple glow to light the sky. As they crested the top of the dune, the fort spread out before them, sunken in the sand by over a century of age and abuse, but still imposing nonetheless. It was shaped like a throwing star, with fingers sticking out at odd angles, and a deep ditch dug all around. Battlements and defensive positions were built along all edges, and on the far side, facing out to sea, two giant cannons pointed toward the water.

"Those don't look vintage Civil War," Wolfgang remarked.

"They're not," Reed said. "Fort Morgan was used during both world wars as an anti-naval battery. Those guns are probably from the First World War . . . defenses against a German naval invasion, I guess."

They walked down the backside of the hill, trudging through the sand. At the bottom of the dune, they crossed yet another fence—this one a split-rail affair that looked more like a decoration than an obstacle. Then they stood outside the walls of the fort. The main gate was open, exposing a tunnel that led into the interior. In the dying light, the tunnel was almost black, gaping like the empty mouth of a whale.

Reed reached into his pocket for his flashlight, but as he did, his phone buzzed. The others heard it and shot him a look. A single message waited on the phone.

ONLY YOU.

The others read the message over his shoulder and exchanged glances. Reed felt the uneasiness grow in the pit of his stomach, drowning out the momentary satisfaction of being right about the fort.

"You shouldn't go alone," Wolfgang said. "You need backup."

Reed shook his head. "We've come this far. If this were a setup, Winter could've taken us out at the ship, or even before."

The looks on their faces told him they weren't convinced, but he wasn't worried about it. He tucked the phone into his pocket, pulled out the flashlight without turning it on, and stepped toward the gate. The others spread out to take cover and wait as he crossed into the tunnel and dove into the darkness.

Each step rang out like a small gunshot echoing off the ancient brick walls. He cast a wary look around him, searching for hidden shooters, cameras, or trip wires. He saw nothing but antique walls, flagstones, and emptiness.

He exited the tunnel into the main parade ground in the center of the fort. A flagpole jutted toward the sky with the Stars and Stripes flapping gently in the breeze at the top. The wind whistled over the walls, but all else was silent. Then his phone buzzed again.

STRAIGHT AHEAD.

Reed clicked the flashlight on. He didn't want to use it, but Winter knew where he was, anyway. He could always turn it off.

Another few dozen strides took him across the parade ground to an interior brick wall fitted with another deep tunnel. He hesitated a moment and shone the light around for any signs of impending death. Once again, he saw nothing—just a smaller tunnel leading into the interior of a very, very old fort.

NOW OR NEVER.

Reed read the text and then shoved the phone into his pocket. He switched the flashlight to his left hand before placing his right over the SIG, then took a cautious step inside the fort.

The tunnel moved into the wall of the fort, tilted downward just a little. Another ten yards away, the wall turned to the left, leading farther into the darkness. Reed made the turn, his hand still gripping the SIG.

And then he saw a figure, little more than a silhouette, forty yards ahead. Reed tilted the light down to avoid blinding the person, and he took a few more steps. The closer he came, the more the figure came into view, and it wasn't what he expected. It wasn't a tall man in a trench coat or a spidery figure wearing a mask.

The figure in front of him was petite and stooped forward. It was an old woman with a cane held in one hand and white hair teased and curled into a crown around an aged face. She wore slipper shoes and a simple white dress with a blue flower print. He didn't see any weapons or other people around. Reed lowered the light even more, feeling suddenly self-conscious about the aggressive way he was approaching this old woman.

Could this be Winter? Really?

"Hello, Reed."

The voice was old, but strong. And familiar.

Reed's heart skipped, and he raised the flashlight as the old woman lifted her head and exposed her face. As light fell over her features, the flashlight almost fell from his fingers.

"Grandma?"

10

Matias worked in the drug cartels his entire life. Some of his earliest memories were of helping his mother smuggle cocaine in and out of Santiago de Cali for local consumers. It didn't pay much—nothing like the rich white customers would pay in Miami and New York City—but it was a good start to what he hoped would become a long and profitable career.

Those were the golden days, back in the late seventies, during the reign of Pablo Escobar. Back when cocaine was the largest industry in South America by a significant margin, and back when everybody—literally every cop, every politician, every school teacher—was touched by that lucrative trade.

Matias had no problem with that. For him, dealing cocaine was just another way to make a living, like selling fish or bananas. Only cocaine paid a hell of a lot better than fish or bananas, and the market was insatiable. Sure, things got messy sometimes. The cartels had good reason to arm themselves with automatic rifles and grenade launchers. Mountains of cash bigger than houses instigated instability between rival operations.

But more than intergang warfare, Matias blamed the government—not just the Colombian government, but the US government—for the violence caused by the cartels. Americans craved cocaine just like they craved movies and rock-and-roll and the new Porsche sports car. All these things were freely manufactured, shipped, and sold in America. Why should cocaine be any different?

It wasn't different, at least not in the minds of the cartels. If the US or Colombian government, or the United Nations itself, had a problem with the white gold of the narcos, they would need guns bigger than the cartels, and they had better be ready to use them. The cartels were willing to fight, and why shouldn't they be?

Cocaine was their business. The lifeblood of Colombia. Or, at least . . . it used to be. Back in the eighties and nineties, almost nothing stood in the way of making millions—or billions—off cocaine. But today, things were different. Today the United States had satellites that could read a man's face from an altitude of eight thousand kilometers. They had spies and hackers and drug-sniffing dogs, and all kinds of checkpoints and chokeholds and complex networks of safeties to prevent the flow of drugs into America. More than that, even the mood of the gringos had shifted. Once upon a time, cocaine was forbidden and mysterious and kind of legendary in its own way.

Now it was derogatory. Scorned by "proper" society. Oh, sure, millions of Americans were still hopelessly addicted—many of them members of that same proper society that scorned the drug. But without the weight of an eager, consumeristic, rebellious culture on their side, moving drugs was a lot harder than it used to be.

For all those reasons, Matias's current job confused him. From the moment he met the mysterious man who called himself "Gambit," Matias knew this job was peculiar. The American didn't want cocaine or any of its wondrous derivatives. He wanted something else—something boring—and as much as Matias could tell, something useless. But Gambit wanted it, and he wanted a lot of it. He wanted it manufactured in absolute secrecy under his exclusive supervision, guarded by enough men with automatic AK-47s to invade a small country.

Matias thought the whole thing was strange, but he hadn't risen this far in his drug-dealing career or earned the generous salary he commanded by passing judgment or asking too many questions. If the American wanted him to bleach flour, he would do it. He had only one question: *Can you pay?*

Gambit could pay. Or at least he always had. But now Gambit had vanished. For almost a week Matias hadn't heard from his strange, secretive employer. Occasionally, Gambit wouldn't call every day, but he never went longer than forty-eight hours without making contact. Matias might not have cared, but it was now approaching the end of the month, and that meant payday. Matias was a lot more concerned about payday than he was in listening to another of Gambit's paranoid phone calls.

Matias stood at the end of the metal building and surveyed the workers. Per Gambit's specifications, every worker wore a full biomedical suit covering their faces and bodies. Before they left the building, somebody would spray them down with a water hose, and the suits were replaced altogether every ten days. Matias didn't understand why. It seemed a need-less precaution for what he was sure was just another recreational hallu-cinogen. Of course, he didn't know for certain. Gambit absolutely forbade anyone to consume the product, under threat of death. And he meant it, too. During a random site visit six months before, Gambit executed a line worker for sniffing the product. Matias had objected, of course. The man was a good worker.

But hey, if the employer said don't touch . . . don't touch.

Matias donned a face mask and stepped down the line, checking various procedures to be sure everything was proceeding according to Gambit's precise specifications. It certainly appeared to be. In fact, produc-tion was up seventeen percent over the prior week—a surplus Gambit was sure to be thrilled over.

If he ever called.

As if on cue, one of Matias's workers appeared at the end of the shed and waved to him, indicating the phone in his private office.

Matias hurried into the small room, shutting the door before lifting the ringing phone off the receiver. His English wasn't great, but it was sufficient. "Gambit, it's Matias."

"This isn't Gambit."

The voice on the other end of the line was certainly American. Male, probably early fifties. Stern and cold and somewhat ominous. Matias didn't recognize it.

"Who is this?"

"Gambit's boss. Call me Fianchetto."

Matias hesitated. Long years of watching his colleagues fall to vicious sting operations had taught him to never accept a person at face value. The DEA loved to set somebody up on a recorded line—entrap them in their own words.

But then again . . . Gambit hadn't called.

"Okay," Matias said at last.

"Gambit will no longer be contacting you. For now, you will deal directly with me. Do you understand?"

"Okay . . ."

"Don't worry. I'm not with the government. Nobody with the government has this number."

Somebody with the government would definitely say that, but Gambit had always assured him the line was secure.

"How's production today?" Fianchetto asked.

Matias knew "production" could mean anything. Even if this was the National Police or the DEA, he could later claim he was talking about coffee. Of course, if the police *were* on the other end of the line, they may try to make him comfortable before leading him into a trap. But if this man really was Gambit's boss, he wouldn't say anything that required Matias to incriminate himself.

So, Matias would answer and then proceed with caution. "Production is excellent. Up seventeen percent over last week."

"Excellent. Gambit told me you were good at your job. When are you supposed to be paid?"

Again Matias hesitated. Shouldn't Gambit's boss know when to pay him? He shrugged to himself. It wasn't incriminating.

"At the end of every month. The usual amount."

There. If this man was for real, he would know what the usual amount was. Or know how to find out.

"Very good," Fianchetto said. "You can expect a little bonus on your next check . . . for all your excellent work."

Suspicious or otherwise, the thought of a bonus excited Matias. If his men didn't know about it, he wouldn't need to share it.

"One more thing, Matias."

"¿Sí, señor?"

"I'm sending in some additional security. Specialists, from Europe. They'll arrive in the morning. You are to cooperate with them without question. Do you understand?"

A cold hand of uncertainty closed over Matias's heart. He glanced across the production floor at the roving gunmen armed with AK-47s. Existing security was already heavy—almost overbearing, in his opinion. Why would Fianchetto send more?

"That really isn't necessary, señor," Matias said. "My men—"

"Allow me to clarify. These men will assist you or replace you. I don't have a preference."

The ice in Matias's chest crept up his spine. He shifted the phone. "Of course, señor. I'm grateful for the assistance."

The phone was silent for a long moment, and Matias thought Fianchetto may have hung up, but then he heard soft breathing—almost a rasp and barely audible. Somehow, it was even more unsettling than the rest of the call.

"Excellent," Fianchetto said. "I think we're going to work well together."

11

Reed's body felt like granite—rock-still, as if he'd forgotten how to breathe. He stood in the darkness and stared at the old woman as he tried to make sense of what he saw, but nothing would compute.

This is Winter?

The old woman took a shuffling step forward, her slippers grinding against the flagstones. She offered him a weary smile. "Hello, Reed."

Reed cast a glance around the tunnel and adjusted his grip on the still-holstered pistol. "You . . . you're Winter?"

She nodded. "For forty-eight years. A long, arduous career."

"But . . ."

"But I'm an old woman?" She laughed a little. It was a quavering sound, but there was spirit in it.

"I was going to say, but you're my grandmother."

"Well, I have to be somebody's grandmother, don't I?"

Reed's face flushed with sudden anger. "You let him die," he said. "You let your own son die."

The old woman's face flooded with so much pain that Reed almost regretted the words. But he didn't take them back because they were true.

"No, Reed. I didn't let him die. If there was anything in the world I could have done, I would have."

"You could've given me the information I needed when I needed it," he snarled. "Back in Georgia, when I needed to know who ordered the Holiday hit. You could've told me. You could've *helped*." His voice rose with emotion, and he checked himself. He had no need to yell. His voice echoed enough in this tunnel.

She sighed and shuffled forward a little. "Things aren't that simple, Reed. As much as I wish they were."

"Aren't that *simple*? Are you kidding me? I haven't seen you since I was six years old. You disappeared. You completely vanished from my life. Now I find out you've spent that time living in the shadows as an intelligence spoof, with supposedly infinite knowledge of all things everywhere. And you did nothing."

Winter snapped her cane against the flagstones. "*That* is not true. That is not true at all. I've done everything I possibly could. By the time I realized what your father was involved in, it was much too late to save him. I worked for the CIA at the time, so I was very limited on what I could do. After I left the agency and started my own firm, I spent decades trying to unwind and hunt down the truth of David's entanglement with Aiden Phillips. When you accepted the Holiday hit, I knew it was probably related, but I didn't have enough information at the time to prove it. So, I tried to push you out and get you out of harm's way. But you know, Reed, you're pretty damn stubborn."

She folded her hands over the top of the cane and shot him a look so disapproving, Reed felt the sudden need to hang his head. He struggled to sort through the deluge of information she'd just unloaded. Clouds of unfamiliar emotions filled his mind, but he pushed them out and pulled himself back to the present.

"You know about Aiden?" Reed demanded. "You know where to find him?"

"I know where to start. But right now, I don't have time to explain. There are two things you need to know. First, if you have any hope of taking down Aiden, you need the help of all your friends. Especially the doctor."

Reed frowned. "The doctor?"

"Mr. Pierce is a doctor of medical science with a specialty in genetic research. He didn't tell you?"

"He may have mentioned it."

"You need him. I'll explain why later. For now, the second thing you need to know is that this is the end. Whatever happens next, whether you bring down Aiden or he brings you down, this is the last roll of the dice. That's why nobody can know I'm your grandmother."

"What the hell are you talking about?"

"I've spent decades as a successful intelligence mogul by shielding my identity. My work relies on a massive network of informants, partners, and friends in low places. None of them would have dealt with me if they knew who I really was—an old widow with false teeth. That's why I used the genderless name, the genderless voice, and all the fake identities. Now I'm stepping into the light, which marks a certain end to my career and also places me in a great deal of personal danger. But more importantly, it compromises my credibility. You know what I'm capable of, Reed. My intel has always been excellent. Not so for Mr. Pierce and the others. All they'll see is a sexy little old woman who isn't to be trusted with serious matters. Young people are like that. They always think old folks are cuckoo."

Reed struggled to keep up with her fast-talking logic. He certainly agreed with her that the others would never trust her. Hell, he wasn't sure if he trusted her. Winter had been a faultless, absolutely reliable source of intel. But . . . this woman?

"What's your point?" Reed said.

"You'll never bring down Aiden alone. You need me, and you need the others. You need them to trust me. That's why we're meeting alone, so we could have this talk before they meet me. It's also why I set everything up with the pizza boxes and the battleship and the RV in the lot. I needed Wolfgang and the others to be convinced they were dealing with a professional. But it's not enough by itself. If they know I'm your grandmother, they'll think you're only vouching for me because of that. They'll think you've cracked. So, we only tell them what they need to know."

"And what is it they need to know?"

She shook her head wearily. "I'm only going to explain that once to everybody. Trust me when I tell you that things are worse now than they've ever been. None of you are safe. But I have information that may give you an edge."

Reed hesitated another long moment, still dazed. Grandma Montgomery disappeared around the same time David went to prison. At the time, Reed was confused and crushed, and those feelings of abandonment quickly grew into angst and resentment as he entered his teenage years.

Grandma Montgomery was a traitor, he decided. She failed him, just like David, and just like his mother. Just like everyone.

Reed took a half step forward. He felt a tremor in his hand, but he controlled it. "You abandoned me. When Dad went to prison and Mom moved me to California, you were the only family we had. And you *abandoned* us."

Winter sighed, but she didn't look away. She clicked her teeth, and Reed saw them shift. Fake teeth, like she said.

"I never abandoned you, Reed. You just couldn't see me. But I was always looking after you."

"Oh, please. Like I believe that."

"It was in a grocery store parking lot, wasn't it?" Winter said.

"What?"

"There was a fried chicken place next to the grocery store where you used to eat with your friends. That's where the Marine recruiter approached you."

"How did you know that?"

"Because I called a friend, and he called a friend, and that friend called the recruiter and told him about a troubled young man, teetering on the edge of a life of crime. A young man who needed a place to belong."

Reed's eyes burned, and the air around him felt suddenly hot. "You sent the recruiter?"

Winter puckered her lips. "We're never as alone as we think we are, Reed. What happened in Iraq was unfortunate, but I've never lost track of you. I'm not like most grandmothers. I don't feed you candy and buy you Christmas gifts, but dammit, Reed, you're not like most grandsons. We both live in a world most people will never understand. Let's show each other some grace."

Reed stared her down. Winter had deep brown eyes—a lot like David's. A lot like his own. He saw kindness in them, and strength, also.

She's not like most grandmothers. Just mine.

"Okay," he said at last. "I'll hear you out."

She smiled, and the expression brought a strange warmth to Reed's chest.

"We're gonna make him proud, Reed. We're going to avenge your father."

Reed shifted and looked away, then he motioned to the tunnel. "We should go."

She cleared her throat. "One more thing, Reed. Something you need to know."

Her voice bore an edge that chilled him somehow. He squinted in the darkness. "What?"

"There was that fire in Georgia. At your friend's house."

Reed kept his voice steady. "At Kelly's house, you mean?"

Winter nodded, and her gaze dropped to her feet.

"What about it?" Reed pressed.

"You were there. You saw them bring out a body."

"I saw them bring out *her* body."

Winter shook her head. "No, Reed, you didn't."

"What are you saying?"

"Kelly survived the fire. She's still alive, although pretty disfigured. She was badly burned, but she survived."

Reed's face burned. "What?"

"Kelly escaped. After the fire, she flew to Europe, I think. I'm not sure why, but I expect she was looking for the Cedric Muri outfit that was hired to burn the house. Then she came back, and . . ." His grandmother sucked in a long, weary breath and folded both hands over the top of her cane again.

"And *what*?" he asked, his voice wavering.

"She came looking for you. To kill you, I expect. But she found Banks instead. I'm not confident about what happened next, but I'd guess Lucy Byrne had something to do with it. Kelly has traveled with them ever since."

Reed placed one palm against the cool stone of the nearest wall. He saw the burned-out hulk of Kelly's house in Canton again—the ashes, still smoldering, with smoke rising from the remnants of a once-beautiful home. He remembered the yellow children's swing in the backyard. Kelly was three months pregnant and consumed with excitement. He remembered how she held her stomach when he asked about the child.

He'd last seen her while dropping off his English bulldog Baxter at the house for her to look after while he hunted Oliver Enfield. She objected to keeping the dog. He pressed. She finally agreed. And then he drove away. He didn't see the house again until it was nothing but the ashes left by the mercenaries hired to hunt him down and destroy him. Cedric Muri's men, hired by Salvador.

Salvador, hired by Gambit.

Gambit . . . Aiden's right-hand man.

The anger boiled up inside of him again as he suddenly recalled seeing a third woman standing with Banks and Lucy in New Orleans. She wore some kind of all-black Middle Eastern women's garb that obscured her entire body, with just a slit for her eyes.

Kelly.

Reed gritted his teeth and turned back toward the parade ground. "Come on."

"Where are you going?" Winter said.

"To finish this."

12

The dull lights of the fuel station clicked and throbbed overhead as Turk shoved the fuel nozzle into the Jeep and hit the trigger. His back ached from the long miles already behind him, but there were a lot more to go. With luck, he'd make New Orleans by lunch the next day—another few tanks of gas for the greedy Wrangler YJ. He'd need some fuel for himself, as well. Caffeine and food that he could eat without stopping.

The pump finally clicked off, and Turk hung it up, then walked inside for Red Bull, candy bars, and peanuts. Three minutes later, he was back in the old Jeep and firing it up. The chilly fall wind found its way through the gaps in the soft top, but within ten minutes, the heater caught up and kept at least his legs warm as he pumped through the gears and swung back onto the highway.

Turk didn't like the Jeep. It rode rough, required frequent maintenance, and wasn't all that comfortable, yet he couldn't part with it. Something about it—maybe it was the ride, the boxy style, or the general appearance —reminded him of the Marine Corps. It wasn't really much like a Humvee, but it was the closest thing he could afford, and that was good enough.

Reed would never drive something like this. Reed was a damn good

Marine, but he didn't actually enjoy the job, let alone the crappy vehicles that came with it. In his own words, Reed was a Marine simply because he needed something to do.

Not so for Turk. Turk loved the Corps. Every sweaty, shitty minute of it. He loved the grit, and the bad food, and the endless firefights. He loved feeling like he was a part of something bigger than himself, something old and glorious and important. Turk joined the Marines because he truly loved his country and because he believed Jarheads were the toughest soldiers.

So, it broke his heart when he decided not to reenlist. Turk wanted to take another deployment and sharpen his skills as a Force Recon Marine. Maybe find his way to Scout Sniper School like Reed had. Maybe apply for MECEP and become an officer someday. Stay a Marine. Stay proud.

But after that fateful night in Iraq, everything changed. It changed because Turk couldn't shake the feeling that he'd failed. He failed the Marine Corps for not stopping Reed from killing those contractors. He failed Private O'Conner for not protecting her *from* those contractors. He failed himself for not seeing the problem ahead of time and doing some-thing—anything—to stop it.

But more than anything, he failed Reed for not stopping him and not helping him find a better solution. He failed him for not being there to protect him from himself. Reed was a machine: a brutal, relentless fighter who saw black and white and had very little patience for anybody who danced along the line. What Reed did to those contractors made perfect sense. They raped and murdered Private O'Conner, so they had to die. All of them.

Turk should've been there to find a better solution or at least to help Reed bury the bodies. If Reed really had to gun them down, Turk should've made sure he wasn't caught. He should've covered Reed's six just like Reed had always covered his.

But he cowered out. He backed away and let it all happen, and then, at the trial, he didn't even defend Reed. He just answered the questions.

Yes, sir, I saw Corporal Reed headed toward the contractor barracks with his rifle. Yes, sir, Reed Montgomery is a very protective man. Yes, sir, I've seen him kill before.

Turk sucked down a Red Bull before slinging the can into the back seat. In the long years that passed since Reed's trial, Turk had spent a lot of time wondering if Reed held him responsible for the death sentence. Turk was the prosecution's star witness, after all. When Turk finally spoke to Reed, however briefly, his fears were in no way assuaged. Reed was harder and colder than Turk remembered him. More intense, also. Edgier.

What happened to his old friend in those years since Reed inexplicably vanished from prison? What turned him into such a dark, dangerous man? A domestic terrorist, the FBI called him. A blood-spilling maniac.

Turk shoved his foot harder into the accelerator as the Jeep rattled down the highway like a galloping horse laden with tin cups. The speedometer hopped around seventy, eating up the miles with slow, relentless dedication. Like Turk. Eating up the obstacles between himself and the truth, one at a time. He would find Reed and find out what happened to him and why he was wreaking havoc around the country.

And if Reed didn't have a damn good explanation, Turk would bring him in. Again.

13

"I'm guessing I shouldn't call you Granny."

Reed couldn't hide the bitterness in his tone as he walked next to the old woman. She moved with surprising agility on her way out of the fort, the cane clicking along with each of her smooth strides. But still, her legs were half as long as Reed's. He had to hold himself back from a comfortable walk just to avoid losing her.

"Call me Winter, like you always have. The others will do the same."

As they exited the tunnel, Reed caught sight of Wolfgang standing to his left, just behind the shelter of a low hill, one hand on his gun. Lucy wasn't visible, which was more disconcerting. Maggie must've been with her.

Reed waved to Wolfgang and continued with Winter to the entrance of the park. She lifted her cane over the loose gravel and quickly ascended toward the park's gift shop.

"There's cameras," Reed warned.

"I've already disabled them."

Of course you did.

As they stepped onto the sidewalk outside the gift shop, Wolfgang appeared from their left, and Lucy and Maggie stepped out of the darkness directly ahead. They all shot Reed confused, semi-disappointed looks.

Reed gestured to his grandmother. "Meet Winter. My intelligence operative."

They all exchanged glances and then shot Reed looks that said, "Are you serious?"

Maggie was the first to recover, her leadership instincts taking over.

She held out a hand. "Governor Margaret Trousdale, ma'am. It's a pleasure to meet you."

Winter accepted the hand and smiled. "Ah, yes. Muddy Maggie. I know all about you, young lady."

Maggie shook her hand and shot Reed another uncertain look. Reed nodded reassuringly, but Lucy and Wolfgang remained at a distance.

"I know all about you two, also," Winter said, pursing her lips. "So, you can stop being so mysterious, if you like."

Lucy shook Winter's hand a little reluctantly, but Wolfgang didn't move.

"All right, then," Winter said. "We've got a lot to discuss, but this isn't the place. Why don't you accompany me to my hotel? I have a lovely suite at the Battle House."

Wolfgang grunted, his expression disinterested.

"Sounds good," Reed said. "We'll get the cars."

Winter shook her head. "No need. I've got room for everybody. We'll ride together."

Reed felt Wolfgang's discomfort rise another notch, and he smiled at Winter with what he hoped was a measure of command. "I think we'd be more comfortable in our own cars, thank you. We can follow you."

Winter twisted toward Reed, her back stiffening. Ten years seemed to fall off her shoulders without effort. "Let me rephrase. If you want my help, you'll ride with me. A single vehicle is dismissible. Three cars is an entourage. A noteworthy experience. Something a valet or a security guard or a cop might remember. And we don't do things that people might remember."

Reed thought Wolfgang might walk, so he held up a hand and locked eyes with Winter, who didn't blink.

This woman is for real. She has something to offer.

Reed waited another moment, then grunted. "Okay, we'll ride with you. But we're not disarming."

Winter dipped her head slightly. "Of course. This way, please." She set off toward the parking lot.

Wolfgang stepped close to Reed, his voice an irritated hiss. "No go, Reed. I don't know this woman. Frankly, I barely know *you*."

"So, I guess it's no use asking you to trust me?"

Wolfgang said nothing.

"I'm going to say it anyway," Reed said. "Trust me. Winter has valuable intel that we desperately need."

"We?"

"Yes, we. It's we now, like it or not. Winter claims you're an integral part of whatever operation is required to take Aiden down, which, if I recall, is something you're interested in."

Wolfgang turned to Lucy. Maggie was already gone, walking close to Winter.

Lucy shrugged. "She's an old woman. I think you can handle her, Wolf."

Wolfgang remained tense but followed Reed and Lucy to the empty parking lot. Winter produced a phone from her pocket, and a moment later, the roar of a V-8 engine rippled through the air, followed by the flash of lights. Reed felt the urge to reach for his gun but resisted it. He couldn't afford to rattle Wolfgang any further.

Tires ground on pavement, and a brand-new, jet-black Chevrolet Tahoe appeared on the drive, sliding up to the small crowd with a soft rumble. The windows were tinted to the point of invisibility, and the driver didn't open the door.

Winter held out a hand. "Dr. Pierce, you may sit up front if it makes you more comfortable."

Wolfgang circled the vehicle without comment. Reed opened the back door, and Winter climbed in with a strength and agility that once again defied her age. Lucy slid into the far back seat, and Maggie took the middle, leaving Reed to slip in behind the driver.

A combat advantage. Winter is trying to put me at ease.

Reed wasn't a small man by any standard—six foot four and a bulky two hundred fifty pounds, give or take. But the man sitting in the driver's seat dwarfed him. No shorter than six seven, with massive shoulders and a huge, bald head, he was a deep shade of ebony, and his eyes gleamed into the rearview mirror, locking against Reed's.

"Good evening, Mr. Montgomery." He spoke in perfect English with a deep African accent, but with the lilt of a man speaking his second language.

"This is Amadou," Winter said. "My friend."

Wolfgang laughed. "Friend?"

Winter buckled her seatbelt. "Among other things."

"Where you from, Amadou?" Wolfgang asked. His tone was open, but Reed detected a definite tension in his body language.

"Mali," Amadou said.

"North Africa, right?" Wolfgang said. "I've been there. Nice place."

"It is paradise." Amadou's voice boomed like the bass on a quality stereo, filling the car without effort.

Wolfgang grimaced. "I don't know if I'd go that far. Have you ever checked out Sandals in Cancun? It's pretty great."

Amadou shot a semi-lethal glare toward his shotgun passenger. "You're a funny man."

"You didn't laugh," Wolfgang said.

"If I doused you in gasoline and lit you on fire, I would laugh."

The SUV fell silent, and Reed slipped his hand closer to the grip of his SIG. Winter saw the movement and put a hand on his arm. She leaned forward as if to speak, but Wolfgang spoke first.

"That's dark, bro."

Amadou grunted. "I'm a dark man." The hint of a smile flittered at the corners of Amadou's lips.

Reed saw it in the rearview mirror, and Wolfgang saw it, too.

Wolfgang grinned, then chuckled just a little. "Ha! A dark man. Nice, Amadou." The tension eased, and he settled back into the seat.

Amadou shifted into gear and glanced into the rearview mirror toward Winter.

She said, "To the hotel, Amadou."

The Tahoe growled its way up highways and across the bay, arriving in downtown Mobile an hour later. Amadou drove with the ready confidence of a man who knew exactly where he was going but was ready to adjust course at a moment's notice, keeping constant surveillance of every sidewalk and connecting street they passed.

This man was a professional, Reed decided. A professional driver, yes, but probably a full-time bodyguard, also. Not the kind of guy Reed wanted to cross.

The Battle House Hotel was an old establishment situated in the heart of downtown Mobile. Freshly renovated and cleaned until it sparkled, Reed was immediately impressed by the quiet grace and imposing confidence of the seven-story, brick-faced building. Amadou pulled the SUV to the curb and stepped out, speaking momentarily to the valet before passing him a banknote and the keys, then circling to open Winter's door. He held out his hand to help Winter onto the sidewalk, and Reed noticed a gentleness in his gestures, like the protective strength of a mama bear with her cub.

He'd kill for her.

Reed slid out behind Maggie, then opened the back seat for Lucy to climb out. The group piled onto the sidewalk, then followed the steady click of Winter's cane into the gleaming lobby of the hotel.

"The Battle House was constructed in the first decade of the twentieth century," Winter remarked. "It's a lovely piece of history."

Reed would've probably agreed if he had the time to care. As it was, he only wanted answers. He could see in Wolfgang's weary stance that although he had come this far, he wouldn't stay long if he wasn't incentivized.

I hope Winter realizes that.

They all packed into the elevator and rode it to the top floor. Amadou stood in the corner with his shoulders crunched inward, as though the world itself were too small for him.

The bell rang, and the doors rolled open. Amadou led them to a door at the end of the hallway, pausing to conduct some manner of careful search of the door—probably checking for disturbances. He grabbed something from the top corner of the doorframe, inspected it, then unlocked the door. "You may enter," he said to nobody in particular.

Winter walked in first, followed by the others. As Reed passed him, Amadou leaned down and whispered into his ear. "If you or any of your colleagues so much as breathe on my friend, I will break your spines over my knee."

Reed stopped mid-stride and rocked his head back to meet Amadou's gaze. He saw no malice in those eyes, but plenty of confidence. Reed nodded once, then walked into the room and heard Amadou follow before the door thumped shut.

The room was a sitting area, complete with two sofas, a wet bar, and a bank of windows that opened out over the glistening city; connecting bedrooms, and even a dining room linked to the sitting area. Winter stood next to one sofa, and as Reed entered, she faced the entrance of a bedroom and motioned to somebody.

A moment later, Reed heard footsteps. His heart lurched, and he swallowed hard. Banks stepped into the room, her hair held back in a loose ponytail. Her eyes shone brighter than any light in the city, and her body language was calm and composed. Her nose was still discolored from an apparent injury, which was something he noticed when he saw her in New Orleans. Otherwise, she looked fit and healthy.

Banks acknowledged Lucy but didn't look at Reed.

More footsteps followed, and Reed braced himself. Kelly appeared from the bedroom, dressed head to toe in the same black garb, her face obscured from view. She walked straight and stiff, and even though he could see nothing more of her than he had a few days prior, he immediately knew it was her.

Kelly faced him, her deep brown eyes wide open and displaying no discernible emotion. Reed forced himself not to look away, suddenly conscious of the fact that the whole room had fallen silent. Kelly held his gaze, and he saw pain, regret, and boiling anger behind her stare. Then the wall went back up, and she sat down on the sofa next to Banks, her face directed at the opposing wall.

Reed saw the smoke again rising from the ashes of Kelly's beautiful suburban home. He heard the shouts of the firefighters calling him back from the house. He watched them haul the charred, unrecognizable body from the ashes. He thought that was Kelly. He told them it was Kelly. But it hadn't been. So, who was it? It didn't even matter. All that mattered was that Kelly lived, but she had clearly changed. Whatever happened to her was his fault.

"Thank you all for joining me," Winter said. She offered Reed a glance that displayed no comfort or grace—only stern expectancy. "My name is Winter. I'm a former CIA officer who now works as an independent intelligence purveyor. I'm the best in the world, and I've gathered you here because I believe that, in one way or another, you are the best in the world. The team I've been waiting for."

"A team for *what*?" Wolfgang demanded.

Winter squared her shoulders. "A team to destroy the monster Aiden Phillips. And none of you are leaving this hotel until we figure out how."

14

Winter ushered them into an adjacent dining room, complete with a table large enough for them to gather around. Reed sat awkwardly across from Lucy while Kelly and Banks settled down next to her. They seemed at ease with LB, as if there was some developed history there.

As they settled in, a knock rang at the main door, and Winter turned to Amadou. "The food."

Amadou disappeared, then returned a moment later with an armful of savory-smelling, nondescript white packages.

"I hope you enjoy Cajun food," Winter said. "I never come to the coast without indulging."

Maggie didn't hesitate. She ripped into the packages and passed around Styrofoam cartons of rice, jambalaya, and various etouffees. Kelly waved the food away without comment, and Lucy raised an eyebrow.

"What the hell is it?" Lucy asked.

"Don't ask," Maggie said. "Just eat."

Reed accepted a carton of rice and allowed Maggie to ladle a thick helping of an orange topping over it. Fragments of shrimp and unidentifiable meats slid through the saucier parts of the food, but Reed didn't ask. Like anybody from the South, he was familiar with Cajun cuisine and usually enjoyed it.

Reed felt eyes on him, and he looked up in time to catch an icy glance from Kelly. His appetite faded like a dying breath, and he set the carton down. "Can we get on with it?" he asked, turning to Winter.

Winter motioned to Amadou. The big man shut the twin doors to the dining room, then settled into a chair in the corner.

Winter leaned forward. "At this point, I assume everyone is aware of the events that unfolded in Atlanta involving Reed and the late Mitchell Holiday."

Everybody signaled in the affirmative.

"Then I'll get straight to the point. I've brought you here because each of you has played a part in those events and have now assumed an obligation, willingly or otherwise, to see this mess through to the end."

She paused, as if waiting for objections or questions, but nothing except quiet chewing from Maggie and Lucy answered her. The others sat silently, ignoring the food.

"Are you familiar with the name Aiden Phillips?"

Silence again.

"Phillips is, directly or otherwise, responsible for everything that has taken place in the past month. He is the owner and operator of a highly organized, heavily funded criminal organization based, I think, in Atlanta. For the last twenty years, I've worked around the clock in an effort to obtain operational intelligence about this organization—something that could take Phillips down. I've failed on every account."

"What's your beef with Phillips?" Wolfgang said.

"Let's just say it's a personal thing."

Wolfgang grunted. "Personal. Well, I've got bad news for you. I don't do personal. So, thanks for the weird food, but I'll be going now."

Winter folded her slender arms. "Don't you want to know about the package on your doorstep?"

"You admit to putting it there?" Wolfgang said.

"Amadou put it there. But I sent it."

Wolfgang shot Amadou a sideways look, sizing him up again. "You circumvented my security system?"

Amadou said nothing, focusing on his Styrofoam carton of food.

Wolfgang looked back to Winter. "What was in the vial?"

"I was hoping you would know."

Wolfgang folded his arms and stared the old woman down. Reed couldn't tell if he was still suspicious of her or if he was just holding his cards close to his chest.

"Where did you get it?" Wolfgang said.

Winter shrugged. "It's a long story. Short answer is, I stole it from Aiden's operation."

Wolfgang chewed on that for a moment, then took a sip of water.

"Tell us what you know, Mr. Pierce," Winter pressed. "We're all on the same team."

"There's nothing to tell," Wolfgang said. "I ran some tests and put it under a microscope, but that only helped me identify its components, not necessarily its purpose."

Winter scratched her arm. "You must have some idea."

"You're asking me to take a shot in the dark. Scientists don't like guess-work. But if you put a gun to my head, I'd say it was some type of genetic treatment formula. A compound designed to manage or correct a genetic disorder."

"Medication?" Lucy asked.

Wolfgang made a noncommittal shrug. "That's a simplification, but yes. Something like that."

"I don't get it," Maggie said. "What does any of this have to do with catching Phillips?"

Winter held up a hand. "My apologies. Let me start from the beginning. And please . . . eat. If you don't like the food, I'll order something else."

There was a moment of hesitation around the table, then everybody except Kelly ate again.

"The story starts at Vanderbilt University right around 1990. Five men met and founded an unofficial fraternity. Those men were Aiden Phillips, Dick Carter, Liam Holland, Mitchell Holiday, Frank Morccelli, and David Montgomery."

Lucy twitched. "David Montgomery? As in . . . ?"

"Yes. Reed's father."

"Hell of a coincidence," Wolfgang muttered.

"I said this was personal," Winter said. "I didn't say who it was personal *to*. But another name should stand out on that list—Frank Morccelli, Banks's father."

Everybody avoided looking at Banks. She poked at her food and said nothing.

"The other thing you should know about that list is that all those men are dead, except for Aiden and Liam. Liam went missing in 1993, and Aiden killed the other four."

"Banks and I were in Wyoming," Reed said. "We spoke to Dick Carter. He told us the fraternity was some kind of dark cult."

Winter grunted. "It was. At first, anyway. Things got nasty, and Carter moved to Wyoming to finish his degree. But the rest of them stayed and graduated and became involved in their various careers. Frank became a doctor, David went into financial management, and Mitchell started a logistics business in Brunswick, Georgia."

Reed saw it instantly—something he'd never noticed before, even though it stared him right in the face. "They graduated," he said, "but the fraternity didn't die. They still worked together."

"That's correct," Winter said. "I'm fuzzy on the details, but I know David ran the financial side. Mitchell's logistics company provided a mix of operations and money-laundering functions, and Aiden was the mastermind behind it all. The creative genius."

"What were they doing exactly?" Maggie asked.

"Cocaine. I don't have proof, but my research indicates they were smuggling it out of South America. That was big business in the eighties, but by the nineties, regulation and DEA enforcement really intensified. Moving drugs into the States had become incredibly difficult, if still profitable. My guess is that Aiden invented a way to make it happen and then recruited his old college buddies to help him run the operation. He knew them well, and he knew they could keep strange secrets."

"So, Aiden leveraged their individual expertise into a criminal enterprise," Wolfgang said.

Winter gave a slight shrug, but Reed shook his head. "I don't buy it. My father had his demons, but he wasn't that kind of guy. He just laundered some money and cheated on some taxes. White-collar stuff."

"That's only what they pinned him for," Winter said. "Just before you were hired to kill Mitchell Holiday, he was in contact with an FBI agent named Rollick, and I was able to ascertain some general details about the investigation. Apparently, Holiday wanted to come clean. He wouldn't agree to testify before the FBI granted certain protections for Miss Morccelli, but he claimed to know details of an elaborate enterprise that involved multiple parties. Including David."

"He wanted to protect me?" Banks said softly.

Winter nodded. "I'm not sure why. Apparently, he believed his testimony would endanger you. Holiday was your godfather, after all. You were close. I guess he thought Aiden might go after you."

"What about Frank?" Reed asked. "You haven't mentioned her father."

"Frank wasn't involved in the cocaine operation. The best I can tell, he knew nothing about it. At least at first."

"And then?" Banks asked.

"And then the twenty-first century. And then satellites and digital technology and a wave of new complexities that mass drug smuggling couldn't overcome. Aiden's operation collapsed, and whatever came next is what Frank got tangled up in. I don't have details, but I do know that Aiden was in contact with him in the months preceding his death."

"You mean before Aiden killed him," Banks said.

Winter fingered the edge of the table. "As an intelligence specialist, I loathe speculation. According to his death certificate, your father died in a drunk driving accident. But, yes, I think it was a hit job."

"And you think Aiden ordered that hit?" Reed asked. "The same way he ordered the hit on Holiday and poisoned my father in prison?"

"Yes. The Holiday contract I'm very clear on. Aiden ordered it via his front man, Gambit, whose real name was Stephen Yates. I understand Mr. Yates is no longer with us."

"He acquired a bullet in the throat," Maggie said.

Winter grunted. "That's unfortunate. I would've liked to interrogate him. Back to my point, though. Prior to his death, Holiday was in contact with the FBI, and Aiden must have found out, which was why he ordered the hit. It's reasonable to conclude that at some point, both Frank and David also turned on him, which is why they were killed. That leaves the entire operation under Aiden's control. Whatever he's doing, whatever he's invented with that formula, we know it's sinister. We know it's the kind of thing that will get people killed . . . because it already has."

Nobody seemed eager to speculate or draw conclusions.

To Reed's surprise, Kelly was the first to speak, and her mask fluttered over her face as she faced Winter. "Why are we here?"

Winter sat forward. "All of you have a fight with Aiden. All of you want to take him out, as do I. You're here because, for the first time in two decades, I may have finally found his weakness. I need you to exploit it."

15

―――――

"Explain," Wolfgang said, his voice noncommittal. Winter folded her hands over her lap.

"Two days ago, I was in Taylor, Arizona. Small town. There was a shipment of bananas at a grocery store there from Colombia, and—"

"Did you say bananas?" Maggie said.

"Yes . . . Colombian bananas. I received a tip last week to investigate them, so I did. I had a private laboratory run some tests for me, and they found substantial traces of the same formula I sent Wolfgang on more than half of them."

Wolfgang frowned. "Wait. You're telling me you found what was in that vial on *bananas*?"

"On them. In them. On the boxes they were shipped in."

"So, it's some kind of growth chemical, then?" Wolfgang said. "An herbicide or fertilizer?"

"That's your area of expertise, not mine. But I've only found it on bananas shipped specifically out of Colombia. I haven't been able to narrow it down beyond that."

"It could be a ripening agent," Lucy said.

Everybody pivoted toward her.

"What the hell is that?" Reed asked.

"I saw it on TV," she said. "There was this special about bananas on National Geographic. They pick them when they're super green, then box them up and put them on container ships. When they arrive at their destination, they're still green, and they will stay green for days. So they spray this ripening agent on them that makes them turn yellow. It's some kind of gas."

"Without the gas, they don't turn yellow?" Maggie said.

"I don't think so. Not for a while, anyway."

Maggie sat back. "Shit."

"What is it?" Reed asked.

"Something that happened while I was hunting Gambit," Maggie said. "Last week, I closed the Port of New Orleans to flush him out. We thought he was operating out of the port, and we thought that if we closed it, we might force him to expose himself. So we . . . found a way to close the port."

"You faked an environmental crisis," Winter said, a smile playing at the corner of her lips.

Maggie's face flushed red. "Well, yes. We did. And it worked, too. Or at least we thought it did. There was this Colombian freighter due to make port in New Orleans. We cut them off, and they immediately filed a slew of emergency port-entry certificates at every dock from Houston to Tampa. I mean, it was a firestorm of paperwork, so we thought we hit pay dirt."

"What happened?" Reed pressed.

"I had the Coast Guard conduct a 'routine search' of the ship. They boarded her off the coast and found nothing but crates of green bananas. When they questioned the captain about why his company filed so many emergency certificates, he said it was because the bananas would ripen if he didn't get them off the boat and he'd lose the cargo."

Lucy squinted. "But . . ."

"But that's not true," Maggie finished. "Not if you need a gas to ripen them."

"So, there was another reason he was in a hurry to make port," Wolfgang said. "Something else at stake. Did the Coast Guard conduct a complete search of the vessel?"

Maggie shrugged. "They were on board only half an hour. They couldn't have searched the entire ship, but everything looked okay."

Reed pivoted toward Winter. "What's your theory? I know you have one."

Winter pursed her lips. "There's not enough data to be certain, but I think Aiden is using bananas to smuggle something in from Colombia. I don't know what. Maybe it's some new drug. All I know for sure is that if it's worth killing over, it could be his weakness."

"Where is he?" Reed demanded.

"Aiden?" Winter asked. Reed nodded, and Winter tilted her head. "Why do you want to know?"

"Why do you think? We're sitting here playing Sherlock Holmes when a fifty-cent bullet will end the problem. You say you've spent twenty years trying to pin this guy down, and I'm saying you've wasted your time. Let's just obliterate him and be done with it."

Lucy grunted in what sounded like semi-agreement, but Maggie was already shaking her head. "We're not doing that, Reed. If he's smuggling narcotics into the country, we need *proof*. We need to understand his system, understand the drug, and understand the source. Otherwise, someone else will just step into his shoes after he's dead. And besides, that's not justice."

Reed snorted. "Are you kidding me? The man is a serial murderer, a total psychopath, and probably a massive drug smuggler. What exactly *is* justice in this case?"

"A trial," Maggie said, her voice carrying a sudden edge. "A public trial, and then a conviction."

Reed rolled his eyes. "We've been over this, Governor. What do you think he used that underage brothel for, anyway? He has tapes of all kinds of public officials raping little girls. Judges, law enforcement agents, government officials, probably. It's the grease he uses to push his sludge through the pipes. He's untouchable by anything and anybody except a bullet to the head."

Maggie's cheeks flushed scarlet, and her jaw twitched, but she didn't reply.

"Reed's right," Kelly said. "Tell us where the bastard is, and we'll erase the problem. If you want to know where his operation is, or who his friends are, or what his favorite flavor of milkshake is, we'll get that out of him before his last breath. It won't be a problem."

Everybody turned to Winter, but she looked to Wolfgang.

"Doctor?"

Wolfgang ran his tongue over his teeth and didn't speak. He tapped one index finger against the table and switched his gaze between Reed and Maggie, then back to Reed. "I'm inclined to agree with Reed. Whoever owned the brothel deserves to be roasted alive, and I have zero qualms about doing so myself. I'm not in the business of putting people on trial. Having said that, I'm not convinced Aiden is smuggling drugs. The formula you sent me has all the characteristics of a highly complex DNA reconstruction therapy. In simplistic terms, genetic diseases result from damaged and mutated DNA compounds, which self-replicate, perpetuating the disease. When somebody has a condition like cystic fibrosis, it's because their DNA isn't replicating properly. Something is mutated and continues to mutate. DNA reconditioning therapy is used to retrain the DNA to replicate properly, correcting the condition."

"Sounds like science fiction," Lucy said.

Wolfgang shrugged. "In a lot of ways, it is. The point I'm making is that if there's even a *chance* Aiden has discovered a formula that could lead to a breakthrough in this type of DNA therapy, that would be the greatest medical accomplishment since penicillin. An unprecedented, priceless innovation—something we absolutely, under no circumstances, can let slip away. Unless and until we fully understand what we're dealing with, Aiden cannot be touched. We may need him. The whole world may need him."

Reed shot Winter an icy look. "This was your strategy all along, wasn't it? This is why you wanted him here. Because you have no intention of telling me where Aiden is."

Winter shook her head. "I want him here because I think you need him. I'm not manipulating anything. If you as a group decide it's better to simply kill Aiden, I'll help you find him."

Reed looked to Maggie.

She leaned back and folded her arms. "I've cast my vote."

Reed turned to Lucy.

She shrugged. "I'd rather kill him. But I'm no expert on any of this, so I withdraw my vote."

"Kelly?" Reed said.

"We kill him," she snapped. "Nobody that evil has anything we need."

"Okay, then," Winter said. "The tiebreaker goes to Miss Morccelli."

Banks shifted and glanced around the room, pausing for a moment on Reed. "I want him dead," she said. "As soon and as decisively as possible. I can never forget or forgive what he did to my father." She blinked, her eyes rimmed red. "But that can wait a little longer. If there's any chance that Aiden has something that the world needs, I can't allow my desire for vengeance to supersede that need. We'll run down this formula thing first . . . then we hunt him."

Reed clenched his fingers into a fist. Everything inside of him told him this was wrong. It was always best to slay the dragon and walk away.

But if Banks wants this, I owe it to her.

"All right," he said, turning to Winter. "Where do we start?"

16

Amadou swept the dinner remnants off the table with one brush of his giant arm, dumping them into a trash bag and disappearing from the dining room. He reappeared a moment later with a carafe of coffee, a tray of cups, and a basketful of creamers and sugars. The small crowd enjoyed steaming cups of Colombian brew, and Reed didn't miss the irony.

Winter resumed control of the discussion. "It's unclear to me why Aiden would smuggle any sort of medication into the country via bananas. But there's obviously a connection here. So, the first thing we should do is trace the source and learn more about how the bananas are being contaminated. Which means somebody is going to Colombia."

"I should go," Wolfgang said. "Nobody else knows what to look for. But it may get hairy down there. It wouldn't hurt to have some backup."

"I'll go with you," Reed said. "But it may be tricky for me to fly. I'm sure I'm on every watch list known to man."

"You are," Winter said, "but I think there's still time to slip you out on a fake passport, so long as we move quickly. I can provide the documents. Getting back into the country will be a lot trickier, I'm afraid."

Maggie grunted. "I'll take care of getting him back in. If nothing else, I'll send somebody out on a shrimp boat to pick him up. It won't be a problem."

"Good plan," Winter said. "So, Wolfgang and Reed will go to Colombia. I assume one of you speaks Spanish?"

Reed exchanged a glance with Wolfgang and was met with a small, negative gesture.

"I do," Banks said. "I'll go with them."

"No way," Reed said. "It's dangerous down there."

Banks glared at him. "You mean it's dangerous being with *you*. Trust me, I'm aware. But the reality remains that you can't go digging around in a Latin country without speaking the language. You saw me with that crazy arms dealer. I'm pretty fluent in Spanish."

Reed was ready with his next objection, but Wolfgang broke in. "She's right, Reed. We'll need a translator we can trust. And you shouldn't underestimate her ability to look after herself. She's pretty quick with a shotgun."

Something in Wolfgang's tone told Reed there was a story behind the comment, but Banks waved off the question in his face.

"What about the rest of us?" Lucy said. "We're not gonna sit around."

"You're going to Beaumont," Reed said.

"Texas?" Lucy asked.

Reed nodded.

"Why?"

Reed folded his arms. "Aiden is a calculating genius, but to my knowledge, he's no medical expert. What Wolfgang's talking about—genetic manipulation and replicating cells—is crazy, but I've heard of it before."

"What do you mean?" Wolfgang asked.

"When I was in North Carolina, right before you tried to blow my head off in a coffee shop, I was doing some research on Banks's father. Mitchell Holiday had mentioned him several times, and I wanted to know what his connection might've been. I dug up a whole pile of speculative research papers that Frank drafted prior to his death. Several of them mentioned the same sort of DNA repair replications that Wolfgang is talking about."

The room fell still, and everybody avoided looking at Banks. She picked at the edge of the table, blinking back tears, and Reed plowed ahead.

"One of the papers mentioned a research project Frank was involved in, funded by a company called Beaumont Pharmaceutical. I don't know why the name stuck in my mind, but talking about all this stuff brought it back to me. If Aiden has this formula thing, he didn't invent it himself. I'm guessing Frank did, which may or may not be why he was killed. Either way, we need to know more about his research. Somebody needs to pay Beaumont Pharma a visit."

Winter watched him, and Reed wondered if the old woman already knew about Beaumont. Maybe she did. Maybe she knew a lot of things that she was—for whatever reason—keeping to herself. He didn't appreciate that, but for the moment, he would keep trusting her.

"I'll go," Lucy said. "We can try to meet with somebody."

Kelly shook her head. "These people aren't here to talk. I'll go with you. We'll enter the building at night and take a look."

Lucy raised an eyebrow. "Are you kidding? You can't just waltz in there and poke a thumb drive into a desktop. They'll have security and firewalls—"

"Superchick, if I can nab a supercar out of a Saudi prince's private fortress under the noses of two dozen trigger-happy security guards, I can get us into an office building."

Lucy shot Reed a questioning look, and he nodded. "She can do it," he said.

Lucy shrugged.

"What about me?" Maggie said.

"Go back to Baton Rouge," Winter said. "Retake control of your government, and get rid of Robert Coulier before he does any further damage on Aiden's behalf. Then stand by to get Reed back into the country, and prepare one hell of a prosecution against Aiden's operation. As soon as we have the proper evidence against him, you'll have your hands full."

"I thought Reed was going to murder him," Maggie said, her voice carrying the dull disgust of a person who wasn't sold on the plan at hand.

"We'll decide what to do with Aiden when the time comes," Winter said. "Regardless of what happens to him, you'll have your hands full cleaning up his mess. The child trafficking and rape ring by itself will keep you busy for years, but you can't move on that until we have Aiden in our crosshairs."

Reed watched Maggie carefully. The muscles in her jaw twitched, but she nodded once and said, "I'll leave for Baton Rouge tonight."

"We'll have Reed, Wolfgang, and Banks in the air first thing in the morning," Winter continued. "Amadou and I will assist Lucy and Kelly on the Beaumont operation, and we'll all use Governor Trousdale as our central hub of communication."

Everyone exchanged another glance, then Reed stood up. "Fair enough. Let's hunt."

17

Clouds deepened the darkness that fell over the old city. Reed stood in the living room of the suite and marveled at how quiet downtown had become. Atlanta never slept or even quieted much. But there, everything was silent. If he closed his eyes, he could almost imagine that he was a few hundred miles away, standing in the comfort of his own living room inside the cabin next to the lake. Alone. Safe. As close to peace as he would ever come.

Reed rubbed his jaw and found his way to the wet bar. It featured a diverse display of bottled liquors—nothing fancy, but acceptably premium. He shuffled through the vodkas and bourbons until he located a bottle of Jack Daniels, then he poured himself two fingers into a glass. He stared into the amber drink for a moment, then added another two fingers.

Why not?

He found a chair in the living room. Wolfgang lay stretched out on the couch next to him, his body perfectly still, but Reed doubted he was actually asleep. The other doors to the suite were closed. Banks and Lucy took one room, and Winter and Amadou the other. Maggie had already taken a taxi to the bus station. She planned to slip back into Baton Rouge unannounced and catch Coulier off guard.

Reed gulped the whiskey and relished the burn in his throat. It'd been weeks since he'd sat alone and drank himself into oblivion. It'd been weeks since he enjoyed the simple release of stepping into the unknown and embracing the fog. It was better than sleep—better than bludgeoning himself with a baseball bat and accepting the darkness. With the cloud of whiskey consuming his mind, he could let go of his own carefully crafted mental defenses and face the man he truly was. He could picture each one of the twenty-nine targets he'd executed over the past three years, and he could remember what it felt like to end their lives. In this most brutal form of self-punishment imaginable, he could lay down the lies and simply accept himself as the monster he was.

Reed used to sit this way, alone in his cabin, and drink for days on end. He used to wonder how he got there and if he could get out, and what it meant to be good. He used to contemplate the meaning of life and the value of death and a million abstract philosophies to make himself feel better about the bloodshed. He was done with that. Now, he just wanted to drink and not think too much about anything.

And maybe that makes me worse than ever.

A soft murmur broke through his daze. He thought it was a voice at first, but as he blinked back the fog of the drink and sat up, he heard it again. It wasn't a voice. It was a muted sob—almost a whimper. He looked at Wolfgang, but the killer lay still, both hands folded inside his jacket, where they doubtless held weapons. His eyes remained shut, and his breathing smooth.

Reed heard the sound again, coming from another room. He dumped another double into the glass, then walked into the quiet, empty dining room. Swallowing another gulp of whiskey, he turned to the left when he heard the whimper again. Then he saw her. The end of the dining room was framed by a bank of windows and a door leading out onto a narrow balcony. It was dark outside, but at the far end of the balcony, Reed saw a blackened figure nestled next to the rail, leaning down, holding itself, and sobbing.

Kelly.

A tremor shot through his arm, and he hesitated next to the table, feeling a little unsteady on his feet. Kelly leaned over, her head bent and her hair flowing freely in the gentle November breeze. The hijab was gone, and while her face was obscured from view, Reed could make out the twisted scars of the fire on her neck. Her hair was cut short—just barely reaching her ears, with the jagged lines and uneven cuts of a self-inflicted haircut. She held her arms in an odd, cradle-like posture, as though she were rocking something.

The baby.

Reed stepped back, catching himself on a chair, which slid and smacked against the edge of a table. Kelly straightened, drawing her arms to her chest, and she glanced reflexively over her shoulder. For a split second, their eyes met, and the bullet that tore through his mind only milliseconds before burst into a rush of gunfire.

Kelly's face was a distorted mass of burn marks. Her left cheek was swollen, twisting her nose and lifting her top lip into a permanent snarl. Her skin was a blotchy mix of white patches and red spiderwebs, ripping through her once-beautiful complexion and leaving her with the mask of a Halloween monster.

Kelly twisted away. She ducked her head, and the hijab reappeared over her scalp, the light black cloth falling over her shoulders and hiding the burn marks that rippled down her neck. Reed set the glass down and stepped around the chair. The balcony door eased open without a sound, and his face was stung by the wind blowing down the street, fresh off the bay.

He shut the door behind him, and Kelly turned away. It was then that he saw the revolver resting on the railing next to her hands. Four .38-caliber cartridges stood on their butts, lined up next to the cocked handgun. Reed assumed a fifth round must've been chambered somewhere inside the cylinder.

Kelly made no move to conceal the weapon or its obvious application. She faced the bay, her shoulders squared, and her hands buried inside the folds of the garment.

Reed ran his hand along the smooth wood of the rail, taking a step closer, but he didn't speak. He envisioned smoke rising from Kelly's house and saw the flash of red lights spilling over her lawn from the armada of fire engines. Then he saw her body being wheeled out of the house on a gurney. Only, it wasn't her body.

"I killed them," Kelly whispered. Her voice was hoarse and broken, little more than a hiss through her swollen lips.

Reed noticed her knuckles turn white as she gripped the railing on either side of the handgun.

"Two men set fire to the house," she continued. "One of them screwed up and got the gasoline on himself. He was thrashing around in the kitchen when the fire started. I went downstairs, and I knew what happened, but it was too late. So much smoke . . . So much heat . . . I couldn't get out. He burned alive while clawing at the sink faucet." Her voice faded, and she leaned against the rail.

Reed wanted to step forward and wrap her in his arms and pull her close—

And be everything I was supposed to be. Be the man she deserved.

"I flew to Europe and found the other guy hiding in Latvia. Some little mercenary shit. I tied him up and went to work with a knife." Her voice grew in strength, and her arms stopped shaking. "You should've heard him scream, Reed. I had to cut his throat before it was over, just so he'd shut up. It really pissed me off, too. I wanted to keep going."

This wasn't the Kelly Reed knew from before—the exotic car thief who lived on the edge of her luck, pushing the limits of her skills to attain new heights of adrenaline. A woman who surrounded herself with fancy people and fancy things and didn't need any of them. A woman who stole cars because it was *fun*. This woman was broken and bitter and so different from who she used to be that Reed barely saw a resemblance.

"I'm sorry," Reed whispered. He wasn't sure why he spoke at all. The words were worthless, even though he meant them more than he'd ever meant anything.

Kelly's laugh was dry and lifeless. "I'm sure you are. But you know what's crazy?"

"What?"

"I *get* you, now. When we broke up, I hated you for who you were. I didn't understand how a man could kill so easily. Sure, I was devastated to lose you, but it's easier to judge than to understand."

Kelly picked up the gun, and Reed stood frozen as she pointed it at him, only four feet away. Impossible to miss.

"But I understand now," she said, her eyes crinkling as her cheeks lifted into what may have been a smile. "I know what it feels like to take the life of the person you hate. God, it's a good feeling. It's not power, and it's not love, and it's nothing like happiness. But for a moment—for as long as it takes to watch that person die—it's satisfaction. For people like us, that's as good as it gets."

Reed shook his head. "No, Kelly, it's not. It's a long road into a deep, deep ditch. A place you can't climb out of."

Kelly snorted, and her hoarse voice rose in pitch. "You think so? Well, you'd know, wouldn't you?"

The tip of the revolver twitched, and the hammer snapped forward with a sharp *click*, slamming against an empty chamber. Kelly laughed again, softer this time and with more irony. "Well, would you look at that? You're as unlucky as me. Twenty-seven nights in a row." She turned away, flipping the cylinder open and reloading the other four cartridges. "I was never good at math, you know. But a one-in-five chance, twenty-seven times in a row . . . Hell of a thing, isn't it?" The revolver disappeared into her pocket, and she folded her arms.

Reed stepped forward, sliding his hands along the rail until they were inches from hers. He listened to the soft whistle of her breath passing between twisted lips. "If it makes anything better, kill me. For God's sake."

For a moment, nothing but the wind filled the silence, and he thought she might pull the gun again.

Then she shook her head. "Nah. If I killed you, all your guilt and pain would be over. Where's the fun in that?"

Her words stung with viciousness, but none of that hatred reached her eyes. He saw nothing there except the worst sort of pain.

Without a word, she slipped back through the door and into the suite, leaving him alone in the midnight breeze.

18

Winter was as good as her word. She produced three passports with matching credit cards, which looked and felt as real as they came. Reed traveled under the name Mark Morales, and Banks was Frances Hagelin. Wolfgang declined to share his travel name, but when he saw the passport, he gave Winter a long, cold look, and Winter nodded once.

They flew out of Mobile the next hour, equipped with nothing but clothes, a backpack filled with dry foods, a first-aid kit, and a satellite phone. Amadou dropped them at the airport, and they shuffled through security without issue. Their next stop was Miami, where they boarded an Avianca flight for Bogata—Colombia's capital city. After a two-hour layover, they would board a third and final plane for Barranquilla, a port city from where, according to Maggie, the mystery ship had set sail.

"This is thin," Wolfgang said. It was the first thing he'd said to anyone since leaving Mobile.

"You're here, aren't you?" Reed said.

They sat next to each other in cramped coach seats near the tail of the plane. Banks sat several rows ahead, by herself, staring out the window. She hadn't spoken a word to Reed since leaving the hotel, and she wouldn't meet his gaze.

"I'm here because I want the formula," Wolfgang growled. "I have no ambition to join your little war."

"Nobody's asking you to."

The silence that fell between them was pregnant with animosity. After a while, it irritated Reed. "What's up your ass, anyway?" he said.

Wolfgang glowered but didn't answer.

"It's the passport, isn't it? The name she chose." Reed sighed. "If she made you uncomfortable, that was probably her goal."

"Who said I was uncomfortable?"

Reed ran a tired hand over his face. He felt disoriented and altogether uneasy with the status quo. Flying unarmed into the unknown, accompanied by people he couldn't control, wasn't his idea of a good plan. Alarm bells sounded in his head, leaving him edgy and restless.

This is what happens when I don't work alone. Why didn't I ditch the governor last week and go after Aiden on my own?

He looked down the long aisle of seats and caught sight of Banks's head poking up above the seat, her blonde hair a little disheveled against the fabric.

That's why.

Reed slapped Wolfgang on the arm. "All right, then. You sit here and pout. It's a long flight." He stood and brushed the wrinkles out of his shirt, then stepped down the aisle until he stood next to the empty seat beside Banks.

She didn't look up, but her shoulders stiffened.

"May I sit?"

Banks remained fixated on the window, looking out at the cloud-blanketed sky stretching out beneath them.

Reed eased himself into the seat, taking care not to touch her. His stomach twisted into knots, but he wedged his knees behind the next seat and leaned back. For five minutes, he sat silently, his mind rushing for something to say. He wanted to leave Banks in Mobile, but not because he was trying to get rid of her. Reed had finally accepted that Banks was like a force of nature—something he would never be rid of until she wanted to be rid of him, and he was okay with that. He wanted her close, but Colombia was a dangerous place, and he was flying there with the specific purpose of flushing out dangerous people. He didn't want her caught in the crossfire —again.

"How's Baxter?" he said at last.

"Fine."

"Is he . . . I mean, where is he?"

"Long-term kennel. In Jackson."

"Right." Reed chewed his lip and rubbed a thumb against his jeans.

What do I say to her? Is there anything left to say?

"Banks, about the governor . . ."

"What about her?"

Reed's mind spun back to the previous week when he stood on a New Orleans street corner and kissed Trousdale while Banks watched from thirty yards away.

"When I kissed her—"

"Why would I care about that?"

Reed winced. He remembered the happiness and longing in Banks's eyes as she stared at him from across the street. He hadn't looked up after he kissed Maggie. He just did it, and then they walked away, and that was that.

"You know why," he whispered.

Reed could see a reflection of her face in the window. Her nose was red, and dry trails ran down her cheeks.

He touched her arm as softly as he could, but his rough fingers felt clumsy against her smooth skin. She flinched but didn't pull away.

"I only did it because I wanted you to leave," he said. "I didn't want to hurt you."

She snorted and still didn't face him. "You're so good at that, aren't you?"

"At what?"

"Playing God. You really think you're something."

Reed withdrew his hand. "I don't understand."

She glowered at the backside of the seat in front of her. "From the very start, you've called every shot. *You* decide what's safe for me. *You* decide where I belong and when I belong there. *You* decide what risks I can take and how involved I can be and what I know. It doesn't matter what I think or how I feel or what *I'm* prepared to risk."

A lump swelled in Reed's throat. "Banks, it's not like that. I'm trained—"

"Bullshit, Reed. Bullshit." She kept her voice low, but it still carried a brutal edge. "This isn't about any *training*. This is about you controlling the outcome."

Reed gritted his teeth, feeling suddenly frustrated. "Did it ever occur to you why I wanted to control the outcome? Because I wanted to protect you."

"Did it ever occur to you I didn't want or need protecting?"

Banks dug into her purse, producing a pill bottle and swallowing back two antibiotic tablets. For the Lyme disease, Reed guessed. Maybe that explained her flushed skin.

"You're unbelievable, Reed."

His voice was suddenly hesitant. "It's not like that. I've never risked something I wasn't willing to lose . . . until I met you."

Banks folded her arms and looked back out the window.

"Banks, you have to understand. When I met you—"

"You felt something you'd never felt before?" She twisted toward him. "You connected in a way you didn't know was possible?"

He swallowed, then looked away.

"Well, that's great, Reed. That's really terrific. But high schoolers whine about that kind of crap on a dozen bad TV shows. If you truly care about somebody, if you truly want somebody in your life, then you *respect* them. And you haven't respected me. Not even close."

Reed felt two inches tall, with the sudden irresistible urge to disappear, but he had nowhere to go. He just sat as Banks's verbal barrage continued.

"This isn't about the governor. I know a fake kiss when I see one. She should've knocked your ass out. I'm talking about Kelly. I'm talking about when I told you not to say it, and then you texted me anyway saying you loved me. I'm talking about how you abandoned me in Alabama. I'm talking about every time I've told you that this is *my* fight, as much or more than it was ever yours, and yet you continue to push me away like a paper doll while making the plans and calling the shots. You do not respect me, and it's messed up, Reed. It's messed up because . . ."

He reached for her hand, but she brushed him away.

"Go away, Reed. I'm not dealing with this today."

19

Maggie stepped off the Greyhound and brushed her hair behind her ear. Baton Rouge was alive with bustling citizens hurrying past the downtown station, oblivious to their long-lost governor appearing off the bus like an apparition. She smiled and breathed in the deep, forever-humid scent of Louisiana.

Hot damn. It's good to be home.

She fumbled in her pocket for a quarter and came up empty. With a frustrated sigh, she targeted the first person she saw without holes in their shoes and made an approach. "Excuse me. Do you have a quarter for the phone?"

The man appraised her with the semi-sympathetic, semi-condemning glance of the middle-class, then dug in his pocket. He deposited a handful of coins and a stick of gum into her hand and offered a condescending smile. "That's all I have. You should get a job."

Maggie grinned. "Believe it or not, that's where I'm headed next."

She dumped a couple quarters into the phone, then dialed a number from memory. It rang three times, then four. Most people wouldn't answer a number they didn't recognize, but Yolanda Flint wasn't most people—she was the best damn chief of staff this side of the Mississippi, and if Maggie had any sense, she would've taken better care of her.

Maggie stood up straight. She didn't have time for regret. Today was war day, and today she would take the house back.

The phone rang twice more, but Maggie didn't hang up.

On the eighth ring, a sleepy voice finally answered. "Hello?"

"Good morning, Yolanda. It's Maggie."

"Maggie? Are you for real?"

"Pretty real, Yolanda. How's it going?"

"Maggie, oh my god. You're alive! I've been so worried."

"Yes, I'm alive and well. Listen, I know there's a lot we need to talk about. I owe you a big apology for what happened, and probably some lengthy explanations. But it'll have to wait. Right now, I need a favor, and I need you to not ask questions." The line went heavy with hesitation, and Maggie pressed her luck. "I know what you're thinking. Trust me, I'll explain everything. I need you back on my staff."

"Maggie . . . I resigned."

"I know, and I never should've let you. I need you, Yolanda. The people need you."

That would do it. Yolanda was even more a sucker for public service than Maggie.

Yolanda cleared her throat. "Of course, Madam Governor. I serve the people."

Maggie smiled. "Excellent. So, here's what's up. First, tell nobody—absolutely nobody—that you've heard from me. That's important. Second, remember how I'd sometimes get you to sign stuff for me?"

"I don't know what you're talking about, Madam Governor."

Maggie's smile spread into a grin. "Of course you don't. Here's what I need."

Maggie crossed through downtown and made the two-mile walk to the State Capitol in under twenty minutes, stopping just long enough at a street vendor to secure a late-morning shrimp po'boy. War food. She finished the sandwich by the time she reached the bottom steps of Louisiana's towering, 449-foot State Capitol, and took a minute to stare up through the bright sun at the imposing building.

It's definitely good to be home.

She took the steps two at a time, breaking straight for the door, where a tall state policeman held out his hand. "Hold up there, miss. This entrance is for official use only."

Maggie paused. She recognized the cop—it was Officer O'Dell, one of her personal security detail, now apparently banished to menial sentry duty.

"Morning, O'Dell. Damn good to see you."

The cop's placid face turned shocked. "Madam Governor?"

"Yep."

O'Dell seemed unable to move, his jaw hanging slack. Then he rushed forward and wrapped her in a hug. "Ma'am, I'm so sorry. I'm so, so sorry!"

Maggie coughed, patting him awkwardly on the back.

O'Dell seemed to suddenly realize what he was doing, and he released her and stepped back. His face flushed. "Ma'am, I'm sorry."

She held up a hand. "No more apologies, O'Dell. I'm glad I found you. I may need some muscle. Got your gun?"

O'Dell placed a reflexive hand on the sidearm mounted to his hip.

Maggie winked and led the way up the steps. "Perfect. This way."

O'Dell unlocked the door with his keycard, hurrying to keep up with her quick strides. As they passed into the marble halls of the decorative bottom floor, staffers and politicians in dark suits looked up, and the whole building felt quiet. Then everybody started talking at once, and several state politicians hurried forward.

Maggie motioned to O'Dell, and he lunged forward like a protective dog, signaling everybody back.

"Stand back. Stand back, now!"

Maggie turned a corner, and then she saw Yolanda. Her former chief of staff stood in the middle of the hallway, dressed in an immaculate pants suit—her hallmark look. Yolanda's hair was tied up over her head in the classic way only women born in the sixties can master.

"Madam Governor," she said.

Maggie rushed forward and wrapped her in a big hug—a much more aggressive form of greeting than her chief of staff was comfortable with, but that day, she didn't care.

Yolanda returned the hug, then Maggie stepped back.

"You look great, Yolanda. Damn good to have you back."

Yolanda hesitated. "I'm not back yet, Maggie. I still have some big questions."

"I've got some big answers. Did you bring it?"

Yolanda dug in her coffin-sized purse and produced a manila envelope.

"Is it good?" Maggie asked, taking the file.

Yolanda indulged in an uncharacteristic smirk. "It's perfect."

"Outstanding. Let's get this rat."

They set off down the hallway, reaching the elevator a moment later. The building was already buzzing with personnel. Rushing cops stole glances at her while politicians and bureaucrats stuck their heads out of office doors to catch a glimpse of their governor, returned from the dead.

Baton Rouge was alive now. There would be no subduing this secret.

When the elevator doors rolled open on the executive floor, Maggie marched out with the confidence and command of a woman who owned the whole tower. She burst through the twin glass doors of the governor's suite, ignoring the blustering secretary who first coughed a greeting, then mumbled a "Can I help you?"

"Absolutely. You can get out," Maggie said.

She threw the next two oak-paneled doors open and busted directly into the executive office. Former Attorney General Robert Coulier, the acting and soon-to-be official governor of Louisiana, sat in a plush leather chair behind a sprawling oak desk. *Her* desk.

"Morning, Coulier," Maggie said cheerily.

Coulier's ratlike face turned chalky white. A phone cradled against his ear slipped away, and he sat transfixed, as if he were struck by lightning.

Maggie circled the chair and took the phone from his hand, slamming it home onto the receiver. "Nice to see you, buddy. Do you mind getting the hell out of my chair?"

Coulier stumbled to his feet. "Mag . . . I mean . . . Madam Governor. You're alive."

Maggie sat down, brushing her hands over the leather arms of the chair as if she were scrubbing away germs. "Oh, didn't Gambit tell you? Your little scheme failed."

She didn't think it was possible for Coulier to blanch any further, but he did, confirming her existing suspicions.

"Yep," she said, leaning back in the chair, "I know about Gambit. It was a nice gig, wasn't it? Some shadowy guy approaches you with the offer of a lifetime: sell out your state and become governor. I have to hand it to you, Coulier. It was a nifty scheme."

Coulier glanced from Maggie to Yolanda to O'Dell. The burly Capitol policeman stood next to the door, one hand resting on his gun, his shoulders tensed like a bulldog begging to be let off his leash.

Coulier looked back to Maggie. "Madam Governor, you can't be serious. You hired me."

Maggie's smile faded. "My mistake. I guess it wasn't long after you arrived in Baton Rouge that Gambit approached you. After all, what's the point of assassinating a governor if you can't control her successor? So, he put it in your head to have my lieutenant governor framed for the murder of Attorney General Matthews, and then he guided you through the hoops of sabotaging the Secretary of State. Am I right?"

A slow smile spread across Coulier's face. "You know, Madam Governor, these are troubling accusations. But perhaps more troubling are the questions surrounding your own conduct. As attorney general, I'm obliged to represent the interests of the people, even where they concern the actions of their governor. And I must say, the people have *a lot of questions*."

Maggie sat forward, feigning concern. "But Coulier, you're not the attorney general anymore."

His smirk faded into a glare. "You can't fire me. I'm a confirmed official of the state!"

"Fire you?" Mock confusion clouded her face. "I didn't fire you. You resigned. Don't you remember?"

She lifted Yolanda's envelope off the desk and passed it to Coulier. He ripped it open, his fingers shaking as he scanned the document, his focus landing at the bottom, where his signature was clearly affixed in blue ink.

He crumpled the paper between shaking fingers. "This won't work," he snarled. "You can't push me out."

Maggie stepped around the desk until they stood toe to toe. "Oh, I think it will. And yes, I most definitely can. You're done, you scum."

Coulier shook with restrained rage, looking from Yolanda to O'Dell again as if they might take his side.

Maggie snapped her fingers. "O'Dell! Would you do me a favor?"

Heels clicked against the hardwood floor. "Absolutely, ma'am."

"Kindly escort Mr. Coulier *the fuck* out of my state."

"With pleasure, Madam Governor."

20

Barranquilla, Colombia

The cab ride from Ernesto Cortissoz International Airport to the Port of Barranquilla took over an hour. They all packed into what Reed thought was an old Chevy Caprice—years of DIY paint and slipshod bodywork made it impossible to be sure—and sat quietly while the driver crashed out of the airport and through the city, bobbing his head to the latest Kanye West track on repeat. He didn't speak a word of English, but apparently, that wasn't a prerequisite for enjoying the music.

Fair enough. I don't know what he's rapping about, either.

Reed kept his head behind the rear pillar of the car, peering out over the streets through the dusty window. He'd never been to South America before. There were a couple Central American hits while he was employed by Enfield's outfit, but they were all really quick jobs— in and out, with never enough time to look around.

At first impression, Colombia had a lot in common with most developing countries—packed streets, worn-out cars, and *a lot* of people. They pressed in along the sidewalks in a never-ending torrent of bustling bodies —women in dusty dresses, men in business suits, and barefoot children screaming and chasing each other.

Reed squinted through the glass and swept from face to face, marveling at how many of these people wore shoes with holes in them, but they still smiled. It wasn't like that in Atlanta. Hell, it wasn't like that in most places in the developed world. People rushed and frowned and shouted at cabs. They packed into trains and stared at phones and lost themselves in a crushing world of hurry, hurry, hurry.

Maybe, when this is all over, I'll find a pair of shoes to wear forever and settle down in a place like this.

He planted himself into the seat and folded his arms. He knew people in places like this starved and struggled and lived under oppressive regimes that trampled their human rights and ignored their voices. It wasn't as simple as it seemed, but still, there was something to be said for escaping the rat race.

The driver stuck his head above the seat and rattled off something in Spanish. Banks replied with a question, and the driver repeated his inquiry.

"He wants to know which side of the port we're looking for," she said.

"Ask him if he's heard of a freighter named *Santa Coquina*," Reed said.

Banks spoke in Spanish again. The driver seemed to be only half listening. He shrugged and didn't answer.

"Okay," Reed said. "Wherever they ship the bananas, then. Tell him I'll pitch him another forty bucks if he'll shut off this damn song."

Banks glared at him and rattled off something much too short to include both requests. Kanye rapped on.

As Barranquilla faded from downtown sprawl into industrial outskirts, large factories, warehouses, and train yards replaced the high-rises. On many of them, Reed noted sprawling graffiti painted onto the street-side of the warehouses and artfully designed to depict landscapes and people alike. Bright colors and elaborate texts hallmarked the art, adding a splash of brightness to an otherwise drab and dirty part of town. Reed was almost sad to notice a city employee laboriously covering a section of graffiti with white paint.

Why not leave it? It's not hurting anybody.

The Caprice finally squealed to a stop next to the port, and the view in front of them was much as Reed expected—concrete piers shooting out into the muddy water, with freighters of all sizes lined up next to them.

Forklifts rushed about, and cranes lifted containers on and off the ships. A few hundred yards away a row of tankers were being loaded with crude oil before heading north. They found no sign of a mid-sized reefer named *Santa Coquina,* but Reed didn't expect it to be that easy.

He passed the driver a couple colorful Colombian notes from the airport exchange service, then stepped out of the car. Banks and Wolfgang followed as the cab crashed away, still blaring Kanye.

"Where first?" Wolfgang asked, scanning the docks.

"Port master," Reed said. "Assuming there is one. We need a record of what ships sailed in the last two months. That'll lead us to the right ship, then we can find the headquarters of the shipping company that operates her. Then we can . . . look at some bananas, I guess."

"You're not sold on this, are you?" Wolfgang asked.

Reed shrugged. "It's difficult for me to believe that a gene-altering wonder formula is being smuggled into America inside bananas. It's even more difficult for me to understand *why.* But I was outvoted, and apparently, this is a democracy now."

Banks rolled her eyes and set off down the dock. Wolfgang raised an eyebrow and turned to Reed. "And Democracy—not, say, a blonde with a nice ass—is enough to drag you to South America."

Reed held his gaze a long moment, then set off after Banks.

They searched the port for over an hour before a weary mechanic eating his lunch next to the water was patient enough to direct Banks toward the harbormaster. Another two miles and a slew of disheveled shacks later, they located a multi-story metal building that overlooked the river. Almost nobody was around, and a sudden hush had fallen over the port, almost as though it were midnight.

"What the hell is going on?" Reed muttered.

"Siesta," Banks said. "They take two-hour lunches down here. Naps, too, sometimes."

"Isn't that delightful?" Wolfgang said. "Wouldn't mind a nap myself."

Reed approached the headquarters door and tried it. It was unlocked, and he ducked inside without waiting for an invitation. The interior was dark and hot. Rows of filing cabinets lined the far wall, along with a couple of desks laden with old computers. At the end of the room was a stairwell. Banks and Wolfgang followed not far behind, their footfalls soft behind his on the worn industrial carpet.

At the top of the stairs lay another hallway, then a door that was mostly shut with a crack of sunlight spilling through it. Reed slowed, creeping up to the door and unconsciously reaching for his gun.

His fingers met empty space next to his hip, and a wave of discomfort passed over him. He eased the door open and heard a soft rustling sound— smooth and perfectly cyclic. At first, Reed thought it was an oscillating fan, but as the door swung open, he recognized human breathing.

Light flooded in from a bank of dusty windows, with bent blinds hanging at random over each of them. A desk in the middle of the room was piled high with binders and paperwork, and a few more file cabinets stood along one wall.

But what caught his eye was the twin pair of cowboy boots poking out from behind the desk, toes up. Reed relaxed his shoulders and indulged in a brief smile as the rhythmic breathing was disrupted by a faint snore.

"Dear lord," Wolfgang muttered. "Talk about sleeping on the job."

Reed slipped around the base of the desk to find a short man dressed in jeans and a button-down shirt, lying on a yoga mat behind the desk. A worn cowboy hat covered his face, and his hands were perfectly folded over a bulging paunch.

"Aw," Banks said. "He's tired."

Reed sighed and jammed his hands into his pockets, then gently toed the bottom of one cowboy boot. The sleeping man snorted and twitched but didn't wake. Reed prodded a little harder, and the hat slipped off as the man twisted and sat up in a rush. He wiped drool from his chin with the back of his hand as confusion clouded his dark eyes, followed by momentary panic.

Banks held up one hand and uttered a comforting sentence as the Colombian rushed to his feet, the confusion in his face rapidly turning to irritation and then anger. He snapped back a snarling line or two, then jabbed his hand toward the open office door.

Banks shrugged. "He says, 'Go to hell, gringos.'"

Reed held up both hands. "My apologies. We're not here to bother you. We just need to know about the *Santa Coquina*."

Banks never had a chance to translate. As soon as the words *Santa Coquina* left Reed's mouth, the Colombian's face flushed a crimson red, and he exploded into a hurricane of rage. He shouted in Spanish, gesturing toward the door and repeating his earlier insults.

Reed exchanged a glance with Wolfgang. The Wolf sighed and walked to the door, shutting it gently and twisting the lock. The Colombian watched the door close, then made a dash for a nearby filing cabinet. Before any of them could react, he snatched the top drawer open and slid one hand inside.

"Gun!" Wolfgang said, but Reed was already moving. He threw himself across the office and tackled the Colombian from behind. The two of them crashed to the floor as a revolver spun across the linoleum. Wolfgang hurried to retrieve it, and Reed twisted his hostage's arm behind his back until the harbormaster was unable to move.

"Calm *down*," Reed said. "Just calm the hell down, okay? We don't want to hurt you!"

Banks put a hand on Reed's shoulder. "Relax, Reed! He can't hurt you. He's just scared."

Reed released the Colombian's arm, and the man scrambled backward until his shoulders hit the wall.

"Ask him about the ship," Reed said, returning to his feet and keeping a wary gaze fixed on the harbormaster. The man sat in the corner now, his eyes shooting hatred at Reed.

Banks offered an apologetic smile and a gentle touch on his arm. She spoke in soothing Spanish, but the harbormaster continued to glower at Reed. At the end of her appeal, he shook his head once.

Reed stepped forward, squatting in front of him and relaxing his arms over his knees. He assumed what he hoped was a friendly expression and spoke to the harbormaster directly.

"We're looking for the *Santa Coquina*. Where can we find the captain?"

Banks translated, and the harbormaster folded his arms and looked away, his bottom lip sticking out in a little pout. Reed rubbed his thumbs against closing fists. Traditionally, this would be the point where he resorted to breaking bones, but he wasn't going to go that route today. Not on an innocent third party.

"You need to work with me, amigo. I'm not your enemy."

Again, Banks translated. The Colombian muttered what sounded like a curse, but nothing more.

"Ask him if he's heard of El Diablo," Wolfgang said suddenly.

The words had barely left his mouth before the harbormaster looked up. "El Diablo?" he asked, a tremor slipping into his voice.

Reed glanced at Wolfgang, then decided to roll with it. "Sí. El Diablo."

The harbormaster looked from Reed to Wolfgang, then stopped at Banks and spewed a stream of semi-frantic Spanish. Banks struggled to keep up, translating as quickly as she could and motioning for him to slow down.

"He knows the ship. *Santa Coquina* left port a few weeks ago, headed for New Orleans. She never returned."

Reed snapped his fingers, stopping the harbormaster mid-sentence.

"Slow down," he said. "What do you mean, she never returned?"

Banks translated. The Colombian swallowed, then began again, slower this time.

"He says the ship was due back in Barranquilla over a week ago, but nobody has seen her, and they can't reach the crew. There is a woman—the ship captain's wife—who comes here every day asking about the ship. She's panicked. She hasn't heard from her husband since last week when he called her from Mobile, just before sailing back to Colombia."

"This woman," Reed said. "Is she local?"

Banks nodded. "He says she lives nearby."

"Tell him we need to see her. Ask him if he'll call a cab."

Banks translated, but the harbormaster shook his head and stood up, hurrying to his desk and retrieving a set of car keys.

"He says it will be his pleasure to drive us there," Banks said.

Reed turned to Wolfgang and raised an eyebrow. Wolfgang shook his head once, and the harbormaster hurried to the door, waving his hand and rattling off more Spanish.

"He has a truck. He says we can make it there in half an hour."

Reed held out his hand to Wolfgang. "Let me see the gun."

Wolfgang cocked his head to one side, then slid the revolver into his pocket.

"I think I'll hold on to the firepower, Reed. You're a little high-strung today."

Reed glared a challenge, but then pushed past him and followed the harbormaster down the stairs. There would be time to argue with Wolfgang later. Right now, they just needed to find out how the hell a massive freighter had simply disappeared.

21

The harbormaster led them to a pickup that looked like it had been dragged out of a junkyard a decade before. The engine fired to life, and all three of them opted to sit in the bed, where they could most easily exit the truck if necessary. Reed kept a wary eye on the passing buildings and streets as they drove inland from the port, but nothing he saw raised any alarms. Battered shipping warehouses gave way to overgrown fields interlaced with pothole-infested roads. They were south of Barranquilla now, headed northwest toward what Reed guessed was Malambo, based on what little Spanish he could decipher from passing signs.

"We shouldn't be going with him," he muttered to Wolfgang between the creak of the truck and the roar of passing cars.

"Relax," Wolfgang said. "He's more scared of us than we are of him."

It wasn't a stretch for Reed to believe it. The harbormaster cast wary glances over his shoulder every few minutes and had a noticeable tension in his shoulders. Whatever the meaning was behind Wolfgang's earlier reference to El Diablo—The Devil—it struck a deep chord with the man.

Finally, the truck ground to a halt at the outskirts of a small village packed with cottages shoved next to each other with tiny dirt tracks running in between. They piled out, and Reed circled to the driver's window.

"Gracias, amigo."

Wolfgang gestured to Banks. "Tell him El Diablo is in his debt."

Banks wrinkled her brow but translated. The man nodded several times, and his shoulders relaxed a little. Then he drove off without another word.

"El Diablo?" Reed asked.

Wolfgang watched the truck fade away, concern draped over his tired face. "Did you see the graffiti on the way in from the airport?"

"Pretty creative stuff," Banks said. "All over the place."

"Right," Wolfgang said. "And since I don't speak Spanish, none of it meant much to me. Except for one piece on the backside of a brick wall coming out of the city. There was a guy painting over it, but I still caught a brief line. It said *El Diablo, amigo del pueblo*."

"The Devil . . . friend of the people," Banks murmured.

Wolfgang nodded. "I remembered the stories they used to tell about the Medellín Cartel. You know, Pablo Escobar and his crew back in the seventies and eighties. They were massive drug dealers, and it took the Colombian government and the DEA over a decade to shut them down, partly because they never could obtain the full support of the people. Pablo was a bad dude by civilized standards, but to many of the poor citizens of Colombia, he was a hero. He invested in schools and public works. His soldiers provided protection against other cartels. He was a friend of the people."

Reed made the connection. "So you think *el diablo* wasn't a reference to the actual devil, but a nickname for some kind of new drug lord. A drug lord that's both feared and admired by the people."

Wolfgang shrugged. "Why else would the city pay somebody to paint over that specific graffiti? They aren't painting over anything else. And anyway, based on our friend's reaction, I think I was right. El Diablo is a person, and he's both feared and respected."

Reed felt suddenly self-conscious. He'd noticed the graffiti and the city employee painting over it, but he never would've connected the dots the way Wolfgang had. "Good work," he said.

"Something to keep in our back pocket. Now, the wife?"

Reed nodded. "The wife."

Valentina Antonella Mendoza Ramos lived at the end of a dusty track in an even dustier cottage, which really wasn't much fancier than an old blue-collar home on an abandoned street of Detroit. It sat on the Colombian landscape by itself, and there were chickens pecking around the yard. An old dog slept under a tree with all the watchfulness of a mall cop on his last shift before retirement. Wind chimes rang softly from the low porch, and small toys lay scattered amongst tiny footprints.

But despite the signs of life, the house itself was quiet and almost desolate. The curtains were drawn behind the windows, and there was no car in the driveway or voices coming from the home. They approached quietly, and Reed glanced down at the stack of newspapers flung carelessly near the door as if they'd never been picked up after the courier's deliveries. It didn't require Wolfgang's level of critical observation to draw conclusions about the place. If Valentina was home at all, she certainly wasn't living an organized or vibrant life.

"What's the play here?" Wolfgang asked.

Reed started to answer, then caught himself. He remembered what Banks said on the plane about not being consulted or respected.

Time to stop being a jackass.

"What do you think?" he asked Banks.

Though she seemed surprised by the question, she had a response ready. "If the ship hasn't returned, she probably assumes the worst, and she's probably stressed out of her mind. I think we use a very light touch and infer that we're here to help her, which, if we take down Aiden, we will. Because whatever happened to her husband, Aiden is responsible. That's beyond doubt."

"Good plan," Reed said. "Take the lead. You've got a much lighter touch than either one of us."

Banks rapped softly on the door. It rattled in its frame, but the house remained quiet. Then she knocked again. On the third knock, footsteps padded across the floor, followed by a soft Spanish voice. Reed didn't have to be a linguist to hear the alarm and concern in the tone.

Banks replied, then the door creaked open just a little. Reed could see a chain holding it shut as half of a woman's face appeared. She was dark-skinned, with one red-rimmed eye visible through the narrow slot. She stared first at Banks, then the two men.

We should've let Banks go in alone.

But if they did that, Banks would've been left completely exposed to whatever lay inside. On the off chance that something went sideways, Reed wanted to be close enough to protect her.

The woman asked a question laced with suspicion. Banks replied, her voice gentle and her posture relaxed. Another question, and another response. Banks gestured to the two men, one at a time, and Reed heard his name clearly pronounced amongst the Spanish.

The woman's eye darted suspiciously from him to Wolfgang and then back. She shut the door, then the chain rattled and the door opened again, fully exposing the woman. She was beautiful in every sense of the word—tall, with glowing cheeks and long, dark hair. But Reed saw hesitation in her posture before she stepped back and swept her hand inward.

"Welcome to my home," she said in halting English.

Reed and Wolfgang both ducked their heads politely.

"Thank you, ma'am," Reed said. "We're sorry to bother you."

They slipped inside, and the woman shut the door behind them before motioning to a nearby parlor. She gestured to the couch near the window, and they sat without a word as she vanished through another doorway. She soon returned with a tray holding a pitcher of water and three mismatched glasses, then dispersed the glasses to each of them and poured water from the pitcher.

"Gracias, señora," Reed murmured.

She offered a tired smile and sat down on the opposing couch. For a moment, she said nothing, staring at her hands, then she cleared her throat. "Why are you here?"

Reed kept his tone as soft as hers, his shoulders relaxed, and his voice slow. "We're here about your husband."

"You are from America?"

"We're Americans," Reed answered, dodging the implication of her question.

"Sent by the government?"

Reed took a sip of water. "Señora, if you would be more comfortable, we could speak in Spanish. Miss Banks is happy to translate."

Valentina looked through the window at the front yard. "I speak English. My husband, Roberto, was planning for us to immigrate to America."

Reed noted the way she spoke in past tense about her husband and wondered if she assumed him to be dead. Maybe she just meant their plans had changed.

"Your husband is the captain of the *Santa Coquina*? A freighter."

Valentina nodded. "Sí."

"How long has he been a captain?"

"Six months. Not long."

"You must be very proud."

She picked at her fingernails.

Reed set the water glass on the coffee table. "Señora, we're here because we believe your husband's ship was carrying illegal cargo." Her back stiffened, and Reed held up a hand. "Don't worry. We're not accusing him of anything."

"My husband only transported bananas," she said, the defensiveness adding bite to her words.

"We know," Reed said. "Your husband is a good man, I'm sure. But we need to know more about his job and the company he worked for. Can you tell us where they're located?"

"Barranquilla. There are lots of shipping companies."

"Of course. Do you remember the name of the company?"

"No. It changed sometimes. The name, I mean. Different companies joining, moving . . . I don't understand business."

Changing names and shifting companies . . . Just like in New Orleans.

"That's okay," Reed said. "It's not important. What about the bananas? Can you tell me about those?"

A sad smile crept across her face. "Colombian bananas are the best in the world. Sweet when ripe. Full of flavor."

Reed offered an encouraging smile and waited for her to continue, but she didn't. "Did your husband ship bananas for one of the big farms?"

"He used to. But now there is a smaller farm. Someplace in the mountains. Antioquia, I think."

"Is that a city?" Wolfgang said.

"No, no city. It is a department."

"Department?"

"Like a state," Reed said. "It's south of here, in the mountains."

Reed had scanned a map of Colombia on their flight from Miami and remembered seeing Antioquia Department southwest of Barranquilla. It was a rugged and mountainous place, full of tall peaks and low valleys. Hardly ideal farm country.

"Do you remember the name of the banana farm your husband shipped for?" Reed asked.

Valentina stood up. "No, but I have some bananas. My husband got them for free sometimes."

She hurried out of the room and then returned with a small bunch of bananas. They were almost overripe but still bore little stickers. Reed accepted them with a smile and peered at the labels.

Producto de Colombia. Patiño Granjas.

Reed motioned to Banks.

"Product of Colombia," she said. "Patiño Farms."

Reed looked back at Valentina.

"Mrs. Ramos, how long has your husband been transporting bananas for Patiño?"

"A few months. I'm not sure."

Reed leaned forward. "I know you're worried about your husband. We want to help you find him."

Valentina cried and lowered her head into her hands. "No, señor. I know where my husband is."

"Mrs. Ramos, we can't assume he's dead."

"Dead?" She looked up, then suddenly laughed in a short, coughing sound. "My husband is not dead. He is in Santa Marta fucking street whores."

Reed blinked. "I'm sorry. I thought you said your husband was missing. The harbormaster told us you were looking for him."

"I was, but not because I think he is dead. He has done this before—

disappear for weeks on end, making port in some rancid place, where he and his crew sleep with the women and snort the cocaine for a few days. Then he tells me he hit bad weather. It is nothing new."

Reed cocked his head. "Help me understand, Mrs. Ramos. If you knew where he was, why were you in such a panic?"

Valentina stood up and beckoned to them. "Come with me. I will show you."

They followed her into a narrow hallway, and she stopped at a bedroom and held a finger to her lips. Wolfgang slid his hand into his coat pocket as the door swung open, and Valentina stood back, allowing them to look inside. It was a small child's room with toys piled in one corner and a single bed pushed up against the wall. A girl of maybe six or seven years old lay in bed with dark raven hair like her mother's arranged around her head. She slept fitfully with a stuffed animal clutched close to her chest.

It was her face that drew Reed's immediate attention. Despite her beautiful dark skin, her cheeks were sickly pale and streaked with sweat.

"It is my daughter," Valentina said, her voice choking into a sob. "The doctors say she will die."

22

Lucy and Kelly found the headquarters of Beaumont Pharmaceutical nestled in the heart of a business campus on the outskirts of town. The address led them to a tall, nondescript building with blank windows. The parking lot was as empty as a church on Friday night, which was apropos because it was Friday night, and Lucy doubted that anybody was any more interested in being at the office than they were in being at church. As the sun set toward Austin, she parked her rented Altima near the edge of the business park and motioned Kelly to remain in the passenger seat.

"Where are you going?" Kelly demanded.

"To reconnoiter. We need to know what we're walking into."

"We *know* what we're walking into. A damn office building."

Lucy nodded. "It certainly seems so, but I've made a good life for myself on the deadly edge of dangerous by not making assumptions. It'll only take a minute."

"Fine. I'll come with you." Kelly reached for the door handle, but Lucy put a hand on her arm.

"Kelly, darling. I hate to point out the obvious, but this is Texas, and you aren't dressed like a cowgirl. We really don't need the attention."

Kelly glared through the eye slot of her hijab. "Would you prefer I take it off? I'm sure that'll draw less attention."

Lucy's tone softened a little. "I didn't mean that. I just mean this is a one-girl operation. Let me check it out, and then we'll move in, I promise."

Kelly continued to glare, but she took her hand off the door handle. Lucy ducked out of the car and set off toward the main building.

The campus was quiet. Sure, it was five thirty in the evening, which was late for the corporate world, she supposed. Still, she figured there should be at least a few cars left in the lot. Maybe some overworked executives, or even more overworked interns, struggling to finish a mountain of paperwork before beers with friends at the local sports bar.

Truthfully, Lucy didn't know. She knew even less about the corporate world than she knew about grabbing beers with friends after work. The entire scope of normal, civilized life was an enigma to her. Maybe on Fridays everybody quit at four o'clock . . . or noon. Or maybe today was some kind of obscure holiday she'd never observed, which offered everybody a three-day weekend. There had to be an explanation for the quiet, and whatever it was, she was about to find out.

Lucy walked quickly, her subdued black boots clicking against the pavement. She didn't wear her customary black bodysuit. She liked it, and it left her flexible for action, but much like Kelly's hijab, it would draw too much attention. Instead, she wore dark skinny jeans with a black tank top and a leather jacket thrown over the top. A scrunchie held her hair between her shoulder blades and completed the simple—though, if she said so herself, sexy—ensemble. No, still not the most subtle look, but what was a girl gonna do? Go to work looking like a street urchin? No way.

Lucy tilted her head back and stared up at the six-story tower as she approached. It was a big place—the kind of place she imagined to be full of overweight men in cheap suits and bored women who wore too much makeup and always grinned but never smiled. A sterile, boring place with plastic plants and faux leather chairs that were never replaced though they inflicted their users with endless back pain. An insurance establishment. Or a banking headquarters. One of those penny-pinching, oppressive sorts of places. A place that was all about the bottom line.

And that wasn't right.

The thought hit her like a smack to the head, and Lucy rubbed her bottom lip, still staring at the building. She remembered watching a special on TV years back about the pharmaceutical industry and how much money they made. It was hundreds of billions of dollars or more. They pumped out pills like Tic Tacs and charged hefty sums for every one of them, resulting in huge profit margins and unimaginable revenue streams. And they spent that revenue, too. That was the other thing she remembered. Pharma execs balled like freaking rap stars—cars, opulent houses, lavish lifestyles . . . extravagant offices. Not like this chintzy, cheap place. Was it possible she had the wrong address?

"Can I help you, ma'am?"

Lucy spun on her heel, resisting the urge to reach for the razor-sharp knife strapped beneath her jacket.

A security guard stood ten yards away under the shadow of the building, his right hand resting on the grip of a handgun. He wore dark Ray-Bans, leaving her blind to his emotions.

Lucy assumed her brightest smile. "Excuse me, sir. I'm looking for Beaumont Pharmaceutical. Do I have the wrong building?"

The guard said nothing and remained frozen, one hand on the gun, the other held loose next to a radio.

Strange, she thought. Nothing about this guy felt like a rental cop. He was trim and fit, with well-kept hair and broad shoulders. His clothes were clean and pressed, and the gun was worn but clean—the weapon of somebody who was very familiar with its use, care, and capabilities.

No, he wasn't a rent-a-cop at all. This guy was ex-military, for sure.

"Sir?" she asked again. "Is this Beaumont Pharmaceutical?"

"I'm gonna ask you to leave, now."

Her smile broadened, but the warmth in it cooled. She called this her snake grin. Some men found it sexy, while others found it chilling. The second class were the wiser of the two.

"So this *is* Beaumont, then." He didn't move, and she crossed her arms. "Is Mr. Abrams here? I'm told he always works late. I need to speak to him."

The guard looked unsure, as if his training hadn't equipped him for the eventuality of a woman who flatly refused to be intimidated.

"It's a legal matter," Lucy continued. "I'm sure you understand."

The guard's jaw twitched, and she could tell he was evaluating his options, trying to decide if dragging her off the premises by her hair would result in a promotion or a termination. *Not that he could if he tried*, she thought.

"A legal matter?" he asked.

"Right."

"You're a lawyer?"

"Me? Hell no. I'm a paralegal. A gopher, if you will. I just serve papers, mostly. But hey, gotta start somewhere."

She hoped that line would relax him. That sort of "Hey, I'm on the bottom of the ladder, just like you. Help a girl out," kind of thing. But he didn't relax.

"Who do you represent?"

"Maxx, Locke and Howe. I can't share specifics, of course, but I'm sure you recognize the name. Big-time divorce lawyers. Mr. Abrams really should keep it in his pants."

"Mr. Abrams isn't married," the guard said.

Lucy didn't flinch. It was one in a million that there actually was a Mr. Abrams working here and that the guard knew him well enough to know he wasn't married. More than likely, the guard was simply bluffing, and she was going to call that bluff.

"Not Abrams senior. I mean his son, Jim Abrams. You know . . . saucy kid, red Porsche, big-time playboy? Gonna cost him. Can you tell me where he is, please? I'd love to go home."

The guard impulsively glanced around the parking lot, as if somebody would appear out of thin air to help him resolve the situation. His shoulders squared again in an unmistakable challenge. "You don't have any papers with you."

Lucy tapped her pocket. "On my phone. Digital now, like everything else. Now really, where is he?"

Another hesitation. This would be the make-or-break moment, Lucy decided. She had pushed him as hard as she could, and now he would either cave or not.

"Look, ma'am. I'd love to help you, but the building is closed. You should come back on Monday. And this time, come through the front office, okay?"

"So, I've got the right building, then? This is Beaumont Pharma?"

"Yes, you've got the right building. Now, I have to ask you to leave. Nobody is allowed on the premises after close of business."

Lucy shrugged and rolled her shoulders, switching her smile from the snake grin to the "little innocent ol' me" smile. She stepped forward just a pace, green eyes blazing. But the guard didn't fall for it. He stepped back, falling into a flawless weaver stance as the gun cleared the holster and the muzzle rose to forehead height.

"Ma'am! For the last time, leave the premises."

Lucy froze, genuinely taken off guard. She held up a hand. "Right, no problem. On my way." She turned and started across the lot, moving in a quick walk and resisting the urge to look over her shoulder. She knew he was watching her, so she walked away from the Altima, turning down a side street and into another section of the business park before circling back to approach the car from behind, out of sight of the guard. She slipped into the driver's seat without a word and sat still, facing the building and chewing her bottom lip.

"Well?" Kelly asked.

"That's the building," Lucy said. "And whatever's going on in there, it isn't legal."

23

Maggie stood behind her desk, both hands resting on the back of her chair as Dan Sharp stepped into the executive office. He'd lost weight since she last saw him only ten days before. His cheeks hung hollow, and there were dark circles beneath his eyes. Sharp wore baggy sweatpants and a sweatshirt, both an unflattering shade of dark grey, and he was escorted in handcuffs by a tall state policeman with a look on his face that would melt ice.

Maggie met his gaze and swallowed back the urge to react. She turned to the officer, instead. "Uncuff him, and leave us."

"Ma'am . . ."

"Do it."

The cop uncuffed Sharp, then walked back through the door. It smacked shut behind him, and Sharp pushed his hands into his pockets, his shoulders slumping.

Maggie rubbed her hand against the back of the chair and forced herself to face him. He looked five years older than he had only two weeks prior when he was her lieutenant governor. Before she let Coulier and his snake-tongue talk her into letting Sharp take the fall for her own mistakes. Before she stabbed Sharp in the back like an absolute Judas.

Sharp cleared his throat. "Madam Governor, I'm so thankful you're alive."

Maggie stood, stunned. The words refused to register, bouncing off her like Ping-Pong balls. Did Sharp just say he was glad she was alive?

She moved around the desk, wrapping Sharp in a hug before he could stop her. She buried her face into his shoulder and cried a little, pulling him close as he awkwardly stood, his hands still in his pockets.

"Dan . . . I'm so, so sorry. Everything I did was wrong. Everything we did at the port . . . with you . . . I should have *never* ignored your advice. I should have never done any of it."

His hand slid up to awkwardly rest on her shoulder. His touch was soft but formal and distant.

Maggie pulled back, forcing herself to stop crying. She saw no hint of emotion in his features—not even a shade of sympathy. Of course. Sharp's comment about her being alive was perfunctory. Polite. It didn't mean anything had changed or been forgiven.

Maggie motioned to the wingback chair in front of her desk. "Please have a seat." She walked to the wet bar and poured two glasses of bourbon, both doubles, then took a seat behind her desk and handed him a glass.

Sharp leaned back in his chair and took a deep sip of the bourbon. Maggie drained her glass and folded her arms in her lap, waiting for him to speak first.

He licked his lips, then set the glass down with a little shrug. "Prison gin is better."

He smiled just a little, and Maggie tried to laugh, though the sound came out more like a cough.

"Why am I here, Maggie?"

She crossed her hands on the desk. "Dan, I need to tell you what happened. Everything. From the start."

He swirled his drink but didn't sip it. "With respect . . . I'm not sure I care."

"That's fair," she said, "but I need you to hear me out. Not because of what I did, but because I need to know what to do with you."

Sharp snorted a laugh. "Do with me?"

"Yes. I need to know whether to pardon you or not."

"Pardon me? For what I didn't do? Wow. Lucky me."

Maggie winced but kept going. "We have multiple options, Dan. If I pardon you, it's kind of like confirming your guilt. It'll be a mark on your career forever. Actually, it'll probably end your career. But if we wait around a little, and you help me get things cleared up, I think we can have the charges dismissed."

"Really? You arrange false charges against me, with no substance behind them, and now you want to hold them over my head?"

"Not at all. If it were up to me, the charges would already be dropped, but unfortunately, that's something only the attorney general's office can do. Separation of powers."

"Ah, right." Sharp drained the glass. "And you and Coulier aren't on speaking terms."

"Actually, Coulier isn't attorney general any longer."

Sharp raised an eyebrow. "He resigned?"

"In a manner of speaking."

"You pushed him out."

"I did what I had to."

"That'll backfire. He's not a guy to go quietly."

"He doesn't have a choice. Public opinion is on my side. Have you read the papers? I'm a returned hero. The rumors are flying thick, and they'll fly in my favor."

Sharp smirked. "You've finally learned how to manage the press."

"I wouldn't say that. But I've won this round with them, and when the news breaks tomorrow about the house by the lake, I'll have won the next several rounds."

"What house?"

Maggie refilled both glasses, and without preamble, told Sharp the whole story. From the start, back to her earliest secret meetings with Coulier, to her plans to close the port to flush out Gambit's operation. She told him about how Coulier had talked her into setting him up. She told him about the press conference, the bombs, and Reed Montgomery. She told him about Gambit's organization and her and Reed's hunt to uncover the truth. And at the end of it all, she told him about the house by the lake, only a few miles from the Capitol, where children had been held and raped.

Something flashed across Sharp's eyes when she got to the part about the sex trade, but for the rest of the story, he sat placid and emotionless, only moving to take drinks. When she concluded with her confrontation with Coulier, Sharp leaned back and set the glass on the arm of his chair. "You've been a busy bee."

Maggie grunted. "More than I'd like."

"So, what's your ask?"

Maggie sat forward. "I need you back. It's as simple as that. I know I've made some big mistakes, and I've really let you down, but in the process of it all, I uncovered something really, really sinister. Something that threatens my home. I need your help to take it down."

With shoulders slumped, Sharp took a sip of bourbon and sighed. "Just like that."

Maggie nodded. "Yes, just like that. I won't pardon you, but you can resume your duties while the investigation stalls. We'll find a new candidate for the attorney general's office, and within a couple months, we'll have the charges dropped. Put it behind you."

"And in the meantime, I just work here. Like nothing happened."

"Yes. Obviously, you wouldn't be very visible, but you'd be here like before."

Sharp pursed his lips and swirled his drink again. "Or I could call the officer out there and head back to jail. Eventually get a trial date. Then I'd go to court and shine a spotlight on everything that's happened here. Clear my name, and take you out."

Even as the threat left his lips, it wasn't sincere. His tone fell flat and weak.

"We both know you're not going to do that, Dan."

"What makes you so sure?"

Maggie folded her arms. "Because you haven't got it in you to be that angry for that long. I've seen you blow up in rage over something as simple as a fish hook in your thumb, but by dinner, you're over it. Vengeance isn't in your blood. Even now, sitting here, there's no fight in you."

Sharp turned both palms toward the ceiling. "People can change. Jail is a bitter place."

"Perhaps. But even then, I don't really care. I'm not a politician. I don't intend to run for reelection, and I don't care if you take me down, just so long as I protect my home before I fall."

Sharp chewed his lip, and Maggie knew she was right. Daniel Sharp was made of iron, but not the cutting kind. He was made of the blunt, unbending, relentless kind. More of a plow than a knife, pushing forward through rocks and packed dirt, relentlessly working day after day to slowly build something he cared about. And vengeance wasn't something he cared about. It never had been, and even now, as hurt as he was, that wouldn't change.

Sharp shoved his hands into his pockets and walked to the window, just watching the people walk by, then he spoke softly. "You know what bothers me most, Maggie?"

She wasn't sure she wanted to know but knew she had to ask. "What?"

"It's not what you did or what you did to me. Or even that you let Coulier poison your mind. Because if that's all that happened, we wouldn't be having this conversation. You'd resign, tell the truth, and go back to the swamps. And it would be heartbreaking, but Louisiana would recover, as she always has."

He didn't move from the window, and Maggie waited.

"What bothers me most is that *you've* changed. You're not the person who ran for governor. That woman believed in virtue, honesty, and integrity. Hell, Maggie, that was your whole platform."

"I still believe in those things," she said.

"Do you?" Sharp turned from the window. "You just told me you're working with a known domestic terrorist, running an unsanctioned investigation into a man you believe to be a criminal, all while spilling blood all over the state. *None* of this is what Muddy Maggie would do."

"Don't mistake my fading naïveté for a loss of virtue, Dan. Working with Montgomery isn't clean work, but clean work won't cut it this time. Being Muddy Maggie means things get dirty before they get clean."

Sharp folded his arms. "A thousand tyrants before you have justified their means by their ends, Maggie. It's not enough to slay the dragon. You have to do it without becoming a dragon yourself."

Maggie saw the steel in Sharp's stiff posture and knew she'd miscalculated. Vengeance wasn't something Dan Sharp cared about, but virtue most definitely was. For him, the line in the sand was clear—the spot where white turned to black as crisp as a quality photograph. Maggie was on the wrong side of it, and nothing could change his mind.

Maggie kept her voice calm and flat. "I'm sorry you feel that way, Mr. Lieutenant Governor."

For a moment, the confidence in Sharp's body language quavered. His shoulders twitched, and he ran his tongue over dry lips. "Maggie . . ." he said, his voice soft. "Don't do this. Please."

"Are you with me?"

Sharp stiffened again. "Not like this, Madam Governor."

Maggie looked away and walked around the desk, picking up a file and flipping through it just to avoid making eye contact. "Well then, I guess we're done here. Officer!"

The door opened, and the cop stepped in.

"Mr. Sharp is ready to go," Maggie said.

"Yes, ma'am."

Handcuffs clicked, but Sharp said nothing, and Maggie didn't look at him. She waited until the door shut and his footsteps faded, then she dropped the file and crashed into her chair, dropping her head into her hands. The tears came, and she didn't try to stop them. Sharp's words cut through her again and again as if he were standing right next to her, berating her even now. She saw the pain in his eyes and heard the plea in his voice.

"*Don't do this.*"

Maggie wondered if Sharp was right—if she *had* become the dragon she ran for office to slay. But then she thought about those girls alone in the woods in that sordid brothel, and the conviction that first drove her to work with Reed reignited, stronger than ever.

It may not be the best or virtuous way, but working with Reed delivered more results and brought her closer to defeating her enemies than anything else.

"Don't fail now, Maggie," she whispered. "You can't quit now."

The intercom on her desk beeped. Maggie wanted to ignore it, but the LCD screen indicated that the signal came from Yolanda's office. She was probably just checking on her or calling to ask about Sharp. Maggie didn't want to talk about it, but she couldn't afford to cut Yolanda out now. She needed her more than ever.

Maggie hit the button. "Yes?"

"Sorry to bother you, Maggie. There's a gentleman here to see you."

"I'm not taking any visitors right now, Yolanda."

"I know, but he's with the FBI."

Maggie sat up. "FBI? What does he want?"

"He wouldn't say. He only wants to talk to you. I'm sorry."

Maggie's mind spun, and she scooped the empty bourbon glasses into a drawer. What did the FBI want? Was it about Sharp and the investigation? Or was it Reed?

"Maggie?"

"Uh, yes. Give me two minutes, then send him in."

"Okay."

Maggie pulled a pocket mirror from her desk and checked her reflection. A quick adjustment to her hair brought her from vagabond to harried housewife, which was good enough under the circumstances. She couldn't do much about her red eyes or the black circles beneath them, but hell, she'd earned those.

There was a knock on the door, and Maggie stood up. "Come in."

The door opened, and a big man dressed in cargo pants, a T-shirt, and black tennis shoes stepped inside. He was tall and broad, with a boxy build and a close-cropped haircut. The man shut the door without comment and stepped to the middle of the room.

Maggie remained on the safe side of her desk. "Can I help you?"

The man reached into his pocket and produced a cell phone, then tapped on the screen. A recording played, and Maggie recognized her own voice.

"Working with Montgomery isn't clean work, but clean work won't cut it this time."

The man tapped the screen again, and the recording stopped.

Maggie stiffened, then slowly placed both hands on the back of her chair.

"I'm Agent Turkman," the man said. "Where's Montgomery?"

24

Wolfgang shoved past Reed and slid to his knees next to the child's bed. He felt her pulse, then placed the back of his hand over her forehead. Reed watched from the doorway, a lump rising in his throat as he stared at the fragile life hanging by a thread.

"What are her symptoms?" Wolfgang asked.

Valentina looked at Banks, and she translated the unfamiliar word.

"She has fevers," Valentina said. "Shakes. Her breathing is weak, and she coughs. Her knees, elbows, other . . . um . . ."

"Joints," Wolfgang said.

"Sí. They are swollen."

"Does she vomit?"

"No."

"Has she been checked for pneumonia?"

"She doesn't have it."

"The doctors haven't diagnosed anything?"

Valentina put a hand over her mouth. "They think . . . maybe blood cancer."

Wolfgang motioned to Reed without looking up, and Reed knelt beside him. Wolfgang whispered quietly enough that Valentina wouldn't hear. "She's dying. Her heart rate is under fifty beats per minute, and she's consumed with fever."

"Can you treat it?" Reed asked.

Wolfgang snorted. "Are you kidding me? I'm a research doctor, not an emergency room in tennis shoes. She needs a hospital and an army of specialists. Whatever this is, the local doctors clearly can't handle it."

Reed's mind raced. He didn't know what he expected to find at Valentina's house, but this wasn't it. He knew nothing about kids, let alone the things that could kill them, but looking at the child, he knew Wolfgang was right. She was barely hanging on.

Reed turned to Valentina. "Do you have passports? Money?"

Valentina wiped tears off her cheeks. "I have passports. Not much money. We don't have visas."

"Don't worry about that. I know somebody. Go get the passports and pack a few things, but nothing you can't put in a carry-on. Do you understand?"

Valentina frowned. "Who are you?"

Reed sighed. He didn't have time to explain himself. "It doesn't matter. I'm going to get your daughter help, okay?"

Valentina looked from Reed to Banks, then to her daughter. She nodded, and Reed turned back to Wolfgang. "Do what you can for her. Banks, come with me."

The two of them stepped back down the hallway and into the living room.

Reed checked to be sure Valentina wasn't nearby and kept his voice low. "I want you to fly back with them. Make sure she gets to a hospital."

Banks shook her head. "There's nothing I can do for them that the airport won't accommodate. I need to be here. There's obviously something going on."

"I agree, which is why I want you to fly out. I've got a bad feeling about this place, and those feelings are rarely wrong. Please, Banks, don't fight me."

He placed a gentle hand on her arm. She looked into his eyes, and he saw confliction in hers—frustration, but confusion also. She shook her head, but then Reed heard something he hadn't heard in years: an unmistakable growl mixed with the occasional metallic squeak, and an unforgettable pop of rocks shooting out from beneath over-pressurized tires. He ran to the window, lifting the curtain and squinting out into the gathering darkness.

The Humvee was a hundred yards away, crashing down the dirt road toward the cottage. It was jet black, but there were no police insignias on the outside. An antenna was bent over the top and tied off to the front bumper, and behind the glass were two powerfully framed men with locked jaws and dark sunglasses, despite the vanishing sun.

"Wolf!" Reed snapped, whirling around and pushing Banks in front of him. "Evac, now!"

"Copy," Wolfgang said. He spoke without alarm or surprise and appeared from the bedroom a moment later with the child still asleep and cradled in his arms.

Valentina rushed into the room, a worn duffel bag in one hand and two passports in the other. "What's happening?"

"No time. Let's go. Out the back!" Reed pushed them into the kitchen, glancing over his shoulder as the growl of the Humvee's engine grew closer. He snatched a long kitchen knife along the way, holding it close to his side as they passed through the back door and into the yard.

"Quiet!" he hissed. "Move for the trees."

A low hill covered in trees and low shrubs stood about fifty yards distant, with nothing but packed dirt and tangled grass blocking their path. They ran, leaning low as Reed hurried them. The Humvee slid to a stop at the front of the house, then its metal doors groaned open.

Flashbacks of Iraq ripped through his mind. Memories of a thousand rides in identical vehicles, crashing through the desert. He remembered stepping out of the passenger side of a Humvee, with a rifle clamped in one hand and the hellish blast of the desert sun beating down on him, once again lost in some godforsaken place.

Reed knew what a Humvee sounded like when it was headed down to the general store, loaded with bored soldiers looking for pirated DVDs and porno mags. He also knew what it sounded like crashing through obstructions on its way to war. And the sounds behind him were most definitely the latter.

They reached the trees and dove into the brush. Wolfgang held the child close, nestling down behind a tree as Valentina followed close beside him. Her face was pale, and her hands shook as she clutched her daughter's hand. The child blinked sleepily but didn't wake. She didn't have the strength.

"Get down," Reed said, pushing Banks beneath the brush as he collapsed to his stomach. He squinted through the leaves at the house and heard pounding on the front door, followed by muted voices. He couldn't make out the words, but the accents weren't Colombian.

"Were you expecting visitors?" Reed whispered to Valentina, though he knew the answer even before she shook her head. Reed held the knife close, feeling woefully under-armed, then froze as the first figure appeared behind the house.

The man was a combat operative, no doubt about it. He wore head-to-toe black with a rifle clutched across his chest. It was a European piece, maybe an H&K G36 chambered in 5.56 NATO. That made this guy a purpose-built soldier—not some thug with a cast-off AK.

The operator moved behind the house and checked the back door. It swung open without resistance, and he held the rifle to his chest and waited until another identical operator appeared behind him before he cleared the house.

Well trained. Moving in tandem. Taking the occupants from behind.

Ten seconds ticked by before the operators reappeared from the back door, more relaxed this time. They called out to the front yard, and this time, Reed made out enough words to identify a Slavic language—Bosnian or Serbian. Reed didn't speak either, but if you worked in the criminal underworld long enough, you recognized both.

Wolfgang laid the child on a bed of leaves and crept toward him with the revolver clutched in his hand. Somehow, the handgun appeared every bit as inadequate as Reed's kitchen knife.

"ID?" Wolfgang whispered.

"East European operators."

"Police?"

"Definitely not. Mercenaries, I think."

Wolfgang squinted through the trees as a new figure appeared. He was taller than the first two, with hair so blond it almost looked white. He wore the same black uniform but didn't carry a rifle. Instead, he held a handgun and prodded a fourth figure ahead of him in the dark.

Reed's stomach twisted. The fourth man was the harbormaster, and his face was swollen with bloody bruises. He tripped on the packed earth and hit his knees, blood draining from his nose. Before he could get up, the tall man put a boot in his ass, shoving him face-first into the dust. Then the handgun rose, and the tall man shouted something in Spanish.

"Banks," Reed said.

Banks lay next to him, staring at the men. "He's asking about Valentina. He wants to know where she is."

The harbormaster sobbed and choked, rolling over and holding up both hands. His whole body shook as he babbled in Spanish. Reed didn't need to understand the words to recognize the cadence of desperate pleas. Banks gasped and rose onto her elbows. Reed and Wolfgang reached across at the same moment, shoving her back into the leaves.

"No," Reed hissed.

Again, the tall man shouted, and once more, the harbormaster sobbed and shook his head. Then the man raised the gun and fired twice, just like that. Two quick pops of the pistol, and the harbormaster collapsed into the dust amid a growing pool of red.

Banks gasped, and Reed continued to hold her down. He held a finger to his lips as he watched the three men drag the body into the house. A moment later, a flash of orange lit the windows, followed shortly by a trail of smoke.

"No!" Valentina said, wriggling forward.

Reed lifted his arm off Banks's shoulders and grabbed Valentina's shoulder. "Quiet! They'll kill you, too, if you move now."

Valentina watched her home descend into flames, tears shining on her cheeks. The Humvee roared to life again, rumbling back down the dirt track toward the highway.

Reed released Valentina and watched the flames reach higher into the sky.

What the hell am I involved in now?

Valentina held a hand over her mouth. She watched the house but didn't move as the flames devoured the dry timbers with a ferocity that wouldn't be quenched.

Reed pulled himself to his feet, then helped Banks up. He exchanged a glance with Wolfgang. "This just got a lot more complicated."

"You recognized them?" Wolfgang asked. The tone of his voice said he had, also.

"Legion X mercenaries," Reed said. "I brushed up with them in Nashville when Salvador hired them. I guess they're still in the loop somehow."

Wolfgang grunted. "I thought so, too."

Reed unzipped his backpack and dug out a wad of US currency. "Take this," he said, handing it to Valentina. "Fly to Miami and get your daughter to the hospital. There will be people waiting for you to help with immigration. You won't have to come back."

Valentina hesitated, then accepted the money. It wasn't much—five grand, give or take, but it would be enough to hold her over until they could figure out something better. Reed didn't know what happened to her husband, but he was pretty sure the freighter captain wasn't screwing street hookers. More likely, he was somewhere at the bottom of the Gulf, another victim of this tangled mess.

"Go now," Reed said. "Walk until you find a bus. Get to the airport. Don't look back."

Valentina offered a brief bow, then scooped up her daughter and started off into the brush.

Reed watched her go, then held up his hand. "Valentina! One more thing."

She looked over her shoulder. "Sí?"

"Do you know who El Diablo is?"

Valentina's face darkened. "He is a drug lord, deep in the mountains. Cocaine and marijuana. He is scum."

Reed nodded. "Gracias, señora. Go now. America will take care of you."

Valentina vanished into the darkness within seconds. Reed wanted to follow her. He wanted to carry the girl and make sure his bold promises of refuge in America were validated. But as usual, complications took precedent.

"What now?" Banks asked.

Reed turned back to the flames. "Legion X doesn't work for free. Whoever paid them sent them here to erase anyone asking questions about that ship. They burned the house to draw Valentina out of hiding, which means we haven't seen the last of them."

"So, we wait?" Banks asked.

Reed crouched in the leaves and picked up the kitchen knife. "We wait. And when they return, we get some answers."

25

Night fell across east Texas, bathing Beaumont in inky blackness and leaving the business park obscured by shadows. Lucy waited at the edge of the parking lot, where the tree line of an uncleared lot sheltered her from view of the circling guard. Actually, there were at least two guards: one on the outside—her buddy with the sunglasses—and one who walked inside the building, his flashlight glinting through the windows every fifteen minutes as he completed his circuit.

Leaves rustled behind her, and Lucy tensed, reaching for her knife and twisting toward the sound. Kelly appeared out of the trees, still dressed in black pants and a shirt, but without the face mask. The weak glow of the parking lot lights highlighted the good side of her face, leaving the twisted scars of the fire invisible, and Lucy realized for the first time how beautiful Kelly must've been; not supermodel grade, but attractive in a strong, confident way.

Lucy suddenly wondered what Kelly had been like before her world went up in smoke. The fire had obviously altered more than her face—it changed her personality, too. Was she funny back then? Sarcastic? Goofy?

"What?" Kelly snapped. She stepped forward another pace, and the light fell across her distorted cheek, the lifted, twisted lip, the nonexistent eyebrow, and the permanently bloodshot eye that twitched inside a drooping, scarred eyelid.

Lucy looked away, feeling a wave of sadness pass over her. "Nothing. Just making sure it was you."

Kelly settled into the dirt next to her and produced a pouch of sunflower seeds from her pocket. She tore it open with flashing white teeth and offered it to Lucy. Lucy shook her head, and Kelly shrugged before dumping a handful into her palm and fingering them between her twisted lip.

Another minute passed. The outside guard made a circle around the building, and Lucy set her watch as he disappeared around the corner.

"You were thinking how good I must've looked before the fire," Kelly said.

A lump of guilt welled into Lucy's throat. She searched for something to say, but the hesitation was already obvious.

"I was cute," Kelly said. "Not a beauty queen, but I never paid for drinks."

Kelly spit sunflower seed shells onto the leaves, and Lucy sat awkwardly, still unsure what to say.

"I'm sorry," Lucy said at last. "It was a horrible thing."

Kelly grunted. "I'm sure you think so."

"You don't?"

Kelly palmed another pile of seeds. "Horrible is relative, like everything else. When I got caught smoking pot and got kicked out of private school, that was horrible. When my parents disowned me and cut off my trust fund, that was more horrible. When I got busted by Albanian police for stealing bread from a market, that felt like rock bottom."

Kelly chewed the seeds again. One of them slipped out of her twisted lip, and she glanced down, then tossed the empty package into the leaves and dusted her hands on her pant legs.

"What's your point?" Lucy asked.

"Things always get worse," Kelly said. "That's the way of the world. I used to have all these ideas about goodness and justice and even God. I mean, I had religion and everything, which was why I stopped stealing cars and why I broke it off with Reed. I blamed him for being a killer, but the breakup was my fault."

"How so?"

"Because I was holding us both to a standard that doesn't exist. Goodness is just a concept, but evil is real." Kelly's eyes were distant, pointed at the office complex but not really watching. "The devil comes for us all, eventually," she continued. "These scars are pretty bad, but no worse than being locked in a basement, kept a slave, and raped day after day. Seeing that house by the lake really taught me something."

"What's that?"

"Horrible things are gonna happen, regardless. They can happen *to* me, or they can happen *because* of me. When I get my hands on the people who trafficked those girls, trust me when I tell you, horrible things are gonna happen because of me. And in an ironic way, that's a good thing."

Lucy watched Kelly out of the corner of her eye. In the strangest way, what Kelly said made more sense than any number of moral teachings by wise men long dead. And if Lucy was honest, Kelly's understanding of the world wasn't much different than her own. They both believed in evil, and they both felt fully justified in destroying it by any means necessary.

But Lucy still believed in good things, too. There had to be good things, right? Yin and yang. Darkness and light. The sweet and the bitter. What was the point of combatting the bad if there wasn't something good to protect?

"Check."

Lucy looked up. "What?"

Kelly pointed irritably to the building. "Check. Your inside guard just passed."

"Oh, right." Lucy stopped her watched and checked the number. Three minutes, forty-two seconds between the passage of the exterior guard and the passage of the interior guard. That left them another five minutes before the exterior guard passed again, which meant now was the time to move.

"Let's go," Lucy said.

She started across the parking lot, keeping her head low. Kelly followed, her shoes clicking on the pavement at first and then growing almost silent as she adjusted her stride. They slipped up to the front entrance of the building without obstruction, and Kelly knelt at the lock, producing a pick kit from her pocket. Lucy watched with admiration as Kelly's fingers moved in a soft blur. Only thirteen seconds later, the lock was defeated, and they slipped inside.

"Starting the clock." Lucy reset her stopwatch, and they started through the opening lobby of the building, toward the elevators. "Why the timer?" she asked.

Using the stopwatch after they breached the building was something Kelly had insisted on.

"Law of averages," Kelly said, stopping at the credenza and scanning a menu of business occupants on the wall. "You never stay inside a place longer than eleven minutes."

"Why eleven?"

"Because I stayed twelve once and got busted."

"Oh."

"Beaumont Pharma is on the fourth level. They occupy the entire floor."

Kelly eased the stairway door open, and they listened for the tap of heels on the steps overhead. The stairway lay silent, and they hurried upward.

"The interior guard was on the fourth floor," Lucy whispered.

Kelly nodded. "We'll try to get past him. Worst case, I'll take him out."

They reached the fourth-floor landing and stopped at the door. Kelly held her ear against it, and Lucy checked the watch. Three minutes, twenty-eight seconds. Kelly held up a hand, then slowly lowered one finger at a time. When she made a fist, she eased the door open, and Lucy saw the back shoulder of the guard as he stepped past. Kelly lifted her foot, but Lucy held up a hand.

She slipped beneath Kelly's arm and through the narrow slot of the open door. A hallway lay on the other side of the door, stretching out to the right with office doors on either side. The guard walked ten paces ahead, a metal flashlight dangling from one hand while his other was jammed carelessly in his pocket.

Lucy slipped up behind him, moving on her toes like a cat. She closed to within inches of his shoulder blades, keeping perfect pace with him.

Then she jabbed out with her open right hand, driving her fingertips into his ribcage, just beneath and behind his armpit. The move was sharp and forceful and had exactly the desired effect.

The guard grunted in pain and released the flashlight as he twisted toward the disturbance. Lucy grabbed the flashlight on its way down, stooping beneath his swinging arm as he circled toward her. Then she rose again, only inches from his body, too close to push away. With a quick flick of her arm, she raised the flashlight and cracked the barrel over his forehead. The guard went down like a tree, folding to the floor without another sound.

Lucy checked her watch. Five minutes flat. "Clear," she said, but Kelly was already hurrying down the hall.

Kelly glanced at the unconscious guard. "Nice work."

Lucy smiled. "Thanks."

The two women split, each taking a side of the hallway as they hurried one door to the next. Each door was made of wood, with a misted windowpane covering the top half. Next to the doors were names on plates with various fancy titles—executive vice president of sales, director of marketing, senior vice president of operations, and so on. All the doors were locked, and even with the flashlight, Lucy couldn't see inside.

"Can you pick these?" Lucy asked.

Kelly appeared next to her, the guard's keys in one hand. "Don't need to." She held up a bronze key. "Master key."

The first door she tried opened without objection, and Lucy shone the flashlight inside.

The office looked exactly like what Lucy expected in a building like that —square, with faux wood furniture laden with a computer, a series of perfunctory family photographs, and a few office knickknacks. A brass nameplate on the desk read: MATT GREAVERS, SR. VP OF SALES.

The room was clean, orderly, and somehow not right.

Lucy stepped in and swept the flashlight over the furniture, checking the desk drawers and filing cabinets. They were all locked, but when she shook them, nothing shifted or rattled inside.

"Try the next one," Lucy said.

They moved to the next door and unlocked it. The interior was the same—orderly, with the same smattering of photographs, knickknacks, and unremarkable artwork. Pens and pencils rested in cups, and sticky notepads were stacked next to computer monitors. But nothing was used or worn, and nothing was out of place, either. Offices three, four, and five were all the same.

Lucy glanced at Kelly. "Does this feel right to you?"

"Feels like a boring office to me. Time?"

"Eight minutes, forty-two."

"We need to wrap it up. The guard downstairs might radio his buddy for a check-in."

Lucy wasn't listening. She walked back into the fifth office and studied the walls. They were made of cheap, industrial drywall, coated in inexpensive paint. Again she thought back to the TV special about the big pharmaceutical companies and all the money they made. This wasn't adding up. She stepped across the room and ran her fingernail along one wall. With almost no pressure, the nail left a long black streak that stuck out like a trail from a black marker.

Lucy turned to Kelly. "These offices have never been used. None of them."

"What do you mean? There's furniture here. Personal photographs."

"It's all a fake. See how easily I left a mark on the wall? I had an apartment once with cheap paint, and the same thing happened. You could brush against the wall and leave a mark without even trying. But these walls are clean. Every one of them is perfectly clean, like they were painted yesterday."

"Maybe they *were* painted yesterday."

Lucy shook her head. "No. The carpet is clean, too. There are no worn spots in front of the chairs. And those names on the nameplates? At least three of them are Olympic silver medalists. A couple swimmers and a gymnast."

Kelly frowned. "What are you saying?"

"I'm saying this entire thing is a front. There is no Beaumont Pharmaceutical. There never was. It's some kind of shell company used to hide the real operation."

"Okay, that's not especially surprising. So, this was a wasted trip?"

"No. . . ." Lucy walked back into the hallway, looked left, and bit her lip.

"What's the time?" Kelly asked.

Lucy fast-walked toward the end of the hallway, ignoring the question.

Kelly followed, the keys clinking in her hand. "Lucy, we need to go," she hissed. "We're not staying past eleven."

Lucy ignored her, turning the corner opposite of the bathrooms. The hallway ended there, leaving them facing a small sitting room with two chairs, a couple potted plants, and one blank wooden door, bolted shut. "There," Lucy said. "Open it."

"No. We have to go."

"This is it," Lucy insisted, trying the door. It was locked. "You don't hire two guards to protect a bunch of empty offices. Use the key."

Kelly cursed. She fumbled with the keys, then shoved the master into the lock. It wouldn't turn, so she shifted it, wiggled it, and tried again. The bolt still didn't turn.

"Use the picks," Lucy said. "Hurry!"

Kelly knelt in front of the door and produced the picks. Her fingers moved in a blur, but the bolt was stickier than the simple lock of the front door. It took a moment for it to budge, and even then, Kelly had to jar it with her palm before it finally twisted. She stood and dusted off her hands, looking nervously over her shoulder.

Lucy twisted the handle, and the door gave way. She shone the light inside, illuminating a hallway that twisted to the left and led back down the middle of the floor between the two rows of offices.

There were more offices on either side, blocked by doors made of solid wood, with no glass panels or nameplates. Their surfaces were scarred with use, and a quick flick of the flashlight revealed matted carpet worn by heavy traffic and infrequent cleaning.

Lucy tried the first door. It didn't open, so Kelly tried the key, then switched to the pick.

"This is it," Lucy said again.

The first door opened to reveal a tiny, windowless office. A desk in the middle was piled high with papers and a sleeping computer. File cabinets lined the walls, and a bulletin board was pinned with a half dozen memorandums and a marked-up calendar.

"Open another and check it out," Lucy whispered. "I'll search this one."

Kelly looked at Lucy's wristwatch, then hurried out.

Lucy held the flashlight over the piles of paperwork. Several were labeled with the simplistic blue and green logo of Beaumont Pharmaceutical, but she noted an assortment of other logos, as well. She dug through them, then snatched out her phone and snapped pictures.

GRUDEN PHARMACEUTICALS

HUSKY PHARMACEUTICAL RESEARCH

RESILIENT PHARMACEUTICAL

JENKINS LOWE PHARMA

BRILLIANT HORIZON PHARMACEUTICAL

The names were endless—dozens of simplistic logos for pharmaceutical research or distribution companies she'd never heard of. Several were labeled with the tagline "A Beaumont Pharmaceutical Company," while others appeared to be independent. But they all featured Beaumont's name somewhere on the document. She didn't understand most of the legal language, but some pages were labeled "acquisition contract," while others referenced hostile takeovers.

Lucy shuffled through another few sheets, then her fingers touched a thick sheaf of papers that were thicker and more worn than the rest. She lifted the stack and flipped open the cover that read: "Resilient Pharmaceutical - product research results. Blood cancer cure."

"Product research results . . ." she breathed.

What did that mean?

Then it hit her.

Lucy ran out of the room and down the hallway.

Kelly was leaned over another desk, digging through a similar pile of paperwork, her face twisted into a frown.

"I've got it!" Lucy said. "I know what they're doing."

26

Reed, Wolfgang, and Banks knelt at the edge of the tree line for an hour, watching the house burn. Already the home had collapsed, leaving piles of smoldering timbers amid the metal hulks of the kitchen appliances and bed frames.

Reed stared at the wreckage and tried not to think about Kelly and the similar house fire that destroyed her life only weeks prior.

Why all the flames? Why must everything be burned?

He looked at Banks, and a fresh wave of guilt washed through him.

Why did I bring her here? She could take it, but she shouldn't have to.

This twisted world of bloodshed and fire was his world. Banks deserved a bright, beautiful life in some bright, beautiful city full of opportunities and happiness, where boredom was the worst thing that ever happened.

He settled closer to the ground as Wolfgang dug through the backpack and produced a protein bar. The foil wrapper crinkled as Reed whispered to Banks. "Please go back. We have what we need now. We won't need you to translate anymore."

Banks glowered at him. "You don't know that. And if you try to ditch me again, I'm going to castrate you with a sharp rock."

Reed looked back to the house. In the flames, he imagined he saw Kelly thrashing about, desperate to save herself and her unborn child. Only one of them would survive the night. In some ways, neither of them had.

The distant crackle of the fire was broken only by Wolfgang's methodical chewing, and Reed tried to shut out the thoughts. He had to focus.

Wolfgang spoke suddenly, his mouth half full of protein bar. "You known Lucy long?"

Reed shrugged. "We met a while ago. I wouldn't say I know her that well."

"Cool."

Reed drew a deep breath of dirt-scented air, then he frowned. "Why do you ask?"

Wolfgang said nothing, still chewing. Reed thought he saw something in his co-killer's face that looked a lot like he felt—distant and lost, or maybe old memories stirred up by some new stimulant the way Reed's memories of Kelly were stirred up by this fire. He decided to leave it alone, but Banks wasn't so patient.

She poked Wolfgang in the ribs. "Why do you ask, Wolf?"

Wolfgang finished the bar and offered Banks a dismissive smile. "Just curious about the people I'm working with."

"You never asked about the governor," Banks said.

"She's got a Wikipedia page."

"And I'm sure Lucy's read every word of it. Good pillow talk."

"Lucy's gay?" Wolfgang let the question fly like a bullet, and Reed shook his head with a semi-amused smirk.

Banks sat up, grinning for the first time in over a week. "I knew it. You've got the hots for Lucy, don't you?"

Wolfgang scowled, but his cheeks flushed, and he finished the protein bar without answering.

"I'm just curious," Banks continued, her tone playful. "Was it the duct tape or the hot wax? For future reference, I mean."

"Duct tape?" Reed said. "What did I miss?"

Wolfgang sent Banks a lethal glare. "Nothing."

"Oh, no. I'm hearing this one," Reed pressed.

"Back in Mississippi," Banks said in almost a giggle, "Lucy tied him to a chair and dripped hot wax on his balls."

Reed chuckled. "No kidding?"

"It wasn't like that," Wolfgang said.

Banks laughed. "Relax, Wolf. We all love a crazy redhead."

Wolfgang didn't answer, but Reed saw something change behind his eyes. His usual impassiveness faded to dark, and his cheek twitched as his fingers curled into a fist. Nobody moved, and the laughter of only a moment before died in an instant. Reed glanced sideways at Banks, ensuring she noticed the change. She didn't move, but her smile faded.

"Hey, I'm sorry," Banks said. "It was just a joke."

Wolfgang nodded once, and the darkness vanished. "All in good fun," he said.

Banks's lips parted, but before she could speak, a soft rumble rose from the hills beyond the house, and they all looked to the road.

It wasn't the Humvee this time. Instead, a lone motorcycle appeared, driving slowly with its headlight off. It bounced and wiggled among the ruts, the rider struggling to keep it upright at such a slow speed. Firelight flickered off his jacket, and Reed recognized the outline of a rifle strapped to his back.

Another member of Legion X.

"What's the plan?" Wolfgang asked.

Banks spoke first. "He's here for Valentina?"

"Probably," Reed said.

"All right. I'll distract him."

Before either of them could stop her, Banks stepped out of the trees, keeping the smoking wreckage of the house between her and the rider as she jogged into the yard.

"Banks, get back here!" Reed called. She ignored him, and Reed growled a curse, motioning to Wolfgang. "Take the outside! I'll go left and try to get behind him."

Wolfgang broke into a quiet run, circling northward through the trees before turning west. Reed ran south, holding the kitchen knife close as he worked his way around the perimeter of the yard. The rider stopped the bike and put down the kickstand. He lifted his helmet off and held it under one arm, his attention fixated on the smoking home.

Reed ran faster. He was almost parallel with the rider now, fifty yards east of his position. One false move, or one broken stick, would be enough to alert the man to his position, and Reed had no place to hide as he broke out of the trees.

Then Banks wailed. It was a long, mournful sound, followed by a string of emotional Spanish. Reed was relieved to see that her exact position was obscured by the smoke. He stretched his run into a sprint, eating up the yards. The rider slid the rifle off of his back and left the bike, walking toward the house. Reed had thirty yards to go, his footfalls masked by the crackling of the fire. He couldn't see Wolfgang but knew he had to be somewhere on the far side of the home, which meant his underpowered revolver was still out of range.

Reed would have to finish this himself, armed with nothing but the kitchen knife.

He stretched out harder, knowing that at any moment his footfalls would be heard and the gunman would swing toward him, leading with the rifle.

Then the first gunshot rang out, coming from somewhere north of the house.

Wolfgang.

The gunman jerked the rifle into his shoulder and spun toward the sound, turning his back on Reed. He bent low and swept the weapon across the yard as Reed covered the final fifteen yards in a few quick strides. The revolver cracked again, and the gunman tensed. Reed hit him with the full force of a freight train, and the two crashed to the ground in a thrashing heap. Legs and arms flailed as the kitchen knife flew out of Reed's hand, and the assault rifle clattered to the ground. Reed's back crashed into the dirt, then he rolled on top and jerked his right arm free. A powerful right-hook to the gunman's jawbone resulted in a satisfying crack, but he didn't black out. Instead, he twisted and drove an answering punch into Reed's ribcage, then reached to his left thigh and yanked out a combat knife.

Reed caught his knife arm and put his full weight against it, shoving the arm and the blade into the dirt. The gunman's legs flailed beneath him, threatening to sling Reed off at any moment. In the flickering glow of the dying fire, Reed could see the hate in this man's eyes. It was a raging fire that Reed had seen before—most often in the mirror.

This man would never talk. He would never betray his comrades. Reed was locked in a death struggle with a monster—a war dog. And the only thing you could do with a war dog was rip his throat out.

Reed spat blood and saliva into the gunman's face, temporarily blinding and disorienting him. Then he lifted his left knee, taking a risk by destabilizing himself before he drove it full force into the gunman's groin. The man screamed, and his knife arm went limp. Reed drove it into the ground, forcing his right hand against the gunman's knife wrist. The blade fell free, and Reed reached across with his left hand. He grabbed the knife, then swept it across the gunman's neck in one quick, vicious slash. Blood spurted free, and the man gurgled a panicked cry. Reed flipped the knife in midair, catching it by the handle, point down, then he drove it into the gunman's heart, all the way to the hilt.

The body thrashed once, then lay still. The blood spray subsided as the man's heart stopped beating, and Reed sat panting, straddled across the body. He looked down at the mutilated throat and twisted face, then spat again. "Go to hell."

He pulled himself to his feet and dusted off his knees. Deep inside, he could feel the rage of his own war dog, punctuated by unearthly howls that he felt in his very bones. He forced the beast back into a mental cage and wiped blood from his face as Banks and Wolfgang approached.

"You good?" Wolfgang asked.

Reed nodded and turned back to the body. "Never better."

He resisted the urge to look at Banks as she stood silently behind Wolfgang, her hands shoved under her armpits.

This is why I didn't want you to come.

Wolfgang knelt beside the body and went through his pockets, dumping items onto the ground. There was a wallet with an ID that was probably fake, a handful of Colombian currency mixed with Euros, some candy, a radio, a pocket knife, and a small notebook. Strapped to his side was an H&K P30L handgun, chambered in 9mm. Reed found one round in the chamber and another fifteen in the magazine, along with two more identical magazines in pouches on his belt.

Wolfgang rolled him over and found two thirty-round magazines for the rifle housed in more pouches, each loaded to capacity with 5.56 NATO rounds.

"This guy is definitely Legion X," Wolfgang muttered.

Reed scooped up the magazines and handgun and retrieved the fallen rifle. The ACOG medium-range optic affixed to the rifle was clogged with mud, but otherwise, the weapon appeared serviceable.

"Anything in the notebook?" Reed asked.

Wolfgang flipped through it quickly. "Charts, mostly, of the mountains to the south of here, I think."

"Any notes?"

"No. Just some figures."

A light on the top of the dead man's radio flashed once, but the audio was channeled into an earpiece he still wore, so they didn't hear the words. Wolfgang scooped up the radio and pulled out the headset connection, then waited. The radio chirped, but nobody spoke.

"It's a status check," Wolfgang said. "When he doesn't answer, they'll go to ground."

"Give it to me," Reed said.

"You can't answer," Wolfgang said. "They'll know it's not him."

"I'm counting on it," Reed said, still holding out his hand.

Wolfgang reluctantly passed Reed the radio as it chirped again and a distorted voice said something in some manner of East European language.

"What's up, dude?" Reed said loud and clear into the mic.

Wolfgang's eyes bulged. "What are you doing?"

Reed held up a finger, then waited.

The voice came back, this time in English. "Who is this?"

"Genghis Khan. Who's this?"

Dead quiet. Reed waited another three minutes, then switched the radio off and tossed it next to the body. "Right now, he's wondering if his man is dead or if he simply lost his radio and some fool picked it up."

"And that helps us *how*?" Wolfgang demanded.

"Remember who you're dealing with, Wolf. We know these guys are paramilitary mercenaries, which means they operate in coordinated teams governed by military tactics. When I was a Marine, I spent a lot of years fighting on teams like that, and the first thing you learn is that there's a system for everything—a procedure and a playbook. It's how you ensure that even when things go wrong, the mission is accomplished."

"Okay," Wolfgang said, "but how do we know what their mission is? We don't even know why they're here."

"Sure we do," Reed said. "It's obvious. Legion X is an exclusive and very expensive mercenary force. Even if you can afford them, they don't take just any job, and they aren't a hit team. They didn't fly all the way to Colombia to take out a random woman and her sick child. That was probably just a side job. They flew here because Aiden Phillips hired them to protect his primary operation. We rattled his cage back in Louisiana, so now he sent these guys to protect his biggest asset."

Banks looked up. "And now they're going to lead us right to it."

"Not directly," Reed said. "They're smarter than that. First, they'll retreat to a pre-established rendezvous point, then wait for their man. When he doesn't show up, they'll retreat to the primary objective and lead us along with them."

"Right . . ." Wolfgang frowned. "And we find that rendezvous point how, exactly?"

"Easy." Reed pointed to the pile of things from the dead man's pocket. "It's in the book."

27

Brájen Valko stood next to the Humvee and gently switched off the radio. He tapped the device against the open palm of his left hand while he stared out through the trees, back in the direction of the ship captain's burned-out home five miles away. He couldn't see the smoke rising from the ashes, but he knew it was there. He knew his man should also be there. He should've established an overwatch, searched for Valentina, and then checked in. But Valko hadn't heard from him, so he called for a situation report. And now this.

He looked at the radio and considered every angle of his brief conversation with the unknown man on the other end. Valko was a warrior. No, more than a warrior, he was an elite—a highly trained, battle-tested spec ops soldier with names like *French Foreign Legion* and Germany's *KSK* on his resume. He knew how to fight, and he knew how to win. Something he'd learned long ago was that patience served him well, and when time allowed for it, he liked to think slowly.

Somebody was toying with him. He was sure of that. Either his man had lost his radio and some fool had picked it up, or worse, his man had been killed. But by whom?

Valko thought back to his brief phone call with the man who called himself Fianchetto. Valko knew it wasn't actually a name. In fact, he was pretty sure Fianchetto was a chess maneuver. But it wasn't unusual for his clients to use pseudonyms when hiring Legion X, and Fianchetto was paying a lot, and without question. Fianchetto wanted the best—the most elite. Not Legion X's usual ground-pounders, but their unadvertised Special Operations division. Valko was surprised that Fianchetto even knew about Legion X's spec ops team—a team usually hired out by invitation only. But Fianchetto had insisted.

The money was right, so Legion X agreed, and eight hours later, Valko and his men were on board a privately owned cargo plane en route from Budapest to Barranquilla. These men weren't soldiers, and they weren't even commandos. They were something darker and more deadly, collected from every continent and trained to the point of animalistic lethality inside Legion X's secret combat facility in Belarus. The LX Dark Team, as they were known, rivaled the most superior Special Operations operatives of all the world's leading militaries. They were combat enthusiasts—killing machines.

Valko had been Dark Team's commander for sixteen months, which was the longest anybody had ever been Dark Team's commander, to his knowledge. You didn't acquire this job by appointment or popular vote, but by seniority. So, in theory, becoming the boss was pretty simple. You just didn't get killed while everybody above you did, which made this job suitable for only the most insane.

Cracked.

That was the word Sam Judson, one of Dark Team's American operators and Valko's second-in-command, used. You had to be *cracked* to work on Dark Team. Pure greed wasn't enough. You needed bloodlust. Judson should know. He was one of the most cracked, bloody people Valko had ever met.

On his average deployment, Valko gunned down four or five people, to say nothing of the rest of his team. His usual missions consisted of hit jobs, thefts, and security ops, mostly in Europe and Asia, with the occasional African job. Once, he'd even conducted an op in New York City.

But never Colombia. Never for a man calling himself Fianchetto. And never for a job as innocuous and simplistic as assassinating a ship driver's wife and protecting some shack in the mountains.

Valko rubbed his finger across his chin, still staring at the radio. His men waited silently behind him, dispersed amidst the Colombian forest. They stood in perfect silence, totally relaxed, ready and willing for whatever came next.

What was Fianchetto not telling him? When Valko received the call for eight of Dark Team's operators to fly immediately to Colombia, armed to the teeth, he expected it had something to do with drugs—maybe rival cartels duking it out, and one of them called in reinforcements. But upon landing, Legion X headquarters wired his orders, and they comprised nothing that your average mercenary couldn't have managed.

Assassinate this woman. Then proceed to this location and protect it at all costs.

Valko was missing something, and that was a condition he was altogether uncomfortable with. It made him wonder who was lying. He clicked the radio back into his belt and held up two fingers. Judson appeared out of the shadows, moving without a sound even as his iron jaw chewed mechanically, grinding gum between his teeth.

"Staven hit trouble," Valko whispered in accented English. "He's not responding to his comm."

Judson said nothing. He'd worked for Valko long enough to know when his boss had more to say.

"Either he's been hit, or he lost his radio," Valko continued. "We'll proceed to the checkpoint and give him two more hours. Then we move to the primary objective."

Judson didn't so much as nod—he just faded back into the trees, and a moment later, the men began to load their equipment into the two Humvees at the edge of the road.

Valko remained at the tree line, staring into the darkness. A primitive instinct sharpened by years of illicit combat stirred in the darkest part of his soul. A voice, deep in his mind, spoke softly to him, calling out. Setting off alarm bells. Warning him that he wasn't the only killer in these hills.

28

"Where's Montgomery?" the big man asked again. He sat across from Maggie, his dark eyes fixed on her like the glare of spotlights. His phone remained on the desktop, casting a soft blue glow across the FBI shield next to it.

Maggie folded her arms. Her shock at being confronted by this man and hearing his surveillance tape had faded. Her mind worked quickly, examining all angles and putting her back in the driver's seat.

She decided there was no point in trying to bullshit her way out of this. She had no way of knowing what else he'd heard, and he didn't seem like the kind of man who would respond well if she tried jerking him around. But more than that, a sixth sense told her that something was going on beneath the surface of his dark demeanor. Something conflicted and complex. This wasn't your average FBI interrogation. In fact, she wasn't convinced this man represented the FBI at all.

Maggie picked up the badge and corresponding ID card, holding it under the light of her desk lamp. It read: "Special Agent Rufus Turkman, Federal Bureau of Investigation. Washington DC Office."

She ran her thumb over the shield, admiring the detail of the craftsmanship. The credentials certainly looked legit. Maggie flipped the ID wallet closed and folded her hands, deciding to go for the gentle approach. "Who's asking?"

Turkman didn't blink. "*I'm* asking. The FBI is asking."

"I see. Well, I'm afraid I can't help you. I honestly don't know where he is."

"But you know how to find him. And you know what he's up to."

Maggie's mind spun, trying to calculate her next move. There was a lot on the line. She knew from the start that working with Montgomery was dangerous—definitely illegal and likely to land her in yet more murky waters, morally speaking. But she never expected the FBI to approach her so suddenly, let alone put her under surveillance.

"Why are you looking for him?" she asked.

"I'm not at liberty to say."

His response was canned but logical. The FBI probably wouldn't discuss the issue with her, especially if they thought she was somehow involved with Montgomery. After all, they could be investigating him for any number of reasons. The bombs in New Orleans, or any of the many explosive conflicts Reed had triggered all around the Southeast over the past weeks.

So, it made sense for the FBI to poke around, but something didn't feel right. Why was Turkman alone? Where was his backup? And why was the surveillance tape on his phone? It all felt very . . . vigilante, as if Turkman were working outside his FBI mandate.

Maggie decided to take a chance and call his bluff. "Well, Agent, I'm sorry we couldn't help each other. I'll have security show you back to your car." She reached for the phone.

Turkman cleared his throat. "Wait."

She raised an eyebrow. "Yes?"

He hesitated, looking at his badge and licking his lips. "I know Montgomery is in trouble. I'm not here to arrest him. Not unless I have to. I'm here to help."

Maggie cocked her head. "You know him personally, don't you?"

He didn't answer.

"Marines, right?" she said. "You've got the look."

Turkman rubbed his bottom lip with a thumb, still looking away.

Maggie's confidence rose as she felt the shift of initiative sliding her way. "You certainly haven't been a field agent very long. That much is obvious."

He stiffened a little. "What makes you say that?"

"Well, we could start with your slipshod surveillance of a state official, on state property, without the authorization of that state's attorney general. Pretty amateur stuff . . . not to mention illegal."

It was bullshit. Maggie had no idea what legalities were involved with setting up surveillance over a governor. But Turkman didn't either—that much was clear by the further uneasiness in his posture and the momentary panic that flashed across his face.

"It's not like that," he blurted. "I'm not . . . I'm not exactly here on behalf of the FBI. I mean, I do work for the FBI, but I'm not working the Montgomery case. Domestic terror took over, and they're close. They'll catch him any day, now. I'm here to . . . work something out."

It all spilled out in a gushing, semi-emotional torrent. Yeah, this guy was no seasoned field agent. And the way it looked, he'd never become one. But Maggie could work with that.

She leaned forward, assuming her most conversational posture while keeping her tone commanding. "Well, look. I'm a big supporter of law enforcement, but you can't just come down here, poking around and recording things like that. It's the sort of thing that creates interdepartmental mistrust, you understand? Legal dilemmas. Constitutional concerns." Maggie had no idea what she was saying. She just spouted fancy words and hoped Turkman was too uneducated or distracted to catch her at it.

He frowned at the phone, maybe rethinking his recordings.

Maggie pressed her advantage. "Anyway, what do you mean by 'work something out'?"

He avoided her gaze, and Maggie sighed. She made a production of walking to the minibar and pouring two drinks, just as she had with Sharp only twenty minutes earlier. She pushed those memories out of her mind as she returned to the desk and offered Turkman a glass. He didn't take it.

"Look," Maggie said, setting the drink down. "I don't know what you're up to, but it's late, and I'm tired. I'm not making any phone calls or getting bent out of shape at this hour. So, let's just speak frankly. Can we do that?"

Turkman chewed his lip, then nodded a couple times. Maggie handed him the drink, and he took a long sip.

She returned to her chair. "How do you know Montgomery?"

"We served together in the sandbox."

"You were a Marine?" She already knew the answer.

"Yes. Force Recon."

"Impressive."

Turkman shrugged. "Montgomery was impressive. He was a fighter. A really outstanding Marine."

"Until he gunned down five civilian contractors, you mean."

Turkman swallowed.

"Yes, I know about that," she said. "It may surprise you that I know quite a lot about Montgomery."

"How?"

"He told me."

"So, you're working with him."

"You already know I am."

"Right . . ." He hesitated, as if he were looking for the right words.

Maggie took the lead again. "Here's the deal, Agent. Montgomery kidnapped me, which you probably already suspect. He was hired to kill me by a criminal organization I've been hunting here in Louisiana for the past several months. Turns out he and I have similar enemies, and you know what they say about that."

"The enemy of my enemy is my friend."

"Exactly. And it's not a perfect arrangement. There's a lot of legal questions and general moral grey areas. But the guys we're hunting are absolute animals. They traffic children, among other things. We busted their brothel only last week and found four girls there, all under the age of sixteen. Would you like to see pictures?"

Turkman shook his head quickly. "No. I believe you."

"Right. Well, that's why Montgomery and I are working together. I know he's a dark man, and I realize he's done a lot of nasty things. I'll be the first to see him face justice for those crimes, but not until I've hunted down the monster on my plate. Do you follow me?"

Turkman rubbed his lip. He seemed to be wrestling with something, and she let him work it out at his own speed.

After almost a minute, he said, "The real reason I'm here . . . It's just, well, Montgomery isn't on the FBI's most-wanted list anymore."

Maggie frowned. "I don't understand."

"It's difficult to explain, and I can't prove it. I mean, nobody can. It's not the kind of thing you'll find on paper, you know? It's all with Homeland now."

"What are you telling me?" Maggie asked.

Turkman stared at his boots, his commanding air completely gone now. He looked like a kid caught stealing cookies. "I've only been with the agency a few years, but I've seen this before."

"Seen *what* before?"

"Seen somebody, you know . . . taken off the list. Shifted to another department. And when that happens, it means they don't plan to arrest anybody."

"They plan to kill him," Maggie finished.

"Not the FBI, no. But other agencies in the government. Nameless agencies. You have to understand, Montgomery is now considered a domestic terrorist. What's more, he's a former Marine. It's a political nightmare waiting to happen. It's much easier to just erase the problem."

"You're telling me Washington has sanctioned a hit on one of their own?"

Turkman rolled his eyes. "Don't be naïve, Governor. Do you have any idea how many noncombatants we've waxed overseas? You label somebody a terrorist, and the gloves come off. That's just how it works."

"But he's a US citizen."

"He could be the freakin' pope. It doesn't matter."

"And you have a problem with that?"

"Would you have a problem killing the people who enslaved those girls?"

Maggie didn't answer but held his gaze.

Turkman blinked first. "I'm just saying. There's no negotiating with some people. Sometimes, the only way to solve a problem is with a well-placed bullet."

"But . . ." Maggie said.

"But Montgomery was my trigger buddy. He had my back. He would've died for me. And I just . . ." Turkman swallowed and looked down at the carpet.

"You can't let it happen without warning him," Maggie finished.

"Right. If Montgomery's done everything they say, he probably deserves to have his ticket punched. And I won't stand in the way. But first, I need to see him. He deserves a chance to explain himself."

Maggie stroked the arm of her chair and watched Turkman for a full minute. "Rufus, right?"

"Nobody calls me that. I go by Turk."

"Okay, Turk. Can I trust you?"

"Montgomery did."

Maggie interlaced her fingers. "All right, then. Let me tell you a story."

29

Reed was right about the book. Buried near the back, he found notations detailing a rendezvous located six miles southwest of Valentina's house, in a rural part of the department that featured fields of high grass and scattered hills covered in trees. They located a battered Toyota SUV at a neighbor's house, and after Reed hot-wired the starter, they drove to within a mile of the rendezvous point before ditching the vehicle.

"I'd love for you to stay here," Reed said as he climbed out of the Toyota.

"I'd love to be a pop star," Banks retorted. "Good thing our wants won't kill us."

Reed exchanged a look with Wolfgang, who only shrugged and opened the back hatch of the Toyota. The weapons lay inside—the harbormaster's revolver, and the captured H&K rifle and pistol from the Legion X fighter. Reed wondered briefly if the harbormaster would've avoided capture if he had his gun, but he knew the man was damned as soon as Legion X set their sights on him—just like Valentina would've been if she'd been alone. These guys were lethal.

Reed selected the rifle and checked to make sure a round was chambered, then dumped the extra magazines into the pockets of his cargo pants. Wolfgang took the pistol, and Banks grabbed the revolver.

"What's the play?" Wolfgang asked.

"We're looking for intelligence, not a gunfight," Reed said. "We close in, learn what we can, then fall back and contact Trousdale."

Wolfgang set off toward the rendezvous.

Banks glared at Reed. "I told you, I'm going."

"I know. It's not that." Reed ran a hand over his forehead. It was hot in Colombia, even at night, and sweat trickled down his face. "It's about our conversation on the plane—what you said about respect and the way I've treated you. You were right. I'm sorry, and so long as you're around, I'll do better."

She ducked her head. "Thank you."

Reed adjusted his grip on the rifle. "I won't fight you anymore about coming along. I respect your right to choose, but I need you to respect my experience, also. I don't own this war, but I do own the battlefield. I know what I'm doing."

Banks shifted from one foot to the other, then hesitantly held out her hand.

"What's this?" he said.

She shrugged and looked down. "I don't know . . . Shake on it?"

Reed clasped her hand and gave it a gentle squeeze. "Shake on it."

Wolfgang cleared his throat from fifty yards away, and they hurried to catch up. An open field full of waist-high grass covered the rolling foothills that led toward the mountains in the south. The moon was full, shining down over the grass as a gentle breeze wafted past them, and Reed sucked in a deep breath of someplace new and dangerous. It was a familiar sensation, even if the precise flavor was unique, country to country. He wondered how many men Legion X had deployed, and he thought about Aiden hiring them.

He's rattled. And he should be.

"The rendezvous is just over that ridge," Wolfgang whispered, motioning to a tree-lined rise half a mile away. "It looks like an abandoned roadbed on Google Earth, but I can't be sure."

Reed nodded, and the trio fell silent as they reached the end of the field and slipped into the trees. Soft leaves crunched beneath their feet, and the light of the moon split into bullet-beams that shot between the swaying limbs. Reed heard a chattering sound, followed by the creak of tree limbs. A monkey was swinging from one tree to the next, keeping its beady black eyes fixed on them the entire way.

Don't give us away, little guy.

As they reached the base of the ridge, Wolfgang held up a fist, and the three of them knelt in the shadows, listening. Again, Reed heard the distant grind and clink of an approaching Humvee, and a glance over his shoulder confirmed the vehicle driving in from the northeast, headed toward the far end of the ridge. It drove without headlights, rattling across a dry roadbed with its primary antenna bent over the roof and tied off to the front bumper.

They waited until the Humvee disappeared around the end of the ridge, then they crept up the rise, keeping low beneath the trees and taking care to avoid dry sticks and crunchy leaves. The monkey had gone—probably smelling danger in the wind—and suddenly the Colombian landscape felt still and menacing.

They reached the top of the ridge a hundred yards later and settled onto their hands and knees. Reed motioned Banks to hang back, and this time she didn't argue, crouching behind a tree with the revolver clasped in one hand.

Reed and Wolfgang continued to the edge, descending to their stomachs before the ground fell away and exposed a valley floor over a hundred yards beneath.

Both Humvees sat on a dry roadbed, their lights off but engines running. Reed smelled the distant but familiar odor of diesel fumes and wrinkled his nose, watching as one man climbed out of the passenger seat of the second Humvee and approached the first. He was burly, with a thick beard and bulging muscles that tested the limits of his sleeves. He cradled an H&K G36 as if it were a toy and spat tobacco juice across the ground as he walked.

A tall, blond, and pale man appeared from the first Humvee. Reed recognized him from Valentina's house as the man who shot the harbormaster—the one he'd made a mental note about to kill him personally.

The two men met between the vehicles. Their voices were soft, but the air had fallen so still that Reed could make out fragments of sentences.

"...dead..." Burly said.

"...at the house?" Blond asked.

Burly nodded, and Blond twitched in the frustrated way a man does as he mutters a curse. He folded his arms and said nothing while Burly waited patiently.

Reed eased the rifle from beneath his arm, sliding it slowly over the top of the ridge. Wolfgang held out a hand to stop him, but Reed shook his head once and slipped the stock against his shoulder, then leaned down and aligned his eye with the optic mounted on top. The ACOG offered a fixed 2X magnification, bringing both men into focus, even in the dark.

Again, Blond spoke, but this time a gentle breeze blew over Reed's back, obscuring his words. Reed traced him with the ACOG, keeping Blond's neck aligned with the crosshairs as Reed kept his finger just above the trigger guard.

Blond led Burly to the hood of the second Humvee and produced a map from his pocket. He pinned it to the hood of the vehicle with his radio, then traced his finger along it, still speaking.

Reed moved the crosshairs to the map and recognized the outline of Colombia. Blond moved his finger south, down from Barranquilla and into the heartland of the country. He tapped a spot north of Medellín, and Burly nodded.

"What do you see?" Wolfgang whispered.

Reed didn't answer, watching as Blond pulled a pen from his pocket and marked the map, then wrote next to the spot.

"Write this down!" Reed hissed.

"What?"

"Get a pen!"

Wolfgang fumbled in the dark and produced his cell phone.

"Coordinates," Reed said. "Ready?"

"Ready," Wolfgang said.

Reed focused on the map, struggling to make out the numbers, even with the magnification. He read the latitude and longitude that Blond wrote off one at a time while Burly examined the map. Reed made out all but the last couple of numbers before Blond handed Burly the map and turned back to his Humvee. Burly climbed into the second vehicle, and Reed watched him punching the coordinates into a windshield-mounted GPS. Then he motioned to the driver, the diesel engine roared, and the Humvee reversed out of the valley.

Reed lowered the rifle and chewed his lip.

Wolfgang lay beside him and waited until the engine noise vanished into the hills before he spoke. "What do you think?"

"The blond guy is the leader," Reed said. "We saw him at Valentina's house. The other guy is probably his second-in-command. Some kind of lieutenant."

"What do you think they're up to?"

Reed hesitated. "All we can do is guess, but I'd say we made a mistake not hiding the body of their man. They're spooked now, so they're dividing forces."

Wolfgang frowned. "Why would they do that? If they're spooked, you'd think they'd want to rally."

"Not if they had an asset to protect, which they do. The blond guy probably sent his lieutenant ahead to get boots on the ground while he hangs back to make sure nobody follows."

"Smart."

Reed indulged in a little grin. "Smart, but not smart enough. Come on."

They crept back down the ridge and found Banks waiting behind the tree, then they re-crossed the field and climbed back into the SUV. Reed unpacked the satellite phone from his backpack and speed-dialed Maggie's number. Banks poked him with her elbow, and he placed the phone on speaker.

Maggie answered on the fourth ring. "Reed?"

"It's me. Can you talk?"

"Go ahead. Where are you?"

"Inland. We made contact with the ship captain's wife, but she didn't know where he was. *Santa Coquina* never made it back to port."

"Did you talk to the authorities?"

"Never got the chance. Some guys showed up at her house—mercenaries from Eastern Europe. I've encountered them before. They're not cheap, and they don't play. My guess is that Aiden sent them down here to clean things up. We're following them inland now. What's new on your end?"

"I just got off the phone with Winter. Lucy and Kelly infiltrated Beaumont Pharma. The offices were all unused, but they discovered a hidden section inside the building loaded with documents. They took some pictures, and I'm going over them now."

"What kind of documents?"

"Acquisition contracts and merger agreements. Tons of them. Entity dissolution docs, as well. Beaumont is purchasing and then dissolving dozens of other pharmaceutical companies. I've backtracked a few of them, and these are legitimate businesses. Small, but on the books. Beaumont buys them, and then they just disappear. I can't make sense of it."

Reed rubbed his lip, looking out over the fields and sorting through the pieces in his mind, trying to arrange them into a logical picture. "What did Winter say?"

"She's digging into it, but Lucy has an idea. She saw some documentary a while back about another drug company that used to buy up smaller companies this way. Apparently, they waited until these smaller companies were on the cusp of releasing a profitable new drug, then they torpedoed them, claimed the patents, and produced the drug themselves, effectively eliminating expensive research and development costs. One company Beaumont just bought recently developed a new cancer drug, so Lucy thinks they may be doing the same thing."

"That doesn't sound illegal," Reed said.

"It's a grey area."

"What do you think?"

"Initially, her idea made sense, but looking into these companies, it doesn't add up. Only one of them was on the verge of releasing a new drug, and several of them were dissolved altogether by Beaumont within weeks of acquisition. There's no rhyme or reason."

"It's a smoke screen," Wolfgang said, folding his arms. "They're hiding something."

"I agree," Reed said. "Aiden is using Beaumont to shovel something. The acquisitions are probably part of a complex laundering method."

"Money laundering?" Maggie asked.

"Not necessarily," Reed said. "He could be laundering products or logistics. You can hide all kinds of things if you bury them in enough paperwork."

"What if it's drugs?" Banks said.

Reed cocked his head. "Drugs?"

Banks leaned closer to the phone. "Winter said she thought Aiden was moving cocaine into the country back in the nineties, using your father as his money launderer and my godfather as his logistics expert. Clearly, that operation isn't possible anymore. What if Aiden is now moving cocaine through the pharmaceutical system?"

Reed exchanged a look with Wolfgang.

The Wolf scratched his chin, then shook his head. "I don't see how that would work. Hiding cocaine in pill capsules does nothing for you. The end user still has to know where to find it, and if the end user knows, it's only a matter of time before law enforcement knows. I really think this Beaumont thing is about something else. Another part of his operation."

"And there are still the bananas," Maggie said. "We still don't know what the *Santa Coquina* is all about."

Reed lowered the phone and stared out into the darkening night sky. The moon had set, and only scattered stars gleamed from the heavens. He switched the phone off speaker and held it to his ear. "Maggie, it's just Reed."

"What's up?"

"We sent the ship captain's wife to Miami. Her daughter is sick, and the doctors down here think she has blood cancer. I need you to call in a favor with Florida and make sure she gets to a US hospital."

Maggie cleared her throat. "Call in a favor?"

"Right. Call the governor of Florida, or whatever. Get her through customs."

"Reed, that's not how government works. We can't just let whoever into the country, even if we want to. There are laws. Regulations."

"I know that," Reed said, speaking through his teeth. "Which is why I want you to call somebody and take care of it. This woman's child is dying, and I gave her my word America would take her in."

Maggie said nothing. Reed waited her out, and at last, she sighed. "Okay. I'll make some calls. What's her name?"

"It's a long name. I can't remember. Her first name is Valentina. She's flying into Miami out of Bogota sometime in the next twelve hours."

"Okay. Anything else?"

"That's all. We're going to keep digging down here. I'll keep you posted."

"Sounds good."

Maggie's voice trailed off, and Reed waited, but she didn't speak.

"What is it?" he said.

"There's . . ." Maggie cleared her throat. "Don't worry about it. We'll talk when you get back."

"Copy that. I'll check back in twelve hours."

He hung up and turned to Wolfgang and Banks. "Whatever Aiden hired mercenaries to look after, it'll tell us a lot more about his operation than anything in Beaumont."

"So we follow them?" Wolfgang asked.

Reed nodded. "If it's worth hiring Legion X to protect, it's worth looking into."

30

Wolfgang used his phone to locate the coordinates Reed recorded. They pinpointed a spot deep in the Andes Mountains, about 450 kilometers south of their current position, in the Department of Antioquia. It was a rural part of the country, and a quick search of the satellite view on Wolfgang's phone revealed nothing but endless ridges covered in trees, with winding roadbeds, or no roads at all.

The topography brought to Reed's mind movies about the Medellín Cartel—Pablo Escobar's legendary drug gang that pumped cocaine out of the Andes Mountains like water. During the seventies and eighties, those drug gangs ruled the country with an economic grip so powerful that cocaine surpassed coffee as Colombia's chief export.

Those days were over, eroded by time and improved law-enforcement technology. But the mountains were still there, and they were no less a refuge for organized crime than they'd ever been. Amid the endless miles of Andes ridges, what new criminal enterprises thrived like mold in the damp shadows beneath a house? What had Aiden built there that was so valuable, one of the world's most elite and expensive mercenary forces was hired to protect it?

Whatever it is, I'm going to burn it to the ground.

Wolfgang drove, piloting the stolen SUV into the heart of Colombia along wide highways surrounded by endless coffee fields. The air was fragrant with the scent of fresh-tilled earth and growing things, and the countryside radiated a subtle peace that Reed found deeply attractive.

Banks curled up in the back seat and slept, and Reed watched every passing car for signs of police or Legion X. Most of the vehicles he saw were over-the-road trucks laden with shipping containers probably filled with coffee and headed from inland fields toward the ports at Barranquilla.

Or bananas.

The sky softened from black to grey as they reached Sincelejo and stopped for fuel and breakfast. Reed and Wolfgang had barely spoken on the long drive, and Reed didn't mind. He was becoming accustomed to having the co-killer around and appreciated that Wolfgang knew when to embrace the quiet.

Reed took over driving, enjoying a breakfast burrito purchased from the gas station. It was good—filled with scrambled eggs, peppers, and some kind of roast meat that was both savory and tender. Banks woke up and accepted a bottle of water and a burrito but sat quietly as the coffee fields rose into foothills and the Andes Mountains reached for the sky directly ahead.

They turned off of Highway 25 just north of Caucasia, and took a two-lane directly into the heart of the mountains. It was now almost noon, and the sun beat down on the SUV with enough strength to make the ride uncomfortable. The Toyota's AC was broken, and they rolled the windows down as the air thinned. Reed felt a subtle weight on his chest, like a textbook on his sternum, and recalled having felt this way before whenever he visited any mountains. The farther they drove, the thinner the air became, and the more difficult it would be to breathe.

"We're about an hour out," Wolfgang said. "In another two klicks, you'll turn off the blacktop. It's all dirt roads from there."

Reed nodded but said nothing. A strange foreboding had settled on him. Reed wasn't much on gut feelings, preferring to rely on his training and his own wits to guide him through any situation as it unfolded. But something about these mountains made him altogether uneasy. Maybe it was having Banks with him and worrying about her safety. Or maybe it was an instinct that he'd long ignored and should now heed. A voice that warned him of bad things directly ahead.

Reed turned off the blacktop onto a wide dirt road. It led upward, into the mountains, with tall trees leaning over it on both sides and thick undergrowth clogging the ditches. Tire marks scarred the packed dirt, but the air was still, and nobody was around.

Reed stopped the Toyota and sat for a minute, staring up the road. Then he shifted into park and got out, cradling the H&K in one arm as he circled to the front of the SUV and knelt in the roadbed.

Wolfgang followed, surveying the surrounding trees and undergrowth and leaving his door open. "What is it?"

Reed gestured to the roadbed, pointing at twin wide tire tracks that ran up the road, into the distance. "Humvee tracks."

"You sure?"

Reed nodded but didn't comment further. He stood up and walked a few feet up the road, noting another set of tracks that were both wider and deeper than those of the Humvee, leading back to the blacktop. He used his shoe to estimate width and determined each tread mark to be about a foot wide and eight feet apart. The tire prints lay at the bottom of worn ruts—the mark of repeated, heavy travel.

"Semi-truck," he said.

"Coming and going," Wolfgang added, pointing to an identical set of tracked ruts that ran along the other side of the road.

Reed studied them, dropping his boot into the left-hand tracks before walking to Wolfgang's side of the road and dropping his boot into those tracks, also. He frowned.

"What is it?" Wolfgang asked.

"They're almost identically deep," Reed said.

"Meaning?"

"Meaning the trucks were loaded, coming and going."

Reed searched the road again, noting an array of light vehicle tracks and the odd animal track, but only the Humvee and semitruck tracks looked fresh, and only the truck tracks left ruts from frequent travel.

"Maybe they're trucking in supplies and trucking out product," Wolfgang said.

"Maybe. Regardless, half of Legion X is already up there, and the other half is on our tail. We can't linger."

They returned to the Toyota, and Reed piloted it into the mountains, taking care to avoid the ruts. The roadbed was dry, and the Toyota's tires gripped the dirt well, but the vehicle wasn't four-wheel drive, and the last thing he needed was to become stuck.

The farther they drove, the higher the trees rose on either side, and the more they leaned over the roadbed. Occasional monkeys danced amid the foliage while towering wax palm trees shot out of the forest, reaching as high as two hundred feet above the Toyota.

Banks rolled her window down and gaped at the forest and passing wildlife, leaning out and breaking into a grin every time a monkey appeared. The primates seemed completely unafraid of the vehicle or its occupants, and several swung down to the road to watch them pass, their beady eyes blinking with both indifference and fascination.

Reed noticed Banks reaching for the remnants of her breakfast, and both he and Wolfgang spoke at once. "Don't even think about it."

"What?" she said innocently.

"They'll rip your arm off," Reed said.

"Or bite it off," Wolfgang added.

Banks dropped the burrito back onto the seat, and Reed rolled up the windows. It was still hot, despite the shade of the towering palms, but the farther they crept up the road, the more uneasy he became.

"How far?" Reed asked.

"Five more klicks. We should ditch the car."

Reed nodded his agreement and searched for a spot where the ditch next to the road flattened, allowing him to turn into the trees without bottoming out. He shoved his foot against the gas and drove them into the foliage, sending a pair of disgruntled birds squawking and rocketing into the air. The Toyota ground against a fallen log, and Reed hit the brake, cutting the engine and waiting a moment to see if any other disturbed wildlife would make a more deadly appearance.

He heard nothing but the methodical tick of the cooling engine, and he motioned to Wolfgang. They both piled out and immediately began covering their tracks with fallen leaves and restructuring the undergrowth to shield the back of the Toyota from view of the road.

Reed still cradled the rifle and continued to survey the forest. The uneasiness hadn't left his mind, but the wildlife brought him a little comfort. In Reed's experience, wildlife were better judges of impending doom than humanity. Birds and beasts could sense when something bad was about to happen, and they never stuck around to wait for it. So long as the birds and monkeys were around, that probably meant an army of bloodthirsty mercenaries wasn't nearby.

Probably.

Reed and Wolfgang gathered at the hood of the SUV, and Banks joined them. Wolfgang's phone had long ago lost signal, but the map was still loaded, and Reed zoomed in on their position.

The coordinates led to a point about five kilometers away, across a valley and beyond the next ridge. The road wound its way around the base of the first ridge and then crossed a bridge over the valley and the creek below before winding around the next ridge and reaching the target. Fighting their way through the forest and across the creek without the aid of the bridge would be difficult, but Reed was no longer willing to risk taking the road. Whatever lay ahead, if it was worth hiring Legion X to protect, it was worth posting sentries and perhaps security devices to protect, also.

"From this point forward, I'm taking command," Reed said. "Can we agree on that?"

Wolfgang and Banks nodded without comment, and Reed gestured to the map on the phone.

"We're going to circle north and then descend into the valley here, at this beach, next to the creek. If the creek is passable, we'll ford on foot, then climb the ridge on the backside, a kilometer north of the road. I'll take point with the rifle, and Wolfgang will take our tail. Nobody opens fire unless your life depends on it. Try to avoid stirring up the wildlife, and walk precisely where I walk. That's important. I'll be on the lookout for trip wires and mines."

"Mines?" Banks asked, raising both eyebrows.

"Land mines. Explosive devices buried beneath—"

"I know what they are. I just didn't know if you were serious."

For the millionth time, Reed wished he'd sent her back with Valentina. In truth, he didn't expect mines or trip wires. Maybe Legion X would add them over the coming days, but the security of this place was rooted in its isolation and difficult terrain. Even so, a dozen brutal firefights in Iraq had taught him to assume nothing and expect all the worst obstacles. Land mines were just another obstacle to him, but to Banks, a pop singer from Atlanta, the concept must've been terrifying.

"Don't worry," he said. "I know what to look for. Just stick between Wolfgang and me, and don't feed the monkeys." Reed retrieved the backpack from the trunk of the SUV and slung it over his shoulders, then checked the rifle.

Wolfgang circled to meet him at the back of the vehicle and spoke softly. "You should leave her here."

"No. Now that we're here, I'll feel better keeping her close, where I can look after her."

"That's exactly my point," Wolfgang said, his tone dropping. "If things go south, I want you worried about the mission, not Banks."

Reed glanced over his shoulder to Banks. She was busy checking the load in her revolver.

"Just cover my six," Reed said. "I'll worry about the mission."

They wound through the trees and down into the valley, loosely following the path Reed outlined on the maps. He took the lead, keeping the captured H&K rifle in low-ready as he navigated amid the trees and monitored the path ahead. He saw no established trail, or even much clearance between the sprawling undergrowth, which reinforced his confidence that the area wasn't armed with explosives.

Reed thought about Vietnam and the previous generation of warriors who'd fought through the jungles of Southeast Asia, navigating through foliage and undergrowth much more dense than this. Those jungles were definitely infested with explosive devices, to say nothing of pits, booby traps, and tunnels full of heavily armed Vietcong.

In the context of the Colombian jungle, the heroism of those soldiers was much easier to appreciate, and he marveled at the courage it must take to lead a platoon of Marines into those deadly jungles, knowing that at any moment, all of them could be blown to hell.

Reed looked over his shoulder and saw Banks trailing ten paces behind, and Wolfgang another ten behind her. Already they were sweaty and streaked with dirt, and they hadn't even reached the creek yet.

Thankfully, when they did reach the creek, they found it to be clean, with only a couple feet of water coursing through it. Reed splashed through first, motioning for the others to wait until he reached the far side and ducked into the trees. Half a mile up the valley, he saw the bridge—built of concrete and connecting the first ridge with the second. It was broad and reinforced with concrete buttresses beneath, no doubt designed to carry the crushing weight of the semi-trucks.

Reed wiped sweat off his face, then motioned Banks across. As he did, a distant thrashing sound caught his ear, coming from beyond the ridge they'd just descended. It grew rapidly louder, and Reed waved Banks back into the trees and then knelt in the undergrowth, turning his gaze skyward just as a helicopter rocketed over the top of the ridge and came into view.

Reed jerked the rifle into his shoulder, aligning the ACOG with the aircraft for the split second it was visible over the valley floor. In an instant, the helicopter passed overhead and disappeared beyond the next ridge, but for just a second, Reed swept the crosshairs of the optic across it, and that was enough.

The chopper was small and black—some kind of Eurocopter, he thought. Possibly a militarized variant of the EC145, or what the US Army called a Lakota. Reed couldn't be sure in the brief moment he glimpsed the aircraft, but as the sound faded onto the other side of the ridge, he thought he heard the engine slow and then die.

They landed on the other side.

Reed signaled for Banks and Wolfgang to follow, and as soon as they crossed, they began the punishing ascent up the backside of the second ridge. In places, the climb was so steep that Reed had to claw his way up using the trunks of small trees and thicker undergrowth. Banks's face flushed scarlet, and she struggled to breathe as she climbed. Reed remembered her Lyme disease and how at any time, it could flare into an inflammation strike that triggered sweats, loss of energy, and swollen joints. He wondered if the exertion was triggering a flare now, and he paused to let her catch up.

"You good?" he asked softly.

Banks panted and wiped sweaty hair out of her face. "I'm fine."

Reed reached into his backpack and produced a bottle of water. He offered Banks a drink, and she accepted it eagerly.

"Wishing you'd stayed in Alabama?" Reed asked.

She smirked. "You kidding? You fools would still be feeding monkeys without me."

Reed passed Wolfgang the water, and then they all fought the final hundred yards up the slope. As they neared the top, Reed thought he heard distant voices, and gestured for the others to slow. They decreased their speed to a creep, and Reed dropped onto his hands and knees. Little flying insects swarmed around his face, and a giant centipede scurried across the leaves near his hand. Reed navigated around it, then dropped to his stomach as he reached the crest of the ridge.

They faced north, with the sun beginning its descent to their left. Reed slid his pack off as Banks and Wolfgang wriggled up beside him, and he lifted a hand to block out the sun.

And then he saw it.

31

The valley floor beneath them wasn't as deep as the one they'd just climbed out of. It consisted of a floor about two hundred yards wide and a hundred deep, with ridges on three sides that formed a sort of horseshoe. The road that led up from the bridge fed into the open end of the horseshoe, and towering trees leaned over the valley and sheltered most of it from view of the sky.

The helicopter sat on a pad next to the road, its rotors stopped as heat waves wafted from the engine. Reed recognized one of Legion X's Humvees parked near it, and then he saw both Blond and Burly standing near the chopper, conversing with three men dressed in white hazmat suits.

An assortment of other vehicles—light trucks and small SUVS—sat in neat rows under the shelter of the trees. Reed judged them to be commuter vehicles that represented a workforce of anywhere between twenty and fifty people, depending on how aggressively they carpooled. Several South American men dressed in green fatigues paced near the roadway, armed with AK-47s as they completed security circuits around the parking lot before circling to the east end of the valley, opposite the helicopter pad.

And it was at the east end of the valley, at the bottom of the horseshoe of ridges, that the building stood. Actually, there were three buildings—all rectangular, all of equal size, and all constructed out of metal. They linked together in the shape of the letter U—a north building, an east building, and a south building—with the open end of that U facing west toward the helicopter pad and the road. A loading dock was along the backside of the U, and rolling metal doors were at both ends, while industrial ventilation stacks poked out of the roof of the south building.

Covering the entire facility was a camouflage mesh stretched over the valley floor and staked into the horseshoe ridges. The mesh was constructed of a synthetic netting, with little flaps of green and brown fabric attached to it that allowed exhaust to vent from the ventilation stacks, while, from a distance, giving the impression of fluttering tree leaves.

So satellites won't find it.

At the front door of the north building was a semi-trailer. It was the box-van kind, without a truck, and the back doors were shut. Through the open front doors of the north building, Reed could see men moving inside, but he couldn't make out details. The south building was locked up tight, with no windows or gaps in the metal construction, as was the east building. Everything looked new, fresh, and tight.

A purpose-built facility.

Reed lifted the rifle and pressed his eye to the ACOG again. The valley floor was only a hundred yards away, and with the magnification of the optic, he got a clear view of everything happening below.

"What do you see?" Banks whispered.

"It's some kind of production facility," Reed said. "There's two generator shacks built into the mountainside behind the east building. Probably diesel units with industrial cable powering the facility. I've got five, maybe six men visible at the opening of the north building. Looks like they're sweeping up."

Reed moved the rifle to the left—west, toward the helicopter. Blond and Burly had left the chopper, and Blond was busy pointing to spots along the roadbed, the valley walls, and around the parking lot. Three more Legion X gunmen appeared from the trees and slid open the side door of the helicopter. They lifted crates onto the dusty ground outside, and Reed recognized the familiar markings of military-grade explosives and land mines on the outside of the crates.

Great.

One of the South Americans in a hazmat suit followed Blond and Burly around the base of the valley, nodding and occasionally commenting as Blond continued to gesture at the valley walls. Reed caught only a few of the words, and they were all in Spanish.

"What's he saying?"

Banks leaned forward, stretching her neck to get as close to the top of the ridge as possible without sliding down the far side.

"I'm only getting fragments," she said. "He seems to be talking about security . . . outposts . . . explosives . . . perimeters."

Reed lowered the rifle and chewed his lip.

"What do you think?" Wolfgang asked.

"They're establishing a security ring. By this time tomorrow, they'll have trip wires and land mines all over the place. Probably sniper nests, too, or at least some kind of overwatch to guard the road."

"Why?" Banks asked. "What are they afraid of?"

Reed didn't answer immediately. It felt self-aggrandizing to assume he was the reason for all the additional security, but he couldn't think of an alternative explanation. If this was the heart of Aiden's operation, it made sense to be proactive and indulge in some overkill. Maybe Aiden was just thinking ahead.

"Look," Wolfgang said, pointing back to the building.

Reed lifted the rifle again and trained the optic on the rear of the semi-truck trailer. Several men in hazmat suits approached it and unlocked the doors. They swung open, then the men stepped back as a forklift appeared from inside the building and approached the back of the trailer. From his angle, Reed couldn't see what was inside, but the forklift stopped at the open doors, then reversed away from it, carrying a pallet laden with card-board boxes.

Banana boxes.

Reed traced the progress of the forklift back into the building, where other men in hazmat suits quickly transferred the pallet onto a pallet jack and wheeled it into the darkness. The forklift repeated the procedure, pulling pallets of bananas off the trailer while men operated the jacks on either end—pushing the pallets to the tail end of the trailer, and then taking them deeper into the building.

"What the hell?" Reed whispered.

"They're venting something," Wolfgang said. He lifted a pair of binoculars and pointed to the top of the south building. Reed moved the optic and saw an increase of white gas rising from the vents. It filtered through the mesh and rose to the sky, quickly dissipating and becoming invisible.

You don't get gas without heat.

He moved the rifle along the roof of the south building and then swept the outside wall facing their side of the valley. The optic came to rest against an industrial panel inscribed with red markings in Spanish. Mounted in the middle of the panel was a round metal wheel—like a cutoff valve—and beneath it was a large pipe fitting.

Reed couldn't read the Spanish, but he knew what he was looking at. It was the filler nozzle for an industrial propane tank, probably resting inside the building. The fuel source for whatever heat was now being generated to create the vent exhaust.

He lowered the rifle. Instinctually, he knew that all the pieces of this bizarre puzzle were now on the table. He could infiltrate the facility and look at what happened to the bananas once they came off the truck, but he didn't need to. He had enough data at hand to solve the riddle if he just arranged the parts in the right order.

Bananas are trucked to the facility. They undergo a procedure. Then they are shipped to America, under a time crunch. Meanwhile, Aiden is buying up large numbers of struggling pharmaceutical ventures. Why? What's he hiding?

Banks put a hand on Reed's arm, but he didn't move. He thought about the house in the woods and the videotapes. It was a blackmail operation, clearly. Who would Aiden need to blackmail? Who would he need to pressure to move his sludge through the pipes? What was his sludge?

Then Reed thought about Wolfgang's formula—some kind of genetic disease treatment, possibly invented by Frank Morccelli. A medication? If it was a medication, Aiden could sell it, right? For millions. There was so much money in medication. More than millions . . . Billions. But only if the medication *worked*, and then it was a legal operation, anyway. Whatever Aiden was up to, it clearly wasn't legal.

So he's got a potential medication, but it's not a working medication. It can't treat a known disease, so . . .

Valentina.

A chill ripped down Reed's spine. He thought of Valentina's daughter and the blood cancer. And then he thought about what Lucy found in Beaumont: a new treatment for cancer.

"Wolfgang, that formula Winter sent you . . . The one she captured from Aiden's organization."

"Yeah?"

"Was it a medication or a disease?"

"What do you mean?" Wolfgang said.

Reed turned to him. "You said it looked like a genetic therapy treatment. A medication used to alter the unhealthy replication of DNA and heal the process, right?"

"Right. In theory. It's all experimental."

"If you can use a drug to correct a genetic illness, could you use a drug to cause one?"

Wolfgang bit his tongue and thought a long moment, then made a noncommittal rock of his head. "It's possible. If a person was on the edge of a genetic disorder, the misapplication of drug therapy could, in theory, push them over the edge. But it would have to be a growth-type genetic disorder. Not something that altered their DNA, but something that leveraged existing, weak DNA into unhealthy replications. Cancer, essentially. And even then, you could inject a thousand people with the stuff, and maybe only one of them would develop the disease. What are you talking about?"

"I'm talking about Valentina's daughter," Reed said. "The local doctors think she has blood cancer, remember? And remember how Valentina talked about the bananas? She said her husband used to bring them home and they would eat them. What if the bananas made her daughter sick?"

"Sick *how*?" Wolfgang said.

"With the formula, Wolf. I read about it in North Carolina. Frank Morccelli wrote an article about his research with cell replication. He had a theory about curing cancer by using therapy treatments to replicate healthy cells."

"Right. It's not a new idea."

"What if he made it work?" Reed said. "What if Frank invented a therapy treatment that successfully instigated cell replication, but not the healthy kind? What if Frank mistakenly invented a drug that triggered cancer?"

Wolfgang shook his head. "Frank is dead, Reed. He's been dead for years."

"Exactly! We all think Aiden killed Frank, but we didn't know why. Picture this. Aiden, Holiday, and my father are running a drug-smuggling operation out of Colombia. Their operation is failing, and Aiden is looking for a new opportunity. Meanwhile, Frank has graduated from medical school and is busy researching methods to cure cancer using cell replication therapy. He stumbles on some ideas, but he doesn't have the funding to finish the research."

"How do you know about this?" Banks asked.

"It was all in the articles I read in North Carolina. Remember how I told Winter that I first read about Beaumont Pharmaceutical in those articles? I read about Beaumont *funding* Frank's research."

"And Beaumont is Aiden's company," Wolfgang said.

"Exactly. So maybe, when Aiden's cocaine operation failed, he heard about Frank's research and saw an opportunity. If a cancer cure could be invented, the upside would be in the billions. Trillions, maybe. So, he invested in Frank's research, using the shell corporation Beaumont Pharmaceutical."

"You're saying my father was working with Aiden?" Banks said, a tremor in her voice.

Reed shook his head. "Not directly. He probably knew Aiden was behind Beaumont, but that doesn't mean he knew anything about Aiden's dirty practices."

Wolfgang pointed to the facility on the valley floor. "What does any of that have to do with this?"

Reed held up a finger. "Assume that Frank's research failed. He wasn't able to create a therapy treatment to cure cancer, but he stumbled on a formula that triggered it. Not in everybody. One in a thousand, like you

said. Maybe less. So, he calls Aiden and lets him know the project is a fail-
ure, but Aiden sees an opportunity. A chance to make billions."

"By giving people cancer?" Banks said.

Wolfgang connected the dots, and his faced paled. "Yes. Because if you
know what's causing the cancer, you can cure it."

"That's what we're looking at," Reed said. "Aiden killed Frank, as we
thought, and took his research. And then Aiden used that research to create
a drug that gives one person out of a thousand cancer. Cancer he can *cure*."

"So he then invents an antidote," Wolfgang said. "Something that coun-
teracts the effects of his drug. Something that *looks* like a cure for cancer."

"And sells it wholesale," Banks finished.

Reed nodded. "That's where Beaumont Pharmaceutical comes back in.
Aiden produces the cure for his own poison and hides the development of
that cure in a mountain of acquisition paperwork for different pharmaceutical companies. Then all he has to do is obtain FDA approval to market the
drug."

Wolfgang snapped his fingers. "The house by the lake! There was an
FDA official on one of the tapes. Aiden used the brothel as a blackmail
operation to force the approval of his drug."

"Wait," Banks said. "You're telling me Aiden is purposefully poisoning
people with cancer, and then magically curing them with a miracle drug,
all to make it look like he has a miracle cancer cure?"

"Something like that would be worth billions," Wolfgang said.
"Infinitely more than shipping cocaine. If Aiden successfully poisoned ten
thousand people and cured even a third of them, the world would go nuts.
Anybody who had a similar type of cancer would want to try the drug.
Beaumont could charge whatever they wanted for it."

"It's bigger than that," Reed said. "This isn't a one-time trick. Aiden
could repeat the process with other diseases. Other drugs."

"An endless cycle," Banks said.

"A death cycle," Wolfgang said.

They fell silent while looking down into the valley again. More gas rose
from the second building, and the semi-truck was almost unloaded now.
Men in hazmat suits scurried everywhere, while other men in green
fatigues stood back and guarded the operation with assault rifles.

"Why bananas?" Banks asked.

"Why not?" Reed said. "After his years in the cocaine business, Aiden must've had connections down here, which gave him a place to set up this facility. His formula probably has a shelf life, which is why the *Santa Coquina* was under pressure to make port, despite the bananas requiring a ripening agent to turn yellow. The US probably consumes a few hundred million bananas every year. It's a perfect way to distribute your drug in mass, with nobody having a clue."

"And it would be impossible to backtrack," Wolfgang said. "If a hundred people got sick with the same type of cancer, nobody would think to check their fruit consumption. It's foolproof."

"I should've let you hunt the bastard down," Banks muttered.

Reed knew she must be thinking of her father, but he shook his head. "No, you were right about that. This is much bigger than Aiden. Even if I shot him, there's got to be an entire network of people behind this. The machine would churn out poison for weeks. Thousands could die. We have to pull this thing out by the roots."

"How?" Wolfgang asked.

"We get proof," Reed said. "Look at the facility. The north side is the treatment building where they poison the bananas. The east side is probably a warehouse where the bananas wait to be trucked out again. But the south building—the one with the vents—is the lab where they manufacture the poison. That's where we'll find ingredients and recipes. That's where we'll find proof."

"So, we have to get inside," Wolfgang said. "We have to get samples."

Reed nodded. "And we have to do it quickly, before our Legion X friends bottle this place up like Guantanamo Bay."

32

They retreated off the ridge to a clear spot between the trees, where Reed scraped the leaves aside and sketched out the valley floor with a stick. "Our objective is to infiltrate the south building and get a sample."

"Shouldn't be difficult to get in," Wolfgang said. "It's just a metal building. I'll go."

Reed looked up. "I was thinking you should hang back with Banks. There's no reason to risk more than we need to. If things go bad, I'd feel better knowing you were together."

Wolfgang shook his head. "You're forgetting about the guys in the hazmat suits. Whatever is inside that lab, it's not safe to handle. We don't know what we're walking into, but by far, I'm the best prepared to handle it. And besides, you'll be working on the chopper."

"The chopper?" Banks asked, but Reed already knew where he was headed.

Wolfgang picked up a stick and sketched an X where the helicopter pad sat.

"*If* things go bad, the last thing we want is that bird in the air. It'll be hell enough trying to get out of here on foot with all those gunmen down there. Doing it while they have an eye in the sky would be suicide. I'll infiltrate the building, obtain a sample, and snap some pictures. You disable the helicopter. Best-case scenario, I get out without fireworks, and we slip away. But if things go bad, we'll want it on the ground."

Reed envisioned the aircraft near the road and agreed with Wolfgang's logic. Reed hadn't observed any exterior weapons mounted on the helicopter, but it didn't really need any. With an open side door, a well-trained shooter could take them out like sitting ducks.

"Wait." Banks held up a hand. "I know I'm not a soldier or whatever, but wouldn't it make more sense to do this at night?"

Reed and Wolfgang shook their heads in unison.

"Usually, it would," Reed said, "but we've got two things working against us. First, Legion X brought all the tactical goodies to the party. I'd bet money they're equipped with infrared scopes and night vision. So, they'll be able to see us, and we won't be able to see them. And second, they're going to work right now securing the valley. By nightfall, they could have land mines, trip wires, and motion detectors all over the place. If I had the proper gear and a few trained operators at hand, I'd wait for nightfall. But as it is, our best chance is to move quickly."

Reed traced more lines in the sand, outlining the roadbed, the parked cars, and the semi-truck trailer. Because the helicopter was on the far side of the valley, he would have to follow the ridge behind the building and to the other side of the road before descending to the valley floor—or else descend on this side and walk across the facility parking lot like a fool.

Reed wasn't a fan of either option. So much movement in such close proximity to the enemy drastically increased his risk of exposure. But again, they couldn't afford to wait.

"I'll take the chopper," he said. "I'll follow the ridge to the other side and then slip up behind it. Wolfgang, you take the pistol and infiltrate the building from behind. There should be less security in back."

"What about me?" Banks asked.

Reed made a mark in the dirt at the end of the ridge they stood on, where it was closest to the roadbed.

"You'll hide here and keep the revolver. If all goes well, we'll rendezvous at your position as soon as Wolfgang gets out."

"And if doesn't?" she said.

Wolfgang and Reed exchanged a glance.

"If shit hits the fan," Reed said, "I'll grab a vehicle and, you know, we'll haul ass."

They all stared at the crude map in the dirt, then Wolfgang let out a laborious sigh. "You're going to be the death of me, Reed. No doubt about it." He kicked dirt over the map, then checked his pistol. "Let's do it."

Reed departed first, cradling the rifle in low-ready as he jogged through the trees to the bend in the horseshoe, then ran along the east ridge. Below him, he could see the backside of the east building, and his earlier suspicions about it being a warehouse were confirmed by an open rolling door and dozens of stacked banana pallets inside.

He checked his watch as he turned again, this time onto the north ridge, and knew that Wolfgang and Banks would split about now, each deploying to their separate positions.

A knot gathered in Reed's stomach—a not unfamiliar nervousness of impending action. No matter how many times he picked up a gun and charged headfirst into a fight, that feeling never left him. Over the years, he'd developed mental blocks that allowed him to remain focused despite the nerves, but he'd never been able to completely shut them down, and he wasn't sure he wanted to. Reed had met men who'd developed that level of callousness, and they were barely alive—like death angels who harmonized with nothing except bloodshed.

He could work past the nerves of being shot at, if it meant staying at least a little connected with his humanity. But what worried him most was Banks. In a mission like this, he would usually be alone, free to abort and vanish as soon as he needed to. But with Banks on the far ridge, alone and armed with nothing but four rounds of underpowered .38 Special, direct abortion wasn't an option. If shit hit the fan, he had to get her out.

Which is why shit can't hit the fan. This has to work.

Reed breathed easily, wiping sweat from his forehead. He'd seen no sign of the Legion X operators or any other security forces on the ridge, but he knew that would change after today. The hired guns with AK-47s might be untrained enough to leave the ridges and high points near the facility unguarded, but Legion X knew better. They would put overwatches in place around the ridge with clear shots down the road and over the entire facility.

He knew they would because *he* would.

When in doubt, always take the high ground.

As he reached the end of the north ridge, Reed slowed and moved easily from tree to tree, keeping in the shadows. He stepped carefully over dips in the earth and gaps between brush—exactly where a trip wire might be strung—then froze as a shadow moved in the trees.

Long practice had taught Reed to notice the way shapes and shadows moved in the natural world. Forests, deserts, and cities all have their own unique rhythms of noise and movement—a sort of heartbeat. In the forest, everything moved with the wind, turned toward the sun, and practiced a certain harmony that was as recognizable in Colombia as it was in Georgia.

So when something moved against that harmony, it stuck out, and the tail end of a shadow that moved against the wind twenty yards ahead caught Reed's eye. He slowed, kneeling in the leaves and raising the muzzle of the rifle. Again, the shadow moved—a twitching hard line that contrasted against the random curves of leaf shadows on the ground.

Then he heard the tapping sound, like pebbles dropped on the leafy floor. Reed crept forward, moving around the trees and giving the disturbance a wide berth until he circled far enough to bring it into focus. A man stood on the sheltered side of a towering wax palm tree, an AK-47 resting against the tree trunk as he dumped pistachios out of a plastic baggie into his mouth and crunched them like a beaver gnawing on a tree. Fragments of the nuts rained down over the leaves, resulting in the little tapping sounds Reed heard before.

Reed couldn't approach the slope leading down to the chopper without crossing in front of the sentry. He didn't want to kill the man, but a glance at his watch confirmed that Banks would be in position now, and Wolfgang would make his intrusion at any moment. Every minute that ticked by increased the opportunity for Wolfgang to be noticed, the alarm to be sounded, and the helicopter to take flight.

Reed circled back the way he'd come, positioning the wax palm between himself and the sentry before he began his approach. Each step was calculated, choosing hard sections of dirt with minimal leaves and no sticks. Twenty yards became ten, and then five. More pistachio fragments hit the ground as the sentry completed his noisy snack, and Reed closed to the backside of the tree. He thought momentarily about the knife in his backpack—the weapon he'd used to kill the Legion X operator outside Valentina's smoldering cottage.

No. I'm not killing this man.

Whoever the gunman with the AK was, he wasn't a deliberate participant in Aiden's death cycle. He was just a local in need of work who took whatever job he could find. Whatever it took to feed his family.

He's still gonna have a hell of a headache.

Reed leaned his rifle against the backside of the tree, then circled quickly to the front, moving in a rush and closing in on the sentry before he had time to react. The AK fell to the forest floor, and Reed grabbed the man by the left shoulder, then cocked his fist and drove the heel of his hand directly into the man's forehead.

The sentry's head snapped back against the wax palm, and he crumpled to the forest floor as limp as a rag doll.

Find another job, buddy.

Reed knelt next to the body and sifted quickly through his pockets. He found a cell phone, a wallet, a pair of car keys, and more pistachios. And then the AK.

Reed scooped up both rifles and started down the slope, still taking care to avoid sketchy spots with poor footing or potential trip wires. He found a path this time, well worn by the sentry on his way up and down this part of the ridge, and Reed made it to the bottom in less than two minutes.

The Lakota helicopter sat fifty feet outside the tree line on a flat patch of dirt with a crude white H painted on it. Thirty feet to the left was Legion X's second Humvee, and Reed wondered where the first vehicle was. Burly had taken the second one there, leaving Blond behind, apparently to wait for the men who killed his operator to show up.

Blond had later taken the Lakota to the facility in the mountains. So, where was the first Humvee? Was it still en route with the rest of the Legion X team?

Reed decided he didn't have time to worry about it. He knelt behind a tree at the base of the ridge and cast a quick look around the valley floor. Blond, Burly, and the handful of other Legion X operators who had arrived in either the helicopter or the Humvee were nowhere to be seen, and neither were the men with AK-47s he'd seen before. As Reed leaned out from the trees, he thought he heard voices from the far side of the parking lot, at the other side of the valley floor, and he concluded that Blond and his men must be scoping out positions for their security equipment.

He turned back to the helicopter and surveyed it from tail to nose. The aircraft sat with its rear pointed almost directly at him, one door open, each of its four rotor blades drooping and swaying a little in the breeze. Up close, it looked a lot bigger than it had from a distance, and also less destructible.

Reed didn't know much about helicopters. During his time with the Marines, he'd ridden in a helicopter on a couple occasions, and the only thing he'd learned from either experience was that Marine pilots were too crazy, even for him. He had no idea how to go about disabling the Lakota, but even a rudimentary understanding of physics informed him that if either the main rotor or the tail rotor failed, the aircraft wasn't going anywhere. The tail rotor would be easier to reach, and being smaller might be easier to damage. Reed scanned the valley floor again for signs of sentries or Legion X, then slung the H&K over his back, cradled the AK, and dashed for the chopper.

He made for the sheltered side of the aircraft, keeping it between himself and the facility and bringing the AK to eye level as he reached the open side door. A quick sweep of the rifle covered the rear of the chopper, but nobody was inside. Reed checked the cockpit and likewise found it empty. Then he retreated to the tail and examined the rotor.

The Lakota featured a tail with two elevator planes shooting out on either side, and the rotor itself mounted between them, about eight feet off the ground. The bottom end of the blade came down to head-height for Reed, but even if he stretched, he couldn't reach the middle portion where the rotor was bolted to the tail. He shielded his eyes and examined the setup, noting the metal hydraulic pipes housed behind the rotor's axis.

If I could break one loose, the controls might fail.

Reed reached for the rear elevator plane, ready to haul himself up onto the tail so he could reach the rotor. Then he heard a chorus of shouts, followed by gunshots from the facility. Reed turned and saw two Legion X gunmen running for the lab, weapons drawn as more pistol shots snapped from inside the building and men shouted.

Wolfgang.

Reed turned back to the helicopter, his heart pounding as combat instincts took over. When all else failed, one thing never did—brute force. He slapped the selector lever on the side of the AK to full-auto and unloaded on the Lakota. The gun chattered and spat fire from his hip, spraying .30 caliber slugs through the open door and across the inside of the aircraft, blasting out the windshield and ripping through the cockpit. The noise of the rifle blocked out the gunshots and shouts from the building, but out of his peripheral vision, Reed was aware of two Legion X gunmen turning his way.

The AK clicked over an empty chamber, and Reed slung it down. Before either man could react, he circled the helicopter and threw himself at the parked Humvee. More shouts were followed by the pop of controlled rifle fire, and bullets slammed into the far side of the vehicle. Reed jerked the door open and hopped in, flicking the ignition switch from Engine Stop to Run, and waited as the glow plugs mounted inside the Humvee's engine warmed.

More bullets struck the Humvee, and Reed heard a low hiss from a back tire, but it didn't matter. The vehicle was fitted with run-flat tires, armored walls, and bulletproof glass. He smacked the steering wheel and gritted his teeth. The sounds from behind him confirmed that Legion X was aware of his presence. He had only seconds left before they reached the Humvee.

The light above the ignition switch turned orange, signaling that the glow plugs were now warm and the diesel would start. Reed shoved the switch to start, and the big engine fired up, growling like a caged beast ready to break free.

Reed slammed the gearshift into reverse and shoved his foot into the accelerator. The back tires spun, and the Humvee rocketed away from the helicopter, its back end pointed toward the lab as Reed stared into the side-view mirror and steered with one hand. Something thumped against the rear of the Humvee, then the passenger-side rear tire hopped over what Reed guessed to be a body. He ignored it all, guiding the vehicle directly into the closed metal door of the lab.

The rear bumper collided with the door in a screech of metal on metal, tearing through it as Reed kept his foot on the gas. As soon as he entered the building, he was conscious of gunshots and shouts from all around him, and a red light flashed overhead. Reed slammed on the brake, then kicked his door open. He was immediately confronted by one of the local gunmen, who brandished an AK but seemed stunned by the sudden appearance of the Humvee.

Reed shoved his H&K through the door and yanked on the trigger. The man went down under a ravaging blast of bullets, and Reed screamed out the door, "Wolfgang! Let's go!"

He slammed the shifter into drive and looked ahead. Through the shredded metal door were two Legion X operatives training their weapons on the front end of the Humvee from behind the cover of parked vehicles. Bullets smacked against the armor and ricocheted off the bulletproof windshield.

Reed shouted again over his shoulder. "Now or never!"

The door behind him screeched open, and Wolfgang flung himself inside, landing on his stomach with his back legs still protruding from the rear door.

"Go! Go! Go!"

Reed hit the gas. Metal screamed against metal again, and an unearthly crunching sound filled the cabin of the Humvee as the rear door was shoved shut by the building's passing doorframe. Wolfgang shrieked in pain but remained inside as Reed turned for the nearest gunman, roaring directly at his position.

"Get inside!" Reed shouted.

Wolfgang pulled his legs in just before Reed sideswiped the operative's cover vehicle, sending it crashing toward him and cutting off the gunfire. But more rifles opened up from behind, and a hail of bullets struck the Humvee on all sides. Reed jerked the wheel to the left and shoved his foot into the floor, then tilted his head to the side to look up the ridge.

Banks.

She was sliding down the far end of the south ridge, half-falling, half-running from tree to tree in a cloud of leaves and dirt as the shouts and gunfire continued.

He hit the road and turned left, rounding the corner around the base of the ridge and slamming on the brakes. The Humvee slid to a stop, and Reed threw his door open. "Come on!"

Banks reached the bottom and burst onto the road, snatching open the same door Wolfgang had entered through and crashing on top of him. Wolfgang cried out again, and Reed hit the gas.

Dirt exploded on all sides of the Humvee as the back door smacked shut and Banks shouted something about blood. Reed looked over his shoulder and saw the floorboard behind him slick with crimson as Wolfgang huddled in one seat, holding his leg. Even with a glance, Reed could see a long, jagged rip that ran the length of his outer thigh, probably caused by the lab's doorframe as Reed fled the building.

"Did you get anything?" Reed asked.

Wolfgang gritted his teeth and shook his head. "Got . . . caught."

Reed looked forward, mapping out the path ahead. Another fifty yards, and he would hit the bridge, followed by the endless dirt road out of the mountains, probably with Legion X on his heels.

Reed turned the corner and again slammed on the brakes as the Humvee hit the bridge. Thirty yards ahead, at the other end of the bridge, the second Legion X Humvee blocked his path, four more operators piling out of it with rifles at the ready. As soon as they made eye contact, they opened fire, and a hail of lead smacked the front end of the Humvee. Reed ducked instinctively as the windshield turned milky white under a barrage of hits. None of the small-caliber rounds penetrated the thick glass, but within seconds, the crumbling outer layers rendered the glass a solid wall of white, impossible to see through.

"What are you doing?" Wolfgang shouted. "Go!"

But Reed couldn't go. If any other vehicle sat at the other end of that bridge—a pickup truck or a van—he could smash through it without trouble, slinging it aside and powering through. But hitting another Humvee head-on would bring him to a bone-crushing stop, and long before he could maneuver his way around it, Legion X operatives would enter his vehicle by force.

More bullets ricocheted across the Humvee, and one front-tire hissed. Reed reached for the gearshift, sliding it into reverse as another sound reached his ears: the deep, throbbing roar of a helicopter.

33

Reed's blood ran cold, but he hit the gas as his left-hand mirror succumbed to gunfire.

"Is that the helicopter?" Wolfgang shouted.

Reed said nothing, turning to the right-hand mirror and jerking the wheel just in time to miss a giant pothole. Then the right-hand mirror was also blown away, and a moment later, the rear of the Humvee slammed into what must have been another vehicle. Metal crunched, and men shouted. Reed's head slammed into his seat, and the gunshots outside the Humvee were now only feet away.

And worst of all, the steady *whap* of the helicopter was growing louder. He was sure now that whatever he'd done with the AK wasn't enough. The bird had left the ground.

"You said you'd get the chopper!" Wolfgang shouted.

Reed ignored him and put the Humvee back into drive. "Heads down!"

He located the two quick-release pins holding the windshield in place. After snatching both free, he drove his palm into the backside of the compromised glass, and the entire panel pivoted on its bottom-mounted hinges, smashing into the hood of the Humvee and clearing his view.

Reed hit the gas again. Once more, gunfire burst from the bridge, and Reed ducked as a bullet ricocheted off the Humvee's A-pillar. Wolfgang shouted, and the *whap* of the helicopter grew louder, buzzing directly overhead.

Reed kept one eye above the dash and hurtled toward the bridge. Then, at the last second, he jerked the Humvee to the right. "Hold on!"

The bumper of the vehicle crashed into the brush at the right side of the bridge, and then the front tires left the dirt. Reed felt his stomach fly into his mouth as bullets skipped across the roof, and the nose of the Humvee dropped like a rock. The front tires hit dirt again, and they crashed downward, hurtling along on a demented roller-coaster ride that ended at the bottom of the ravine.

Trees smacked against the doors, and the Humvee hurtled over rocks and fallen logs. Reed clung to the wheel with both hands and kept his foot planted into the accelerator. The diesel motor churned, and everything turned to a blur, then water exploded over the hood as they struck the river.

For a moment, they lost traction, sliding into the mud as water surged up to the bottom of the doorjamb and leaked onto the floorboard. The back end of the Humvee left the bank and slid across slick rocks as the current shoved them downstream. One wheel locked against something solid, and the other three bit. Water washed over the hood and rushed in through the open hole of the windshield, soaking Reed in a moment as the Humvee plowed downriver.

Bullets continued to strike the roof, but they found their mark with less force now, and directly ahead was a bend in the ravine that would bring them shelter—if they could make it that far. His ears rang so loudly he couldn't hear the chopper anymore, but he knew it had to have been close. They could outrun the vehicles, but they couldn't outrun the bird. Not in an open gorge.

Get to the bend, then ditch the vehicle.

The tires slipped, and Reed looked down to see two inches of water in the footwell, still lapping in from the doorjamb. He had plenty of experience in Humvees, but they all involved desert climates. How deep could the river get before the diesel choked out?

Reed turned the corner of the gorge, and suddenly neither the chopper, nor the gunfire, nor the depth of the water mattered. He slammed on the brake, but it was already too late. The weight of the water pushing from behind drove them toward the drop-off directly ahead as white mist rose from the crashing waterfall falling over it.

"Bail!" Reed shouted, but again, it was too late. The front end of the Humvee dropped straight down. Reed grabbed the wheel to hold himself to the seat as his vision blurred around the wide pool the waterfall emptied into twenty feet below. The front bumper made impact in a roar of white spray, and the heavy vehicle shot down like a rock. Water surged in through the open windshield and rushed over Reed's head as he sucked in a last lungful of air. Everything turned black and icy cold.

Reed kicked free of the floorboard and pushed off from the steering wheel. Above him, a trace of light shone in from one of the back windows, and Banks's foot rocketed past his head. Then Reed heard metal groan, and the Humvee toppled forward again.

Banks's soft hand clasped around Reed's as the roof of the Humvee crashed into the surface and more water rushed in through the open windshield. He couldn't see Wolfgang anywhere—everything was dark, and now the entire vehicle was flooded with water.

Reed's lungs burned, and each heartbeat sent throbbing pain through his skull. He reached up and felt the familiar profile of a Humvee's rear seat and followed that outline to the back door. It was still shut, but his fingers found the latch, and he kicked out with one foot.

Banks thrashed next to him, panic ripping down her arm like a shock wave. Reed gripped her hand and kicked the door again. It gave a little beneath his foot, and a third blow shoved it into the blackness beyond.

Reed pulled Banks downward toward the door. She fought back, and her flailing free hand struck him in the jaw. Reed's head spun, and the world around him slowed.

I'm losing consciousness. I have to breathe.

Reed jerked Banks's arm, not giving her the option of fighting him as he grabbed the bottom side of the doorframe and pulled himself through. Banks thrashed but followed, and they cleared the doorframe and kicked into open water.

Bright sunlight streamed in from overhead, glimmering through the water like Heaven itself, just out of reach. His body shook, and darkness closed in from the edges of his vision. Reed shoved off from the overturned Humvee and pushed upward.

They broke through the surface, both gasping for air as water from the nearby falls sprayed their faces. Reed thrashed to stay above the waterline as Banks panicked and started to sink. He pulled her up by the arm, going under himself for a moment before breaking through again.

Reed gasped down more air. He shook his head to clear it and saw the edges of a wide pool all around him, with jungle trees leaning over it. They were in the middle, forty feet from either bank. Men shouted in the distance, and the endless *whap* of the helicopter echoed from the sky.

"Wolfgang!" Reed shouted.

His eyes were still blurred with water and grit. He shouted again, still holding Banks above the surface.

Then Reed saw him. Wolfgang floated face-up, a trail of crimson staining the water near his leg as he drifted out of the pool and back into the river. Reed shouted again, but Wolfgang didn't answer or move.

The roar of the helicopter burst from the top of the waterfall. The aircraft hovered only a hundred feet up, swaying and dipping erratically as if the pilot struggled to control it. But the side door was open, and the outline of a rifle poked out.

"Swim!" Reed shouted, pulling Banks as he kicked toward shore.

Banks gasped for air but began to kick. Reed dug in with both arms, planting his face in the water and reaching for shore with everything he had. As he twisted his face to suck down air, he heard a rifle shot from the helicopter, and a bullet struck the water a few feet away. Out of his peripheral vision, he saw the pilot continuing his fight with the controls, but the next bullet struck only inches from his ribcage.

"Go!" Reed shouted, pushing Banks ahead. The shore was only twenty feet away now. Then ten. Soft mud scraped his sternum as he reached for the shore, then another two gunshots struck the water so close to his ears, that for a second, all he could see was a wall of white spray.

Mud squished beneath his knees, and Reed grabbed Banks by the hand. He rushed for the wall of trees only feet away, Banks stumbling behind him.

Almost there.

Then Banks slipped, and her fingers broke away from his as her knees hit the mud, and she caught herself on one elbow. Reed slid to a stop and turned back, reaching out for her hand. Banks grabbed his arm and clawed her way back to her feet, and then the bullet struck home.

Reed didn't see the blood or hear the gunshot. Banks just froze, and a twisted grimace of unprecedented pain crossed her face. Her cheeks flushed pale, and she stumbled, almost falling.

Maddened fear crashed through Reed like nothing he'd ever felt before. He rushed forward and wrapped both arms around Banks, feeling hot blood streaming from her side as he jumped for the trees. They hurtled to the ground, just inside the jungle. Dirt, leaves, and rocks exploded around them, and they rolled, crashing between trees and sliding to a stop under the shelter of the thick canopy. Bullets zipped at random through the leaves, smacking into trees and hitting the mud as Reed rolled to his knees, still clutching Banks. He pulled her into his chest and thrashed deeper into the brush, kicking aside a snake and finding shelter behind a massive wax palm as the bullets flew wider around him. Banks lay in his arms, not moving or making a sound.

Momentary desperation clouded his mind, and he shoved it back, refusing to surrender to panic. "Banks! Can you hear me?"

Reed moved his hands along her side, searching for the wound and finding it just above her hipbone, six inches to the right of her spine. He couldn't find an exit wound, and when he checked her pulse, it felt weak and slow.

Reed set her down on the leaves that were now coated in her blood, and he rolled her onto her stomach. He pulled her shirt up to examine the wound. It wasn't large—probably inflicted by a 5.56 caliber round—and the fact that Banks was still breathing told him the bullet hadn't obliterated any vital organs. But if he didn't stop the bleeding, none of that would matter.

Reed tore the backpack off and ripped through the contents, spilling Colombian currency on the ground as he dug out the first-aid kit. It was small—not at all the right kind of trauma kit for a situation like this, but it would have to do.

He located a roll of gauze and a tube of antibiotic ointment. After coating a wad of the gauze in the ointment, he twisted it into a tight roll and forced it into the bullet wound. The gauze was too large for the hole, but it needed to be. He kept pressing until a full inch of gauze penetrated the wound, then he wound a roll of medical tape around her stomach, pulling it as tight as possible over the gauze.

Pressure is the key.

If he could keep enough pressure on the wound to stop it from bleeding, he might buy enough time to get help.

As he worked, Banks lay motionless—still breathing but unresponsive.

"Stay with me, Banks. Don't you dare let go!"

After exhausting the tape, Reed ripped his shirt off and tore it into strips, quickly wrapping them around her body, cinching them tight, and adding more pressure to the wound. As he finished the last knot, shouts rang out from behind him—all in Spanish. Reed looked over his shoulder and saw men in green fatigues flow onto the bank of the pool, all wielding AKs. They pointed toward something down the river and shouted, then they ran in that direction.

I can't save Wolfgang now.

The panic that lay at bay behind a practiced armor of discipline overwhelmed Reed's mind. He pressed harder against Banks's wound as he thought about his options. Banks had hours, at most. A gutshot was one of the worst ways to die. It rarely killed you quickly, but it almost always got you in the end. She needed expert medical care long before then—antibiotics, fluids, and surgery to remove the bullet.

The phone.

Reed returned to the backpack and snatched the satellite phone out. His fingers smeared blood over the screen, and it almost slipped out of his hands. He wiped the phone against his pants leg and punched in a number.

The keys didn't illuminate in green, and the phone didn't make little beeping noises as he was accustomed to. He thought it might be turned off, but when he tried the power button, a dead battery symbol flashed across the screen.

He bit back a curse and forced himself to remain focused.

Think. There's always a solution.

Reed pictured the maps of Colombia on Wolfgang's phone and thought about the nearest city or hospital. It would be dozens, if not a hundred kilometers away, and even if he could reach the hidden Toyota, he could never hope to make it to the end of the road without being spotted by the helicopter.

I need help, now. Here, in the jungle.

Then he remembered what Valentina said about the people in the mountains—deep in the mountains, far from civilization.

Reed scooped Banks up and pulled her closer to his chest, breathing soft words of comfort just in case she could hear him. Then he turned away from the river, deeper into the forest, and broke into a run.

34

The afternoon stretched into evening, and Reed kept running. His boots sloshed water and wore blisters on his feet, and flying insects stung the exposed skin of his back and arms. Trees blurred together, and the ravines rose and fell, at times leaving him running along the bottoms of gorges, and at other times forcing him to claw his way up steep inclines, still clutching Banks.

She rode in his arms like a corpse, her head rolling and her arms dragging the ground whenever he bent to slide under a tree. Her blood stained his chest and pants, but her heart continued to beat, and the bleeding had subsided.

The voices of the men on his trail and the beat of the helicopter's rotors faded behind him as darkness fell over Colombia. Reed had no idea how far he'd run or how far he had to run. He only knew which direction he was headed—deeper into the mountains. Deeper into Antioquia Department.

As the last light faded over the mountains, Reed stumbled and began to give out. He was in good shape, and years of regular workouts during his time as an assassin had strengthened the muscles in his arms, chest, and legs into cords of steel that had more than once saved his life. But nothing lasts forever, and as he crashed into a tree and stumbled to his knees, he knew he was reaching his limit.

All around him was darkness. The trees blocked out the sky, and no hint of the moon or the stars broke through the leaves. The occasional rattle of a small animal scurrying across the leaves ripped through the forest like a burst of gunfire as Reed laid Banks on the leaves and leaned against a tree, wheezing.

He was thirsty, and every part of him hurt. His eyes slowly adjusted to the darkness, allowing him to recognize the outlines of trees or fallen logs, but the blackness of this place was so deep and perfect that even those vague shapes blended together, and Reed could barely see his own hand in front of his face.

"Banks?" Reed rasped. His tongue felt thick in his mouth, and his lips were so dry they cracked when he spoke. He felt her wrist again. The heartbeat was still there, but slower and softer than ever. If he leaned his ear close to her mouth, he could hear her breaths, but they were ragged and far apart.

"Banks . . . my god," he whispered.

Again Reed felt for her wound. The blood around it had dried, forming a thick crust that improved the effectiveness of his battlefield bandage, but Reed wondered how much blood she'd lost and how desperately she needed fluids.

How long did she have? An hour? Two?

I should never have brought her. This is all my fault.

Reed slouched against the tree. The scurrying creatures around him were now joined by a host of other forest sounds so otherworldly that Reed wondered if he was imagining them: the call of a strange bird in the trees; the flap of its wings as it took flight; then the creak of a tree as it settled down again. Reed closed his eyes, and more forest noises joined that of the bird: the creak of strange insects and the cries of distant primates. Probably more monkeys, like the ones Banks saw on their drive into the mountains.

Banks. He'd failed her. He'd brought her to this distant, strange place to try to end this war, and all he'd done was make her a casualty. Reed screamed. He shouted at the treetops until his throat went dry. He didn't care who heard him anymore. The Legion X operators had given up chasing him hours before, but even if they followed, he didn't care.

Maybe he should have surrendered to them. Maybe they would've saved Banks in exchange for his own life.

No. It was a bizarre, stupid idea, concocted by his delirious mind on its way out of existence.

She's going to die. I'm going to die. And Aiden will live on, as always.

Reed threw his head back and screamed again, slamming both hands into the ground. He blinked at the sky and thought he saw light—a bulb not far away, but just out of reach. Then the light faded. He placed a hand on Banks's arm and cursed himself for the last time. He should've made for the SUV. Run for the road. Maybe he would've found help.

The scream tore through the night from deep in the trees. It was a long, shrill, bloodcurdling sound that chilled Reed to the very bone. He sat upright and froze, not moving and wondering if the scream, like the light, was all in his head. But then the sound came again, louder this time and more immediate—more a roar than a scream, but so ferocious it sounded inhuman.

A jungle cat.

Reed sat motionless, running his tongue over dry lips.

Is it a tiger? No, tigers are native to Africa and Asia, not South America. This must be some other breed of hunting feline. A puma?

The scream repeated once more, and much closer now, just on the other side of the trees. It was so loud it seemed to shake the leaves on the ground.

A jaguar.

Reed's exhaustion of just moments before vanished in a flood of adrenaline as the thump of heavy feet echoed through the trees. He snatched Banks up and ran again, crashing forward through the dark, heedless of what lay ahead. The easy lope of the big cat's feet pounded not far behind him, but the jaguar didn't scream again. The big cat was closing in, stalking his prey, breathing in the rich scent of human blood.

Reed thought about the trees but instantly scrapped the idea. He knew little about jaguars, or big cats in general, but he knew they could climb. He knew their paws were equipped with razor-sharp claws that were equally as effective at gripping tree bark and shredding skin.

He would never have a chance in a tree, struggling to climb while holding Banks. He didn't have a chance running, either, but without a weapon, he had no choice.

Reed hurtled forward, and again he thought he saw light ahead. But this time, even when he blinked, the light didn't fade. It was vague and soft, almost like a brighter shade of black that was only visible because everything around it was so dark.

With every stride, the footfalls of the big cat thumped a little closer behind him, and Reed suddenly had the idea that the jaguar wasn't even running that hard. He was just loping, easily keeping up with his prey while conserving energy. Time was on the jaguar's side, after all. Before long, Reed would collapse, and the cat could then pounce on an almost defenseless prey. A good meal, dirty or otherwise.

Two good meals.

Fear and fresh adrenaline surged through his body, and Reed ran for the light. It grew a little brighter with each stride, still not so much a light as a contrast, but enough for him to focus on. The jaguar screamed again— softer this time, yet so much more chilling than the first cry.

The contrast ahead grew brighter as he saw a break between the trees. He hurtled forward as the loping of the cat closed to within yards, then Reed broke out of the trees and fell over a shallow ditch, rolling into a roadbed. Dirt and sticks bit his back, and Banks tumbled out of his arms. The black sky above was lit by stars that were just bright enough to provide the contrast he'd notice before, and the jaguar crashed through the trees behind him, followed by another roar. A hungry roar. The final roar.

Reed clawed backward and flailed around for any sort of weapon, but his fingers found only sand. He flung it desperately in the direction of the roar as he saw the outline of the cat break through the trees. It soared out of the darkness with its front paws spread, teeth bared, only seconds from crashing down on top of him.

Then the gunshots started, bursting out of the trees behind Reed, the rapid pop of an assault rifle sending consecutive three-round bursts blasting over the roadbed. The cat screamed again and hit the dirt, flailing feet away from Reed's legs. Blood sprayed into the air, and then a final gunshot struck the cat in the side of the head, sending it rolling into the ditch. The jaguar lay motionless as Reed continued to claw backwards, gasping.

Boots thundered against the dirt, and all at once, a small army of men burst from the forest. They wielded assault rifles and wore green fatigues, like the men at the facility. Only these men were large and well fed, and weapon lights shone from the ends of their rifles.

Reed shielded his eyes as a barrage of shouts assaulted him, and Reed understood none of them. He put both hands up as the sharp end of muzzle-breaks prodded him in the ribs. The Spanish shouting continued, then an individual voice boomed above the rest, and the voices all stopped at once.

Reed kept his hands up. The weapon lights dimmed, pointed toward the ground as a boot struck him in the side.

"¿Quién eres tú?" somebody said.

Reed looked up, keeping his hands above his head. A South American man stood next to him, a pistol pointed at Reed's head. The men around him pointed their weapon lights to the ground, but the glow was still strong enough for Reed to make out details of their faces and their gear.

The green fatigues were splotched with camouflage, like old army BDUs, but these men weren't Colombian army. They wore no hats, and they carried outdated weapons—AK-47s, AK-74s, and an assortment of American castoffs. But the detail that really caught his eye was the little patch they wore on their arms, just below the shoulder. It was round, made of black fabric, with a red insignia stitched onto it. The face of a devil.

Reed swallowed as the man with the pistol kicked him again and repeated the question.

"El Diablo!" Reed said. "Take me to The Devil."

35

The men exchanged a round of looks, then somebody put a boot between Reed's shoulder blades and shoved him into the mud. His arms were wrenched behind his back and tied in place with zip ties, then a black hood slid over his head.

"The woman!" he said. "Bring the woman!"

He was answered with a kick in the ribs, then hauled to his feet. Brush tore at his legs as they pushed him through the trees, then he heard the familiar squeak of a vehicle door swinging on weary hinges. Men shouted, and an engine fired up. Reed was shoved into what may have been the bed of a pickup truck or a big SUV, then the vehicle rolled forward. Reed counted voices and thought four or five men rode nearby. By the fresh air that still blew across his arms, he concluded the vehicle to be a pickup, with some of the gunmen riding next to him. He lifted his head, and once more, a boot crashed into his ribs. Reed recoiled, and his arms landed on something soft, wet, and furry. The jaguar. The men brought it with them, but why?

The truck bumped along rough roads, and Reed kept his head down. He could only pray that they also brought Banks and that she wasn't being kicked back and forth across another truck bed like a hockey puck. She wouldn't survive that, and without immediate medical care, she might not survive much of anything.

Minutes slipped into half an hour or maybe more. Reed lost track of time and focused on keeping his breathing calm and listening for any telling details about the men around him. They didn't talk much, and when they did, it was all in curt Spanish. Weapons clicked against the side of the truck, and from time to time, he heard a sloshing sound as somebody took a drink. His mouth was so dry his tongue felt like wood, but he decided not to mention it. These men were edgy enough.

At last, the pickup ground to a halt, and more Spanish shouting commenced. There seemed to be some kind of exchange—questions, followed by answers, followed by what must've been a joke because everybody laughed and somebody toed Reed again. Then the electric whine of a motor was followed by the clink of an automated gate rolling open, and the pickup started forward again up a hill.

Reed could feel the incline, and he braced himself against the tailgate as the truck left the rutted roadbed and hit smooth asphalt. The air tasted fresher, too, with the unique fragrance of fruit blossoms and mown grass. Five minutes passed, then the truck stopped, and boots hit the ground. The tailgate slammed down, and harsh hands closed around his legs, jerking him out. Somebody shouted in Spanish, and Reed recognized the voice of the man who first spoke to him back in the forest. The leader, probably.

Reed stumbled on his feet, and a rifle barrel poked him in the spine. They shoved him off the asphalt and onto gravel, then his feet crunched onto a manicured lawn. They pushed him along for a hundred yards before he smelled the familiar odor of chlorine.

A pool?

Gentle water ran in the background, lapping over stones or other obstructions. The man with the rifle shoved him another several paces, then a surprise kick to the back of his right leg drove him to his knees. The hood was snatched off, and blinding light flooded his eyes. Reed dropped his head, conscious of the rifle muzzle still only a breath from his back. He twisted his hands inside the plastic ties and cast a quick look around without lifting his head.

Men framed him on either side, and at least one stood behind him—

the asshole with the rifle. He kneeled on white concrete, and only a few feet to his right was a brilliant blue pool illuminated by underwater lights. The running water he heard earlier was from an artificial waterfall on the far side. Water ran down fancy, polished stones and landed in the pool in a gentle stream. It made him thirstier, but he didn't move.

A rifle butt smacked Reed in the back of his head, sending a wave of pain radiating through his skull and driving his face down again. He tried not to fall as soft steps approached him, and everybody became suddenly still. Reed kept his face down and breathed measured breaths, ready for whatever came next.

A rifle muzzle slid beneath Reed's chin and pushed his head up. The man standing in front of him was altogether what a police description might call *medium build*, with a slim but gently muscled frame. He was Colombian, or at least South American, with neatly groomed dark black hair that was combed to one side. He wore a men's nightshirt, made of black silk and belted at the waist, and he held a beer with one hand while the other hung casually at his side.

The man watched Reed a long time, his dark face almost completely impassive. After taking a sip of a beer, he muttered a single word in Spanish. One of the men behind Reed rushed forward and collected an outdoor chair from the pool deck, then positioned it behind the man. He sat down, brushing something off his nightshirt, and then leaned back. His knees fell apart, fully exposing his crotch inside the nightshirt. Reed looked away, and a sarcastic smile spread across the man's lips.

He took another sip of the beer and then spoke in flawless but heavily accented English. "Who are you, gringo?"

Reed licked his lips. They were so dry it was difficult to speak. The rifle prodded him in the back, and one of the gunmen snapped at him in Spanish. Reed tried again and managed nothing more than a dry hiss.

Again with the rifle, but the man in the chair snapped his fingers and said something curt in Spanish. The gunman ducked his head and disappeared behind Reed, reappearing a minute later with a bottle of water. He uncapped it and grabbed Reed by his hair, yanking his head back and dumping water between his lips. Reed gulped it down as quickly as he could, only swallowing about half of it as the rest drained down his bare chest and sprinkled the concrete. The bottled emptied, and the man let go of his hair. Reed coughed and looked down.

"You are welcome," the man in the chair said. He hadn't moved since sitting down—still leaned back with his knees spread, his hands resting casually on the arms of the chair. The picture of condescending confidence.

"Thank you," Reed said. His voice still croaked, but at least he could now feel his tongue.

The man took a sip of his beer, then grunted. "Who are you?"

"My name is Reed. There was a woman with me. Is she—"

"My men have your woman, gringo. Right now, we speak of you."

"She needs help," Reed pressed. "She's been shot. Please."

Reed looked up, and the man took another long sip of his beer. He smacked his lips and burped, never taking his eyes off Reed. "Do you know who I am?"

Reed held the man's gaze. "You're El Diablo. The Devil."

The man swirled the beer in its bottle. "Sí. I am The Devil. The king of these mountains. A man to be feared, some say. So, why are you here?"

"I came for help," Reed said. "The woman was shot. She needs medical care."

"And why would I help a criminal?"

Reed wasn't sure if the comment was calculated or if this man somehow knew a great deal more about him than he should. Or perhaps the man was simply being sarcastic because he himself was a criminal. Reed didn't have time for mind games.

"I'm not a criminal."

The man's eyes widened in indignation. "You lie! You killed the jaguar —the great jungle cat. It is illegal to kill a jaguar."

"I didn't kill it. Your men did."

"My men?" Diablo snorted a semi-disgusted, semi-sarcastic sound. "They shot it to save your life. Had you not been so muddy, they would've known you were a gringo, and they would've let you die."

"I'm grateful. And I'm sorry about the cat. Please, help the woman. She's dying."

"Sí, she is dying. She is shot. Did you shoot her?"

"No. Somebody else. Please. She needs help *now*."

"She will receive nothing until you answer for the death of my cat."

"Your cat?"

"This is my jungle. My world."

Reed dropped his head, thinking quickly. Extensive experience with men like this had taught him that big egos usually only responded to one of two things—submission or defiance. It was a brutal roll of the dice with no predictable outcome. If Diablo was looking for submission, defiance might anger him. But if he was looking for defiance—looking for Reed to prove himself to be a man worthy of respect—then submission would disgust him.

If only I had a rifle and three seconds to use it. You'd be begging to help me.

Reed tried submission first. Diablo had already expressed disgust for Reed being white. It seemed unlikely he expected Reed to prove himself. "You're right," Reed said. "I killed the cat. I'm sorry. You can kill me. Just save her life. Please." Again, he met Diablo's gaze.

Diablo licked his lips and flexed his fingers, then flicked the mouth of the beer bottle toward the pool. "Mátalo."

Two men grabbed Reed by his bound arms and dragged him toward the pool, his knees scraping against rough concrete. Before Reed could fight back, they had him on his stomach, his face inches above the water. A rough hand closed around the back of his skull and forced him downward.

"Wait!" Reed shouted. "I can help you!"

Water closed across his face, and Reed thrashed. The chlorine burned as it flooded his nostrils. He coughed and kicked out with both legs, striking somebody in the shin. Then he twisted and brought his head above the surface just long enough to suck down half a breath. His head was forced down again, and someone kicked him in the ribs hard enough to drive the air out of his lungs.

Darkness closed around the edges of his mind, and all he saw was Banks's face. He saw her at the club in Atlanta, where they first met. She sat on a stool and strummed her guitar, singing with that voice of an angel that first made him stare.

I wish I'd never gone into that bar. I wish I'd never met her. She deserved better.

Reed thought about the fear in her voice as they crashed down the side of the ravine in the Humvee, and rage clouded his mind—guilt mixed with self-hatred and a blinding refusal to quit.

I won't let her die.

Reed collected all that remained of his waning strength and made one last push. He twisted on his hip, bringing his legs off the concrete before he drove two powerful kicks into the first thing his feet found—more shins. A hand left his back, and Reed completed the roll, landing on his back and shoving off the concrete with his bound hands.

His face cleared the water, and he gasped in air, even as he saw his would-be killers closing in on him. A rifle butt rose over his face, two feet up and ready to begin its life-ending descent.

Reed shouted, "I know how to get your drugs into America!"

The rifle began its arc downward, and Reed closed his eyes. His neck rested on the edge of the pool, his body once again pinned in place by the overbearing pressure of two gunmen.

The rifle butt would snap his neck. They wouldn't need to drown him.

Reed braced himself, then Diablo shouted, "¡Espere!"

Reed opened his eyes and saw the butt of the rifle hovering over his face. Nobody moved, and Diablo's face appeared between the others. The sarcasm and casual disregard of only moments before was gone, now replaced by anger—and maybe a little interest.

Diablo growled, "Speak quickly, gringo."

Reed blew water from his mouth and gasped for air. "Your drugs. I know how hard it is to get them to America."

"And?" Diablo said.

Reed noted that he didn't even try to deny the existence of drugs. This man was the real deal—a Colombian drug lord—a man who owned the police, owned an army, and was completely unafraid to execute a man on his own pool deck.

"I have a friend," Reed said. "A powerful friend, in government. She can look the other way."

Diablo rolled his eyes. "You have no friend, gringo. Only a dying wish."

He turned away, and Reed threw all his cards on the table.

"She's the governor of Louisiana. If you help me, I can get your drugs straight into New Orleans."

36

Diablo stared at Reed, then he sucked his teeth and walked out of sight. A moment later, Reed heard fingers snapping, and the gunmen hauled him back to his knees and shoved him in front of the chair again. Diablo sat, his legs spread as before, but this time Reed saw no humor or indulgence in his face.

"You have one minute."

"My friend is Maggie Trousdale, the governor of Louisiana. If you help me, she can look the other way while your men offload drugs at the coast. There are miles of swamps—rural places where you can use shrimp boats or—"

"I *know* about Louisiana, gringo. It is no Miami."

"No, it's not, but you and I both know you can't bring your drugs into Miami anymore. The DEA is all over you, aren't they? It's not the eighties anymore."

Reed sucked down ragged breaths to catch up from his near drowning. He wasn't sure how much of what he said was actually true, but he speculated it wasn't a long shot. Diablo was a drug lord, yes. The king of the mountains, in his own words. But he was no Pablo Escobar. The Pablo Escobars of the world had gone by the wayside decades ago. And why? Because it wasn't easy to move drugs into America anymore. And if you couldn't get drugs into America, how much harder must it be to make money?

"Even if you speak the truth about your friendship with this woman, why would she help you? It could destroy her."

"My friend understands the value of flexibility. And she owes me a big favor."

Diablo snorted. "Two gringo lives aren't worth much. But if you want my help, that's worth a *lot*."

"I know," Reed said. "Which is why you'll be able to smuggle a lot. Hundreds of kilos, right into America. But you have to save the woman. She needs medical care, quickly."

Diablo finished the beer in a long pull. He ran a sharp tongue across his lips, and Reed suddenly noticed how devilish he actually looked. A pointed tongue and ears that stuck up slightly, like horns.

"The woman," Reed repeated. "If she isn't saved, I can't help you."

"If you can't help me, I will kill you."

Reed shrugged.

"Anybody can make claims," Diablo said. "How can you prove it?"

"Get me a phone," Reed said. "I'll call her right now, and we can set it all up. But first, the woman."

Diablo leaned forward. "Who is this woman to you? A lover?"

Reed looked down.

"What is her name?"

Reed didn't answer.

"It is nothing to me, either way," Diablo said. "I would as soon kill a white woman as a dog. Actually, I'd rather save the dog. But I am a businessman, not a monster. If there is profit to be made, I'm willing to deal."

"Then get her the medical help she needs. And get me a phone."

In a cold, reptilian way, Diablo stroked his lip once with a long finger, then he rattled off a string of Spanish to his men, and two of them left for the house. "I cannot promise she will live. She has lost a lot of blood."

"She'd better live," Reed said, "or you get nothing. I don't care if you kill me. I don't care if I never leave these godforsaken mountains. I only care about her."

Diablo laughed. "What is your name, gringo?"

"Reed Montgomery."

"Well, Reed Montgomery. You have balls. I'll give you that."

"So I've been told. Now get me a phone."

Two of Diablo's men cut Reed's wire tie bonds but kept rifles trained on him as they guided him across the pool deck and up two marble steps to the back veranda. It was then that Reed first took serious notice of the house, and he couldn't deny being impressed. If he hadn't been so worried about Banks, he might have admired the sprawling two-story structure, with giant windows, massive doors, and a back porch that was bigger than his entire cabin back in Georgia.

As it was, he only cared about calling Maggie. This harebrained scheme of his, quickly concocted while running from Legion X after the Humvee fiasco, was anything but a surefire solution. Finding El Diablo was a stroke of luck, and convincing him it was in his best interest not to kill Reed was perhaps a further stroke.

But convincing Muddy Maggie Trousdale to become a direct accessory in the trafficking of drugs was a near impossibility. In desperation, Reed was eager to write whatever big checks Diablo demanded in order to save Banks's life. Now he had to cash those checks, leaning on virtual leverage that really didn't exist.

She's got to help me. She owes me this.

The two gunmen prodded Reed into a chair while Diablo disappeared inside the house. He returned a minute later with a satellite phone and two bottles of beer. Reed gratefully accepted one and sucked half of it down, still thoroughly dehydrated from his romp through the woods.

Diablo sipped his beer, standing back from the table, then he gestured to the phone.

Reed picked it up, dialing Maggie's number from memory.

"On speaker," Diablo said.

Reed shot him a challenging look, but the casual slouch of Diablo's shoulders and the way the two gunmen stood back, rifles held at the ready, dismissed any hopes Reed had of intimidating him. This gangster didn't actually believe Reed knew the governor or could negotiate a smuggling operation. He was just curious, and maybe bored, and maybe concocting some kind of demented punishment for Reed after calling his bluff.

Reed hit the dial button, then the speaker button. The phone rang three times, and he took another slow sip of beer, forcing himself to remain calm. It must be past midnight in both Colombia and Louisiana. Maggie would still be awake, though.

Answer, dammit.

Four rings. Five. Diablo smirked, but Reed didn't break eye contact.

Six rings. Seven.

Diablo cocked his head toward the guards.

Then Maggie answered. "Hello?"

"It's Reed." He kept his voice calm and continued to stare at Diablo.

Maggie must have heard something in his tone, or maybe the unknown number cued her suspicion.

"How are you?" she said cautiously.

"Banks was shot. We're being held captive in the mountains by a Colombian drug lord. I'm calling on his behalf to make a deal."

Maggie stayed quiet. Reed wasn't sure if she didn't believe him or if she was simply trying to process what he'd said. Reed had deliberately left Wolfgang out of the conversation and prayed she wouldn't mention him. The last thing Diablo needed was more leverage.

"Am I on speaker?" Maggie asked.

Smart woman.

Reed's silence was as good as an acknowledgment.

"Who's there?" Maggie demanded. Her tone assumed a commanding edge—her executive voice. Reed had heard it before.

"They call me El Diablo," he said, sliding into a chair across from Reed. "Who are *you*?"

Maggie didn't miss a beat. "This is Governor Margaret Trousdale of Louisiana. Are you holding American citizens against their will?"

Diablo actually grinned. It was that sharp-tongued, toothy smile. The devil smile. "They never asked to leave."

True enough.

"What do you want?" Maggie said.

Diablo folded his hands but didn't answer.

Reed took over. "Banks needs medical care, quickly. Our host is offering to provide the care, and free us, in exchange for a favor from you."

"What kind of favor?"

Diablo said, "I want you to open your borders and allow my merchandise to enter your country, unmolested."

Reed tried to put himself in the room with Maggie and imagine what must be going through her head. He didn't have to speculate long.

"Are you fucking kidding me?" Maggie said.

Diablo laughed. "I really don't know if you're the governor of Louisiana or a homeless woman speaking from a payphone. But this is by far the most interesting night I've had all year."

"None of your 'merchandise' is entering my state," Maggie said.

Diablo shrugged. "My merchandise is already in your state. I was only looking for expansion. But okay, it's all the same to me. I'll kill them both."

Reed grabbed the phone and took it off speaker. Diablo continued to grin and didn't move to stop him as Reed walked back to the edge of the pool. The two gunmen raised their rifles, but Diablo waved them back as Reed pressed the phone to his ear. "Maggie, it's just me."

"Reed, what the hell is going on?"

"It's just like I told you. Banks was shot, and now we're hostages of this drug lord. I need your help."

"Reed, I'm not helping him smuggle drugs into Louisiana!"

From the veranda, Diablo leaned back in his chair and interlaced his hands behind his head. Reed wondered if he was drunk or simply deranged. Either way, Reed was running out of time.

"Maggie, listen to me," he said, dropping this voice to barely above a whisper. "You don't have to let him move much. Just a few kilos. Just enough to get him to help Banks and let us go. She's dying."

"I'm sorry. I'll do whatever I can, but I'm not aiding a drug smuggler. That's nonnegotiable."

Diablo ran a hand through his hair and let out a devilish chuckle. He looked like a coiled snake, hissing and ready to strike.

"We found the facility," Reed said, his mind clicking back into gear.

"Aiden is manufacturing cancer-inducing poison and pumping it into the country by the truckload."

"What are you talking about?"

"I'm talking about death, Maggie. A lot of it. Wolfgang believes Aiden may have found a way to fake a cancer cure, which is where Beaumont comes in."

"Is Wolfgang not with you?"

"He was captured by Aiden's men. Maybe killed. I don't know. You need to get me out of this, right now. Thousands of lives are at stake."

"Tell me where the operation is. I'll call the president."

"Not happening, Maggie. If you don't help me save Banks's life, you'll get nothing from me."

"You can't be serious . . ."

Reed snapped. "I'm deadly serious. Don't think for a moment that our partnership means more to me than Banks's life. Nothing does. I swear to God, Maggie, if you don't help me, I'll kill you. I'll find you, no matter how long—"

"Shut up, Reed," Maggie said. "I know your spiel. I've heard it before, remember?"

"Then you know I mean it."

The line went silent, and Reed glanced back at Diablo. The drug lord sipped on another beer, tapping absently at a cell phone. Reed might have another ten minutes or only ten seconds. There was no way to know.

"If you don't do this, thousands will die," Reed pressed. "Do you understand me? I'm not bullshitting."

"And you're willing to let that happen?" Maggie said.

"Are *you*?"

Reed waited out her silence, watching as Diablo tossed the phone down, then turned to his men.

Now or never.

"Put the thug on the phone," Maggie said.

Reed hit the speaker button and held up the phone as the two gunmen turned toward him and raised their weapons.

"Hold on!" he said. "She's ready to talk."

The gunmen didn't move, and Reed approached. He set the phone on the table between the chairs.

Diablo grunted. "Governor?"

"Save the woman," Maggie said. "Then we'll talk."

"Do you take me for a fool? First, you prove your identity, then we make a deal. *Then* I save the woman."

"She could be dead by then."

"Maybe."

"In which case, we make no deal. That can't be good for business."

Diablo picked at the label on his empty beer bottle.

"You can always shoot her later," Maggie said.

Reed flinched but didn't move. The rifle muzzles of Diablo's two gunmen hovered inches from his head.

Diablo smirked. "Whoever you are, you're a shrewd woman."

"I have to be, talking to scum like you."

He laughed. "Okay. I'll take care of the woman. Tomorrow, we talk again."

"She better be alive."

"And *you* better be the governor of Louisiana."

The phone clicked off, and Reed held his breath, unwilling to move and unable to think. Would he bite?

Diablo stood and snapped his fingers at his men. They lowered the guns and rushed forward, wrenching Reed's arms behind his back and tying them with wire ties again.

"Okay, gringo. I will do what I can for your woman. But you better pray to your gods that this friend of yours comes through, or your lover will wish she had died."

37

Maggie set the phone down. The knot that never seemed to leave her stomach tightened, and she had the sudden urge to puke. But she couldn't. Not only because she hadn't eaten today but also because Turk was sitting across the table.

"Well, that's not good," Turk said.

More than anything, Maggie was furious at herself for taking Reed's call while Turk was in the room. After sharing the details of Reed's campaign against Aiden with Turk, she'd won over his support—or, at least, convinced him not to immediately turn the whole thing over to the FBI.

In a strange way, she was glad Turk turned up. If they were going to bring Aiden down, they would need an investigative specialist to guide them through the legalities of assembling evidence and arresting Aiden. Turk may or may not be the man she needed, but he was the man she had, and she had been willing to run with that.

Until this. Until Reed called, and against all of her better judgment, she answered the call with Turk in the room. He'd only heard part of the conversation before she walked out, but that was more than enough.

"What are you gonna do?" Turk said.

Maggie wished she knew. A part of her suspected that Reed had made up the entire story about Aiden's cancer-inducing drug to manipulate her help with this drug lord. But on the off chance that he was telling the truth . . .

"Would the FBI investigate?" she asked.

"Investigate what?"

"The facility in Colombia."

Turk shook his head. "Not without a mountain of evidence and somebody in the state department willing to lean on the Colombians. You have neither."

Maggie bit her lip. She knew the answer before she asked, but she needed Turk to say the words and follow her own train of logic—a train that led to only one logical conclusion, no matter how messed up it was.

"I know somebody in the DEA," Turk said.

Maggie looked up. Was Turk threatening her? But she saw no malice in his face—just patience, and maybe concern. "Okay. How would that help?"

Turk shrugged. "He's not a field agent. He works in administration. Really ambitious guy. A little cutthroat, too. I worked with him by proxy on a drug bust in Virginia a while back."

"Your point?"

"I don't have a point, just an observation."

"Which is?"

Turk leaned forward. "When it comes to ambitious bureaucrats in the DEA, the ends justify the means."

Maggie held his gaze. Was Turk saying what she thought he was saying?

"Is this friend of yours discreet?" Maggie asked.

"So long as he's well fed."

Maggie looked out the window, back over the skyline of Baton Rouge. She thought about all the moments she'd sat in this chair and had these sorts of conversations over the last year. Saying things without saying them. Asking questions without asking them. Dancing along the line between criminal and hero, all in the name of bringing bad people down. It had almost cost her everything, yet here she was, asking questions without asking them. Connecting the dots with invisible ink.

"Let's give him a call," Maggie said. "This might be the biggest meal of his life."

38

Diablo's gunmen dragged Reed to some manner of a cellar a hundred yards from the house and threw him in, arms still bound. Reed landed on his face and rolled onto his side, smelling damp earth and mildew. The door slammed shut, and inky black darkness like that of the jungle closed around him. It was thick and suffocating. Reed rolled onto his butt, panting and looking toward the door. Not even a crack of light spilled from beneath it, but it was still nighttime in Colombia. In a few hours, the sun would rise, and maybe then he'd be able to see.

Reed thought about Banks, gutshot and pale, bleeding out in the forest. Was it too late? He didn't know how long he'd run through the trees before encountering Diablo's men, or how long he and the drug lord spent next to the pool, trading verbal shots like poker players, both hiding their cards.

Banks could be dead by now. The thought was too painful to admit, but in the back of his mind, Reed knew it to be true. The last time he'd seen her was when the jaguar was shot. She lay limp and unconscious on the road, unresponsive to her fall or the gunshots that followed. From there, a bumpy truck ride to Diablo's mansion may have jostled the bullet in her gut or started the bleeding again. She couldn't lose any more blood. She'd lost enough, and like Reed, she would be dehydrated anyway.

What about her Lyme disease? Would that make her weaker?

For the millionth time, Reed cursed himself. He cursed himself for everything that had happened since he was born. Some of it wasn't his fault, but most of it was. How far back did the dominos stand? Which was the first to fall?

Maybe it was that hot night in Iraq when he first chambered a round and settled his crosshairs over a noncombatant—somebody he wasn't ordered to kill, but chose to kill, because it made sense to him. Maybe the decision to impose his own understanding of morality on the world around him was the first domino to fall.

Or maybe he was kidding himself. Perhaps the first domino fell years earlier, long before he was a Marine, when his mom moved them to Los Angeles and he stood outside school with other junior high schoolers and took his first puff of weed.

Reed never believed that things like weed, alcohol, and rock music created the people they were associated with. He never believed that individual actions sealed a person's destiny or defined them. But maybe all those little things slowly built him into the man he was. Maybe all those little choices, even if they felt right in the moment, led him here.

Or maybe he should have just left Banks in Alabama, regardless of her protests. Maybe this train wreck wasn't the result of a million bad decisions, but just one or two.

If she dies, I'll never forgive myself.

Reed thought about Banks in the nightclub in Atlanta and her little yellow Super Beetle in North Carolina. He remembered what it felt like to make love to her on the floor in front of a crackling fire. The way she sang and laughed and how everything she felt and believed she wore on her sleeve. Banks wasn't simple—she was just honest. Transparent. Because she knew who she was, and she had nothing to hide. A *good* person. A person he'd give anything to escape life with, if only life would let him go.

Sweat trickled down Reed's face, and for the first time in his adult life, Reed wished he could cry. He hadn't cried in years, but sometimes he wished he knew a way to release his pain and anger other than snapping necks and pressing triggers. He took a long breath of the dampness around him. He'd been here before, many times. Not in this cellar, and not in Colombia. But Reed was no stranger to the pressure of his back against a wall, and he knew exactly what to do about it.

If Diablo saves Banks, then we negotiate our release. And if he doesn't, I'll introduce him to the real Devil.

Reed scooted his butt across the floor until he felt a brick wall against his back. His arms and shoulders ached, but it felt good to lean against something. It gave him enough physical stability to calm his mind and think about the big picture.

Wolfgang.

The Wolf was either captured or dead. Regardless, if Reed expected Maggie to negotiate with Diablo, Reed would need proof of what he'd seen at Aiden's facility, and if Wolfgang was held captive there, Reed owed him an attempted rescue.

Reed closed his eyes and breathed in. He held the breath and pictured himself behind a rifle, staring down the scope at a target a thousand yards away. This was his calm place. Not a happy place or a peaceful one, but a place where he could shut out everything he felt and feared and was confused by. It was a place where he could focus only on his target and finding a way to hit it.

Banks. Maggie. Diablo. Wolfgang.

The four corners of a strange puzzle. And in the middle? Aiden Phillips's facility.

Reed released his breath slowly, breathing through his nose and focusing on the intersection of the crosshairs. He imagined the little rise and fall of those crosshairs and the way heat waves shimmered over his distant target. Whenever he pictured himself in this position, he always saw the desert through his scope, like in Iraq.

Banks. Maggie. Diablo. Wolfgang.

Reed thought about the facility. He thought about Legion X, and the helicopter, and all the guns. He pictured the way the road led up to the horseshoe ridges, and how those ridges restricted access to the valley.

He thought about what it would mean to rescue Wolfgang and get the evidence he needed. It wasn't a job for a lone man, no matter how tough he was. It was a job for a dozen men, heavily armed and ready for blood. A job for an army.

Reed drew a half breath and held it. The crosshairs in his mind froze, and he pressed the trigger. He knew what to do.

39

Reed lost track of time before Diablo's men returned, but when they dragged him out of the cellar into oppressive sunshine, he judged it to be late afternoon. He stumbled as they pushed him across the yard, again prodding him at gunpoint. The wire ties bit into his arms, and once more, he felt so dehydrated it was difficult not to throw himself into the pool as they passed, but Reed remained calm.

He'd regained control of himself during his time in the darkness. One of two things was about to happen: either Diablo was about to take him to Banks and she was going to be okay, or Diablo was about to die.

Beyond that, he didn't need a plan. He'd take things one step at a time.

Diablo waited on the veranda, but this time he wasn't alone. Two beautiful Colombian women accompanied him, both dressed in skimpy bikinis, with their skin bathed in sun lotion. They regarded Reed through condescending, disinterested brown eyes as he approached, and Diablo didn't so much as look up.

He was drinking again—liquor this time, accompanied by a cigar. The nightshirt was replaced by white golf shorts, boat shoes, and a shirt that was only half-buttoned, exposing a muscled chest traced with a number of jagged scars.

Reed wasn't impressed. He stopped at the foot of the marble steps and waited while Diablo took a long puff of the cigar.

"Sleep well?" Diablo asked. He knocked ashes off his cigar and stared at Reed, his gaze stopping from time to time at the scars on Reed's bare chest and arms. He took a sip of his liquor. "Who are you, gringo?"

Reed held his gaze. "Just some guy."

Diablo's devilish smile was more subdued than the night before, probably because he was more sober than the night before. "I doubt that very much." He puffed the cigar, then ground it out against the table and set his drink down. As he stood, the two women moved to follow him, but he waved them away and muttered a curt command in Spanish to the two gunmen.

Reed felt metal against his arm, and then the wire ties were cut away. Relief flooded his strained and aching muscles as he pulled his arms from behind his back and flexed them. His wrists were marred and bruised by the bonds, but Reed offered Diablo a brief nod of thanks.

Diablo motioned toward the sprawling green yard to the right of the house. Reed hesitated, looking toward the mansion and thinking about Banks. He wondered what twisted game Diablo was playing now and decided that if he planned to kill him, he wouldn't have cut him loose.

"Relax," Diablo said, as if reading his thoughts. "Your woman lives."

A flood of relief and hope rushed Reed's mind so strongly he knew it must be visible.

Diablo motioned to the yard.

"Show me," Reed said.

Diablo sighed and reached into his pocket. He tapped on a phone and then held it out to Reed. The phone displayed a video feed of a bedroom. Banks lay amid a stack of plush pillows, hooked to an IV with a heart monitor blipping next to her. Her stomach was wrapped in clean bandages, and a doctor leaned over her.

Reed squinted at the image, searching for indicators of deceit, but Banks's skin was no longer pale—a glow had returned to her cheeks, however weak, and her chest rose and fell smoothly.

Reed returned the phone, and Diablo set out across the yard. Reed reluctantly followed, conscious of the gunmen ten yards behind, and sure their rifles were still trained on his back.

"Your woman was shot just above her hip bone," Diablo said. "The bullet missed her spine and her kidney, which is lucky. The doctor was able to locate and remove the bullet and stitch up the damage. However, her intestines were severely damaged. There is a substantial risk of sepsis. Do you know what this means?"

Reed nodded, impressed by Diablo's detailed understanding of the injury but perpetually suspicious of a punchline.

Diablo walked with his head down, his hands clasped behind his back. Brilliant green grass crunched beneath their feet, and as they circled to the side of the house, Reed noticed a spread of flower gardens adorning the hillside next to a sprawling driveway.

"I have sent a man to Bogotá to purchase specialized antibiotics. You do not have these medicines in America. They may save her."

"Thank you," Reed said.

Diablo started forward again. The two of them reached a crest in the yard, and suddenly the ground fell away, revealing the rolling glory of the Andes Mountains. The sun set on Reed's right shoulder, and in the far distance, he saw the glimmer of a sprawling city, resting amid the slopes of the mountains. It was massive, spreading out on either side and glimmering in the golden light.

Reed drew a deep breath and allowed himself to enjoy the view.

Diablo folded his arms.

"Medellín," he said.

The city of Pablo Escobar.

Reed was quiet, but Diablo must have noticed the recognition on his face. "You've heard of it?" he asked.

"I've seen *Blow*," Reed said.

Diablo chuckled. "Americans. They know everything from movies."

Reed continued admiring the view as the sun faded behind the mountains.

"Medellín is not as it once was," Diablo said. "When I was a child, it was full of bloodshed and gunfire. Today, it is a thriving city, full of tourists and music. A safe place."

"How disappointing," Reed said. He couldn't resist.

Diablo shoved his hands into his pockets. "It is very disappointing, gringo. It is disappointing because Colombia has polished her brightest cities like prized trophies to display to an internet world, while allowing her villages and slums to remain crippled by poverty. Medellín is a shame because Medellín is a half-truth. Medellín makes the world think the days of the narcos are over, while only the gunfire has subsided."

"I was under the impression that you were a narco," Reed said.

"In your American mind, it may seem so. But I am no gangster. I do not murder people on the streets. I am a businessman—a philanthropist, as you say. I produce cocaine and export it to the profit of my people."

"El Diablo. Amigo del pueblo," Reed quoted.

Diablo didn't seem surprised that Reed knew the phrase.

"Some may say so. My drugs bring millions into my country—a true export. Those millions build schools and pave roads and provide food in places that the government does not care about. Those millions bring hope to my people."

"And a mansion full of voluptuous Colombian women for you."

Diablo shrugged. "The politicians in Bogotá indulge as much. As you say in America: 'The ends justify the means.' Based on last night's proposal with your friend in Louisiana, it would seem that you agree."

Reed's jaw tensed, and Diablo shot him a challenging look. The devil was alive in his eyes again, but Reed wasn't fooled by this man. His monologue about the needs of his people was moving, for sure, but it was shortsighted and ignorant. Reed wanted to point out that the millions of dollars Diablo supposedly invested into schools and roads were paid by homeless, destitute addicts in America. He wanted to underscore the fact that Diablo wasn't assuaging suffering, he was only transplanting it.

But Diablo still held Banks, and Reed was still a prisoner. There were more pressing matters at hand than high-minded moral debates.

"Are you going to let us go?" Reed said.

Diablo started back toward the house, and Reed followed.

"My offer is the same as before. If your friend truly has power, and if she can move my product into your country unmolested, then I will let your friend go."

Reed shoved his hands into his pockets and grunted. "I'm afraid that's not going to be enough. Not anymore."

Diablo stopped. "Excuse me?"

"The deal has changed," Reed said. "I can get your drugs into America, but I'm going to need more from you than my own freedom."

"And what makes you think you're in a position to demand that?"

"I'm not demanding, Diablo. I'm simply expanding the deal. I have something else to offer. Something you'll definitely be interested in. But if I offer more, so must you."

Diablo grinned, but the casual warmth of his posture only moments before was long gone. Reed saw ice in his eyes—the promise of hellfire to come if Reed pushed too hard.

"What else?" Diablo said.

"Do you have a map?"

"It's here," Reed said. He bent over the iPad resting on Diablo's kitchen table and pointed to a spot in the mountains. It was easy to identify, based on the horseshoe shape and the glint of sunlight against the chrome bumpers of parked cars, half-hidden under trees. If Reed zoomed out and moved the satellite image, he could trace the road around the base of the ridge, through the forest to the bridge.

Examining the spot, Diablo adjusted the view with one finger and shook his head. "I see nothing."

"Zoom in. Here." Reed adjusted the map, focusing on the mesh that stretched across the valley floor. At first glance, it looked like foliage, but if Reed squinted, he could make out the metallic outline of the U-shaped metal building beneath it.

Diablo saw it. Reed knew by the way his shoulders tensed.

"How far?" Diablo asked.

"A few miles."

"They are making drugs?"

"It seems so," Reed said. "Competition. Right in your backyard."

Diablo looked back at the map. He adjusted the angle a few times, then stroked his chin. Reed sucked on his fourth glass of water and glanced around the interior of Diablo's kitchen. It was massive, and everything in it was covered in either marble or stainless steel.

"How did you find this?" Diablo said.

"By accident," Reed lied. "My friends and I came to Colombia to go hiking. We like birds. Yesterday we stumbled on this place by mistake, and they responded poorly. That's where the woman was shot."

"You said *friends*," Diablo said. "There was another woman?"

"A man. He was captured."

Diablo sucked his teeth and studied the map. "Why are you telling me this?"

"Because I need to get my friend back, and you need to eliminate competition. It seems we can help each other."

"You want my men to rescue your friend?"

Reed shook his head. "I want your men to provide a distraction. I'll rescue my friend."

"You?" Diablo laughed. "I thought you were just 'some guy.'"

"I am. But sometimes some guys know how to shoot."

Diablo folded his arms. "You know what I'm thinking, gringo?"

"What?"

"I'm thinking I should kill you and your woman, and be done. This whole thing smells sour to me. Like a DEA plot."

"I'm not DEA."

"The DEA would say that."

"I'm not."

"Maybe. Whatever you are, I will not risk lives on your say-so. If these people in the mountains are competitors, I will deal with them in my own way, when the time is best. You've already told me where they are. You have nothing left to offer."

"Of course I do."

"And that is?"

"A way to authenticate and guarantee the cooperation of the Louisiana governor. And if you'll help me rescue my friend, I'll double the shipment size. Twice as much of your product smuggled into America."

Diablo cocked his head. "You can guarantee the governor's cooperation? How?"

"It's a little trick I learned recently. You film somebody doing a naughty thing and then use it against them if they try to backstab you."

"You have a film of your governor?"

"No, but you can make one. I'll have her agree to conduct a video call with you right in her executive office with the flags in the background. She'll agree to help with your drugs, and you can record the whole thing. Then, if she tries to back out, you can send the tape to the DEA."

Even before Reed finished, the smile crept across Diablo's face like a rash slowly consuming his features. Then came the dark chuckle. "She may be a friend of yours, gringo, but you are no friend of hers."

Reed shrugged. "It's a surefire system. Either she agrees and you move your product, or she doesn't agree, and you kill us."

"You seem terribly confident. Perhaps you already have leverage over this woman."

"I don't. But I trust her."

"Trust is a strange thing. For some, it is cheap, and for others, it is expensive. But for everyone, it has a price."

Reed motioned to the iPad. "So call her, and let's get this show on the road."

40

Maggie required less convincing than Reed expected, but he thought he knew why. After a brief conversation on Diablo's satellite phone, she agreed to the video call.

She better have a plan.

Diablo blacked out the camera on his end and used an electronic voice scrambler for his communications, then propped his iPad up on the counter and set it to record the call. Maggie beeped through a moment later, sitting behind her executive desk in the State Capitol. The blue Louisiana state flag stood behind her on one side and the Stars and Stripes on the other. She looked exhausted and wore no makeup, but she sat upright with the commanding air of a woman who still assumed control of the situation.

"Who am I speaking with?" she said.

Diablo lifted the voice scrambler to his lips and spoke quietly. His voice was amplified by the speaker on the other side and came out in a computerized monotone. "You know who I am."

"I know who you *say* you are. Why can't I see you?"

"You don't need to see me. You only need to speak the words I want to hear."

Maggie sat straight-backed and stared into the camera. "Very well. I'm prepared to offer the passage of your merchandise into my state in exchange for the safe and healthy return of my friends."

"You're going to have to be more specific," Diablo said.

Maggie tensed, but something in her eyes told Reed that she was more relaxed than she appeared.

She does have a plan.

"Okay," she said. "*Specifically,* I agree to allow the passage of one hundred kilos of your drugs into my state in exchange for the safe and healthy return of my friends."

"One thousand kilos," Diablo said. "That is my price."

Maggie shook her head. "That's too large a shipment. I can do as much as five hundred, but you will have to split the shipments. It's too dangerous to attempt that much at once."

"No," Diablo said. "I am no fool. As soon as your friends are returned, there is no guarantee you will protect the second shipment."

"You're recording this, are you not?" Maggie said with a condescending lift of one eyebrow.

"Yes, but destroying you wouldn't move my drugs, would it? One shipment. One thousand kilos. That is the price, or your friends die."

Maggie's face turned dark, but she nodded once. "One thousand kilos. But then our business is concluded. Understand?"

"Understood. I will contact you in the coming days to arrange passage. Your friends will accompany the shipment. If at any point you try to back out or attempt to double-cross me, they die. Understand?"

Maggie nodded again, and Diablo cut the video feed. He looked up at Reed and chuckled. "You are either a very great fool or a very great businessman, gringo."

Reed drained the last of his water and slammed the cup down. "I'm just a man trying to get home. Now, where's my army?"

Diablo made a call, and fifteen minutes later, he led Reed out the front door of the mansion to where a Mercedes G-Wagon waited in front of the house, diesel fumes gathering beneath the bumper. The two goons with AKs waited at the foot of the front porch steps, and a driver sat behind the wheel, smoking a cigarette.

Reed stopped at the foot of the stairs and looked up at the house. He didn't know which room Banks was housed in, or if she was even still at the house. Diablo could have moved her while he was locked in the cellar. But Reed pictured her behind one of the curtained windows on the second floor and imagined she lay on the bed inside, covered in sheets and sleeping fitfully—at war with infection, maybe fighting a losing battle—desperate for the medication Diablo promised.

"When do the antibiotics get here?" Reed asked, still looking at the window.

Diablo stood two steps above him, and Reed saw the devilish smile out of the corner of his eye. It was subdued, as if the demons inside Diablo were drunk and half-awake. But it was there, reminding Reed that this man wasn't his friend.

"My man left for Bogotá last night," Diablo said. "It's a nine-hour drive."

Reed looked away from the window, facing Diablo, unblinking and holding the man's gaze. "Funny. If the antibiotics are so special, you'd think you'd keep them close by."

"You'd think," Diablo said.

"You better hope she lives." Reed's voice was flat, but he couldn't hide all the edge behind it.

Diablo laughed. "It does me no good to let her die, gringo. I still have drugs to move."

"If she dies," Reed said, "moving drugs will be the last thing on your mind."

The devilish smile melted, and Reed saw something deeper in Diablo's face—respect, maybe, but also something darker.

"Get in the truck," Diablo said.

Reed stepped across the drive to where the two gunmen waited. They regarded him with the obvious disgust of men deprived of an opportunity to drown somebody, their fingers held close to the triggers of matching AK-74s. Reed looked at each of the men, then moved to walk between them. One blocked his path, and the other pulled a black hood from his pocket.

"I'm sorry, my friend," Diablo said from behind him. "Of course you understand."

Reed evaluated his options quickly, but he knew he had none. He and Diablo stood in a deadlock, neither trusting the other, but neither was willing to resort to a nuclear option that would kill them both. For now, Reed was better off playing along.

He allowed one goon to pull the hood over his head, and then they forced him into the back seat of the G-Wagon, climbing in on either side. Reed heard Diablo climb into the front seat, then the doors clanged shut, and Diablo said something in Spanish. The interior of the SUV was hot and stuffy, and everything smelled like cigarettes. Reed struggled to find a comfortable spot on the leather seat as the SUV growled and then turned down the driveway. He felt the elevation dropping away as they wound down the mountainside, and five minutes later, the crunch of gravel replaced the smooth hum of asphalt. Reed didn't even try to speculate on where he was.

His plan was the same as before—use Diablo's men to flatten Aiden's facility and rescue Wolfgang, then get the hell out of Colombia. He would probably have to wait until he was on a drug boat headed north to split from Diablo's men, and he might have to wait until they reached Louisiana. Regardless, the only thing to do was roll with the plan and hope Diablo did the same.

Reed listened to the jungle sounds through the open windows, noting the calls of foreign birds and the occasional cry of a primate. The air was thick and humid, making it even more difficult to breathe through the hood, but he didn't complain.

After half an hour, the SUV ground up a short hill, and the sounds of distant voices rang through the windows. Gravel crunched beneath the tires as they ground to a stop, and then the doors opened. Diablo snapped an order in Spanish, and the hood slid off Reed's head.

He blinked in the bright light of midday and quickly scanned his surroundings. The SUV sat in the middle of a jungle clearing, with towering trees on all sides and an assortment of huts, mobile buildings, and RVs parked around the edge. There were probably a dozen buildings in total, all spread around a space the size of a football field and butting up against the steep side of a mountain.

Men were everywhere, leaning against trees, slouching on beach chairs next to campfires, sipping beer, and playing cards. Reed counted at least thirty of them and noticed several more walking in and out of the huts and RVs. Scattered among the crowd were weapons: AKs, AR-15s, submachine guns, heavy rifles, and shotguns. Crates of food and ammunition joined the mess, stacked under slouching sheds and packed into rusting metal shipping containers.

Reed surveyed the scene, then looked at Diablo.

The drug lord bared his teeth. "Meet your army, gringo."

When the goon next to Reed pushed him out of the SUV, damp mud squished beneath Reed's boots. Diablo led him across the clearing to the nearest fire, and as he approached, the men around the fire raised their beers, cheering but not standing. Diablo grinned and slapped several of them on the back, working his way around the circle and chattering in warm Spanish. Everybody he encountered seemed excited to see him, and somebody passed him a cold beer.

Diablo held out his hand toward Reed, beckoning. Diablo's smile reminded Reed of a senator running for reelection—high-wattage and fake as hell.

Reed approached, keeping his shoulders stiff and his head up.

"Gringo," Diablo said, "this is Santiago, my captain!"

A big Colombian looked up from his seat, his mouth full of chips and a beer in one hand. He regarded Reed with the semi-interested look of a man appraising a piece of meat, then looked away without getting up.

Diablo slapped Santiago on the shoulder, his face still blazing with the politician's smile. He said something in Spanish, and Santiago shrugged. Diablo laughed again, but the light in his eyes changed. The wattage faded, replaced now by the fire Reed had seen earlier. He threw his head back and laughed, smacking Santiago on the back. Then his right hand flashed beneath his shirt, and a revolver appeared out of nowhere. Diablo placed the muzzle against the back of Santiago's head and pulled the trigger so quickly even Reed was taken off guard.

The gun cracked, and the front of Santiago's face simply vanished in a cloud of red. He crumpled forward, his face landing in the dust as a shocked silence fell across the clearing. Diablo looked down at the body, grinning from ear to ear, then he shoved the revolver back into his pants and shouted at the crowd. "Perro gordo!"

A roar of raucous laughter filled the jungle, and the men around the fire slapped each other on the shoulders. Their faces turned red with mirth, and several of them spat on the body.

Diablo held his hands up and continued to grin. The roar grew louder, and Diablo tilted his head back, beckoning toward himself like a rock star basking in applause after a hit performance.

What the hell is this?

The laughter continued, now joined by the blare of a stereo and a few drunken whoops. Diablo swigged his beer, then approached Reed and put one arm around his shoulder, pulling him to the side. Diablo tilted his head back to meet Reed's gaze. The devil had returned.

"You see, gringo, these are *my* men. Not Santiago's men. Not their mother's men. Not even God's men. These are El Diablo's men. And that's why I'm going to let you borrow them. Because I know if you try to screw me, they'll rip you to shreds."

41

For the next half hour, Diablo circled the clearing and greeted his men, slapping shoulders and knocking back half a dozen beers. He led Reed along with him, and even though Diablo spoke only in Spanish, Reed gathered the gist of his introduction. Words like "gringo," "loco," and "soldado" were used frequently. Reed—the crazy white soldier.

Fair enough.

After Diablo completed his circuit, he brought Reed to the hut nearest the mountain that seemed to be the operational headquarters of his little army. Diablo called into the house, and a muscular, shirtless Colombian wearing a pistol and a black headband appeared. He was scarred and missing one eye but not wearing a patch.

"Gringo, meet Cristian. He is my new captain."

Diablo smacked Cristian on the arm, and to Reed's surprise, the man offered his hand. Reed took it and was impressed by the grip.

Cristian's good eye stared into Reed's soul. "Welcome to Colombia, amigo." He released Reed's hand, and Diablo motioned them into the house.

All the windows were open, and a squeaking ceiling fan rotated overhead, but it was muggy inside. An assortment of recliners and battered wooden chairs surrounded a large table laden with junk food and warm beer. Cristian cleared a space, and Diablo called over his shoulder to one of the gunmen from his house. The man brought his iPad, and Diablo cued up the satellite map from before.

"Tell Cristian about this facility," Diablo said.

Reed took the iPad and located the spot in the mountains, then quickly relayed to Cristian what he'd already told Diablo—all the details about the facility, the road leading up to it, and the security on-site. Cristian seemed neither fazed nor surprised by the information, and Reed wondered if he already knew about the facility. When Reed finished his discourse, he placed the iPad on the table and folded his arms.

Cristian turned to Diablo. "What are your orders?"

Diablo ran his serpent tongue over his lips, then looked at Reed. "The gringo has a friend held inside this facility. He wants him back."

"You want us to help?" Cristian asked.

Diablo drew a breath, but Reed answered first. It was time to regain some initiative. "I'll get my friend back. I don't need help. What I need is a distraction and some firepower."

Cristian turned to Diablo again, but Diablo didn't comment. He motioned for Reed to continue.

Reed picked up a pen and used it to point out different locations on the map. "The key to the entire place is the bridge. There's no way into the valley except by the road, and if the bridge were blown, there would be no easy way out of it, either."

"You want us to blow the bridge?" Cristian asked.

Reed shook his head. "We don't need to blow it. We just need them to think we might. The facility is protected by a dozen or so locals with assault rifles and at least eight highly trained mercenaries from Europe. If you attack the bridge with enough ferocity, the bulk of that force will be drawn away from the facility to repel your attack, leaving an opening for me to infiltrate the valley."

Cristian shot Diablo a quizzical look, and Diablo smirked at Reed.

"You are very tactical for 'some guy.'"

Reed shrugged. "I play *Call of Duty*."

Diablo chuckled. "Okay, so you want my men to rain hellfire on this bridge, allowing you to rescue your friend. But you promised me this facility would be destroyed."

"It will be," Reed said. He pointed to another point on the map. "This building here, on the south side, is their lab. I understand most drugs involve a cooking process?"

Diablo made a noncommittal shrug.

"There's a large propane tank inside this building," Reed continued. "They use propane to cook their product, I guess. After rescuing my friend, I'll place a bomb next to the tank on a timer. Even an average size propane explosion would be enough to bring down the entire facility. I trust you have some C4 lying around?"

Diablo grinned at Reed. "*Call of Duty*?'"

Reed held his gaze. "*Battlefield*, sometimes."

Diablo stroked his lip, peering at the map, then he looked at Cristian.

"We have the explosives," Cristian said. "So long as my men are dug in along the road, there should be little risk for them. But I have a question."

Cristian picked up the iPad and adjusted the view, then pointed to a spot in the valley where the faint outlines of a capital letter H were painted on the dirt in white.

"They have a helicopter?"

Smart guy.

Reed nodded. "They do. An unarmed Lakota. But it's damaged."

"Unarmed and damaged or not, it could be a serious threat to my men," Cristian said. "We should send soldiers with you up onto the ridge. They can take it out with RPGs."

"An RPG would be much too inaccurate at that range," Reed said. "And besides, your men would never make it up the ridge. The mercenaries I mentioned before brought land mines and trip wire–triggered explosives with them. By now, they'll have littered the entire ridge with enough ordnance to blow your men to hell. There's no chance they could make it to the top."

"But you can?" Cristian challenged.

"I know what to look for," Reed said. "And the defenses are designed to prevent an army, anyway. Not one man. I can make it to the bottom of the horseshoe on the east side and establish an overwatch."

Cristian's brow wrinkled. "Overwatch?"

"It's a sniper's term," Reed said. "It means high ground with a clear shot." He zoomed in on the map and pointed at a spot at the bottom of the horseshoe, with a clear field of fire over the parking lot and the helipad. "Here is good. From this position, there is no direct line of fire from any other point along the ridge, which gives me a little shelter from sentries placed along either side. Also, the bottom of the horseshoe faces east, which means that if we attack at dawn, the sun will be at my back, obscuring my position and clarifying my targets. As soon as your men draw out the security force, I'll take out the helicopter. All I need is a good rifle."

"You're going to take down a helicopter with a rifle?" Diablo said.

"Can't fly without a pilot."

Again, Cristian and Diablo exchanged a look.

Reed pressed his advantage. "Once the chopper is grounded and the mercenaries are cleared out, I'll take the facility and rescue my friend. On my way out, I'll set off the explosives. Then we haul ass."

"Haul ass . . ." Diablo said with another chuckle.

Reed returned the smile, keeping his just as cold as Diablo's. "Just like *Battlefield*. Now, show me your rifles."

―――――――

After a little more convincing, Diablo agreed to the plan and surrendered Reed into Cristian's custody. The drug lord returned to his G-Wagon, sucking down another beer on the way, and two minutes later, he disappeared into the trees.

Reed raised both eyebrows at Cristian. "Stressful job you've got."

"Stressful world we live in."

"Not so much for Santiago."

Cristian rocked his head toward the back of the house, and Reed followed him through a dirty hallway to a slouched back porch that faced the steep side of the mountain behind it. The back of the yard was thick with undergrowth and leaning trees, but between the brush, Reed saw the face of a shipping container, half-buried in the mountainside. The door was painted black and chained shut.

Cristian approached it with casual nonchalance, then unlocked the padlock with a key from his pocket and jerked the chain out. "When you play *Battlefield*, do you ever find piles of weapons hidden in the jungle?"

"All the time," Reed said, keeping his tone even.

Cristian shot him a sideways glance, then jerked the door open. "I'll bet you never found a pile like this." He hit a switch mounted just inside the shipping container, and bright light flooded the interior. Reed stepped through the door and drew a deep breath of gun-oiled air, and in a millisecond, he felt better about everything.

The container was filled to the brim with weaponry. Rows of rifle racks lined either wall, packed tight with assault weapons, submachine guns, and shotguns. Above the rifle racks were shelves stacked with handguns— everything from modern SIG Sauer pistols to WWII-era Russian Nagant revolvers, all piled at random like forgotten toys at the end of a long playdate.

The middle of the container was occupied by a lengthy table stacked to the breaking point with boxes of ammunition, knives, canteens, and body armor. And along the back wall of the container, another rifle rack was filled with what Reed was looking for—precision rifles, complete with optics.

Reed glanced at Cristian and offered a short nod.

The Colombian motioned to the container. "Mi casa es tú casa, amigo. Help yourself."

<hr />

Reed spent half an hour selecting his equipment. While the sheer volume of the weaponry in Cristian's arsenal was impressive, the actual quality, condition, and vintage of the firearms were all lacking, particularly where rifles were concerned. There were no modern sniper rifles, and most of the assault weapons and submachine guns were Russian-sourced AKs and Bizons.

Only the pistols reflected any sort of modern technology, and Reed quickly determined that this was because the SIGs had been taken from the bodies of Colombian national police officers. Everything else, much like the rifles, was old and predominantly Russian.

He started at the back of the container and located a rifle first. He selected the best of a row of precision weapons—the SVDS model of Russian-built Dragunov sniper rifles. It featured a synthetic folding stock and some type of wide-angle scope he'd never heard of. Altogether, it was a lot clunkier and heavier than his custom-built AR-10 back in Georgia, but it was clean and rust-free and came with plenty of 7.62x51R ammunition—a heavy-hitting caliber similar to the American 308 that would more than meet his needs.

Next, he moved to the assault rifle racks and picked out the cleanest AK-74 he could find. An updated version of the legendary AK-47, the 74 featured a zippier bullet and a more refined action, without sacrificing any of its predecessor's reliability. This particular rifle was equipped with some kind of fix-magnification optic, similar to the ACOG on the G36 he stole from Legion X. He selected half a dozen 30-round magazines loaded to capacity with steel-core ammunition to go with it, and grabbed a SIG M11 chambered in 9mm on his way out.

He piled all the gear near the door, then returned inside and dug through the junk on the table until he found a holster for the SIG and a chest rig to hold the extra magazines. Last of all, he selected a Russian-made KAMPO bayonet, which was really more of a combat knife. It wasn't as sharp as he would've liked, but a little polishing would add an edge, and he didn't plan on shaving with it anyway.

When he returned to the clearing loaded with the gear, he found none of the casual revelry he'd seen when Diablo was present. Some men still slouched around fires or ate at scattered picnic tables, but most of them were busy cleaning guns and loading trucks.

Cristian approached from the main house, a backpack slung over one shoulder, and cast a surprised look at Reed's armful of equipment. "Anything else?"

"Water," Reed said. "And food that won't upset my stomach. I'm not accustomed to local cuisine."

Cristian led him to a table and offered him some kind of shredded meat on fresh tortillas. It was savory and rich, and Reed washed it down with two liters of water while watching Cristian's men continue to load guns into the beds of two pickup trucks.

"They will be your road crew," Cristian said. "I will lead them personally."

Cristian unslung the backpack, pulling back the zipper and dumping the contents onto the table. It was C4—a good pile of it, with a two-part electronic detonator system consisting of a radio-powered trigger and an electronic igniter.

Reed sorted through it, checking each component and examining the explosives, then he nodded. "It'll do."

He shoveled more food into his mouth and slouched against the table. His body was still sore and bruised from the catastrophe in the Humvee, and his mind was numb with constant strain and endless churning thoughts. He knew his plan was good and that it could work, but one piece of the puzzle still bothered him. He could reach the valley floor and rescue Wolfgang and blow the facility, but if Wolfgang was injured, or if Reed was taking fire when he fled the building, he'd need a quick way out of the valley that didn't require use of the bridge. A way to haul ass, like he'd told Diablo.

"Can somebody else lead your men?" Reed asked. "I may have another job for you."

Cristian frowned. "What do you mean?"

Reed pointed across the clearing to a pile of equipment heaped against the side of a storage container. Amid battered cots and abandoned buckets, he identified an aluminum stretcher like the kind you might find mounted to the roof of a medical Humvee. A metal sled, more or less.

"Do you see that stretcher?"

Cristian nodded.

"I'm going to take it with me, tied to a rope, to the bottom of the valley. The other end of that rope is going to be tied to a truck on the far side of the ridge, where a second road crosses through the jungle. You'll be in that truck waiting for my signal. If things turn bad, you can pull me out."

Cristian scratched his chin and cocked his head. "Why me? I should be with my men."

Reed swigged water but didn't answer. In his mind, he calculated the length of rope he would need to reach the backside of the ridge, where another dirt road wound through the jungle. He'd noticed it on the satellite map, but the roadbed must've been three hundred yards from the bottom of the valley on the other side of the ridge. He would need a lot of rope.

Reed savored the relief of the water and cleared his head of the technicalities of the operation, focusing instead on the key components of the plan.

Knock out the facility. Rescue Wolfgang. Get Banks. Then get the hell out. Four easy steps.

"Amigo . . ." Cristian folded his arms, and Reed saw indecision in his face. Uncertainty, perhaps.

"What?" Reed asked.

"I don't know what kind of deal you have with Diablo, but . . ."

Reed swished the water in his mouth and said nothing.

Cristian cast a hesitant look at his men, then cleared his throat. "These men are loyal to Diablo, as am I. We will die for him, if necessary, but we don't want to."

"You want to know if I know what I'm doing," Reed said. He set the bottle down. "Your boss is holding a woman. Somebody very important to me. I made this arrangement with him to get her back."

Cristian kept his arms folded.

"I know what I'm doing," Reed said. "More than anyone you've ever met."

"From *Battlefield*?"

"From a lot of battlefields, in a lot of places, with a lot worse odds than these."

Cristian considered the answer. "It's not that I don't believe you. It's just that these are my men. It's my duty to look after them. Surely, you must understand this."

"I do understand it. It means you're a good guy who's not trying to screw people over. And in case you're still wondering, *that's* why I want you in that truck." Reed wiped grease on his pants and finished the water. "Now, show me a place to test these rifles. We move just before dawn."

42

Wolfgang didn't know how many hours—or days—had passed since he washed up on the riverbank, stunned and bleeding, with a busted right leg. The last thing he clearly remembered was careening off the waterfall with Banks screaming next to him and Reed shouting for them to bail. He recalled pushing his door open and hurling himself out of the doomed vehicle only a moment before it hit the water, but after that, everything was a blur.

Wolfgang ran a dry tongue over busted lips and stared up at a black ceiling. All around him was darkness, and in the distance, voices and the sound of machinery carried through the walls. He lay on a metal cot without a mattress, his hands and feet chained to its four corners. His entire body throbbed. He recalled injuring his leg during his escape from the lab, but the fall from the Humvee must have worsened the injury, and Wolfgang was now sure that his right femur was busted. The pain was intense and ceaseless—so acute that the ceiling overhead swam, and he couldn't even focus on the fact that he was desperately dehydrated.

Where was he? Back at the facility in the mountains? Probably. But what about Reed and Banks? Had they escaped?

Wolfgang closed his eyes and tried to block out the pain. It was almost impossible, but if he focused hard enough on a specific image, he could minimize the throbbing and fill his consciousness with a mental painkiller. It was an old trick he learned years before, during some of the darkest moments of his life, and the image was always the same—taken from even earlier in his life, during one of its brightest moments.

Wolfgang saw a woman. She was petite, with deep red hair and a slight button nose. She stared up at him under long lashes, and her cheeks glowed a deep red. The woman looked a little like Lucy, but to Wolfgang, she was infinitely more beautiful. To Wolfgang, she was the most beautiful woman on the planet and always would be. She stood next to a window, overlooking a bright city full of a million lights, and when she looked up at him, he felt a warmth and a longing stronger than the pain.

He focused on the memory with his entire consciousness, picturing himself standing a few feet away just as the woman turned around. Her hands wrapped around a railing near the window, and a small crowd of other people—tourists and locals alike—stood near them, having ascended to the top of the tower to enjoy the view, just like the woman had. They formed depth to the memory and made it feel more present, but he couldn't remember their faces. He didn't need to. Only her face mattered, and he focused on it.

He took a step toward her, and she blinked. A tear hit the carpet, and he held out a hand. "Megan?"

The woman smiled, just a little. He pictured the little lift of her lips and the flash of her eyes as though she were standing right in front of him, and it flooded him with a deep warmth so powerful it completely masked the pain of his busted leg. Wolfgang surrendered himself to the memory as he held out his hands and she rushed into his arms. The world around them faded, and they spun around and around until the lights turned to a blur, and the people vanished, and the city was gone. They stood in outer space now, just the two of them.

Together. Forever.

Something hit Wolfgang in the leg, and a wave of pain rocketed through his body. The woman faded from his view, and he screamed, writhing on the bed as reality rushed in like a tidal wave. His eyes snapped open, and he saw the room, but it was no longer dark. A light shone from overhead, and a big man stood next to him, leaned back, one foot stamping down on Wolfgang's thigh.

Wolfgang screamed again and jerked his leg. The big man's boot bit into his flesh and ripped at the wound, shoving down until the ceiling spun and darkness crept in from the edges of Wolfgang's vision. It was like being run through a meat grinder, feeling his body crushed and crunched—an unbelievable, consuming agony.

The big man lifted his boot and stamped it down on the floor. Wolfgang panted and shook, his head throbbing. A chair scraped on the floor next to him, and the big man sat down. Wolfgang was aware of it, but he couldn't really see the man.

Then he felt something rest against his leg again. Not a boot—a hand, this time. A big hand with strong fingers that wrapped around his injury and squeezed. The pain was nothing like the dominating surge of only moments before, but it was sharper and somehow more menacing.

"I'm Valko," the man said. His voice carried a faint East European accent, and Wolfgang vaguely remembered the tall blond man from the valley floor.

Wolfgang panted but didn't answer. He struggled to bring the woman back to his mind, but she was gone like a vapor in the wind, leaving nothing but the pain.

"What is your name?" Valko asked.

Wolfgang didn't answer, and Valko squeezed again.

Bullets of pain raced up his leg and through his spine. He screamed and tried to twist away, but it was useless. The chains kept him lashed to the bed.

"You have a compound fracture in the middle of your right femur," Valko said. His voice was calm and unfeeling. "The bone is completely shattered, and fragments of it have broken through the skin. The pain you feel results from those fragments tearing through your muscle. The harder I press, the deeper the injury. Do you understand?"

Wolfgang panted.

"Tell me your name," Valko said.

"Go," Wolfgang said.

"Go?"

"Go to Hell!"

Valko squeezed, and the edges of reality faded into a blinding red agony. Wolfgang shook, but he didn't scream. He clenched his jaw, and instead of blocking the pain, he embraced it, letting it fill his consciousness and become the very meaning of his existence. He let it take over everything, just to prove to himself that it wouldn't kill him.

"You think you're funny," Valko said, "but I'm a minister of pain. What you feel right now is just the tip of the iceberg. Do you understand me?" Valko leaned forward, his hand still tight around Wolfgang's shattered leg. "Who is the other man?"

Wolfgang managed a laugh. "Wrong question."

"Wrong question? What's the right question?"

"The right question," Wolfgang panted, "is *where* is the other man? If I were you, that's what I'd be worried about."

Valko lifted his hand and folded his arms. Wolfgang's head still throbbed, but his brain now blocked the edge of the pain—an automatic, biological protection mechanism that blurred everything into a numb fog.

"Is he a soldier?" Valko asked.

Wolfgang didn't answer.

"Is he a mercenary?"

Wolfgang licked his lips. "No."

"Who is he?" Valko leaned forward, bringing his face inches from Wolfgang's. Despite the brain-numbing fog, Wolfgang recognized the stench of tobacco and coffee on his breath.

"Who is he?" Valko demanded.

Wolfgang forced a joyless grin. "The guy you didn't count on."

Valko slammed his hand down on Wolfgang's thigh, and this time the pain was too much. It shattered his mind, and Wolfgang screamed. Then everything went black.

43

Darkness saturated the jungle, and Reed stood at the edge of the clearing, smoking his third cigarette of the night. One of the Colombians had provided them, and the wash of nicotine filled his lungs and took the edge off his nerves—a welcome respite after days of stress and fatigue.

Reed's three weapons lay on a picnic table in front of him—the SIG Sauer handgun, AK-74, and Dragunov sniper rifle. He'd put fifty rounds through each, checking function, reliability, and accuracy, and determined them all to be serviceable. From now on, the weapons wouldn't leave his sight, and nobody but him would touch them. He would only use the magazines he'd tested, and he'd inspected every round of ammunition he planned to carry, ensuring that none were corroded or misshapen. It was the best he could do with battered, surplus weaponry he didn't know the history of and hadn't spent months acquainting himself with. Plenty of times he'd survived on less, but he still didn't like it.

Reed sucked down a deep lungful of smoke and held it, staring at the weapons as the clatter of the preparing Colombians filled his ears from fifty yards away. He blocked out the noise, the details of the approaching operation, and his concerns about the firearms, and for the first time in two days, he allowed himself to think about Banks.

Even after years of taking lives and risking his own life, Reed had never felt guilt or fear like he'd felt holding Banks in the jungle, feeling her life slip away. As she struggled for breath and her blood drained into the dirt, the crushing reality that all of this was his fault bore down on his shoulders like the weight of the world, and Reed knew that if she died, he would kill himself without a second thought. It wasn't a noble thing or even a misguided belief that taking his own life would reunite him with her disembodied soul. Reed knew about Heaven and Hell—those spiritual destinations of the afterlife, forever separated from each other, with eternities of utopia and torment reserved for each. He knew where a person like Banks would go, and he knew where he would go.

No. He wouldn't have killed himself to see her again. He would have done it because, in the simplest terms, he couldn't live with himself if he watched her die. It was a strange sensation for a guy who made his living by snuffing out lives. Maybe, in a twisted way, it was the most demented thing for him to prioritize her life over the lives of his targets.

Reed didn't know or have the mental energy or the emotional self-awareness to unravel the ethical questions. He just knew that Banks was the only thing left on the planet that he cared about, and whatever happened, he was going to protect her.

He exhaled a dense cloud of smoke. He knew he should sleep, but he didn't trust the Colombians enough to let his guard down, and he couldn't shut off his mind anyway.

Cristian stepped out of the darkness ten yards away. "Are you hungry, amigo?"

One final drag of the cigarette, and Reed pictured the blond man and the burly man from the valley—Wolfgang's current captors, and maybe the men responsible for shooting Banks. They were his next targets. Men who were now damned and would very soon transition to that spiritual destination reserved for them.

"I'm good, Cristian. You should get some sleep. We leave in five hours."

They started up the trucks an hour before dawn. Cristian and another Colombian piled into a two-door Toyota pickup, and Reed jumped in back on top of the stretcher and a mountain of rope. He glanced up at a black sky as they passed two truckloads of heavily armed gunmen who would assault the bridge, and he thought about first light.

Reed was aware of a long, infamous history of early morning attacks. The Japanese at Pearl Harbor, George Washington at Trenton, and the Allies at Normandy. There was a reason first-light strikes often resulted in devastation. The enemy was either asleep or just concluding a long night of vigilance that left them fatigued and disoriented. They were hungry, groggy, and their thought processes were slow. Even with the rush of adrenaline that accompanied the sounds of gunfire, it took time for them to react. It took time for them to find weapons and locate the enemy. Even Legion X, as trained and lethal as Reed knew them to be, wasn't immune to the laws of nature, and he was going to destroy them for it.

Cristian drove, taking them west of the encampment down a series of winding dirt roads for almost an hour. The jungle leaned close over the road on both sides, leaving deep pools of shadows between the trees that were occasionally illuminated by glowing animal eyes. Reed watched them and thought about the slain jaguar from the previous night. It now felt like days ago, but he wondered if there were other jungle cats in those trees, and if cats were like humans.

Do they avenge their dead?

After turning down a new road, Cristian extinguished the headlights, and they bumped along in near-perfect darkness. Reed's eyes adjusted, and he held the AK over his lap as his mind switched into combat mode.

This wasn't the road he'd parked the stolen SUV on. Per his directions, Cristian took a long, indirect route from Diablo's encampment to a narrow, dirty track that ran just east of the horseshoe ridge. From there, Reed could scale the base of the horseshoe and establish an overwatch over the backside of the facility, with a clear field of fire over the entire valley. Cristian and his truck would wait on the track, ready to yank him out as soon as he recovered Wolfgang and deployed the bomb.

Another two miles passed, then Cristian pulled the truck to the edge of the road and cut the motor. Reed listened to the sounds of the sleeping jungle. He didn't hear any voices or the distant rumble of an approaching Humvee, but all these things weren't far away.

Like sleeping bears.

Reed climbed out of the truck and put the chest rig on first, tucking spare magazines for the AK and the Dragunov into its front pouches. He strapped the pistol and the knife around his waist, slid on the backpack laden with the bomb, and slung the Dragunov on top of it. Lastly, he picked up the AK, then lifted the aluminum stretcher from the back of the truck.

"Make sure the rope stays loose," he said. "If I yank on it, that means I need more slack."

Cristian stared at the massive pile of looped rope and chewed his lip. Reed knew he wasn't sold on the plan, but so long as he followed orders, he didn't need to be.

Reed knotted one end of the rope to the front of the stretcher, then gave Cristian a reassuring pat on the shoulder. "Got the radio?"

Cristian lifted his shirt, exposing the radio clipped to his belt.

Reed nodded. "Keep the rope untangled, and wait for my signal. We strike in about an hour."

Cristian grunted, then to Reed's surprise, he offered his hand.

"Good luck to you, amigo."

They shook once, then Reed lifted the stretcher and started into the trees.

The base of the ridge on the east side of the horseshoe was steeper than the south side, where Reed, Banks, and Wolfgang had previously ascended. Reed had avoided the river altogether by making his approach from the east, but that didn't make this climb any easier. After reaching the bottom of the slope, Reed looked up over a hundred yards to the top, marked by a sky that was now grey instead of black, and he drew in a long breath. He saw no direct path between the trees, which meant he'd need to weave his way with the stretcher, keeping the rope as clear as possible and avoiding land mines and trip wires the entire way.

Starting up the ridge, Reed breathed easily, keeping one hand on the AK and the other cradling the stretcher beneath his left arm. He fought his way halfway up the steep mountainside, then cut his speed in half and chose each step with care.

In the inky blackness, trip wires would be as invisible as spiderwebs, and land mines would be undetectable lumps, carefully buried beneath a bed of rotting leaves. But as steep as the mountainside was, Reed believed it was unlikely that Legion X would've descended through the trees to lay traps. His greatest threat now was a sentry, posted at the top of the ridge to guard against intruders, armed with a powerful flashlight and an automatic rifle.

The farther up the mountainside Reed climbed, the slower he moved. Every little while, he stopped and crouched behind a tree, just to listen. Occasional bird calls or the snap of a twig in the darkness signaling the passage of an animal were all that broke the stillness.

He climbed on, keeping as close to the ground as he could while trying not to bang into anything with the stretcher. The last hundred yards were the most difficult, as the terrain steepened and the trees grew farther apart, leaving him less cover. He slowed to almost a crawl, walking only on his toes and avoiding sticks and low brush.

Finally, the crest of the ridge became visible a few yards ahead. Reed waited again behind a tree, listening, then he knelt and rested the stretcher on the leaves, picking up a stick instead. With each step he took, Reed swept gently with the stick and prodded the ground, feeling for wires or the metallic bulk of land mines. On the third step, he felt resistance on the stick, and as he knelt next to a tree, he saw the wire. No larger than fishing line, it raced between the low brush and terminated on either end at a large tree.

Reed withdrew the stick and studied the trees, quickly noticing small packages strapped to their bases. C4, probably. Enough to knock him off his feet and maybe kill him. He rerouted to avoid the wire, then repeated his pattern of sweeping and probing, noting one more wire and what may have been a land mine before he finally reached the crest of the ridge.

The valley floor spilled out before him just as the brightening sky turned from grey to orange. It looked exactly as he had left it, save that one of the Humvees was missing, and the helicopter sat on its pad with a shattered windshield. The grey outlines of half a dozen gunmen paced around the parked vehicles, rifles held across their chests as they systematically patrolled the facility grounds. None of them were Legion X mercenaries, which meant those guys were hidden around the facility, asleep inside, or posted as sentries along the ridge. Maybe at the bridge, also.

Reed returned to retrieve the stretcher, navigating along a new path, which ensured that the rope behind him would avoid contact with trip wires or land mines. It rustled softly in the leaves as he pulled it—loud enough to put him on edge but no louder than the passing animals bouncing through the leaves.

When he returned to the ridge, Reed rested the stretcher behind a tree and crouched on the dirt. A glance over his shoulder confirmed that the sky behind him had turned red at the edges and orange in the middle. He had maybe twenty minutes before the blaze of the sun poured over his shoulders, which meant it was time to send the first signal.

Reed dug into his pocket and produced a short-wave radio, identical to Cristian's. He turned it on and handpicked channel 9, then depressed the call button, held it for a full second, and let go. On the other end of the line, the Colombians in the trucks would hear a single, digital *bleep* and know it was time.

Reed turned the volume up on his radio, just barely loud enough to be audible if he held it against his ear, and he waited. Seconds passed. Almost half a minute. Then the digital bleep was returned.

He switched the radio off and pocketed it. About twenty yards ahead was an ideal shooting position—sheltered on either side by thick trees and clogged with enough brush to obscure his exact position, while still providing a clear view of the valley. He remained in a crouch, took a hesitant step toward it, then froze. Something—maybe a sensation, a distant sound, or just an instinct—told him to stop. He slid behind a tree and looked through the forest, searching for the disturbance and wondering if he'd imagined it.

His nose wrinkled, and he realized what had alerted him: the smell of human urine nearby. Reed turned his head into the wind, tracking the smell to the right of his designated sniper's nest. A figure in the trees, as dark as a shadow, stood holding a rifle and staring right at him.

44

Reed didn't move. His first instinct commanded him to run or fight, but years of aggressive training and combat experience overrode that instinct and kept him perfectly still. The man he saw in the shadows, thirty yards away, wasn't brandishing his rifle. Reed had seen him, but maybe he hadn't seen Reed.

Seconds slipped by, and Reed held his breath and kept his finger only a flick away from the trigger of the AK. The man in the shadows stared into the forest with his rifle held at low-ready, the stock sandwiched under his right arm, his right hand on the grip, his left hand on the forestock. Prepared for action, but not yet taking aim.

The figure leaned forward, and Reed realized he must have heard something and was now searching for the source of the disturbance. This wasn't one of the Legion X guys. They would've taken immediate cover and waited for another noise to give away their prey. This must be one of the Colombians—local guns, like Diablo's people.

The man leaned forward a little farther, and a first ray of sunlight broke across his cheek, revealing sleepy eyes and dirty hair. He carried the rifle as he'd been taught, but he wasn't prepared to use it. He was just trying to stay awake.

Yet, if he keeps looking, he'll see me.

Gunshots cracked in the distance. A long strip of rattlesnake-like fire. The sentry stiffened and raised his gun, looking away from Reed and toward the source of the noise.

The bridge attack has begun.

The sentry turned, rushing away from his post and toward the valley floor. He reached to his belt for a radio, but the facility below was already alive with action. A low but shrill alarm rang out from the facility, and then the gunmen on patrol took cover behind parked cars and directed their rifles at the mouth of the valley.

The sentry unclipped his radio and raised it to his lips. That was when Reed hit him, dropping the AK to the forest floor a split second before he snaked his left arm around the man's throat and drove the KAMPO up to the hilt between his ribs. The radio hit the dirt, and the man fought, but Reed snatched the knife out and stabbed again, twisting and pulling this time.

He wasn't going to take another chance of knocking a sentry out. The man wretched a couple more times, but then his body went into shock, and his jerks became irregular and unfocused. Reed pulled the knife free and tightened his arm around his neck, pulling in and holding until the body grew limp. Then he slowly lowered him to the forest floor, loosening his hold until the sentry lay lifeless in the leaves.

Reed wiped the knife on his leg and jammed it back into his sheath. He didn't have time to second-guess his choice. The roar of a Humvee rumbled from the valley floor amid the shouts of running men. Reed scooped his AK back up and hurried through the trees, following the path he'd already identified to his chosen overwatch.

Reed slid to his knees, resting the AK on the ground and unslinging the Dragunov. He chambered a round into the big rifle and deployed the bipod as he surveyed the valley floor. Four Legion X soldiers piled into their surviving Humvee, quickly joined by a pickup truck loaded with local gunmen. Both vehicles turned toward the road, and Reed looked back to the buildings.

Come on, come on . . . Use the helicopter.

The distant commotion of Diablo's approaching gangsters was louder now—a ceaseless roar of reckless gunfire as their two trucks lurched up the road toward the bridge. Reed slid onto his stomach, pulling the rifle stock into his shoulder. In a millisecond, the presence of the sniper rifle and the blast of gunfire took him back to Iraq, and the momentary wash of memories was enough to disorient him. He shut them all out, casting a nervous glance around the trees before he flipped the safety off and swept the crosshairs over the valley floor.

There.

Four men, all dressed in the black fatigues of Legion X, ran toward the helicopter. Two of them carried assault rifles, while a third sported an H&K MG4 machine gun, and the fourth was armed only with an MP5 submachine gun strapped across his chest.

The pilot.

Reed swept his crosshairs across the valley floor, checking for additional targets or threats while the helicopter crew approached the aircraft. He returned his focus to the bird, watching as the four men threw open the doors and piled in. Two guys took the back, squatting on the floor and keeping the doors open as the second guy with the assault rifle took the co-pilot's seat, and the guy with the MP5 took the pilot's seat.

Reed breathed in. Breathed out. Shut out the world around him and focused on the men in the small aircraft. He knew there were other snipers —Legion X guys—on the right-hand ridge, providing overwatch into the valley and sniper cover over the road. Extensive experience told Reed he had two shots with the Dragunov before those snipers opened fire on the backside of the ridge, unable to pinpoint his exact position but eager as hell for a lucky shot.

Two shots. Two targets. The pilot and the co-pilot.

Reed relaxed and settled the crosshairs over the pilot's ear—above his chest plate and below his helmet, three hundred yards away. He rested his finger on the trigger and drew a deep breath, then let half of it out and held it. The helicopter's engines whined, and Reed watched the rotor gain speed. The aircraft twitched, and its left runner skipped over the ground.

Then Reed fired.

The blown-out glass of the pilot's door provided no protection against the heavy Russian bullet. His head exploded in a cloud of red, and even before his body slumped, Reed pivoted to the left, aligned his sights, and squeezed again.

The co-pilot pitched forward, faceless, and the aircraft slammed into the ground. The engine continued to roar, and the blades turned, but both men in the back bailed out. Reed swung the rifle to the right and pulled the trigger again, pushing his luck with a third shot against the guy with the machine gun.

The Legion X operator took the bullet in his hip and pitched forward as the MG4 flew out of his hands. Bullets snapped through the trees, just over Reed's head. He heard gunshots from the ridge to his front-right and rolled to his left as a branch was shot away from a nearby tree and crashed to the ground. Reed fast-crawled on his stomach away from the overwatch, dragging the Dragunov with him as random bullets continued to zip through the trees over his head.

He found cover behind a wax palm and pivoted the Dragunov around the base of the tree. From the north ridge of the horseshoe, muzzle flash—small arms fire, probably from AKs wielded by local hired guns—lit the jungle in two places.

Amateurs.

Reed swept the crosshairs along the ridge, identifying the locations of both shooters. There would be a third shooter, probably a Legion X sniper, at the end of the ridge. But this man was smart enough not to waste ammunition and give away his position. He'd wait, hoping for Reed to shoot first. But with the sun blazing in over Reed's shoulders, the Dragunov's muzzle flash would be indistinct.

Reed fired—once, then twice. Both AKs went silent, and the bullets zipping through the trees ceased. Just after Reed's second shot, the crack of a high-powered rifle boomed from the end of a ridge, and a bullet slammed into the wax palm he was leaning against.

Reed snapped the rifle to the left, placing the crosshairs over the spot where his instincts told him the sniper lay, and he pulled the trigger. The Dragunov slammed into his shoulder, spitting another 7.62 slug across the valley floor and into the trees. Reed rolled to the left as soon as he fired, carrying the rifle with him and taking cover behind another tree. But no return shot sounded from the ridge.

Reed lifted the scope back to his eye and swept the ridge. All was still amid the trees, with nothing but the incessant fire from the bridge battle filling the air. Something moved amid the brush, and he pivoted the scope down to focus on the object. An AR-10 sniper rifle slid down the hillside. Reed leaned back from the rifle and took a long breath, scanning the valley floor for more combatants, but even the hip-shot machine gunner had fled the valley.

Ditching the Dragunov and hurrying to his feet, he again scooped up the AK on his way to the stretcher. As before, he carried the stretcher beneath his left arm, yanking to ensure the rope held plenty of slack, then he turned down the ridge and rushed for the backside of the facility.

45

All hell broke loose in the valley. Valko's first warning of the impending attack came as the sounds of automatic gunfire echoed out of the jungle. He was already awake—enjoying a second cup of coffee and reviewing plans for a new field of land mines on the far side of the bridge, when Judson burst into his mobile office.

"Two trucks loaded with fighters, moving on the bridge," Judson said. His voice was calm, but Valko saw a light in his eyes that told him Judson was excited and ready for blood.

"Load a truck with the local guys," Valko said, snatching up a rifle and moving to the door. "I'll take the Humvee."

By the time Valko reached the Humvee with three of his riflemen, the roar of approaching gunfire was deafening. Judson had already left for the bridge, driving a pickup loaded with local security contractors Valko had found upon arriving at the facility.

Valko ordered his driver to follow, then shouted into his radio. "Bosko, what do you see?"

Legion X's sniper was positioned at the end of the north ridge, where he had a clean overwatch of both the valley and the road. "They're almost to the bridge," Bosko responded. "I see two trucks and maybe twenty-five combatants. Looks like local guns."

Valko cursed. Local guns. Maybe Fianchetto had more to worry about in Colombia than Valko first thought. "Romano!" he shouted into the radio. "Take Griswold, Beckham, and Pelkov, and get that bird in the air!"

"Copy that, Valko," Romano radioed back.

Valko grabbed the dash of the Humvee as it hurtled down the road, out of the horseshoe valley, and toward the bridge. He heard the distant crack of Bosko's rifle from behind and knew the sniper was already engaging the enemy.

Judson parked his truck across the bridge and positioned his contractors behind it. Valko directed his driver to fill the remaining gap with the Humvee and then piled out with his men.

Already, a hail of bullets assaulted both vehicles, skipping off the concrete surface of the bridge and slamming into glass and sheet metal. The endless storm of automatic gunfire coming from the jungle was immense. It was as if every one of the two dozen gunmen assaulting the bridge were armed with Miniguns. Valko attempted to lean out from the back bumper of the Humvee and return fire, but as soon as he exposed a shoulder, a blast of bullets skipped off the vehicle's rear quarter panel and whizzed past his face.

Valko looked back to the valley, cursing as a lucky shot nicked his leg. It was barely a scratch, but his inability to return fire disillusioned him. It made him feel out of control, like the entire situation was melting down in a matter of seconds.

"Romano!" he shouted into his radio. "Where the hell are you?"

The helicopter pilot didn't answer, and as Valko looked to the sky, he didn't see the Lakota rising over the ridge.

A low hiss broke through the gunfire, followed by the familiar whooshing rush of a rocket-propelled grenade hurtling across the bridge.

"Take cover!" Valko shouted, throwing himself to the ground.

The Legion X fighters huddled around the Humvee and moved with practiced ease, shielding themselves behind the bulk of the armored vehicle. But the local contractors dug in around the pickup never heard the command. The RPG struck the edge of the bridge ten feet from the pickup and detonated with a ground-shaking boom. The truck slammed against the Humvee, and shards of windshield glass rained over the concrete.

One of the local guys closest to the blast was blown backward, a hole the size of a basketball torn through his chest, and two more lay on the ground in growing pools of blood, screaming and clutching shrapnel wounds.

Valko clawed his way through the glass, reaching Judson and shouting over the din. "Go back and find Romano. We need that chopper in the air!"

46

The rope dragged across the ground and slapped against foliage as Reed followed the sentry's trail down the inside of the ridge. Adrenaline surged into his blood, supercharging his every move. From the end of the valley, the familiar blast of an RPG detonated, and he thought he heard screams amid the gunfire. Smoke rose over the ridge, black with soot and burning tires, and Reed couldn't help but be impressed by the ferocity of Diablo's soldiers.

Pour on the heat, guys.

The facility loomed out of the valley floor a hundred yards ahead. As Reed drew closer, he dropped to his knees and rolled beneath the edge of the mesh shielding the building from aerial view, still dragging the stretcher along with him. After another ten yards, he descended into a crouch behind a tree, directing the AK at the rear door of the facility.

Shouts rang from the building, followed almost instantly by the gunshots. Bullets tore through the foliage around him, but Reed didn't budge. He recognized the distinct note of pistol-caliber submachine guns, and at a distance of a hundred yards, set to full-auto, the shooters might as well throw rocks at him.

Muzzle flash illuminated the gunmen—two near the door, and two more firing from windows near the roof. Reed moved the AK quickly, sighting through the Russian-made optic mounted above the receiver and pressing the trigger with smooth, successive twitches of his index finger. The AK barked, and bodies hit the floor as the submachine guns fell quiet.

Reed ran, abandoning the stretcher fifty yards from the bottom of the ridge and breaking straight for the loading dock built along the backside of the facility. Again, gunfire burst from an overhead window, and Reed slid to a stop at the base of the loading dock, slamming the AK's selector switch to full-auto before unleashing a hail of bullets through the building. The AK's steel-core ammunition tore through the sheet metal like it was paper, and more screams rang from inside. Reed dumped the empty mag and slammed a fresh one into the receiver, then hoisted himself onto the dock and barreled through the open back door.

The interior of the building was paved in concrete, with a high ceiling crisscrossed by catwalks and offices. An abandoned forklift sat near the door with a trail of blood leading away from it and into the darkness. Behind the forklift were the bananas—hundreds, maybe thousands of boxes of them, stacked together on pallets to form a Manhattan of towering rows eight feet high, with narrow walks in between them. Reed had never seen so many bananas. They filled the warehouse, stretching out to both sides and disappearing into the darkness.

He kept the rifle at eye level as he moved into the shadows, sweeping the catwalks and offices, and moving from cover to cover. He reviewed his mental outline of the facility—how the bananas entered through the north wing of the U-shaped building, where they were treated. Then they were moved here, into the warehouse, where they were stored before being shipped out again. The south building, the final wing of the facility, was the lab. So, where would Wolfgang be?

Not in the lab, that was for sure. And not in the treatment facility, either. Legion X would want him in the most isolated, secure part of the facility, farthest from the road.

He's in one of the offices.

Reed ran to the nearest staircase and swept the warehouse floor one more time before lunging up the metal stairs, which had zero protective cover if somebody burst into the room. For the moment, everybody seemed to be either dead or involved in the shootout at the bridge, but that didn't mean a new gunman couldn't burst in at any moment.

Reaching the top of the steps, he turned to the offices, kicking the first door open and leading with the AK. The cheap plywood door caved in, revealing a dusty office with a desk and filing cabinets, but no prisoner.

After clearing the interior in under two seconds, he moved to the next office. It was also barricaded by a plywood door that collapsed under a booted kick, but the inside wasn't empty. A window stared out over the mountain slope at the back of the horseshoe, and on the floor, the bloody corpse of a hired gunman lay. His body was shredded by at least three rounds from Reed's AK, and a fallen MP5 submachine gun was next to him, along with a litter of empty shell casings.

Reed toed him with his boot to ensure he was no longer a threat. The body didn't move, and Reed hurried to the final two offices. The first featured an open plywood door and an interior stacked with file boxes, but the last was guarded by a metal door, shut and locked with a padlock. Reed stood back from the door and smacked it with one fist. He waited but heard nothing inside.

The padlock was new and clean. It looped through a hasp that was screwed in on one side into the door and the other into the doorframe. The door, the hasp, and the lock were all made of thick steel—unbreakable by force and impervious to gunfire. But the doorframe itself was made of aluminum, and Reed knew aluminum to be a relatively soft metal that was anything but impervious.

He checked over his shoulder to the floor of the warehouse, but it lay empty and silent, so he flipped the AK backwards in his hands and slammed the solid spruce stock directly into the lock. The hasp pulled against both the door and the doorframe but didn't move. He slammed a second time, and then a third. On the fourth blow, he noticed the screws loosening in the doorframe. Four more strikes, and they tore free.

Shouts rang out from one of the connecting buildings, and Reed swapped the AK around in his hands again. He tore the shattered remains of the hasp away from the doorframe, then twisted the knob with his left hand, still gripping the AK with his right.

The interior of the last office was small and windowless. Light streamed over Reed's shoulder and into the room, spilling over a stained linoleum floor and exposing the only two pieces of furniture it contained—a chair and a metal cot.

And on the metal cot lay Wolfgang Pierce. His face was pale, and he was chained hand-and-foot to the four corners of the bed. Reed's nose wrinkled at the stench of blood and rotting flesh, and even before he stepped into the room, he knew Wolfgang was badly injured.

As Reed approached, his eyes fell on the swollen mass of Wolfgang's right thigh. His knee was twisted to the right at an unnatural angle, and although thick bandages covered the leg, those bandages poked up at random, as though something was rising out of his leg.

Bone.

Wolfgang's swollen lips parted, and he tried to speak, but Reed heard nothing.

"Don't talk," Reed said. "Just nod if you understand."

Wolfgang nodded weakly.

"Is your leg broken?"

A nod.

"Compound fracture?"

Another nod.

Reed thought quickly as the shouts of people closing in on the back of the facility grew louder, and he pulled the door shut. This wasn't a fortress; he couldn't hope to keep Wolfgang alive while Legion X operatives still breathed in the facility. They had to get back down the stairs and out to the stretcher, but before Reed could do that, he still had to take care of the lab.

One step at a time.

Reed knelt down and quickly moved the bandage. The swollen mass of Wolfgang's leg was beyond horrifying—the skin was purple and black, with fragments of dirty and shattered bone poking through. The odor of rot grew stronger, and Reed replaced the bandage.

"You've got to walk," Reed said. "I'll hold you up and get you down the stairs. Then we move to the exit." Reed unclipped the AK's two-point sling and adjusted it to maximum length. He wrapped one end around the ankle of Wolfgang's shattered leg, then grabbed him by the upper arm. "Grit your teeth. This is gonna hurt."

Reed tugged, rolling Wolfgang off his back and onto his side. Wolfgang shook and let out a choking cry but held back a scream. Leaning over him, Reed snaked the free end of the AK sling up his back, pulling until Wolfgang's broken leg bent at the knee. Again, Wolfgang cried and shook, but Reed hooked the end of the sling to the back of his belt, suspending his leg into a flamingo-bend that would keep it from dragging on the ground. Without waiting or warning, he grabbed Wolfgang by the shoulders and pulled him into a sitting position on the edge of the bed. Wolfgang screamed as he rolled over his shattered thigh. The AK sling rode the edge of the bed and pulled at the injury, and Wolfgang's eyes rolled back in his head.

Reed smacked him on the cheek. "Stay with me, Wolf!"

Doors blew open, and boots pounded against the warehouse floor beneath. Reed slapped a hand across Wolfgang's mouth, clamping it down and holding his breath. Men spoke, all in Spanish, and excited cries and shouts rang from one end of the warehouse to the other.

More local guns.

Reed held up a finger and whispered. "I'm going to hold you up on your good leg. We're going to get down the stairs. Understand?" Wolfgang nodded, and Reed unholstered the SIG and pressed it into Wolfgang's left hand. "You see somebody, you waste 'em."

Wolfgang's eyes were so blurry, Reed doubted he could recognize his own mother, but he still wanted as much lead as possible flying toward the bad guys. There were no friends in the warehouse below. Only targets.

Reed grabbed the AK with his right hand and slid his left arm beneath Wolfgang's arms and around his back. "On three. Don't scream."

He pulled Wolfgang close and counted under his breath. When he reached three, he moved upward, smooth and fast, and Wolfgang rose with him. The SIG hit the floor, and Wolfgang crumpled over in shaking agony. Reed thought he might collapse, but at the last second, Wolfgang's good leg stiffened, and he held himself up. Teeth ground, and he shook, but The Wolf didn't fall.

Reed gave the SIG a sideways glance, but he knew he couldn't afford to stoop and retrieve it. Now that Wolfgang was up, he had to keep him up. They staggered to the door, and Reed used the muzzle of the AK to nudge it open. It swung on smooth hinges, and the voices below continued—a chatter of stressed Spanish.

Reed led Wolfgang through the door and looked off the catwalk to the warehouse floor. Two Colombians, both dressed in green fatigues and carrying MP5s, surveyed the bloody mess of the floor, standing about twenty feet apart and thirty yards from Reed's position.

Reed held his breath and rested the muzzle of the rifle on the catwalk railing. Reaching up with his free fingers, he grabbed the selector switch, tugging gently downward from full-auto to semi-auto. The switch clicked into position, making a small metallic sound that rang through the quiet warehouse like a gunshot of its own. Both Colombians looked up, but it was already too late for them. Bent at the knee and still bracing the end of the rifle against the catwalk, Reed brought his shoulder into the stock, his eyeline equal with the sights and his finger against the trigger. It was one smooth motion, carefully calculated and followed by a quick shot, an adjustment of the sights, and another quick shot.

Both Colombians hit the concrete with gushing holes torn through their chests. Their weapons clattered to the floor, and Reed straightened, lifting both Wolfgang and the rifle as he moved to the stairs. With each step, Wolfgang shook and bit back a cry, but he moved his good leg the best he could, supporting the bulk of his weight as his suspended foot slammed at random into the steps, sending tremors ripping through his body.

Reed hurried, critically aware that Wolfgang could pass out at any moment or another wave of gunmen could rush the warehouse. He reached the foot of the stairs and turned for the first available cover—a double-stacked tower of pallets wrapped in shrink wrap.

He barely made it to their sheltered side before two things happened simultaneously—Wolfgang passed out, and the lights cut off, drenching the warehouse with darkness.

Legion X had arrived.

47

As soon as the lights snapped off, Reed knew he had trouble. The same logic that demanded he attack the facility after sunrise also meant that the odds were now against him in a darkened warehouse. Even with the back door open and sunlight streaming in, substantial sections of the warehouse were completely shrouded in shadow, giving a decided advantage to anybody dressed in black and equipped with night vision or an infrared optic.

Reed lowered Wolfgang's limp form to the ground, then cradled the rifle in both hands. He listened intently for footsteps or the creak of a catwalk overhead. He heard nothing, and for a second, he wondered if the power had been cut from another part of the facility.

No. I heard the switch.

Moving away from Wolfgang, Reed slipped into the maze of stacked pallets. Everything smelled green and earthy, like a grocery store's produce section on steroids. He crouched closer to the floor, shrinking away from exposure to the catwalks, and he crept forward, keeping the rifle held close to his shoulder. All was silent, but that only confirmed his fears about another man in the warehouse.

Reed calculated quickly. His opponent would be armed but wouldn't fire until he had a clean shot, which meant Reed would probably never hear the gunshot. He was most vulnerable to the catwalks, where a shooter could easily lie prone and wait for Reed to expose himself between the pallets. But the catwalks featured only a single access point, which was the stairway he and Wolfgang used previously. Reed already knew nobody was hiding in the offices, so that meant he was safe from overhead.

He's down here with me. Searching.

With the AK at eye level, Reed kept his finger resting against the trigger as he cleared one aisle, then the next. With each step, he listened for an answering footstep or the click of gear on a harness. He blinked away sweat trickling into his eye and cleared the next aisle, moving between the tightly stacked pallets and keeping his footsteps imperceptibly soft.

Then he heard the click. It was faint, like the flick of a safety, only it wasn't a safety. Reed slung himself to the left, instinctively moving behind a banana crate only a second before the click was joined by the metallic smack of a grenade hitting the pavement. He clamped his eyes shut and turned his head away. A shockwave of disorienting force washed over him and hurled him to the ground as the warehouse rang with a deafening boom.

It was a flash-bang, and when Reed opened his eyes, all he saw was blinding white light. His ears rang, and the floor around him felt unsteady, like the deck of a rocking boat. But despite the violence of the blast, Reed's instincts and quick movement sheltered him from the bulk of the explosion, and his vision quickly returned. In a microsecond, Reed calculated the arc and travel time of the grenade, turned his rifle toward his attacker, and clamped his finger down on the trigger.

The AK rattled out a short blast, and somebody screamed. A figure clothed in all black stumbled out from behind a pallet, twenty yards away, blood streaming from his arm. Before Reed could deliver a killing shot, Burly appeared out of the darkness.

Reed swung the AK to face his attacker and fired again. Burly slid behind a pallet, and the bullets zipped harmlessly through midair before the AK clicked over an empty chamber. Pulling back into the shadows, Reed kicked the mag out and reached for another. Burly opened fire, and Reed ducked to the ground as bullets ripped through the pallets, blasting a purée of banana across the ground.

Reed clawed his way backward, jerking a new magazine out of his chest rig and slamming it into the AK. He cycled the action, then returned to his feet and rushed for the first gunman—the one who slung the flash-bang. A trail of blood marked the way, leading into the shadows from the point where Reed's bullets first made impact. Reed couldn't hear Burly following him, but he knew the big man wouldn't be far behind and may have grenades of his own—fragmentation grenades that would do a lot worse than disorient him.

The trail of blood turned a corner around a pallet, and Reed ground to a stop, holding his breath. Once again, the warehouse had fallen eerily still, but this time, if he listened closely, he could hear wheezing from the wounded Legion X mercenary. The sound was too faint and indistinct to place, but it wasn't far away.

Reed lowered the AK and looked up to the pallets. They loomed over him, glistening in shrink wrap, their tops about ten feet off the ground. He quickly calculated Burly's distance and speed and made an instant decision. It might get him killed, but if he stayed on the ground, the odds were against him.

Reed lifted his left leg and got his shoe into the gap between the top and bottom banana boxes, then braced himself with his free hand and pushed up. His right foot left the ground, and he swung his hand and AK over the lid of the top pallet before pulling himself up. The entire move was smooth enough to remain almost silent, and in a little under three seconds, he lay on his stomach atop a row of banana pallets.

The cardboard creaked a little under his weight as Reed wriggled softly forward, pulling his legs up behind him. The closer he came to the far side of the row, the louder the grunting of the injured mercenary. Slowing to a worm's crawl, he moved as softly as he could off the first pallet and onto the second. Ahead of him, the row of pallets looked like a cardboard road, shooting off into the darkness with occasional gaps where a forklift path cut between them.

Reed reached the other side of the row and looked down into the gap. The mercenary lay there, huddled into a corner with his rifle cradled in his lap, pointed at the entrance of the alley. Blood streamed from two wounds in his left arm, and a third in his ribcage, where a bullet passed through an opening in his body armor. He held pressure against the rib wound with his left elbow, but blood streaming from his arm pooled next to him, and his face was pale.

He's got five minutes. Ten, max.

Reed lifted the AK, resting the bottom of the magazine over the top of the pallet, and turned his head back to the entrance of the alley. He couldn't hear Burly, but he knew the killer was still nearby, somewhere in the shadows.

Hunting.

Reed slipped the KAMPO from its sheath on his hip and moved a little closer to the edge of the pallets. They shifted beneath him, and wood creaked against loosening nails. The mercenary twitched, sweat dripping off his upper lip, then he sat up and brandished the rifle, its muzzle swaying.

Reed took the knife by the blade, holding it like a paper airplane as he rose onto his elbow. Only ten feet above and ten feet away from the mercenary, he was so close he could smell the man's sweat. Reed cocked his wrist back and slung the knife. It spun through the air, heavy and wobbly, more like a hatchet than a knife. As soon as he released it, Reed dropped to his chest, disappearing behind the top edge of the pallet. The knife struck home, and the mercenary shouted. It didn't sound like a pained shout as much as a surprised cry, but it had the desired effect. He jerked, and his gun fired, spitting bullets out of the alley and into a facing row of banana pallets.

Burly's footfalls resounded immediately, booming from a nearby forklift path. He called to his man in a foreign language—German, maybe— and the man called back.

Reed raised the AK and pointed it toward the mouth of the alley. The wounded mercenary beneath him continued to groan, but Reed didn't risk looking over the top of the pallets to confirm his predicament. Boots thumped, and Burly appeared around the end of the alley, his gun raised and his meaty face tensed behind the sights of his weapon.

Five quick shots from Reed tore through the air, ripping through Burly's neck and face and hurling him to the ground. He'd barely hit the concrete before Reed was on his knees, twisting back and shooting into the alley.

The wounded mercenary never had a chance. He took two rounds to the face and one in the neck before crumpling back, his chest drenched in a waterfall of blood.

Reed kept the rifle up, sweeping the forklift paths and listening for more boots. He swung two legs off the edge of the pallets and dropped into the alley, quickly confirming that both mercenaries were dead before he recovered the KAMPO, took a pistol from Burly, and rushed back to Wolfgang.

48

Valko knew something was wrong. Even as an endless barrage of gunfire tore through the jungle and blasted the mouth of the bridge, the severity of the firefight didn't translate into genuine aggression. Hundreds of rounds and several rocket-propelled grenades had been hurled at his men, even as they dug in behind parked vehicles and defended the bridge. But the horde of attacking Colombians didn't advance.

They just dug in, more like defenders than aggressors, and poured on the heat.

Valko dropped behind the parked Humvee and swapped the mag in his rifle. He slammed home a new one, then depressed the call button on his radio. "Judson, come in!"

Since deploying his second-in-command ten minutes before, Valko hadn't heard from Judson, and the Lakota still hadn't taken off. Something was very wrong.

An RPG made contact against the Toyota pickup Judson had left behind. It detonated, sending a hail of shredded vehicle parts shooting into the air as two more of Valko's incompetent local gunmen hurtled to the ground, one of them missing an arm. Valko cursed and radioed Judson again, but again there was no reply.

A growing uneasiness rose in his chest. All of this felt wrong. If the army of fighters assaulting the bridge were sincere in their attempt to take the facility, why weren't they moving forward? For that matter, why had they attacked so brazenly in the first place, charging up the road and firing into the air like a horde of drunken thugs?

On first impression, Valko had chalked the reckless assault down to just that—the strategy of drunken thugs. But as Judson failed to answer a third call, Valko knew he'd miscalculated. This wasn't an attack at all. It was a distraction. And he'd fallen for it.

"Back to the truck!" Valko shouted, raising the rifle and taking a quick shot at an attacker as the man exposed himself from behind a tree. The target went down, blood streaming from his chest, and Valko jerked the driver's-side door of his Humvee open. He started the engine as two of his surviving operators piled into the back seat, then shoved the transmission into reverse and slammed on the gas.

"Where are we going?" one of his men asked.

"Back to the facility."

"What about Judson?" the man pressed. "He's covering it!"

Valko jerked the Humvee around, slammed it into drive, and roared back onto the road. He could think of only one reason his second-in-command wouldn't answer his radio. Judson was dead, and that left the facility fully exposed.

49

When Reed returned to Wolfgang, he found him unconscious and limp, like a dead animal. He checked his pulse to ensure he was still alive, but the crimson blotches creeping up Wolfgang's neck confirmed his earlier suspicions that blood poisoning was underway.

Diablo better have more of those antibiotics.

Reed checked his watch, then thumbed the two-way radio. "Cristian, come in."

"I'm here, amigo."

"All good on the truck?" Reed asked.

"All good. Are you ready?"

Reed keyed the radio to respond, but a new sound from outside the facility arrested his attention. It was the all-too-familiar groan of a diesel engine, punctuated by the pop of gravel beneath oversized tires.

A Humvee.

Reed snatched the AK and broke into a run down the length of the warehouse, weaving between stacks of pallets as he navigated to the south wing of the facility—the laboratory.

The south building connected to the warehouse with a set of double metal doors set in a blank wall. They were windowless and flat grey, with a red warning sign in Spanish mounted above them.

The growl of the Humvee grew closer, and Reed tried the handle. Both doors were locked, but there was a keypad mounted on the wall next to them. He'd encountered locking mechanisms like this before and knew there were generally two types—the type designed to secure a sensitive area against intentional intrusion, and the kind designed to block casual and careless people from wandering into a danger zone. This keypad was the second kind, which meant it was as easy to defeat as stripping a couple of wires and bypassing the code.

Reed made quick work of the wires with the KAMPO, cutting them free of the pad and stripping away the insulation with his teeth. He began to systematically cross wires, listening for the click of the lock as the Humvee ground to a stop at the front of the facility. Then he heard the shouting voice of a man calling orders.

The blond guy.

Reed continued to cross wires as the clock in his head ticked like an omen of doom. He gave himself sixty seconds to breach the lab and place the bomb. If he couldn't make it before then, he would have to extract and leave the building standing.

Not happening. I'm finishing this.

The lock clicked, and Reed dropped the wires, shoving the double doors open before they could relock. He barreled through to the other side, rifle raised, and immediately ground to a halt. The enormous room had a high roof, and desks were built along both walls. Some sort of conveyor belt assembly line filled the middle section. Bottles, vials, and tanks of unidentifiable substances crowded shelves and filled bins, and along the left wall, near the filler port Reed had seen from outside the facility, was a large propane tank the size of a sedan.

Bright fluorescent lights lit up everything, driving away shadows and making the place feel cold and harsh. But what caught his attention were the ten men and women dressed in full hazmat gear, standing at the far end of the building, huddled near the assembly line, their eyes wide behind plastic face masks.

Unmoving, they stared at Reed. His muscles tensed, and his finger tightened around the trigger, but then he stopped himself. These people weren't combatants. They probably had no idea what horrific poison they were brewing in this godforsaken place.

"Get out!" he yelled, jerking the rifle. The crowd of lab workers shifted, and a woman screamed, but nobody moved. Reed flicked the selector switch on the rifle to full-auto and tipped the muzzle upward, just above their heads. He squeezed off a burst, blasting penlight holes through the metal wall behind them.

Everybody screamed and broke for the door. Reed repeated the blast as he ran down the aisle to the left of the conveyor belt. Doors hurtled open, and the crowd rushed out, but their panicked voices were now joined by the shouts of Legion X mercenaries outside.

Reed snatched the backpack off, quickly removing the detonator from the top and tucking it into his pocket. Then he ran for the propane tank, shoving the pack beneath it until it rested out of sight amid dark shadows.

No sooner had he placed the backpack than gunshots burst from the doorway the lab workers had fled through. Reed hit the floor as bullets slammed into the conveyor and ricocheted off the metal shelves, then he jerked the AK toward the gunfire and clamped down on the trigger, dumping the entire mag at the door. Empty cartridge casings rained across the concrete, and more pinholes of light opened through the face of the building as shouts echoed through the lab.

Reed didn't wait for Legion X to reappear. He lurched to his feet and ran as fast as he could back through the double doors, slamming them shut as he passed. Small-caliber rounds struck the doors just as they closed, but as the latch clicked into place, Reed heard the lock follow suit. When he tried the door, it wouldn't open.

That'll buy me a minute.

Rushing back across the warehouse, he swerved between the pallets and found Wolfgang right where he'd left him. He dropped the AK and grabbed Wolfgang with both arms, manhandling him over his shoulder before he dashed for the back entrance of the warehouse.

The double doors to the laboratory clattered but didn't open. Shouts rang from the other side, followed by the meaty thud of a man body-slamming the doors. They still didn't open, but Reed knew it was only a matter of seconds before Legion X forced or blew their way through.

He hustled down the steps of the loading dock, holding Wolfgang in place with one arm while he struggled for balance with the other. The blood rushed in his ears as he started the ascent up the hill. Wolfgang was dead weight, bearing down on Reed's shoulders as he fought his way between the trees. He could see the stretcher up the hill, and he poured all his energy into reaching it.

Reed dropped Wolfgang in, laying him on his back and stretching out his busted leg inside the stretcher's rails. Then he dug the radio from his pocket. "Cristian!"

Nobody answered the line as the familiar boom of a breaching charge echoed behind him. Men shouted, and he snatched the pistol from his belt.

"Cristian!"

Still no answer. Reed looked over his shoulder and into the mouth of the warehouse fifty yards behind. The shadow of approaching men flitted between the banana boxes, and he opened up with Burly's pistol, firing at random through the warehouse door.

Legion X took cover, diving behind pallets as Reed emptied the handgun. The slide locked back just as Cristian's garbled voice crackled over the radio.

"Amigo?"

"Pull now!" Reed shouted, hurling himself on top of Wolfgang and grabbing the stretcher with his free hand.

"Pull now?" Cristian asked.

"Now! Now! Now!" Reed screamed into the radio.

Voices boomed from the warehouse, and Reed looked over his shoulder. Men ran out of the shadows, brandishing rifles and dashing for the door. They'd have a clear shot at him in under two seconds, and he'd be riddled with bullets before he finished his next breath.

Reed gritted his teeth and closed his eyes, and then the rope attached to the stretcher pulled taut, and Reed took off. Dirt and dead leaves exploded in front of him as the stretcher careened through low brush and hopped fallen limbs, shooting up the side of the ridge like a rocket leaving a launchpad. Gunshots cracked behind him, and bullets zipped over them, but Reed planted his face next to Wolfgang's lolling head and clung on for dear life. The stretcher tipped and almost rolled as it shot over the edge of a stump, but Reed leaned quickly to the right, and it slammed back into the dirt again, gaining speed all the time.

The gunshots behind him grew distant as the side of the mountain flashed past. In what felt like the blink of an eye, Reed was at the top of the ridge, shooting past his sniper's nest and still zipping between the trees. He reached for the radio, but a sudden bump sent it spinning out of his hand and into the trees.

And still, Cristian and his truck kept pulling. Only fifty yards ahead, Reed saw the other side of the ridge and remembered the steep drop beyond it, all the way to the roadbed far below.

Reed clawed the KAMPO out of its sheath and slashed at the rope. The dull blade ripped at the fibers, and Reed cursed himself for not sharpening it as Cristian continued to pull. Reed cut again, his nose and throat clogged with dirt and forest debris to the point he could barely see. More strands of the rope parted, but the stretcher careened onward, now only twenty yards from the drop-off.

Ten yards.

After a final, frantic slash with the knife, the rope snapped under tension, and the stretcher spun sideways, slamming into a tree only feet from the drop-off. Reed coughed, clawing debris out of his eyes. His arms shook, and the overwhelming relief that flooded his system was only over-shadowed by the shouts of Legion X in the valley below, clambering up the mountainside.

He rolled off the stretcher, wiping his face with one sleeve and retrieving the detonator from his pocket. It was undamaged, and the red warning light flashed on, just as it was supposed to when he disengaged the safety. Voices carried out of the valley, and Reed imagined the blond man rallying the remnants of his shattered army to ascend the backside of the horseshoe and find the man on the stretcher.

Too late, bastard.

Reed pressed the detonator. It clicked softly, followed by a silence so perfect that it felt like a minute, not a split second. Then the earth itself seemed to lurch forward, like an overpowered car blasting off the starting line. Fire leapt into the sky from the valley below—a giant orange orb that reminded Reed of the nuclear explosions he'd seen on TV, except this blast was littered with torn bits of sheet metal, metal beams, machinery . . .

And bananas. Thousands upon thousands of bananas.

50

Diablo's gunmen accompanied Reed as he approached the mansion. They stood on either side, AK-74s held at waist level and pointed at him. Prior to trucking him back to the mansion, they'd patted him down and taken the KAMPO, his only remaining weapon. Reed didn't object because he didn't need the KAMPO to break their necks.

He followed the walking trail around the side of the house and to the veranda. Diablo sat, kicked back with his feet on a stool and a margarita in one hand. The Colombian women were there, still dressed in bikinis and fawning over him like he was the prince of the world.

Reed still wasn't impressed.

Diablo sipped his drink and stared at Reed. The devil flashed in his eyes. "Some guy," he said.

Reed's body hurt all over—strained and battered by the combat and his reckless ascent up the mountainside. He was dehydrated again, and he was so tired he thought he could sleep on his feet, but he wasn't out of the woods yet, and he couldn't afford to let his guard down.

"You know we get the American news here in Colombia," Diablo said.

Reed said nothing.

"I like American news. It's like a reality show full of all kinds of games." Diablo sipped his drink and ran the devil tongue over his lips. "Do you know what they're talking about on the American news these days, gringo?" He sat forward, and his smile widened. "Chaos in Atlanta. Gunfire on the streets of Nashville. Explosions in downtown New Orleans."

Reed shoved his hands into his pockets.

Diablo watched him, then a dry laugh rustled from his throat. "But what do I care about American news? It's just a reality show, right?"

Reed shrugged. "Always has been."

Diablo finished the drink and stood up. "You did a number on that place in the mountains. Cristian said it burned to the ground. He said you tore through it like one of your American superheroes."

"He exaggerates. I just wanted my friend back."

"Ah, yes. Your friend. We are treating him. I don't know if he will walk again, but we can take care of the infection."

"Thank you."

Diablo stepped down from the porch, and as he approached Reed, the smile melted from his face. "I have saved your woman. I have helped you save your friend. Now, you will move my drugs, as you promised."

Reed held Diablo's gaze and gestured to the house with his chin. "I want to see her."

Diablo's eyes remained like black pits into the afterlife. "I don't think you heard me, gringo. I've done enough favors for you. Now, you—"

Reed took a sudden step forward, cutting the distance between them in half. The two gunmen tensed, jerking the rifles into their shoulders.

"Cards on the table," Reed said, speaking softly but with an edge sharp enough to slice stone. "You're right about one thing. I'm not some guy. I'm *the* guy. The guy who could break your neck before your goons could find their triggers, and the guy who's going to move your drugs, as promised. So let's skip the part where you piss me off over something stupid."

The gunmen exchanged a glance, unsure what to do next. Reed didn't blink, staring into Diablo's devil-soul with no hint of fear or intimidation.

Diablo stared right back, just as steady, but with a twitch in his upper lip. Then his posture relaxed, like a stiff towel exposed to steam, and his easy-going grin returned.

"You're so serious! I'm only yanking your chain. Of course you can see your woman." Diablo stepped back, motioning to the house, but he didn't turn his back on Reed.

The hallway to Banks's room was paved with expensive carpet, the walls lined with rare paintings. Reed walked without care of the mud crumbling on his boots, following the directions of Diablo's maid to the room at the end of the hall on the left. He paused outside the door and ran a hand through his hair. Dry mud and blood crumbled off, and he straightened his shirt, suddenly very self-conscious.

He put a hand on the doorknob and hesitated, then twisted. The door swung open without a sound, revealing a sun-bathed room on the other side, a four-poster bed in the middle. Banks's head rested on the pillow, her dirty-blonde hair strewn around her face. She was clean, and a healthy glow had returned to her cheeks.

Reed stopped in the doorway and watched her as she slept. In an instant, every memory he'd ever formed of Banks returned. The first night he met her at that Atlanta nightclub. The innocent joy in her smile when she unexpectedly encountered him in North Carolina. The betrayal and anger in her eyes when she again encountered him in Nashville. The agony of conflicted emotions in her reddened face when he kissed Maggie in New Orleans. And the fear that dominated her scream as the Humvee rocketed off the waterfall in Colombia.

In the few short weeks he'd known Banks, he'd seen her transition through almost every facet of the human experience—passion, happiness, terror, and remorse. He'd caused most of those emotions, but what he felt now, watching her sleep, was so much deeper.

He took a cautious step forward, a voice in the back of his head reminding him he had done this to her. He should feel guilt for the pain and suffering his private war continued to rain on her, but all he felt was longing. Longing to touch her hand, to lean in close . . .

A floorboard creaked under his foot, and Banks's eyes fluttered open. She stared right at him, momentarily confused and disoriented, then clarity filled her face. She sat up slowly, her face flushed.

"I love you," Reed said before he could stop himself. "And I'm never apologizing for that again."

Banks held out her hand.

Reed ran to her, sliding onto his knees next to the bed and pulling her into a hug. She grunted in pain but rested her chin against his shoulder and pressed her face into his neck.

Neither of them spoke, just holding each other in the stillness. Despite the pain and the uncertainty of being thousands of miles from America with a drug lord holding them hostage, Reed had never felt more at home.

51

The ship that waited for them in Barranquilla was old and nondescript—a small freighter with a mile of tangled registration documents, all pointing to a network of phony corporations and shipping companies. In that way, Reed guessed, Colombian criminals weren't all that different from American criminals.

Diablo himself drove with Reed, Banks, and Wolfgang from his mansion to the port, in an upgraded Cadillac Escalade that would make a rapper blush. It was a twelve-hour drive, but Diablo seemed intent on keeping his eyes on Reed as long as possible.

Nobody said anything during the trip. Reed rode in the back, with one arm around Banks, while Wolfgang lay on an air mattress in the cargo area. A goon monitored Reed from the back seat, while Diablo and his driver rode up front. Two Chevy Suburbans accompanied them, doubtlessly loaded with more goons.

This guy.

When they reached the port, it was a little after midnight. Diablo informed Reed that the ship was loaded with bananas, and Reed didn't miss the irony. He watched while Wolfgang was taken aboard on a stretcher, and then five of Diablo's men followed, all carrying bags that only barely concealed their arsenal of assault weapons.

"Safe voyage, gringo," Diablo said.

Two of the goons escorted Banks onto the ship. It was no secret that she was still a hostage, and that if Reed tried to pull any games, she'd be the first to die.

Reed faced the smaller man, keeping his tone cool. "You better not try anything stupid, Diablo. I'm damn hard to kill, and I've got a damn long memory."

Diablo grinned, his lips spreading across wolfish teeth in the most unsettling smile Reed had seen yet. He motioned to the ship, and Reed found his way up the scaffolding stairs onto the main deck. The vessel was rusty and littered with maritime paraphernalia. Through the open cargo hatch, Reed could see into the main hold, where maybe a hundred thousand bananas rested in crates.

And a thousand kilos of cocaine.

He found Wolfgang resting on his air mattress across the deck and knelt beside him. "How are you feeling?"

Wolfgang's eyes were hazed, a side effect of the heavy painkillers Diablo's men had given him, but his leg was bandaged, and the flush of infection had left his body.

"I'm alive," Wolfgang said.

Reed nodded. "When we get home, we'll get you to a hospital and see about some surgery. I'm sure they can fix your leg."

Reed wondered if he even believed his own words. It had been days since Wolfgang experienced the compound fracture that still shattered his leg. How much longer before he'd never walk again?

Reed started to stand, but Wolfgang whispered, "Reed?"

"Yeah?"

Wolfgang licked his lips, casting a nervous glance around the deck. "You have a plan, right?"

Reed chewed his lip, circulating through a list of canned responses of the reassuring variety. "Not really. But I do my best work on the fly."

Wolfgang closed his eyes. "That's what I was afraid of."

Reed squeezed his shoulder, then stood as the ship's big diesels groaned to life, and they churned away from the dock. He looked back to the entrance of the cabins but didn't see Banks, so he walked to the railing instead and stared down at the black water. It lapped against the sides of the ship, reflecting the moon as they plowed upriver and toward the Gulf—toward Louisiana and whatever lay waiting for them.

SUNDOWN
THE REED MONTGOMERY SERIES Book 7

Sometimes falling on your sword is the only option.

Armed with critical intelligence and surrounded by a team of ruthless operators, elite assassin Reed Montgomery is ready to deliver a death blow against the criminal empire that destroyed his family.

His greatest enemy, Aiden Phillips, leads that empire, and Reed is ready to rip him down.

But Aiden didn't come this far or rise this high just to go down without a fight. He'll shelter behind an army of killers, using humans as shields while targeting Reed's closest allies and friends.

Because Aiden believes every man has his price, and he knows what Reed treasures most.

The last battle of this bloody war may cost Reed everything.

Get your copy today at
severnriverbooks.com/series/reed-montgomery

ABOUT THE AUTHOR

Logan Ryles was born in small town USA and knew from an early age he wanted to be a writer. After working as a pizza delivery driver, sawmill operator, and banker, he finally embraced the dream and has been writing ever since. With a passion for action-packed and mystery-laced stories, Logan's work has ranged from global-scale political thrillers to small town vigilante hero fiction.

Beyond writing, Logan enjoys saltwater fishing, road trips, sports, and fast cars. He lives with his wife and three fun-loving dogs in Alabama.

Sign up for Logan Ryles's reader list at
severnriverbooks.com/authors/logan-ryles

Printed in the United States
by Baker & Taylor Publisher Services